Praise for *The Ramshead*

M000313289

"THE RAMSHEAD ALGORI̶̶̶̶̶ ̶̶̶̶ ̶̶̶̶̶ O̶THER
STORIES is strongly recommended for any speculative-
fiction readers interested in experiencing a fresh new voice
in the genre."

—*Booklist*

"Science and the supernatural converge to form quirky and
original hybrids in the 11 stories in Kabza's latest... Kabza's
well-drawn characters... are recognizably human, and their
emotional authenticity lends gravity to these tales' wildest
flights of fancy."

—*Publishers Weekly*

"KJ Kabza seems to specialize in altered states, dream states,
and has a range from flights of fancy to gut-wrenching
terror... You will treasure this collection.
RECOMMENDED."

—Hugo-nominated magazine *Abyss & Apex*

"Eleven stories with eleven compelling characters driven by
passion and love... Each story in this collection raises more
than one philosophical question."

—*Tangent*

"THE RAMSHEAD ALGORITHM AND OTHER
STORIES' mix of science fiction and fantasy travels the
futuristic and fantastical, yet always returns to relationships.
KJ Kabza's characters struggle against oppressive restriction,
loss, or isolation, yet unexpected turns of complex
humanity offer redemption (should they choose to take it).
Recommended for any fan of complicated people moving
through intriguing places."

—Scott H. Andrews, Five-Time World Fantasy Award
Finalist Editor-in-Chief of *Beneath Ceaseless Skies
Magazine*

"Almost all of these stories function wonderfully on their own, at their current length, and make you want more; there are at least six stories that briefly detail and suggest worlds colorful, intriguing and distinctive enough that the reader would jump at a novel-length exploration of their settings... A strong, promising debut...bursting with both ideas and emotion. "
—*RT Book Reviews*

"I can't come close to approximating the crackling language or incandescent imagination that KJ Kabza displays in these stories. So instead I'll say this: he's really f***ing good. Literate, smart, sometimes gentle, sometimes devastating, these stories will set your brain on fire."
—Cecilia Tan, author of *Daron's Guitar Chronicles* and the *Magic University* series

"Kabza's stories take us to realms where the mundane becomes magical and the weird perfectly ordinary. His writing pushes the lyricism of Bradbury into edgy and odd places to create powerful work that is wholly original, delightfully strange, and emotionally resonant."
—LJ Cohen, author of the *Halcyone Space* and *Changeling's Choice* series

"In these stories, KJ Kabza creates whole fantastic worlds that combine the universe-building of Jack Vance with the odd logic of fairy tales. These are a great read and unlike anything you've read before."
—Craig Shaw Gardner, New York Times bestselling author of *Batman* and *Temporary Monsters*

"KJ Kabza's endlessly fertile, often delightfully twisted imagination is vividly rendered on the page by his confident prose. Whether they be poignant, haunting, comical, or horrifying, every single story in THE RAMSHEAD ALGORITHM AND OTHER STORIES will linger in your

mind long after you read it."
—Fonda Lee, award-winning author
of *Jade City, Zeroboxer,* and *Exo*

"Reading KJ Kabza is like reading early Roger Zelazny crossed with early J.G. Ballard crossed with—oh heavens, I don't know what. His prose sparkles with colors you've never seen."
—Jeffrey A. Carver, author of The Chaos Chronicles and *Eternity's End*

"THE RAMSHEAD ALGORITHM AND OTHER STORIES is a highly imaginative mix of genre stories with the feel of classic fables—but unwinding with unique plots, characters, and magical/science-fictional gadgets. Reading this fantastic variety of stories left me hungry for the next book by Kabza!"
—Linda D. Addison, four-time Bram Stoker Award winner and author of *How to Recognize a Demon Has Become Your Friend*

For Anh--
   I hope you enjoy the reading as
much as I enjoyed the writing!
                -best, Jack (KJ Kabza)
                         7/12/18

THE RAMSHEAD ALGORITHM

AND OTHER STORIES

KJ KABZA

PINK
NARCISSUS
PRESS

Author's Note

It's pronounced "RAM'S head," as in, the head of a ram.

This book is a work of fiction. All the characters and events portrayed in this book are fictitious, and any resemblance to real people or events is purely coincidental.

THE RAMSHEAD ALGORITHM and Other Stories
© 2018 Pink Narcissus Press

All rights reserved. No part of this book may be reproduced in any form or by any means without the prior written consent of the Publisher, excepting brief quotes used in reviews.

"The Leafsmith in Love." First appearance: *Beneath Ceaseless Skies*, Issue #39, 2010.
"The Color of Sand." First appearance: *The Magazine of Fantasy and Science Fiction*, Jul/Aug 2013 issue.
"The Ramshead Algorithm." First appearance: *The Magazine of Fantasy and Science Fiction*, Jul/Aug 2011 issue.
"Steady on Her Feet." First appearance: *Beneath Ceaseless Skies*, Issue #168, 2015.
"The Flight Stone." First appearance: *Daily Science Fiction*, July 11, 2013.
"The Soul in the Bell Jar." First appearance: *The Magazine of Fantasy and Science Fiction*, Nov/Dec 2013 issue.
"Heaventide." First appearance: *The Magazine of Fantasy and Science Fiction*, Nov/Dec 2012 issue.
"All Souls Proceed." First appearance: *Flash Fiction Online*, 3/2016.

Illustrations and cover design by Dante Saunders

Published by Pink Narcissus Press
Massachusetts, USA
pinknarc.com

ISBN: 978-1-939056-13-9
First trade paperback edition: January 2018

CONTENTS

DEDICATION

For my husband,
who keeps insisting that I'm "right up there
with Harlan Ellison"

INTRODUCTION

A few years back, I decided I'd had enough of fatuous comparisons. Bret Easton Ellis was not the Brat Pack's version of F. Scott Fitzgerald, Brett Gardner is not this decade's Roy White, and Harlan Ellison is not science fiction's Don Rickles. Ellis is Ellis and Ellison is Ellison.

Still, the mind likes comparisons. So it struck me as odd that when I first started reading stories by KJ Kabza, I kept thinking of Roger Zelazny.

Was the comparison just superficial? There's that little "z" in his last name, and the "J" in his name is short for Jack; Zelazny loved to use names like "Shadowjack" and "Donnerjack." Perhaps... but probably not.

I thought the comparison had more to do with the verve and energy that both writers brought to their early work —"The Ramshead Algorithm" was damned near electric to the touch and its flawed first-person narrator put me in mind of the tall, judo-practicing poet of Zelazny's "A Rose for Ecclesiastes," while the sandcats in "The Color of Sand" reminded me of *Eye of Cat*, and for some reason, "For a Breath I Tarry" often seemed to lurk in the corner of my eye as I read Kabza. Both writers dream big.

Also, there's the penchant for tales that take us on travels through imaginative lands, a theme not just in Zelazny's Amber novels, but also in *Roadmarks* and *Damnation Alley*. Kabza makes this theme explicit in "Heaventide." His stories take you places you've never been.

And both writers wrote of families. Zelazny, of course, gave us Corwin's strange, powerful royal family in the Amber novels, while Kabza gave us some smaller—but equally strange—families, most strikingly in "Ramshead." Keep an eye on sisters as you read through this collection. They show up frequently.

But I sit here now, having read the eleven stories in this book —some for the first time, others for the first time in half a decade—and no, Kabza is no Zelazny. Nor is Zelazny any Kabza. (And anyone who read the introduction to *Four for Tomorrow* can tell at once that I am no Ted Sturgeon.)

What KJ Kabza is is a fine storyteller who shows vivid and roving imagination, an easy knack for characterization, and a steady hand on the wheel of his narratives. These tales vary a lot in theme and setting, in mood and tone. I'm loath to do the usual introductory maneuver of saying a few words about each story because some of them work better without any foregrounding—you do well to find your own way without having me tip you off whether to expect a work of science fiction or of fantasy (or of something in between). However, do note that that I found these stories more effectively enjoyed at intervals, rather than bingeing on three or four at a time. Each piece collected here is its own boat, a separate vessel. Hopping too quickly from one to another takes you in too many directions all at once and gives you less pleasure from each journey.

And may you enjoy these journeys as much as I have.

—Gordon Van Gelder
December 2017

THE LEAFSMITH IN LOVE

The first thing Jesper noticed was her parasol, twirling like a ghostly pinwheel beyond the branches and webs. He was instantly intrigued. On previous occasions, when watching all the visiting women on the Red Path, he had often told himself, *If I were a Lady with a lacy parasol, I would be entranced by the decorative absurdity of it and play with it constantly, not stand there dumbly beneath it like a worm beneath a mushroom.*

Compelled by its beckoning clockwise motion, he wove between the trees and smithing with the skill of a hart. In minutes he was behind her, three paces from the edge of the pink gravel clearing. The bench opposite her was empty, and she was conversing with herself in a quite lively manner.

"Indeed," she was saying aloud, "but I do not know their names. All I know is that I have truly never seen so queer a place in all my life. We could simply name them ourselves, you know." The parasol slowed, paused, and began to thoughtfully spin in the other direction. "Oh certainly not! They would never come up with something suitable." She laughed. "Zuhanna, from whose head do you pull such ideas? They don't care a bit. It's clearly too splendid for them to understand anyway. If they would only open their eyes and look around—and around and around and around...!" With this, she tossed down the parasol, hopped up from the bench, held out her arms, and spun.

Jesper's heart quickened. Lady Zuhanna's eyes were closed in overflowing joy, her palms upturned to the sweet spring air, her quick feet pirouetting her in a rhythm that was almost a dance, savoring this one silly, spontaneous moment.

And as he watched her, Jesper, the Master Leafsmith of Holdt Castle, finally fell in love.

Around them, the Arboretum sang and rustled and clicked. Jesper's heart rose up, past the gleaming webs, the thousands of clockwork creatures on uncountable hybrid branches, the interlocking cogs nestled in the forest's crown. A flock of real birds rushed overhead, and a score of ticking dragonflies took flight; they settled around her blooming petticoats in a ring, baffled by the spinning laughter in their midst.

She tripped and fell.

Jesper rushed to her side and the dragonflies scattered. He knelt on the crushed feldspar and extended his elbow. "My Lady!"

Her face was red. Her fine hand settled on his arm, and she looked up at him in sheepish acknowledgment. A few of her hairpins had come loose, and the careful fresco of braids coiled about her head had become paunchy and lopsided.

Oh—she was unspeakably lovely.

They stood. "Thank you, kind sir," she said bashfully. "I'm sorry. I'm so clumsy, and I get so carried away."

"Not at all. Are you injured?"

"No." She did not remove her hand from his. She looked down and smoothed her rumpled frock with the other. "I'm afraid I cannot say the same for this silly old thing."

"I am sorry."

"I am so foolish. Have you seen where I placed my parasol?"

"It's lovely. I mean, yes, it is over here."

"Thank you." She pulled away to fetch it, and the

rhythm of Jesper's heartbeat quickened, like that of a pendulum set too short. She picked up her parasol and blew on it, ineffectually, unable to disturb the pink dust or hundreds of tiny metal springs the smithing invariably shed. "I don't believe we have met?"

Jesper raised a reverent hand to his top hat. "Jesper. Jesper Leafsmith."

"A Leafsmith! O marvelous, delightful!" She held up her battered parasol and swiveled toward him. "You help keep this place, then?"

Jesper smiled and his body warmed. "My Lady, I have built this place."

Her mouth opened. She said nothing, then mutely looked about her.

A proud flush crept over the entirety of Jesper's skin. "I started with a section of ordinary Arboretum, a space near an abandoned ore mine. The webs you see, along with the occasional plant made wholly of smithing, are maintained with Animus distillate and Elementalic cleverness. I am no Elementalor myself, so the machines that grow themselves along with the wood are not wholly my province. But all the accompanying smithlife is mine."

She took a step closer to him, her eyes shining. "Papa gave me a magnificun scope one St. Adelayde's Day, when I was twelve years. I loved that scope. I'd take it to Papa's swamp, and I would spend hours watching all the wiggly, squiggly things in a drop of water. Tell me, what is it like? To see that way always?"

Jesper felt a sweat prickle along his covered scalp and under his arms. She was lauding him with her eyes. "It is not always. Only when I wish."

She took another step closer. "I have been wondering, Leafsmith. How do you make a clockwork ladybug? I would love to know. I am so intrigued."

His knees begged him to sit down, but his feet were

somehow affixed to the feldspar. "There are many ways. In brief, I take a living ladybug, look deep into it, and replicate the gross moving parts in tiny brass. I use a special branch of mathematica to calculate where to place static runes upon the moving clockwork, to channel the distant energy that powers it. But I have many machines to aid me, including a Sight Translationer."

"A Sight Translationer?!"

"It is a rare mechanism. It requires Fractional distillate, which few alchemists are skilled enough to reduce."

"Fractional distillate! Listen to you talk! There is so much about magics I do not know, and I have only three days to secretly learn it all, before we leave for home. Papa will only let me study Elementics back in South Tairee, and I am only any good with Earth." She took another step closer; she had reached him now. Her parasol began to spin again, and her face warmed and opened like a sunflower. "So you must hurry and tell me absolutely everything you know."

"I..."

"Shall we sit? These benches are so queer, with their little jointed feet. Are they able to walk about? That is awfully clever. Could we ride an ambling bench as we talk?"

"You may not, I dare say," interrupted a voice, and Jesper's body tightened.

Princess Kanna, clothed in a gown more intricately executed than any of her interpersonal machinations, stepped off the Red Path and into the gravel clearing. "You're conversing with Jesper, sweet coz. Our dear Leaf-smith has a mechanical heart, and it holds less feeling than a stone." She laughed. The over-sweetness of the sound made Jesper's teeth ache. "He only sits and visits with his Wood-tinkers, in his cottage in the heart of the wood, which no courtesan is invited to see."

Lady Zuhanna's spinning parasol stilled, and a heavy veil of adult seriousness dropped over her face. "I beg your pardon, Leafsmith. I should not have been so nosy. Excuse me for being so forward."

Jesper reached toward her. "Please—"

The Princess strolled forward and patted Jesper's arm. "No need to pretend at manners, Leafsmith." She waved her hand at Lady Zuhanna. "And you, shoo! Your Papa is looking for you. I'd stay down in the library as he says. You'll get nowhere filling your head with butterflies and steam-powered rabbits."

She curtsied. "Yes, coz. Good morning."

"Good morning."

Jesper watched her trod away over the Red Path, her body held stiffly, looking straight ahead at nothing, like any world-weary Lady at court.

For this, Jesper hated the Princess more than ever.

As soon as Lady Zuhanna had vanished from sight, the Princess slid close to him, running her palm up the length of his arm. Her breath in his ear sickened, like too much honey. "What is this I see, Leafsmith? You are a man after all? Or are you just play-acting? She is a plain, empty-headed fool. And so are you, for thinking you can freely insult your Princess by admiring her so."

"Perhaps we two fools would make a good match, then."

Princess Kanna hissed. She stood on her toes and forcefully pressed her ripe body into his, hugging his arm with her softness. "What madness do you breed on your lonesome in that secret woodland hut? All the men of this castle would slaughter their mothers, and rightly so, for but a single one of my smiles—all but you. You wound me, Leafsmith. All this time you've been saving your arrogant love, and you finally fall for—her?"

"I beg your pardon." Jesper gracefully stepped away. "I seem to have somehow stood too close."

She narrowed her eyes. "I do not appreciate being

mocked."

"No-one does, Princess."

Princess Kanna put her hands on her hips and pertly swung them just so, a motion that made Gentlemen faint yet always left Jesper cold. "I deserve to be mocked least of all. You may not have her, Leafsmith, not as long as you dare to think her lovelier."

"It is not wise to fall for me," said Jesper gravely, feigning he had misinterpreted her jealousy. "Your father would never approve. You are the heir and I but a working craftsman, and twice your age besides."

She bared her teeth. "Tell me I am the more beautiful!"

Jesper touched his hat. "We must not converse about such things. The court will talk. Good morning, Princess."

She stamped her foot. "I order you to tell me!"

Jesper touched a solemn finger to his lips and slipped back into the trees where she could not follow.

He fled to his hidden cottage, his poor human heart throbbing with fear and desire. He would die before saying so, but in his secret and ungentlemanly opinion, the Princess was as desirable as a Witch-rash in a personal place. In one of his secret and ungentlemanly notebooks, he in fact cultivated a wicked collection of verse on the subject. He thought of writing some now, to strengthen his resolve, but what he truly wanted to do surprised him.

He wanted to make a ringauble, as a gift for her so enchanting cousin.

And why not? It might enrage the Princess dreadfully.

Whistling the preemptory Build, Jesper entered his adjacent greenhouse and began to search for something suitable to start with.

★★★

The ringauble was completed by sundown—a simple pot containing the sleeping bulb of a flower nestled in smithing soil. Lady Zuhanna's three-day visit did not give Jesper much time, but he knew that the Princess was watching, so he must wait to present it to her.

The next afternoon, during Princess Kanna's daily one-of-the-clock nap, Jesper readied a cloth sack and trotted to the southeast wing of the castle, where the Perennial Tower stood. He eschewed the locked door at its base, and like a love-struck boy, instead hid surreptitiously in the topiary.

He glanced about the deserted shrubbery, then retrieved a steam-powered condor from the sack and roused it. As the condor sputtered and clanked, Jesper placed a Scrygonfly and the lip of the ringauble pot in its talons, then issued his instructions in a sub-audible mumble. The condor flew up to the third-floor balcony and correctly placed the ringauble on a pedestal, but misheard Jesper otherwise and placed the Scrygonfly on the edge of the roof without winding it first. Close enough—Jesper bolted from the bushes and fled.

He waited in his hidden cottage. He pretended to work on the blueprints for a hydroelectric mangrove, refining the nanodynamos in the xylem, but he did little other than stare at the lines. No-one else could make a ringauble quite like this, and when she saw it, she'd know who sent it.

When he felt the prickling behind his eyes, he attuned his sight so fast to the scene observed by the Scrygonfly's ommatidia that he saw nothing but gray static at first. Then, from the roof, he was watching the Princess' sweet cousin step out onto the balcony.

She bent to stroke a morning glory blossom, then noticed the ringauble. "Oh!"

Jesper's breathing quickened. She stepped to the pedestal and set her hands upon the ringauble's terra-cotta pot, her dark eyes dancing in curiosity.

The potting soil, a bricolage of microscopic gears watered with Animus distillate, parted with a whisper of clicks to reveal a steel shoot. Before her eyes, the invaginated tube grew and thickened and sprouted brass self-constructing leaves, and in twenty seconds, the top of the stalk swelled and darkened. Her mouth parted, as if she were burning to ask it a question.

The bud swelled to the size of a man's fist, then abruptly opened to reveal spiraling rows of stained glass petals, firing microscopic pistons, and droplets of molten gold dew.

She squealed.

"What on earth are you on about now?" Princess Kanna stalked out onto the balcony. "*What*, Zuhanna?"

"Oh! Look, look!"

The Princess pushed her aside and snatched up the pot. "This frivolous bauble? Pah. It's a trifle. It's presented to all our guests."

Lady Zuhanna reached out to it, mesmerized, and touched the edge of a brass leaf.

The music box in the flower's bulb tinkled to life at the contact, and the petals trembled as the ringauble chimed the bars of a love ballad.

Lady Zuhanna's eyes went wide, and Princess Kanna let out a haughty laugh. "Oh, I see what's happening here. It's that foolish Leafsmith."

Lady Zuhanna, bewildered, pulled back her hand. "Foolish?"

"Oh yes." The Princess looked down at the smithing in her hands, the power of Jesper's love harnessed and turned into song by the runes on the terra-cotta. She knowingly shook her head. "Our Leafsmith has been secretly admiring me for years. I suppose, if you are a simple craftsman, seeing a beautiful princess strolling about every day in your own backyard is too much. He has been making wanton eyes at me since I was thirteen years."

Jesper gaped. That lying, miserable harpy!

Lady Zuhanna nodded, confused and crestfallen.

"He knew I'd come out here with you this afternoon," the Princess continued, "because he knows our most honored Ladies always stay in the Perennial Tower's Silver Suite. And besides which, he has these little mechanical insects that he sends to follow me about and scry on my comings and goings. I don't know whether to feel amusement or pity."

"He... he loves you?"

"Oh yes," sighed Princess Kanna, in a tone as plaintive as it was infuriating. She indifferently set the pot, still chiming its love, upon a railing. "He gives these things to visitors all the time, but he only gives the ones that sing to me. This is the third this week. Though he's usually not so insolent as to present them to me in front of other people. I suppose you must matter little to him."

Lady Zuhanna bit her lip and nodded.

Beyond the ommatidia, the Princess yawned and went inside. Lady Zuhanna sadly touched the ringauble once more; it fell silent, and she slipped inside after a disappointed sigh.

The scene dissolved as Jesper's anger overwhelmed his focus. So the Princess would play this way, would she?

You may be quick on your feet, Princess Kanna, but you forget—my very profession is in miracles and engineered delicacy.

And my devices are far more clever.

★★★

Jesper made himself wait another precious day. Around ten of the clock the next morning, he walked the Silver Path to Arachnotropolis, where Kellin, Master Wood-tinker, was at work. Kellin was frowning under his heavy beard and winding, by hand, a large number of spiders whose runes had become too worn to do any tapping. He didn't even look up as Jesper approached. "Master Fluff-brains. Come to lend me a hand today? Or are you still stuck on that mangrove?"

"Still stuck."

"Frivolity in a sea of frivolities." Kellin replaced the freshly ticking spider in its web, where it scurried about and rearranged the strands of metal to its ineffable liking. Kellin plucked a stilled body from another web nearby. "We can't even use a hydroelectric mangrove, you know. Rithick told me the drop in the river isn't great enough."

"A sapling, perhaps."

"No matter. What's news?"

Jesper cleared his throat. "The visiting King Ethin of Snow-on-High has asked that I give his daughter a lesson."

Kellin stopped breathing for a moment so he could accurately insert his microkey. He wound the spider by rubbing his fingertips together a bare sixteenth of an inch. "The Lady Zuhanna? Poor man. At least she's not destined for his throne. No amount of education, even if it culminates at Holdt castle, is going to get *her* head out of the clouds."

"Yes, well, he seems to think it will do her good." Jesper watched Kellin replace the spider and select another. "He asked that she receive an interdisciplinary lesson in Earth-Metal Elementics."

"And you can't do Elementics," finished Kellin with a sigh. "Passing the knife, are we? That's fine, it'll get me out of this tedium."

"Can you be at the seventh joint at one-thirty of the clock?"

Kellin set the wound spider back in its web with a grunt of assent. "Certainly." He plucked another from an orb web. "Pardon me for not touching farewell, but if I drop this microkey, it'll take an hour to spin one out again. Good morning, Jesper."

Jesper touched his top hat. "Good morning, Kellin."

Next, Jesper walked the Red Path until he came across an idle page boy, who was holding a stone to his ear and listening to it tick. Jesper asked him to tell the visiting Lady Zuhanna at exactly one-ten of the clock that she would be late for her lesson at the seventh joint on the White Path if she did not hurry.

He then set a Scrygonfly at the seventh joint, and worst of all, tried to occupy himself until the timekeeping oak could thrum half-past one. When it did, he was already in position, within an iron Banyan tree seventy paces distant. At the sound of the oak, he attuned his sight to the distant scene.

Two long minutes later, the White Path crackled with the sound of running feet. Lady Zuhanna, out of breath, missing her hat, and one button at her neck undone, skidded off the path and stumbled onto the bare dirt. "Oh my! Good sir, excuse me, can you tell me where the seventh joint is?"

Kellin, who had been sitting on an ornamental rock, stood up and dusted off his palms. "Lady Zuhanna. Good afternoon." He touched his top hat, a battered thing with a distinct dent in the middle. "My name is Kellin Woodtinker, and I have been told to give you your lesson."

Lady Zuhanna dug in her clutch for a fan. She could not find one, gave up, and fanned herself with the clutch instead. A few strands of hair were stuck to her forehead, and Jesper yearned to carefully brush them back with his fingertips. "Yes, about that. I seem to have forgotten I had something scheduled. Excuse me, I think I am late."

"Only slightly. And if you've never walked the White Path, finding your way can be confusing."

"Could you please remind me what I am here for?"

"Your lesson on Elemental Earth-Metal dynamics."

Lady Zuhanna straightened and redoubled her clumsy

fanning. "Oh! I thought I wasn't—well—Papa must have—well! Splendid! Yes, oh yes, please do!"

Kellin nodded and, in his blunt way, promptly began. "This patch of bare ground, of which there are fifty in the Arboretum, is what we call a joint, or a place where the currents of elements cross. Common natural examples would be a swamp, for an Earth-Water joint, or in the center of a lake, for Water-Air."

"Excuse me, have you seen my clutch?"

"Uh... Lady, you are—"

"Oh. Yes. Here it is, obviously. I'm sorry, do continue."

Kellin pointed at the bare earth. "The numbered joints in the Arboretum refer to the places where our subterranean network of living metal comes together in large bundles, like a sort of root or pipe, and nears the surface. It's easier to get to this way; we can write runes in the dirt, speak the Power Tongue with no leaves to obscure our words, etc."

Jesper had meant to let Kellin go on for several minutes, but he could make himself wait no longer. He drew a breath, stepped from behind the smithing, and approached the White Path. He rehearsed in his head. *Oh, Lady Zuhanna, I thought you were studying in the library. Kellin, something's come up—I'll take over now. No, you can go on, the lesson can cover something else. Well you see, my Lady, I wanted it to be a surprise. That's why nobody else needed to know we were meeting like this. Of course it's all perfectly innocent—I am just giving you a lesson.*

"First," said Kellin, beyond the Scrygonfly's transmitting eyes, "I'll show you how to feel where the metal comes up through the earth. With a little practice, you don't even need to feel; you can just sense. Anybody can do it, even those who don't have the instinct for Elementics. We can find our joints this way in the dark, or any place where we have lots of webs growing up out of the ground with the trees." Kellin knelt in the dust. "Place your palms on the ground... here."

Jesper hastened his steps. He pushed through some loosened copper vetch and stepped onto the White Path. He prepared for the most casual near-sprint of his life, but before he could even begin, he was hamstrung by a frightened cry behind him.

Jesper whirled. Right at his back, feet clacking on the limestone, was one of his steam-powered wolves. But instead of ambling across the gravel and back into the forest, it went utterly mad, hoping forward and back, tail pin-wheeling like a riled attack dog's. It jumped forward, teeth bared; the air rent with a scream and the ugly sound of ripping fabric; the wolf danced away with a mangled petti-coat in its gleaming jaws, only to drop it and lunge back in.

Scrygonfly forgotten, Jesper lunged after it, legs firing like pistons and hands out and ready for The Touch. The Words were loaded on the tip of his tongue when, five steps from the unknown Lady, the wolf rocked back and let out its thin, piping artificial howl. Jesper threw himself at the smithing, his hat flying off, his palm connecting with its burning head, speaking the Words and feeling the beast grow slack beneath him, but nine more of the things, equally crazed, burst onto the path from the trees.

Something wet rained onto him, and he prayed it was only leaked oil.

He stood and lunged again at the nearest wolf. It snorted steam and danced away, mocking him with its lolling, multijointed tongue. Jesper used the Words to speak a lasso and snare its uncrushable neck. It fell, yelping; he pulled it towards him, its steel body squealing across the limestone, before palming its head and speaking it silent.

"Oh, you brute, you horrid, horrid brute!"

Jesper's anxiety flared up into full, burning horror. The maddened wolves had set themselves on none other than

Princess Kanna, who was definitely not taking her customary afternoon nap, but was instead engaged in beating off her indestructible attackers with a small handbag.

She was unharmed, but her fine gown had been ripped to scandalizing shreds.

Jesper shoved into the thick of them, caring not a damn if they snapped at him and only thinking to cover the Princess' shame. He tore off his tail coat and flung it over her. "Your Highness!"

And as suddenly as they had descended, the wolves bolted and vanished with a squeal and a hiss of steam.

Reddened and panting, the Princess curled up and pulled Jesper's coat around her, the embroidered tails dragging in the dust. It still wasn't enough. Under the remains of her gown, wholly half of her legs lay naked to the air. Face burning, he stammered something, stripped off his waistcoat, cringed and tried to further cover her. She feebly protested. He insisted.

He heard the sound of running feet, and a strong masculine voice crying, "Hallo!"

Jesper gasped, had no time to think, and flung himself over Princess Kanna to prevent anyone from seeing her exposed body.

Kellin, with Lady Zuhanna in tow, rounded a corner of the White Path. In a sudden hot moment, Jesper realized what they were seeing: a nearly-nude Princess, panting and flush, gown in savage ruins, with Jesper undressed, hatless, and pressing his body atop hers.

Lady Zuhanna's hands flew to her mouth.

"This is not as you think!" Jesper cried.

Lady Zuhanna turned and ran.

Jesper cursed, shouted, railed in unnamed tongues as Kellin rushed forward and stripped off his own tail coat. Jesper's ravings were joined by Kellin's cruel tongue-lashing: "Have you gone mad? What in Heaven's name are you trying to do? You could be executed for such indecency!"

Nearly in tears, the Princess interrupted. Breathless explanations were exchanged. Others in the Arboretum, alarmed by the cries, soon arrived on the scene. Gentlemen fell over themselves to help cover the Princess. Page boys were sent for another gown. Rumors ignited and went flying. And to the tittering onlookers, the smug, secret smile Princess Kanna gave Jesper before being led away was all the clarification they needed.

It cleared up some things for Jesper, too, and not at all in a way he would have liked.

Some hours later, after a forest-wide search, Jesper had his employees bring him all of his wolves for a thorough examination. Jesper inspected them in his greenhouse, alone. He'd tell the King that there had been a flaw in the engravings, causing the first wolf to both behave like the pack leader and persuade the others to engage in rough play with the wrong species.

He'd tell no-one, however, that alchemical analysis uncovered traces of six kinds of distillate—Summon, Wolf, Conglomerate, Mind-Read, Denude, and Goal-Disperse— and as Princess Kanna loved to boast, the only people with free access to distillate of any kind were those in the Royal House. But even if Jesper did tell someone, who would want to believe? The rumor of a forbidden daylight rendezvous was too outrageous to resist.

Jesper wrapped his lonely arms around a wolf and laid his head down upon its cool body. Lady Zuhanna would never consent to being courted now.

★★★

Jesper locked himself in his cottage and admitted no-one. His windows stayed dark and silent into the deepening evening and throughout the clicking night. The next morning, it was the same.

He did not eat or sleep. Perhaps he worked, but it was

better to call it mourning: he designed ringaubles, over and over, each more ostentatious and impossible than the last. He wrote her name in the Power Tongue, and spoke it, so she would feel an anxious longing pull at her soul, without knowing why. It was the best he could do.

Two hours past sundown, on Lady Zuhanna's last night at Holdt Castle, Jesper realized that this was not so.

He could do better. He was a Master Leafsmith, and in love, and at least one of these things was unstoppable.

***

The seeds were easy—in addition to those newly made, Jesper already had thousands, and three quick cycles in the Von Neumann Apparatus could multiply any of his stocks by nearly a hundred-fold. Stealing a ten-gallon barrel of Animus distillate should have been far more troublesome, but the door to the Royal Storeroom was left unguarded, and the tediously frequent repetitions of Princess Kanna's name in the logbook hinted at why. The locked Storeroom door would've stymied most thieves, of course, but the lock's secret inner workings were no match for Jesper's Leafsmith sight and skill. With a few calculations and runes scratched into its brass plate, the lock opened of its own volition.

Once equipped, Jesper took the long way around to the Perennial Tower, his cartload of supplies tip-toeing behind. He stopped at the base of the structure, directly over a lone thread of submerged metal webbing. The empty night around him sung with crickets and sleepless clockwork. Though torches flickered on distant parapets, the nearby tower was dark. She would be sleeping.

A pity—she would have loved to see this.

Jesper beckoned to his cart. It stepped forward, and from it Jesper plucked a wind-up Ravenous. He set the greedy creature on the ground, and once it had eaten away the grass along with a good-sized hole in the soil, he locked its jaws and returned it to the cart. Then he lifted his nine-pound sack of indehiscent mechanacia seeds over the hole and poured.

He wrote the necessary containment runes in the freshly bared dirt.

Finally, Jesper positioned the cart above the hole and opened the tap on the distillate drum. In the Power Tongue, he said, "Grow."

The seeds needed no urging. The distillate hit, the first roots plunged down, the web line was touched, and all Heaven and Hell broke free. The dirt blew apart with the force of it; clacking trees under snapping leaves under tinkling loads of flowers rose up to the stars in a plume of percussive, frenzied song. Glass petals and iron twigs rained down. Living crickets fled. Jesper stumbled back and fell right on his rear, mouth momentarily unable to close, wondering if ten entire gallons had been strictly necessary.

A light blazed in her room.

A bronze leaf the size of a mixing bowl crashed to the earth by his feet; he scooped it up as he stood and placed it over his top hat as a helmet. Before his nerves could fail him, he grasped a still-growing branch and climbed.

He dodged rusted thorns, jagged edges of peeling bark, poison ivy covered in crushed glass. His hands grew black with oil; his soles grew scratched by the rough steel. The column of squealing life kept growing, reaching out vines to the Perennial Tower and anchoring them into the mortar, covering the windows and beyond with impenetrable brass clusters of fleur-de-lis.

Jesper reached the open window to her bedroom, hesitating, but even as he watched, a branch grew straight inside. He climbed along it and disembarked. The interior was bright with lamps. The bedclothes were pushed aside in a hasty awakening, though a cotton dressing gown was tossed over a nearby chaise lounge. The wardrobe door was cracked, and the comb from the dressing table had been knocked to the floor.

The room was empty.

"Lady Zuhanna?"

Jesper turned in a baffled circle. He wandered through an open doorway into a sitting room, untouched and immaculate. Other than her cousin, it seemed she'd had no visitors. "Lady Zuhanna?"

Jesper doubled back and entered the washroom. The signs of her were everywhere—balled-up towel on the floor, discarded stockings draped over a changing screen, hairpins scattered everywhere like Arboretum springs—but she was nowhere near. He went again to the sitting room and through a second doorway into an antechamber. The cuckoo clock read past midnight. Jesper did not understand.

He stepped out onto the balcony off the sitting room, but the ringauble was gone.

He placed his blackened hands on the railing and looked down. The distillate drum had emptied; the cart had skittered back, out of self-preservation. The tower of clicking, interlocking steel was taller than the one he stood in, wobbling perilously in the favonian breeze.

Useless.

Jesper pulled off his leaf helmet, set it carefully upon the railing, and descended the tower via the inside stone staircase. Outside, he paused by his soaring marvel, watching it whir and clack and expertly go nowhere.

The door behind him in the Perennial Tower opened, and a dozen castle guards came charging out. "Halt!"

Jesper turned to the forest and bolted, cursing his careless mooning, but perhaps he should have saved his breath for running. A pair of guards easily overtook him, and he went down, violently, onto the grass. They chained his wrists and hauled him to his feet. The rest caught up, and a gloved hand grabbed his jaw and forcefully raised his chin to let its owner get a look at his face.

"...Is that... Master Leafsmith?"

"How could you—did *you*—"

"What in Heaven's holy name—"

They dragged him back to the Perennial Tower. Jesper hung his head. In the nearing castle, lights blazed up, and more guards stampeded closer. He was hit with a wave of polished armor and astonished inquiry, and the queries rose into an angry din of indistinct demands. There was no fighting against it. Jesper did not bother. By now, he had no honor left to defend.

The crowd around him suddenly quieted. Heads rose and turned, and the guards obediently pulled apart, like the sea at the nose of some great Leviathan. "I don't give a care that my rooms are closer, next time, you fetch Father! Now where is the sniveling rat that has disturbed my rest?"

The last chagrined guard stepped aside. Princess Kanna, clad in a satin dressing gown, shoved past him. Her gaze fell on Jesper. Wrathful judgment blazed up in her eyes.

His idea, and only way out, made his crippled pride breathe its last. His heart numb with humiliation, he knelt in the wet grass at her feet. He removed his top hat and bent over until his forehead touched her tiger-skin slippers. "My sweet angel."

The wrath on her face hesitated. "I... beg your pardon?"

Jesper let his tears fall into the soft fur, though they were not for the Princess; oh, not at all. "My sweet angel. My Princess. I beg you, forgive me. I have made an arrant fool of myself this night. I could hold back no more. I have been waiting too many long and lonely years, with too lonely and heavy a heart to keep silent for even one more day."

"Keep silent?"

He lifted his head to be better heard over the uncomfortable shuffle of booted feet. The false confession was filth on his tongue. "My angel, have mercy. I stilled those wolves for you on the White Path, but had Hell itself besmirched your innocence, I would have done the same. Has my steady, cold demeanor not told all? I love you. I love you, and I cannot have you. So I try, endlessly, to pretend. But after yesterday, when I thought I'd lose you to my own faulty lupine smithing... to my own mistakes..."

Her uncertainty melted, and her eyes opened wide in enlightened pleasure. "You... you try to pretend?"

The guards averted their eyes, shifted their weight, ashamed by his naked emotion. A few looked pained and nodded in knowing sympathy. Jesper could only plunge in deeper. "Of course! O Princess, have you never seen a looking glass? How can you bear your own beauty and power? The light of you consumes me. Your perfection is what I aspire to each time I sit before my drawing board. The whole of my Arboretum, sweet one, which so rightly bores you, is merely my feeble attempt to emulate... you."

Princess Kanna grinned. She glanced down to retie the belt on her dressing gown, taking her time to fuss with the knot. "I thought so. I always knew there was something funny about you, Leafsmith. Did you really think you could fool me for much longer?"

"I did."

She gestured in dismissal at the newly grown steel. "And this?"

"The strange consequences of my vanity. I have hid this thing for too dangerously long, and something ugly came over me. I planted this monstrosity, and I was going to ascend it and cut through the Perennial Tower to your rooms, but looking up at it, I realized what foolhardy thing I'd done, and I lost my nerve."

The Princess nodded and combed her hair back with her fingers. "And my dumpy, thick-headed cousin?"

Jesper closed his eyes in pain, and the tears poured. "Only my misguided attempts to make you jealous, my angel."

Princess Kanna laughed. "Well, I certainly hoped you've learned your lesson, Leafsmith."

"That I am a fool?"

"And a rather pathetic one, at that. You are no different from any other man, after all. Guards, let him go. He did this out of love for me, which is laughable of course, but pitiable and understandable. Go to your wretched, hidden home, Leafsmith. Your shame, and what they will say about you in the halls of my castle, is satisfaction enough for me." The guards removed the manacles and backed away. "You can clean up this frightful mess in the morning."

Jesper nodded, not looking at her, and turned to go. He headed back towards the Arboretum and his lonely sanctuary, his cart following him at a respectful distance.

Once within the black embrace of the branches, he moved through the dark on the unnamed path. A handful of mechanical bats swooped by, the breeze from their silk wings icy on the last of his tears. From its place on the hill, the timekeeping oak rolled out a single great boom. Elsewhere, the Arboretum danced on, but the sounds felt rote and empty. These stones migrating across his path, those Nibblers mining a fallen tree for ingrown steel—this was not life. This was desperate, hollow artifice.

Jesper reached his cottage. A light he'd left burning shone through the slats in the shutters. He opened his door —there was no reason to ever lock it—and went inside.

He stepped in something that crunched.

"I am afraid that I have spilled quite a lot of your sugar," said Lady Zuhanna.

Jesper's breath left him.

"I thought that I could use a cup of tea while I waited for you," she explained, blushing while turning round to face him, "and that you mightn't mind since it would only be a few small tea leaves, but I couldn't find any tea leaves at all in your entire kitchen, and the last place I decided to look was behind the sugar because at home that's where Ethy keeps them, and I thought perhaps you might too. But then I knocked it over somehow, and then those things came from somewhere, and now the sugar's crawling with them. Are they ants, or something mechanical? And where do you keep your broom? I've looked all over for that too."

Jesper still could not speak, too overwhelmed by the simple fact of her standing in his secret sanctum. As if she belonged there...

Lady Zuhanna nervously fiddled with a lacy appurtenance on her gown. "I'm quite sorry. Oh! How rude of me, to have you just standing there like that. Won't you come in?"

Jesper groped behind him for the doorknob. He pulled the door shut and stepped in further, feet crunching over spilled sugar intermingled with fragile clockwork ants, but he didn't care a damn about the ants. He cared that she wasn't leaving, but rather, breathing faster at his approach. And he cared, most powerfully, that she leaned forward, oh so slightly, when he set his still-blackened hands on her arms.

She looked up at him, eyes wide as a frightened kitten's. "I couldn't sleep. I didn't even get undressed; I just lay in the dark and thought and thought and thought, about the things Kanna said that did not fit together well, and about what Papa said when I showed him the ringauble you made, and I heard a frightful noise and lit a lamp and remembered what Goodman Kellin taught me—how to see where the steel comes up through the earth—and when I saw what was happening outside, I knew what it meant, and I ran down the stairs, and... and... but you weren't... and then..."

Jesper's hands began to shake, or perhaps it was her

who shook. He licked his lips and tried to speak, but the very breath stuck in his throat, even as Lady Zuhanna's flush deepened.

"And—" The pitch of her voice rose as she spoke, growing ever more panicky and frightened. "I looked at the metal in the ground, and I said to myself if *I* were a Master Leafsmith and I lived over a web like this but in a secret place, I'd be where there was no metal at all, and I followed... that is... I wanted to... I mean, your cottage—" Her lower lip began to tremble. "I'm so sorry—I just thought—"

Jesper kissed her.

The clockwork ants carried away nearly half of the sugar before they were willing to let each other go.

***

"You know," said Lady Zuhanna cheerfully, as they walked arm-in-arm on the Silver Path to the castle, "my dress is now absolutely covered in these oily black marks. Perhaps you should have washed your hands before expressing your intentions. Oh, look! The sky is turning light. You can just see it through the... the... my word, what is that, exactly?"

"It's a hedge maze. The solution changes, depending on where the spiders decide to weave their webs. A gap in the bushes one day becomes an impassable wire net the next."

She squeezed his arm, urgently. "You must make one for Papa and I that is twice as large."

"My Lady, it will be my dearest pleasure."

She did not lessen her grip. "And you must make us a timekeeping redwood. And a whole pack of wolves, and coyotes, and—and a herd of unicorns, with diamond horns that grow themselves. I am certain you will devise a way. And! Papa and I have a frightfully unattractive swamp. Can you do something to our swamp?"

Jesper rubbed his chin thoughtfully to hide his smile. "Could your father have use for some hydroelectric mangroves?"

"I am certain he could." The light in her eyes rose more brightly than the awakening sun. "And, of course, you must teach me every single thing you know about every single thing you do. And all about hydra-eclectic mangroves, and nightingales made of gold, and ferns that water themselves. Or oil themselves. Whichever."

Jesper squeezed her hand, his joy too overwhelming to articulate.

They exited the Arboretum. Lady Zuhanna pulled away and set her hands on his arms, as if instructing a child. "Now. You must meet Papa and I in two hours, right at the castle gates, and—you said all you needed to bring was seeds and a number of papers?"

"My stock, blueprints, and notebooks. All else is replaceable."

"And we shall sneak you away and go for a long voyage on a ship, and we shall arrive in South Tairee—" her eager grip tightened anew as she spoke— "and you shall build us the most fantastical Arboretum that the world will ever know, and my elder sister can do whatever she likes about ruling the country someday, but you and I shall live in the same little house at the center of your new strange and magical woods for ever and ever and ever."

Jesper's eyes clouded with tears.

"Won't that be fun?"

He kissed her again.

When he could finally bring himself to pull away, he hastily wiped his face and said, "But there is one more thing that you must do before we leave Holdt."

"There is?"

Jesper nodded. "Before you leave to meet me at the main castle gates... touch the column I planted last night outside your bedroom window."

"Touch it?"

Jesper pointed. From where they stood, the Perennial Tower was visible; Jesper's accompanying creation, swaying precariously, sparkled in the new light. "Yes. Don't you remember what happened when you touched the first ringauble I made you?"

Lady Zuhanna's lips curved into an impish grin. "If I'm not there to touch it a second time, that stupendous tower will just sing on and on and on until they figure out how to dismantle it, won't it?"

"Well..."

She laughed. "Oh, Kanna will *hate* that. It's the sweetest gift you could give to me. Stars, but my cousin is a great crashing tedious bore, isn't she?"

Jesper laughed as well. The tireless Arboretum sang at his back, the sun climbed higher, and the lawn came alive with servants, page boys, guards, and curious Gentlemen and Ladies who had heard the furtive midnight rumors and come to gawk at the audacious result. "She certainly is, and I am more than glad to leave her. In fact, I'm sure I will miss nothing at all about this place."

"Not even your old Arboretum? It's so lovely."

Jesper made a dismissive gesture. "It is mechanical and empty, a mere echo of the living. But my new Arboretum— that one will finally have a soul at its heart."

Lady Zuhanna cocked her head. "How does one cultivate such a soul?"

He gave her one last parting kiss. "That, my Lady, is what *you* will be teaching *me*."

THE COLOR OF SAND

Where the sea, sand, and sky come together and kiss, there once lived a boy named Catch. He lived in a driftwood hut on the edge of the dunes with his mother, so far from the village that they had no neighbors, save for a sandcat.

The sandcat lived in a hole ten feet away, and had not been happy when Catch's mother had first come there, shamefaced with her baby clutched to her chest, resigned to living in such a place alone. But although the sandcat had said, "I am Bone. This is my dune. You will go away," Catch's mother set her mouth, dried her tears, and placed little Catch down in the dunegrass so she could gather driftwood for a shelter. She said her name was Fairday, and that she was staying. She was that sort of woman.

Every morning, when the light licked the tops of the dunes bright gold, Catch and his mother would walk west to the beach, and then north or south along the shore. Every so often, Catch's mother would swoop to the flat sand and pluck up a fragment of something from the sea wrack. When Catch was small, he copied her and gathered anything; later, beginning to understand, he only gathered pebbles; later still, she showed him what lay in her hand and said, "Like this."

They were stones, but not stones. They were too translucent. Held up to the light, they shimmered with pinks and oranges and reds, like water beneath the setting sun. Held in the palm, they exuded a soft warmth. Catch even sniffed one once. He lacked the words to describe what he smelled, but he knew what it was not. This was not a thing of the sea.

"Where do the pieces come from?" he finally asked.

Catch was five. His mother's age was unknown. "Someplace past the ocean," she said. "Maybe from under it."

"Are they from another beach?"

"Maybe."

"Are they rocks?"

Fairday reached into the pocket of her dress, as though touching them could help her think. "No, Catch. They're something different. They're stranger than rocks."

"Are they jewelry?" Catch asked, when he was seven. "When we go to the Equinox Markets to sell them all and trade—people buy them because they're pretty?"

Catch's mother shook her head. "They are very beautiful, but they can't be cut or polished. So I suppose you could wear them as jewelry, but only if you liked their natural shapes."

When Catch was ten, he asked, "Are the pieces magic?"

It was three weeks before their trip to the Autumn Market. They were sitting in the hut, listening to the drizzle outside, sorting through baskets and baskets of pieces. Thin, yellow, small, triangular, heavy, shimmering, orange, irregular, smooth, red, thick, square, round, shiny, bright, warm, glowing. Their combined heat made the hut toasty despite the fall chill, and the walls of the ill-made shack rippled with refracted, water-patterned light.

"They're a mystery," said Catch's mother. She sounded almost sad. "One of the great, enduring mysteries of the Langdown Coast. I always saw foreigners buying them in the markets when I was a little girl, and foreigners are buying them still. You'll almost never see another person around here bothering with them. Whatever else they are, in the end, they're just souvenirs."

The neighboring sandcat, with whom they'd long ago forged a comfortable truce, looked up from sniffing a tiny basket of white triangles. "You are wrong," he said. "Catch's guess is right."

Fairday snorted. "Please, Bone."

"No please." Bone blinked his big, gold eyes. "Its name is refulgium. It has easy inside. You take out the easy. You make magic. I thought you knew." His eyes squeezed shut, a sandcat laughing. "Everyone knows."

"Everyone," scoffed Fairday.

"Everyone," Bone repeated. "Wind in her dune. Blood in his dune. Grass in her dune. Cloud in his dune. Crab and Feather and Pebble and Creek in their dunes, and—"

"Yes, fine, everyone," said Fairday, "but if the pieces—"

"—its name is refulgium—"

"—if *refulgium* has genuine magic inside, why have I never seen any of the sandcats using it?"

"Silly," said the sandcat. "I use it right now."

Before their astonished eyes, Bone's throat contorted and bobbed. He opened his mouth, unrolled his long tongue, and gagged. A smooth, pebble-sized red piece, like a drop of solidified blood, clattered into a basket.

When he spoke next, his speech was nothing but the chirps of an ordinary cat.

Fairday put a hand to her mouth.

But Catch, being Catch, plunged his hand into their basket of smooth, pebble-sized red pieces, cried, "I want to try!" and swallowed one up.

Fairday screamed. Bone snapped up his own piece and backed to the doorway, his ruff rising.

"Nothing's happening," Catch said. But then he bumped his head upon the ceiling, and noticed how small his mother and neighbor looked.

The hut shrank. Catch knelt down. The hut shrank

further, and Catch's broad shoulders lifted the roof up and away. When he finally stood, startled and naked in the cold drizzle, the top of the hut's walls scarcely reached his hips.

Fairday screamed again. Instead of running away, she ran forth and clutched her child's leg. She was, you mustn't forget, that sort of woman. "Bone! Where are you, you mangy liar!"

Bone poked his head from his hole. "I am not a liar. You are a human without a throat-pouch. Only a stomach. You swallowed it anyway. Where else did you think it would go?"

"What do we do?"

"Nothing," said Bone. "Wait until the refulgium comes out." To Catch, he said, "Do not eat until it does. Or you will grow even bigger."

"Can we undo it?" asked Fairday. "How do we undo it?"

But Bone pulled his head back inside his hole.

Catch wrapped his arms about himself. He shivered. "Mama, I'm cold."

"You should have thought of that before you swallowed it and split your clothes!" said Fairday, but when Catch's enormous face pinched with guilt, she was immediately sorry. "Hush now. Hush."

Catch hung his head. "I'll be okay. I'll go to Blood. He'll know what to do."

***

Blood lived in a hole five dunes over. He was old, his tawny fur and bobtail spotted with a white so bright, it shimmered. He had always been content to tolerate the two newcomers. They had never made trouble.

"I am Catch," Catch called into Blood's hole. "I will ask you a question about the pieces you... the refulgium that everyone swallows."

Blood was sleeping. "Go away."

Fairday's voice interrupted. "My baby ate one."

"So?"

"He grew big."

"Of course he did." To himself, Blood grumbled, "Ate a red one. What did she expect?"

"How do I make him small again?"

"Go away."

"Please! It's cold. We can't fit into our house anymore."

"So?"

Catch's voice cut in. "I am big now," he called into the hole. "Big enough to crush when I don't mean to. When I climb up the dunes to look for birds' eggs, I could crush everyone's houses."

Blood reluctantly uncurled and crawled up from his hole. Blinking in the drizzle, he regarded the outsiders. "Yes," he agreed, gauging Catch's new height and the size of his feet. "You can make great crushings."

"Now will you help us?" Fairday begged.

"You must eat a black refulgium," said Blood to Catch. "Red makes precision. So if a one wants to make speech, she swallows a red one into her throat-pouch, to make precise words. And if she eats it when she is a child, and there is food inside of her, it makes the food precise and her growing precise. So she grows big." His eyes pinched shut in laughter. "Would you like to try?" he asked Fairday. "You are an adult. So if you eat a red one, you will only grow very, very fat."

"A black piece!" said Fairday. "There are no black pieces!"

"Black makes undoing," continued Blood, unperturbed. "It undoes the other colors. You know none of this? Only color is what matters. Color and size. Richer color makes more power, and bigger size makes the refulgium last longer. When the red piece comes out of you, Catch, it will be smaller. You used some of it to grow big. You see?"

"Yes," said Catch, still shivering. His goosebumps prickled under a sheen of cold rain. "Please. Where can I find a black piece?"

"The beach, silly," said Blood. "But black is very rare. I only found it twice. And a dead one named Seedpod found it once."

Catch sneezed. The rain hung off his nose in tickling drops. Catch's mother, unable to handle her frustration any longer, shouted, "Then what must we do—find where the pieces come from and demand a black one?"

"Yes," said Blood, and added, "Your idea is good. If anyone tries to stop you, Catch can crush them."

***

Since their hut had no roof, Catch still had no clothes, and they had no better plan than Blood's, Catch argued that going into town and hiring a boat to hunt for black refulgium was the only course. "With what, you poor, stupid boy?" Fairday said bitterly. "We have no money!"

"No, we don't," agreed Catch. "But we have refulgium. And now we know what some of it does. Maybe we can trade."

So Fairday, who once more set her mouth and dried her tears, combed through the hut's ruins for refulgium, gathering a little bit here, a little bit there, until her pockets clinked with every step. Catch lowered his hand, she grasped a finger, and they walked to town.

The muddy road was empty on so dreary a day, but dreary days or no, towns are always bustling, so once inside the edges of the village, Catch and his mother came across a lot of startled people. The strangers stared, or made unkind remarks, or laughed. But Catch, being Catch, was determined not to care. He stuck out his monstrous tongue and growled until they paled and stepped back.

"Stop it, Catch!" said Fairday. "You cannot be a sandcat here. Can't you think before you act? You're already frightening enough like that. Now come. We must go to the harbor."

In those days, the wildest, jauntiest, devil-may-care-est seaman was a close-shaven man named Shamus Fleece. He was too beautiful for the sea, the town ladies said; so beautiful that it wasn't fair that his rich and childless wife should have him all to herself. They tried their best to tempt him to stray, and truth be told, Shamus Fleece was an easily tempted man. As a wave leaves sea wrack behind, so Shamus left a trail of smitten and broken hearts.

Fairday knocked on Shamus's dock-shack door, knowing this full well. Even so, when Shamus answered and she beheld that wild and beautiful face, still she felt his pull.

"I need to hire you and your crew for a job," said Fairday.

Shamus's handsome mouth froze into a brittle, uneasy smile. "Fairday." His eyes darted left and right. "I thought we agreed. You were never to come here, outside the Equinox Markets."

"We did agree," said Fairday, "but there's been a complication." She pulled a round, dark red refulgium from her pocket. "Believe me, I'm only here because you're the best. Listen—I can pay you."

Shamus slapped her hand. The refulgium bounced upon the dock and into the choppy sea. "Stop it. I don't want your trinkets, and nobody else does, either. If you don't leave—"

"Catch," Fairday called.

Her mammoth child, still naked and shivering, stepped from around the corner of Shamus's dock-shack.

"If I don't leave," said Fairday, "I'll tell the whole town who sired this new, unnatural monster in their midst. And I am not leaving unless it is on your ship, to go to the places I ask you to take me."

Shamus looked up at Catch. And up. Blinking in the

rain, he was startled to discover that the giant's face had a familiar beauty in its depths.

"Catch?" he asked, disbelieving.

Catch, being Catch, stared back down with the placid courage of a sandcat. "What is your name, coward?"

Shamus Fleece bellowed out a great, startled laugh. He slapped Catch on the leg. "Saint Meer's Third Eye, but he's hot as coals, isn't he?" To Fairday, he held out a stiff hand. "We have a deal. Be back here at tide-up tomorrow. Until then, I suggest you get some charity at the Temple. They might have a winding sheet that fits him."

***

Shamus's men were spooked by the new job. The woman, her hair wild and dark as tempests, would not speak to them. The boy, so gigantic he wore twin funeral shrouds as a toga, was as fearless as a sandcat. And Shamus Fleece, that great gallivanter of the Langdown Coast, was both cowed by their presence and closemouthed about their destination. He charted the course himself. The navigator, on a night when Shamus grew careless and left his cabin unlocked, took a peek at the charts and logbook, and immediately spread the terrible gossip. They were headed to Final Atoll.

"What's Final Atoll?" Catch asked. With his great height, he'd heard the sailors whispering in the rigging, and only had to turn around to confront their guilty, wind-worn faces.

"It's the deadliest," one confessed. "The worst. A man who sails to Final Atoll, them's the final waters he wets his boards in."

"Why?"

"Why?" echoed the sailor, baffled. "Because it's a mess. Rocks and wreckage miles and miles long, one big ring o' nightmares."

"The Devil's Shore," another put in. "No settin' foot

on it while you're alive."

Catch's stomach knotted with worry. He'd seen the icy politeness with which Shamus treated Mama. Shamus was a bad man—or at least, a man who didn't care for his employers. "Why are we headed there?"

"Why *are* we headed there?" the sailor shot back. "You and your mama are chartin' this wreck, ain't you?"

In the heart of the night, when Shamus stepped on deck to think an insomniac's thoughts, Catch, who was too big to sleep belowdecks, rolled over under his sail blanket and caught him. "Why are we sailing to Final Atoll?"

Shamus frowned. The starlight lifted his exquisite face to preternatural heights of beauty. "Who told you we were?"

"Everyone."

Shamus sighed and ran his fingers through his lustrous hair. He lowered his voice. "Your mama told me what you're about—this business with your magic rocks. Well, everything wrecks on Final Atoll, and those beaches are next to inaccessible. I'd bet there are some real finds on it. And plenty of your black... whatever... on its shores. So the plan's for us to get close enough, put you and your mama in a skiff, and have you make for the beach, where you can gather your special rocks to your heart's content. And if there are no special rocks to be had there after all, then we can still go ahead and sail to whatever other places your mama had in mind. Eh?"

It sounded like a good plan. And Catch, having grown up with the sandcats, could not recognize a lie. "That's a really good idea. Thank you, Mr. Fleece."

Shamus grinned and looked east, to the faraway shore on which the pining town ladies waited. "Don't mention it."

★★★

They dropped anchor and readied the skiff the night before, stocking it with plenty of supplies. "Your lunk of a boy eats a lot, don't forget," said Shamus cheerfully, "and besides, it's a long row to shore."

Fairday was unhappy. The beach was a mere smudge. "Can't we get any closer?"

Shamus pointed to a dark spot in the water. A wave broke there, spraying frothy ocean with a boom. "Not a chance. Only a shallow skiff, with a pair of sharp-eyed people, can make it."

And he insisted it was so when the time came, when he and his men lowered Fairday and Catch, and only Fairday and Catch, down to the swirling waters. With Catch's unnatural height and strength, he maneuvered the craft with ease. Fairday kept her eyes on Shamus Fleece's vessel, face pinched with uncertainty.

"Is something wrong?" Catch asked. He tried a few pulls of the oars and said, "This isn't bad at all."

"Let's pray it stays that way," said Fairday.

Catch pulled them on. The waters grew choppier, and more than once the skiff banged on sunken stones, throwing Fairday from her seat. The third time it happened, her vision spun from the impact, and for a few moments she couldn't trust what she saw. It appeared as though Shamus Fleece's ship had pulled up anchor and was leaving.

But when her vision cleared, she wasn't wrong.

She ordered Catch to turn the skiff about and pull with all he had. He did, but not even a giant can outrun a fully rigged ship. It was hopeless.

Panting, Catch rested the oars on the gunwale, eyes wide and baffled. Fairday buried her face in her hands and wept. "Stupid," she sobbed. "So stupid."

"Don't cry, Mama," said Catch, helplessly. "I'll think of something."

"Oh, Catch," cried Fairday. "I'm so sorry." She pulled her handfuls of refulgium forth. "We only have enough food and water for three days. We have no choice. Something might help, and you've tried already—I'll go next—which do you think I should swallow?"

"Not a white one," said a muffled voice.

Catch peeled off the canvas from the top of their supplies. Blinking in the center of the bags, tightly curled, lay Bone. "The white ones make the unlikely happen. You eat it and very bad things might happen to your body. Or very good things. Maybe you will shrink. Probably you will grow thorns everywhere and die."

"Bone!" cried Fairday. She scooped up the heavy sand-cat into her arms, and Bone's eyes popped wide as his ears flattened against his skull.

"No please," he said, wriggling.

"Bone, how did you get here?"

"I hid on the ship."

"Why did you follow us?"

Bone merely looked up at her. A sandcat's reasons are his own.

"Never mind," said Catch. "What should we do?"

Bone wriggled out of Fairday's arms. His ruff rose, then settled. "We should go to the..." He paused at the unfamiliar word. "Atoll. The hollow island. Maybe there are many pink ones."

"Oh! I have pink ones!" Fairday displayed a handful of pink triangles. "See?"

Bone sniffed them. "We need more. Pink makes the big. We need a big wind to push us home, and many red ones to make the wind precise."

Fairday shook her head. "If the sandcats have all known so much magic all this time, why aren't they... I mean, why aren't you...?"

Again, Bone merely looked at her.

Thinking back, Fairday realized that, for as long as she had lived near the dunes, there had been no storms, no floods, no hurricanes or gales. Only gentle rain.

And the creek never dried out. The game was always

plentiful. The winters, while cold and snowy, were never cruel.

The hairs on Fairday's arms prickled.

Catch put his oars back in the water. "I'll go as fast as I can."

★★★

Not even Catch's great size and strength could smooth their final approach. The currents and rocks became so treacherous that the skiff overturned near a gravel sandbar. They salvaged what they could, and with the boat holding Fairday, Bone, and the sodden supplies, Catch half-floated upon it and half-pushed it to shore, cutting his shins and feet on countless barnacles and stones.

Final Atoll was vast and cruel, a gravel beach as gray as thunderheads. Nothing grew but a few sickly wisps of dunegrass. The shore itself was scarcely as deep as Shamus Fleece's ship was long. On the other side, it dropped off once again into sea—an inner sea of so calm and deep a blue, Fairday could believe it supernatural, and that this was the Devil's Shore after all.

Bone leaped from the boat. "Ah," he said, nosing in the gravel. "Many refulgiums. Do you see? We will have all the red and pink ones very soon."

Fairday ignored him, first fussing about her son, who was sitting on the beach and wincing over his many minor wounds. Fairday used a little of their fresh water to clean them, as little as she dared. "Wait, Bone."

"Forget about the refulgium," said Catch. "What's that?"

Fairday followed where he pointed. In the heart of the supernatural sea, a mountainous island stretched its tooth-colored towers to the sky.

The island hadn't been there a moment before.

Fairday did not know how to answer. Averting her eyes, she hunted for refulgium.

True to Bone's prediction, they had enough red and pink pieces within minutes. The search for black refulgium, however, stretched on. Now and then they took a break and straightened, staring at the island that had, until they'd set foot on the Devil's Shore, been invisible. But their curiosity was fruitless. They could not ask questions of each other, and no friend or foe crossed the inner sea to meet them.

Nor did the shore offer what they sought. Fairday and Catch found refulgium in a whole spectrum of colors—not just pinks and whites and yellows and reds and oranges, but greens, blues, browns, violets, and golds; indigos, lavenders, and aquamarines; and exotic melds of color they had no name for. A navy-blue piece nearly had them fooled, and Fairday swatted it out of Catch's hand before he could pop it into his mouth. But as the sun began its gentle dive down the sky, Fairday's long-practiced eyes finally plucked a bit of gravel from its surroundings, and her fingers followed suit. She held it aloft. A black piece, smooth enough for Catch to swallow without harm.

But when he did so, nothing happened.

"Perhaps it takes time," said Fairday. They sat on the gravel to wait.

They waited there the whole night, past sundown and moonrise. Bone dug a trench in the gravel. Catch flipped the skiff over it for meager shelter. They huddled in the darkness, listening to the booming waves, and nothing changed.

At sun-up, Catch said, "It isn't going to work. We have to row to the island. Maybe they'll know how to help us."

★★★

The Final Sea (or so Catch dubbed it) was as luminous and deep as cobalt glass. The waters were sluggish, and their little skiff made barely a wake.

The Final Island (or so Catch dubbed it) was steep and deathly silent. No songbirds sang from its fruit-laden branches, and no columns of smoke rose in the distance.

The pier they tied their skiff to was deserted of all other craft, and the rope they tied it with was frayed soft by weather.

"Hello?" called Fairday, the first to disembark.

The Final City did not answer.

They entered the narrow, winding streets. Fairday called, Catch carried supplies, and Bone sniffed walls and doorways. Every structure was too clean to be real; every road, paved with perfectly fitted stone, was deserted.

"Did they all die?" Catch wondered.

"I do not know," said Bone. His ruff rose. "The magic smell is very strong. Stronger than death."

High up, in a tower window, a face disappeared behind a curtain.

They climbed higher. To either side waited secret wonders: empty courtyards echoing with the bubble of running water, walls covered with iridescent butterflies, gardens that produced fruit that smelled of roasted flesh. The impression of vanishing faces grew. Movement flickered at the corner of each eye, like the shadows of gulls passing overhead.

The road ended in a courtyard. A wide set of steps led into the last tower of all.

A slender woman, her face etched with wisdom, waited at the top of the steps. Her pale garments didn't so much hang from her as float.

"You again," she said, to Bone.

Bone flattened his ears.

"What do you want?" she asked.

Fairday gaped at her sandcat neighbor. "Wait. You've been here before?"

"No." Bone's ruff puffed erect. "I am Bone. I am here with two people. I do not know your name."

Fairday blinked, and the woman was standing beside them. She peered at Bone. Her eyes were a sandcat's gold. "I am Sun." She straightened. "Forgive me. I mistook you for someone else."

"I am Bone."

"Yes. I'm sorry."

"Who could you have mistaken him for?" Fairday demanded, then hastily added, "If I may ask. Since I didn't think anyone came here."

The woman waved a hand dismissively. "Not anymore. But we are long-lived."

"I am Catch," said Catch. "I did something stupid and ate a red refulgium, but I don't want to be a giant, not really. Can you help us?"

"Catch!"

The woman smiled. The lines in her face etched more deeply, and Fairday saw not only wisdom there, but pleasure. "I see you're a very direct fellow."

"I apologize for my son," said Fairday, taking one of Catch's monstrous fingers in what she hoped was a firm, authoritative grip. "He was raised in the Langdown dunes with the sandcats."

"Indeed," said the woman, her smile growing. Other people, many old, all beautiful, appeared in the courtyard. Not walked or drifted from doorways: appeared, as though they'd been there all along and had merely stepped from behind the sunbeams. "We don't often have visitors in Cairnachh, civilized or otherwise. Would you like to come inside?"

When Fairday thanked her, and said that yes, they would, the courtyard became a cool and airy receiving room, and the sunny flags became soft cushions around a low, well-laden table.

Fairday put a hand to her mouth. Bone stood on his hind legs, placed his front paws on the table, and leaned forward for a sniff.

His ruff settled. "The food is not magic." He removed

a fowl from a plate with his teeth, dragged it to the floor, and crouched over it, crunching the bones with obvious satisfaction.

Catch's face lit up. "You may," Fairday whispered, "but for Moon's sake use a *plate*."

The company settled around the table. Fairday watched them and copied their table manners: take communal food with the left hand, eat from one's own plate with the right. "Thank you for your hospitality."

Catch took food with both hands, but to his credit, he did place it on a plate before eating it. The low table was too low for his great frame, and Fairday's heart stung with the sight of him hunching over so far, trying to join them on their level. "Yeah," said Catch. "Thank you. And thanks for helping us undo what I did. It was a dumb mistake and I'm sorry I made it." He put a whole loaf of bread in his mouth, then said, "Bone said I had to eat a black one to undo it, but we found a black one and I ate it and nothing happened. Why?"

Sun shook her head. "You swallowed the red refulgium too long ago. The antithesis must be taken soon after the primary magic is applied."

"So what do we do?"

Sun smiled. "You ask as if we know."

"Well, of course you know," said Catch. "You magicked us in here. You're wizards. You make the refulgium. Don't you?"

They all smiled, but their eyes were sad. Some glanced at each other, or at their plates. "We did," said Sun. "Once."

"What ha—" Catch started to ask, but Fairday jabbed him with her elbow.

"I suppose you could swallow a blue refulgim," said Sun, "to shrink you directly. But without knowing the exact shade or size of the refulgium you swallowed, this could be a dangerous choice."

"Gold," an old woman next to Sun said, "to turn back time."

"Lime," an older man next to her said, "to focus his willpower and make his will reality."

"Tawny," said the oldest man of all. He was seated at the far end of the table, and the only person present who was so very old that all his beauty had been washed away.

"Tawny?" Sun asked.

"The color of sand," he said.

While everyone else murmured approval, Sun spoke to Catch and Fairday. "We use sand-colored refulgium in magicks that deal with truth. If you swallow some, Catch, you'll have your true form restored to you."

Fairday exhaled in relief. She leaned over to hug her child, what little of him she could embrace.

Catch grinned. "Thank you. Thank you so much."

"Grigor?" Sun asked. A middle-aged man stood, bowed, and disappeared. "He'll fetch you a piece."

"Thank you," Fairday echoed. "I cannot tell you how grateful we are. We won't bother you any further, after this. Our friend... er, our neighbor... our... well... Bone has helped us gather red and pink refulgium, and we'll start our journey home tomorrow."

Sun shook her head. "I'm afraid not."

"Is tomorrow a poor time to sail?"

Now all the company exchanged glances. Sun looked at Fairday, then away, her brows raising and lowering.

"What?"

"We don't have visitors often," said Sun.

"You've mentioned."

More glances rippled around the table. Sun licked her lips. "That is... we have many questions about the world outside."

"We are poor people to ask," said Fairday. "We come from the sand dunes. Which I have mentioned."

The glances became strained with distress. "I'm sorry," said Sun. "What we mean is... we would very much like your company."

"We can stay a little while, Mama," said Catch. "Can't we? We still have a few days before the Market."

But the discomfort in those wise and ancient faces spoke far more than their delicate words alone could. Fairday stood. "You would have us be prisoners."

"No," said a woman, swiftly. "Scholars, to join us in Paradise."

Fairday swatted Catch lightly with the back of her hand. "Get up, Catch. We're leaving."

"I'm afraid you're not," said Sun, biting her lip.

Fairday whirled to go. But the sumptuous room had no door.

"Cairnachh is rich with mysteries," said the oldest man. His tone was anxious, almost pleading. "Think of the wonders you could spend your lives unraveling, delving through miles of libraries—"

"I said we come from the dunes!" Fairday cried. "None of us can even read!" She swept an arm violently, to indicate the island, the inner sea, the distant Devil's Shore. "We never asked for any of this! We don't want your mysteries!" She blinked back tears and fury. "We just want to go home!"

"We are going home," said Catch, uncertainly. "Right, Mama?"

Grigor appeared. Everyone fell silent, shifting uncomfortably on their cushions, rich food forgotten. Grigor walked around the table to Fairday, and with great ceremony raised his fist, turned it over, and opened his palm to reveal a refulgium the color of sand.

Nobody spoke a word.

Bone padded over. He sat and groomed his front right paw. Between licks, he said, "I have a bargain to make with you."

The whole company looked down.

"I will stay. Fairday and Catch will leave."

Catch opened his mouth. "Oh, Bone," Fairday whispered.

"And why would we strike this bargain?" asked Sun.

"They are stupid," Bone explained, serenely. He set down his right paw and went to work on his left. "They can tell you nothing. Who eats a red one, anyway? Honestly. But I am Bone. I am a sandcat. I know about the refulgiums. I live with the refulgiums. I like them. I will listen to your new refulgiums tell me secrets. You will make the big and precise wind for Fairday and Catch to ride home. You will listen to me. I have a dune. I am Bone."

Catch's face crumpled. Fairday bit her fist.

The silent glances of the old ones went around again, but now their expressions fluttered with too many motions and nuances to follow. They finally faced their visitors as one.

"I'm forced to admit it," said Sun. "Your argument makes sense. You would probably be the only worthy scholar in your party, after all. We agree to your bargain."

★★★

After a long, sleepless night in a decadent bedroom that would have put an emperor to shame, Fairday and Catch rode with Sun and the oldest man back out to Final Atoll. The skiff could comfortably seat four hale sailors, but since Catch had not yet swallowed the sand-colored refulgium, it was a tight squeeze. It was tighter still thanks to Bone, who had calmly followed them to the dock that morning, but neither Fairday nor Catch was about to refuse his final, wordless offer of company.

They disembarked, carried the boat over the harsh gravel, and set it upon the far shore in silence. The rocks and waves gnashed and foamed. While the oldest man scratched lines in the gravel and the hull of the skiff with red and pink refulgium, Sun reached into her pocket and said, "I have a farewell gift for you."

"We have it already," said Fairday, glancing at Catch. He and Bone watched the oldest man draw the magic lines with bright-eyed interest. "He wants to wait until we've crossed the sea, in case something goes wrong, and we need his size and strength to row."

"I'm not talking about that." Sun drew forth another refulgium, marbled in red and brown, as small as Catch's precious tawny piece. "Blood and earth. Family. If ever you are separated from your child in some way—or he from you—swallow this. The blood that binds you, and the earth you share, will bring you close again."

Sun pulled up Fairday's palm and dropped the piece upon it. It felt so warm. Like a tiny ball of life.

Fairday tucked it away, feeling both grateful and ashamed.

"Step inside," said the oldest man. "All's ready."

Fairday knelt by Bone. She held his ears and kissed his forehead. "Thank you," she whispered. "Thank you."

"You will have my dune now," said Bone. "I am Bone."

Fairday blinked her tears into his fur. When she let go of his ears, a little piece of her stayed behind, hard and bright and warm as what lay in her pocket.

Now Catch knelt and bent over the biting gravel. His own tears ran freely, but his face was empty. Nose to nose, he and Bone regarded each other.

Delicately, Bone extended his tongue and ran it over Catch's broad, smooth cheeks.

"I will honor your dune," Catch whispered. "I am Catch."

"You are Catch."

Catch backed away and stepped into the boat, never taking his eyes from Bone's.

Fairday joined him. The oldest man whispered something behind them, a little shimmer of red and pink dropped to the shore, and the waters were flying away beneath them, under a cushion of whistling air.

***

The little skiff slowed and lowered, gradually, until by mid-morn it moved no faster than an ordinary boat, and the tops of the waves spit against its belly. The tawny-green smudge of the Langdown dunes rose against the horizon. The skiff came ashore, grounding to a stop with a final hiss.

For a moment, Fairday and Catch sat in silence.

Then Catch looked at his mother, shrugged, and pulled the precious refulgium from his pocket.

He smiled at her and swallowed it.

The transformation was soundless and smooth, like the evolution of a cloud. Catch shrank and shrank, until he was swimming in his funeral shroud toga. Billowing fabric closed over his head, leaving nothing but a startled, wriggling shape beneath. Fairday nearly moaned with relief. She fought through the cloth, parting it to pull him out.

A sandcat kitten, wide-eyed and flat-eared, emerged.

Fairday screamed.

The sandcat leaped clumsily from the fabric. He made it to a seat with the grace of a poorly handled puppet, scrabbling his claws for purchase. Fairday sobbed. She knelt in the boat and put her face in her hands, and the voice that cried, "No, no, no, no, no," was hers.

The sandcat looked down at himself, astonished.

Fairday raised her head. "You bastards," she wailed to the sky, to a hidden world beyond the edge of the wind. "You bastards."

***

Fairday returned to the wreckage of her driftwood hut, the sandcat kitten in her arms. As she began so many years ago, so she began again; but now her shame was deeper, and her loss bitter beyond measure.

Once she could bear it, she took the sandcat to wise old Blood. He showed the kitten how to swallow and expel an ordinary pebble into and out of his roomy throat-pouch, and then placed a tiny red refulgium in the sand at his feet. The kitten gulped it down and coughed. "I am Catch," he said, spitting up sand.

Fairday wept anew.

Blood was very interested in their story. Everyone was. However, nobody was surprised. "Of course Catch is a sand-cat," was the common response. "He was always a sandcat."

Many weeks later, Fairday worked up the courage to speak with Blood, alone. After bribing him with a hefty portion of smoked fish, she told him about the strangers' other gift. The little coal of warmth still lay in her pocket, and had lain there ever since. She couldn't bear to take it out. "Sun said it would bring my family together," she told Blood. "I've been thinking. Blood... if I swallow this... will I..."

Blood gazed back at her, unperturbed. It was early winter now. The slanted sun pushed its watery light through the dunegrass, over sand dusted with white. The air was still but cold. Every whisper hung as steam.

"Do you think I'll become as he is?"

Blood blinked, slowly. He did not answer.

"Should I do it?" Fairday asked.

Blood said, "You live in the dunes. You have a dune. You do not want to go back to the village." He closed his eyes, his face pinching up. "You are silly. Your baby is happy. We are happy. You live here with everyone who is happy. This place is the happiest."

Fairday decided to be brave. She smiled. Her fingers sought the Final Gift, and she decided to swallow it that night, in front of Catch, after dinner.

She was, you forget, that sort of woman.

★★★

Catch nosed a pebble across the floor. "Ready?" he

asked.

Fairday tried to nod, but her new neck was not made for it. Her throat made a strange chirp when she tried to speak. But, because Catch was Catch, he just pinched up his face at her and showed her the obvious trick of swallowing and keeping a thing in one's throat-pouch.

When she finally had the refulgium in place, she swallowed, coughed, and said, "I am Fairday."

Catch squeaked and licked her chin.

She laughed. So did Catch. Awkward barks chirped through the driftwood hut. "Is it okay for us to laugh like this?" Fairday asked.

"I guess," said Catch. "I mean, we're sandcats. Isn't the whole point of this doing whatever we want? We're free, Mama. We don't have to scrounge every day and go to the Markets anymore."

Fairday licked his face until he purred.

They pushed open the door and stepped outside, Fairday unsteady on her wide and loping legs. It was night now, but the moon was full and high, and everything looked fresher and deeper: the texture of the dunegrass, the dark of the ocean, the color of sand.

"So this refulgium is supposed to bring family together, right?" Catch asked as they walked. "Does that mean if I had any sisters or brothers, or uncles or cousins, they'd turn into sandcats when you swallowed it, too?"

"I don't know," Fairday said. "I don't think anyone here knows. Red and brown is too rare."

"I guess we don't have any family that's still alive, then," said Catch. "Otherwise they'd appear here, too. Right? Since if you eat it, it brings family together?"

Fairday looked at her son. Then, though her feet were still clumsy, she ran back to the hut.

He was waiting for them by the shack, sitting with his head held high. The firelight from the cracked door traced a dancing path down his back.

"I am Bone," he announced. "I was away, but I am back. How am I back? I smell you. You are Catch and Fairday. Catch, you were always a sandcat. Fairday, why are you a sandcat?

"I smell Shamus Fleece. I smell his fear. He was here, running, moments ago. I met him on the big boat. We were going to the Final Atoll. I did not like him. I am glad he is afraid. Why is he here? Why does he smell like sandcat now?

"I do not understand. You will explain. You will give up my dune to me. I am Bone."

They covered his ears with their tongues.

★★★

They spent a final night in the hut, drowsing by the dying fire. Fairday and Catch told their tale.

Then Bone said, "I have a story, too."

He rolled to his feet. He coughed, gagged, and unfurled his long tongue, but it was not a single red refulgium that dropped to the floor. A whole rainbow of colors pattered onto the packed earth, scattering jewels of reflected firelight across the rude beams.

Fairday and Catch stared.

"I do not wear clothes," Bone said. "I do not have pockets. I research many things in Cairnachh. I must keep all the many things in my throat-pouch."

His eyes closed and his face pinched in pleasure.

"Thank you for bringing me home. I know things Cairnachh does not. I will tell them to you now."

THE RAMSHEAD ALGORITHM

Beneath the four of us was a patch of bare earth, which Yuri had anchored into reality with a screw he'd muttered. Beyond our tiny island of the rational, the lines, as they say here, ran crooked: unknown suns rocked in the sky in polynomial smears of light. The walls of vegetation surrounding us reiterated with themselves, morphing each second into something different. The sudden paths in the undergrowth pulsed, as if breathing, before being swallowed by life again. Unchallenged by screws, The Maze reigned.

"Are we anywhere close?" I asked them.

A worker from Trail Crew 64, a translucent thing covered in dexterous pseudopodia, spoke up. Her voice came from the vibrations of a million cilia. "I think so. I didn't have my curvessor with me when I noticed the damage, but I'm sure your problem is starting somewhere here in the 64th cycle. We shouldn't need to tune into another cycle to find it."

I scratched my thigh. Something burned there, like the bite of an insect, though the insects in The Maze aren't exactly real either. "Well, if you're wrong, I've fixed problems on a lot of other cycles before. We should be able to figure it out without involving yet another Trail Crew."

Yuri thumped the bare earth with a triumphant set of talons. To the being from Trail Crew 64, he said, "Space-Cowboy-Hero Ram can fix anything."

They all turned to admire me. I scratched my thigh again and pretended not to notice. I'd been doing this for a decade, and I probably could fix anything by now. But the "Ram of Earth" folktales that were starting to go around were bad enough, and I didn't want to fan the flames.

"But what's wrong with your leg?" asked Yuri. "You are injured?"

"No. I just—" The fabric beneath my hand felt hot.

An injury would've been preferable.

Slowly, I slid a hand into my pocket, feeling for my vial of silvery spirit water. I withdrew it. Inside the stoppered container, 2,000 times stronger than glass, my spirit water was boiling.

Yuri tossed his ox-like head in alarm. "Cowboy-Hero —"

"Sorry, everyone," I blurted. "It's just a chaos knot here that needs untying, you'll be fine—I think I see a tree that won't change over there—gotta go—"

I turned side. I closed my eyes and tuned into the 98th cycle, not letting my rational eyesight ruin my sense of irrational impulse that could be my only guide in this place. I almost twisted my ankle in a small hole, ran over something wooden and hollow, made a turn at full speed, ran through something wet, and jumped.

I crashed through brush, and was suddenly running over consistent, grassy ground.

I stopped and opened my eyes. Trail Crew 98 HQ. Our hard-won clearing, anchored over acres, where all the Trail Crew workers from the planets on our shared plane of reality camped and recovered under the familiar laws of physics.

I ran expertly through the compound, past the ancient, central Spindle and its contradictory shadows, and past Perihana'ii's hut and its plume of smoke. Above the compound, the lines ran crooked, too; fifty feet up, the smoke from Perihana'ii's fire splintered into colors, or stars, or schools of frightened fish.

I ran into one of the private bathing houses and took the fastest bath of my life. While I splashed and cursed and dropped the soap, I ran through a mental list of options, all of them bleak. I was the only crew member from Earth in the entire Maze. My permanent two-way portal to Earth had just been officially approved. Only six outside people had even been to my world so far, and none of them were on my crew and therefore plane of reality, and none were even anywhere near the First East Iteration, the family of realities to which I belonged. And no one here at HQ could master the illusion of a human shell yet.

Better hurry.

After I jumped out of the bath, I shoved my work clothes in a duffel bag, then took out my $1,000 shoes (Christian Dior) and gave them a fast look-over for anything telltale. Any green blood? Bone shards? Thanatos sap?

Nope. Chemicals first, then: deodorant (Michel Germain, Sexual), aftershave (Perry Ellis, 360), summer scent (Issey Miyake, L'Eau D'Issey). Beneath the manufactured finesse, the smell of myself dissolved.

Clothing second: from a garment bag hung on a hook, Yves Saint Laurent (various collections). Boxers, jeans, socks; undershirt, button-down shirt, watch (Rolex, Cosmograph Daytona); aforementioned $1,000 shoes.

Hair last. I went to a mirror, a piece of polished tin nailed to a post. Meticulous and stupid: dry, gel, comb, sculpt.

If my portal were taken from me—

I stopped the thought, grabbed my bags, and ran outside, along the crescent-shaped bank of alarm pools that made up an edge of the compound. Each tiny pool, scrying the health of the two-way portals we watched over, lay clear and calm.

Except, of course, the farthest and newest one.

Mine.

I reached it, dropped my bags, and wiped my calloused palms on my $450 jeans. I typed on the boiling surface, wincing at the heat, seeking and discarding the incorrect times and places until the surface cooled with the single moment that contained the danger to my monitored portal. The stilled spirit water condensed into colors. I leaned forward.

My alarm showed me a place near my portal's entrance (or exit): a large kitchen done in white tile and stainless steel. Someone I knew too well was approaching from the adjoining hallway, his ruthless monologue preceding him in compacted commands, as if by Doppler effect. He entered the kitchen. Juan followed at his heels.

I'd always feared that it would end like this.

"Also," said my father to Juan, "phone Martinez about the meeting with Bill next week. Tell him it's on Thursday, and if he says that I said Wednesday, claim that I didn't."

My father rifled through the kitchen cupboards. Juan followed after him, taking notes on a legal pad. "Also, reschedule my fitting with Richard for next Monday. Imply that he's an arrogant shit for wrongly assuming that I'd gain weight, but be subtle about it. Work in an ambiguous comment about how some people, like his wife and daughter, do in fact pork up and spill out as they get older."

Juan scribbled. My father opened a cabinet, disregarded the eighteenth-century Plymouth porcelain within, and moved on to another. "Also, talk to the Bentley people about Alan's car. Make sure they use the dead oak from the side yard when they do the finishing in the interior. Ask if they can work in the part where he carved his initials. If they say they can't, tell them that I am not paying two hundred thousand dollars for a goddamn car that won't be paneled with my firstborn's favorite goddamn climbing tree."

My father finally pulled a meal-replacement bar from one of the cupboards and slipped it into a pocket of his

Givenchy suit. "Oh. And call a landscaping company about the hedge maze out back. I want it ripped out tomorrow morning."

There.

My hands clenched the spirit water and the image dissolved.

Somewhere behind me, I heard Yuri's distinctive, loping gait. Of course. He'd seen my boiling vial, and he'd be heading to Perihana'ii's hut to alert her. But I knew she'd just curl her tail helplessly and say there was nothing they could do, that my world was still too foreign. Ram of Earth was on his own.

So be it. Gripping my bags, I edged around the crescent's horn, to where the vegetation breathed and liquefied into itself.

I turned side.

This time, my way back to Earth was via a narrow winding road, wreathed in vines, blood in their veins in lieu of sap. Somewhere, children sang. The road forked and slithered, as all roads here do, and I coalesced The Maze's split-up cycles by feeling which fork was more interesting— and taking the opposite.

The bloody leaves around me gradually turned green. The distant singing faded. The tunnels retracted into the rectilinear walls of a hedge maze, first shaking, then pulsing, then almost still, save for the wind. The path turned from dust to grass, and a colored sky emerged above me. Blue. The smears of light overhead contracted into a single star.

I took another cold turn, and I was out.

I stood at the southernmost edge of a monstrous, hilly lawn, which sprawled up and away under the warm California sun. The slopes of it went on and on: orchards, gardens, fields, and flowerbeds; winding paths and statuary; benches, gazebos, secluded guest houses, and tennis courts; pools and granite fountains; artistic vistas and sculpted trees;

plants from around the world.

The hike up took twenty minutes.

At the top, a mansion lords over it all. I picked an entrance and stepped inside, into a scripted life where I am called Ramshead Jones, my father's net worth is $48 billion, and I am required to add glamor to the family name by being the hedonistic party boy.

And Jesus, do I hate it.

★★★

I entered my rooms and grasped the first idea that came to me. I rummaged in my bags for a phone, and when I found one, I rang the direct line to my brother's secretary.

"Patty Cheng."

"Patty—thank God. It's Ramshead."

"Good morning, Ramshead! How are you?"

"Where's Alan?"

"He's in a meeting right now."

"I hate to ask you this, but I need you to take him out of it. Tell him to come home. Immediately."

Her voice cooled into seriousness. "I'll go get him right away—hold, please?"

"Yes."

She put me on hold. I began to pace. The other people at that table would frown at each other when Alan left, and within a few hours, NASDAQ would probably quiver.

Whatever.

The line clicked to life. "Jesus, Ramshead, what is it?" asked Alan, out of breath.

"I can't talk about it over the phone. Please."

"Dad."

"No."

"Hanna."

"No."

"Jesus, Ramshead!"

"I can't. Just please—come home."

"What—you?"

"Please!"

He paused. "You? Ramshead Jones?"

"Alan—"

"What could *you* possibly need from *me?*"

"Don't do this to me now! I need you!"

"Is that so. This wouldn't happen to have anything to do with your latest fall from the planet, would it?"

"Alan, damnit, I *cannot* talk about it here!"

"You've been gone over two months this time, Ramshead. Doing what? Just what is it that you do, when you're away?"

"Come home, you hateful son of a bitch!"

Icy silence from the other end.

"I will come," Alan finally said. His pitch was even and calm. "And you will get down on your knees and thank God that I'm even bothering to deal with a parasite like you."

He hung up.

Well—at least he was coming.

I ran downstairs and outside, to await him on the mansion's main steps. I had to move the portal. I had to move the portal. In less than twenty-four hours? I took my copy of *Trail Crew Emergency Screws* from a pocket and thumbed through the pages. At least I found it quickly.

Screw 8: Moving a Portal from Without

Required blocks:
1: A tongue unknown
2: A tongue rare
3: A life unknown
4: A life rare

"Seriously?" I yelled at the book. An endangered animal, the sacrifice of a life that never was, and a language nobody can speak. With the screw itself to be spoken in a language *almost* nobody can speak. Christ, how could I do this?

I looked up at the sound of an engine, watching from across our green and empty front lawn: a Mercedes-Benz S550, powerful and purring. It moved with skillful violence. It swung over the long curve of the driveway and right up to me, at the bottom of the main staircase, where it whispered into silence.

I slid the book into a pocket. My brother climbed out of the car.

Alan strode up the steps, a flame of hunger and hate smoldering from within Armani Privé. He is too short, too broad-shouldered, to look much like our father, but he moves like him: hard, fast, relentless. He is not attractive. He wishes he were.

Alan crucified me with his eyes. "And?"

I opened my mouth.

"*And?*"

I said, "The backyard," and turned and ran into the house.

Alan followed me, saying something, but I ignored it and kept moving. In one minute I was through and out on the back lawn, waiting. I listened to him stomp through the hall behind me.

"There better be a fucking flying saucer in the middle of the fucking carp pond!" He banged out of the house and bent over, huffing, hands on his knees, hairline glistening with sweat. The scent of Calvin Klein's Obsession rose. "What the hell, Ramshead?"

I pointed south.

"What!"

I ran down the backyard. Alan cursed and followed, all the way down, until the house receded onto lofty hills. Below us, the wind pulled through the hedge maze, stretching east and west into hissing green infinity.

Behind me, Alan stopped.

I turned. "Come on," I demanded.

"Talk to me, goddamnit! What is it!"

"Come here."

"Talk to me!"

I felt my hands coil into fists. Around us, plum trees drank in the sun and couldn't care less. "Alan. I have to—" My tongue was sandpaper. "I have to show you something."

"You haven't showed me shit. You've dragged me all the way across the property when we could've just taken the service road down here. Do you have *any idea* what you pulled me out of?"

I started to shout, but he shouted me down. "Do you even care what it is the rest of us do, day after day, every day? Or can you not get past your own pampered little bubble?"

Alan paused for a gulp of air, and I felt my long-cultivated magnetism rise. The portal was too close. Around me, its exuded zap began to spin. Not like this.

"I swear to Christ, if you ever do this to me again, I will tell Patty that you have died." He drew a cell phone from a jacket pocket. "Now if you're done with your shitty little cry for attention, I have a lot of explaining to do."

"You haven't even looked at it yet!"

He raised the phone to his ear and spoke to me, coldly, as it rang. "Looked at what? There's nothing to see here."

I clenched my right fist and turned a screw. The zap spun into the first degree of visible, crackling over my fist and forearm like blue lighting.

Alan froze.

I raised my crackling fist. The sudden, humiliated fear in his eyes made me feel large and ashamed. I was ready to say, "Alan—I beg you—don't make me force you."

But Alan's wide eyes settled on the zap, and he blurted, "It's about the hedge maze."

My fist dropped like a dead bird. "It's *what?*"

Alan shut his phone and put it away, all the while staring at my hand. The zap fizzled into invisibility but I could still feel it circling. "The hedge maze. Isn't it."

I stared at him. I did not know where to start.

Alan took a step back. The humiliated fear had not gone away. "Don't make me get any closer to it."

"I... I won't."

"What have you seen?"

"Huh?"

"No. Don't tell me." He stepped back again. "What do you know about it?"

I stared at him again. The sweat around his hairline had thickened into beads. "What do *you* know about it?"

"Ramshead—don't." His voice was nearly pleading. "Let's not."

"When we were kids," I said quietly, "you told me it was haunted. It took me years to even work up the courage to get close to it. Did you actually see something, Alan?"

One of his hands fluttered out, looking for something supportive to grip. It brushed useless, reedy branches. "No."

I took a step toward him. "*I've* seen something. And I've been inside."

Alan swayed, as if he were about to faint; then sat down hard on a nearby rock as the color drained from his face.

"Look—I won't say any more. But I really need your help. And you don't want to know what'll happen if you decide not to give it. Please. I'm begging you, Al."

He shivered and said nothing.

I sat down on the grass. The zap still circled me, as if it could find refuge in my skin, but I ignored it.

Alan finally swallowed. "And?" he whispered.

I brushed off some invisible zap. "And?"

Alan asked, "What do I do?"

I let out a breath. "Thank—"

"Just tell me."

"Really. If you want to know what's going on—"

"I don't."

"Well, in case you're ever curious what—"

"I won't be."

Self-consciously, I looked down. I fiddled with the cuffs of my shirt. I wanted him to be curious—to demand that I explain everything, because all those years of secrets, my secrets, still loomed between us.

But I couldn't say that.

Instead, I looked up. "All right. I need you to find two things for me."

Alan reached a trembling hand into his jacket and pulled out his leather-bound, paper appointment book. He removed a pencil from the spine. "Go ahead."

I watched him transcribe as I spoke. "I need you to find me a text, either original or copied, in a language nobody has been able to translate. And I also need you to find someone who speaks a very rare language. Once you find someone, have them call me. Can you do this?"

"Yes."

"As soon as possible."

"Yes."

"Alan, I'm not kidding."

"I know." Alan replaced the pencil, shut the date book, and slid it back inside his jacket. "If I thought you were, I wouldn't've bothered to write it down in *there*."

I reached for something to say but came up empty.

Alan stood and climbed through the plum orchard, back toward the house. I watched him go. I could've walked back with him, but I still didn't know what to say.

I headed back to the house on a different path, so we wouldn't run into each other.

★★★

Alan went back to work. I went up to my rooms and locked the door, to concentrate on how to deal with the other two blocks I'd need for my portal-moving screw.

The "life unknown" was actually not an issue. I am male and healthy, and have plenty of homunculi to spare.

The "life rare" was the problem. I started with some research online, looking for places to call that offered private endangered-animal encounters. But every place's breathless, "Yes! Good morning! Mr. Ramshead Jones—an absolute pleasure—what can we do for you, sir!?" rapidly turned into an, "Ah... I'm afraid we can't allow animal encounters on private property... unsupervised... sir."

An hour later I was out of places to call. I went back online, digging for people who would sell "exotic" animals to private buyers outright. But the red tape here was even worse: you must be licensed, we must process your application, we must meet with you to see if you will be kind to our animals.

No time.

Was there such a thing as buying an animal on the black market?

Hanna would know.

I grabbed a set of car keys—Jaguar, XKR Portfolio, 2004—and headed toward the garage.

***

I drove around L.A. in loops and spirals, making more calls. Hanna has a cell phone, but the number always changes. She also has a house, but she does not like it. She much prefers the endless string of dangerous men that loops around her, so where she lays her head each night is never certain.

I finally got a lead. An ex-boyfriend of an acquaintance I'd met at a party some years ago told me that she was sleeping with a certain vocalist these days whose band was beginning the slide into bloated overexposure. I got an address and drove to his house. They buzzed the gate open for me, not because I knew him personally, but because when I go anywhere, gates always open.

The front door had been left ajar, so I entered unannounced. The interior was a frat-house wreck: broken furniture, shattered lamps, the stench of weed and beer. I heard someone clattering around in the kitchen, swearing in a masculine voice: "Where the hell does he keep the plates?"

I ventured upstairs, peeking in bedrooms. The remains of the house party reached into every corner: bongs, panties, pornography, designer jeans, condoms, dustings of cocaine, the occasional bass or guitar. One nude, bug-eyed woman with hard, globular breasts, smoking a cigarette in a bathroom doorway, demanding of me, "What the fuck are you looking at, asshole?"

I found Hanna in the master bedroom. She was standing barefoot at the floor-to-ceiling window, the tips of her fingers in the pockets of her tiny shorts, pulling down the low-rise waistband and revealing her tattoos, one fat red star on each hip. She had her weight on her right leg, and was watching the distant street with her head cocked, a strand of dark hair hanging loose from one of her high ponytails.

I cleared my throat. "Hanna."

She started. "Rammy! I didn't see you last night. Were you with the girls in the pool?"

Before I could answer, she grinned and strolled toward me, rolling her hips, making those red stars wink with each rise and fall of her waistband. "Daddy will love it that you're finally partying like you're supposed to, and keeping up the fashionable family image or whatever. Haven't seen you in ages, kiddo. How've you been?"

"I'm fine. Hanna—"

She reached me and curled her arms around my neck. She kissed me on the cheek. "Missed you bunches." She lowered one hand and rubbed it over my stomach. "Did you lose weight?"

I set a hand on hers and pulled it away. "Yeah. I've been really busy. Hanna, I've got something to ask you."

Hanna grinned up at me. I couldn't tell if she wore dark eye makeup or if she were exhausted. "Rammy, relax. We got all day."

"No, we don't." I stepped away from her. "Look, I'm really sorry, but I can't visit this time. I just have to ask you. Do you know where I could buy an exotic animal? In a hurry? I need it by tonight."

Hanna put her fingers back in her pockets and looked down at the carpet. "You mean you don't have time to hang out?"

"No. Tomorrow, maybe."

"I never see you anymore."

"I know—I said, I've been really busy."

"When am I supposed to see you?" She looked up at me, her frown quivering. "You're never at your house. And you know Daddy won't let me go back *there*."

I bit my tongue. Hanna misinterpreted my silence. She looked out the window again and said, "Forget it. You came to the party, and you didn't even talk to me last night. You don't have to say anything."

"I wasn't here last night. I just got here."

"To ask me something, instead of see me. Yeah. I get it." She turned her body away from mine, to face the street again.

I took a breath. "Hanna, you know I care about you—"

"I know you spend all day at *his* house," she said flatly, "instead of ever hanging out with me."

"I never know where you are!"

"You found me now, didn't you?"

"I didn't come here for this. Look." I took out my wallet and pulled out all the cash I had on me, $600. "If you need to pay someone for the information, then here. I'm really serious about this. You're the only one who can help me."

She turned her head and eyed the money. "Why do you need an exotic animal?"

"I just need it, okay?"

"It's a weird thing to ask. What's it for?"

I rolled my eyes. "I need it for a spell."

Hanna cocked her head.

I thought she'd take my bitterness as sarcasm, but she turned her body back toward mine. "A spell? That does what?"

I looked away. She finally reached out and took the cash, and I gratefully pulled back into myself. "I was kidding. Forget it."

"What does it do? This spell?"

"I don't need it for a spell, okay? I was being sarcastic."

"You're a rotten liar."

"Come on. Do you really believe that I secretly know how to cast spells?"

"You seem to."

I didn't reply.

Hanna took out a wallet from her back pocket and flipped it open. For a moment, I hated her for her self-absorption and breezy acceptance of something so strange. Shouldn't she feel something? Betrayal? Shock?

She put the money away. I saw Hanna's hard-copy picture of our mother in her wallet, her serene expression, her narrow, wide-set eyes, her face as cool and evocative as the face of the moon. Leading a life somewhere just as out of reach, for twenty-three years now and counting. For a moment, I hated her, too. Had she stayed around, Hanna might have turned into something other than this.

Hanna said, "You'll have to show me some magic sometime."

I looked at her closely. I couldn't read her expression.

"Can you find an animal for me or not?"

Hanna slid her wallet back into her pocket and offered me that deceptively sunny grin. "Sure can."

"Find me something slow, that won't run away. Like a tortoise or a slug. Or better yet—" I took out my wallet again and handed her a credit card. "Buy it for me with this, if you can. And call my cell as soon as you do, so I know it's on its way."

She took the card. Her eyes glittered. "Do I get a present for helping you? Since Daddy refuses to 'sponsor a whore' and give me money anymore?"

I couldn't say no. "Sure. Buy yourself whatever you want."

She slid up to me and gave me a one-armed hug, while slipping my credit card into the front of her waistband with her other hand. "Love you bunches, Rammy. Call me and we'll hang out sometime for real, okay?"

Her hair smelled like cigarettes, and this close, I could see the redness in her eyes. I hugged her back, as if I could squeeze out everything within her that I had long ago ceased to recognize. "Sure."

★★★

I left the party and got back into the Jag. I drove a winding course through L.A. again, making more calls.

"Alan, it's Ramshead. I'm calling to see how things are going."

"Alan, it's Ramshead. I couldn't get you on your main cell. I'm seeing if you've found any of those things we talked about."

"Hi, Alan, it's Ramshead. I've tried a bunch of your other numbers. Where in God's name are you?"

I finally gave up and called the direct line to his secretary again.

"Patty Cheng."

"Hi, Patty, this is Ramshead."

"Ramshead! Hello. Is everything all right?"

"Yeah. I need to speak with Alan again. He should be expecting my calls, but I can't raise him. Didn't he come back to the office?"

"He did. I think he's here right now."

I was driving east on San Vicente Boulevard, already doing sixty, but at this I upped my speed to sixty-five. "Do you know if he's supposed to be in for the next half-hour or so?"

"He is, as far as he's told me."

"Great."

"Did you want me to get him?"

"No. That's all I needed to know."

We said our goodbyes, and I hung up as I swerved onto Wilshire Boulevard. Alan was deliberately not answering my calls.

I upped it to seventy.

★★★

I parked in the garage, showed my badge to security, and ran into the depths of the building. In minutes, I stood outside the antechamber of Alan's office, sweating and breathless. I wiped my forehead with my wrists, figured that was good enough to make me look presentable, and went inside.

Patty looked up from her desk as I came in. "Oh! Ramshead. I wasn't expecting you. Shall I—"

"Yes."

"I'll tell him you're here."

I did not sit down. Patty smiled at me and busied herself at her computer. It should have taken Alan less than fifteen seconds to come out from his inner office, but thirty seconds passed.

"Would you like to sit down?" Patty asked.

"No."

"I think he's in the middle of something."

I moved to the inner door, but Patty stood up, her smile a warning. "I'm sure he'll be right out."

I fumed and paced. Patty made calls and spoke in a sweet, pleasant voice. She typed at her computer. She put documents into envelopes. I pointedly checked my Daytona, over and over, and in this way, twenty horrible minutes passed.

I stopped pacing. "Patty," I finally said, "I'm really sorry about this."

She waved a hand. "That's all right. I know that things happen, and—Ramshead!"

I ran into his office anyway.

And right there, on the wide coffee table (Thomas Messel, American Chestnut), that lying son of a bitch was having lunch.

With *him*.

My heart seized. The door swung shut behind me. Alan looked up and away, too fast for me to even make eye contact, as across the table from him, my father said dryly, "Good afternoon, Ramshead. I can't imagine that you'd possibly be interested in our business meeting, but please, if you care that much about the Q2 reports, pull up a chair."

My throat was ash. "I need to talk to Alan."

"I don't think you do. We'll see you later, Ramshead."

Alan nodded without looking at me. "We'll talk some other time, all right?"

"Goddamnit it, no!" I shouted. "I *asked* you, and you *agreed*—so what the hell is *this?*"

"A meeting," said my father flatly. "Or is taking him out of one today not enough?"

I tried again to make eye contact with Alan, but he still wouldn't look at me—only down at the details of his Caesar salad.

My father pulled the napkin from his lap, wiped his mouth, and stood. "Ramshead, I really don't want to repeat myself."

"This is important!"

"Like it was this morning? Oh yes—Alan told me all about that. Of all the childish reasons to interrupt his day. Great crucified Christ."

I reeled. "What—what reasons? What did you tell him?" I demanded of Alan, but he wouldn't answer.

"Everything," snapped my father. "Which is to say, nothing much. A bunch of bushes? You pulled him out over your love for a bunch of fucking *bushes?*"

Between us, thousands of truths and unheld conversations loomed.

"But see...," I started. "It's not just... I mean there's—"

"You've got a real problem with moving on and letting go, you know that?" My father adjusted the cuffs of his shirt, to make each one symmetrical and perfect. "I want you to listen to me, Ramshead, for once in your contrary, obstinate life. Your existence is designed to be unimportant. Ergo, by definition, nothing you could *ever* do or want will *ever* be as important as even one, tiny little word spoken within these walls. Unless my house is on fire, you are not to take Alan out of a meeting. Do you understand me?"

I couldn't speak.

"So I suggest that you grow up and accept the upcoming passing of the goddamn topiary. It can't mean anything real to you anyway."

I took a step toward my brother.

My father lunged forward, whites of his eyes visible all around, daring me to take it further.

I turned on my heel and stormed out.

I had trouble breathing. My muscles wouldn't work right. I couldn't see where I was going and moved only on blind instinct, to someplace where there would be no people to see my humiliation. A back stairwell somewhere. I sank to concrete steps and put my head in my arms.

In my pocket, my cell phone rang. I drew it out and stared at the unfamiliar digits, then ground a palm into my eyes to clear them. Maybe it was Hanna's new number. "Ramshead."

"I didn't tell him *everything*," whispered Alan. "Obviously."

I stiffened.

"He'd never believe it. You know that. And anyway— what do you think I am?"

"I think you're a lying son of a bitch who I never should've—"

"I saw something. Okay? Earlier, you asked me if I actually saw something. Well—I did. Every single night for an entire year, after Mom left, I dreamed that I saw everyone I ever gave a damn about—you, Hanna, Mom, Dad—walking into that thing, and never coming out.

"Don't mess with it, Ramshead. I'm begging you. I don't want to know what you're doing, but for Christ's sake, leave it alone. You have no idea what this is connected to."

"Neither do you," I choked, but Alan had hung up.

***

I wasted valuable time collecting myself, then left the stairwell and made it back to the garage. Again I drove through L.A. traffic, growing rougher with the first edge of rush hour. I navigated it the way I turn side in The Maze: on instinct alone, with my mind in some disconnected place.

To protect myself.

This is fine, I told myself. I am fine. Everything is fine. I'm on my own all the time, so how is this any different? It's not. It's going to be fine.

I took out my phone again and called down the list.

"Hi, Sammy, this is Ramshead. Haven't talked to you in a while. Listen, I need a favor... call me back when you get this.

"Hi, Diana, this is Ramshead. Oh, shit. You're in

France this month, aren't you? Never mind.

"Hey Vic. It's Ramshead. I think you told me once that you have an uncle who teaches at UCLA. He's in the Linguistics Department, right? This'll sound weird, but can you give me his number? Call me back."

I went through my entire phone, leaving messages and getting actual answers from no one.

So now what?

I went to the house. Not my father's house, but rather the "little cottage" that he had given me on my eighteenth birthday, in which I, and not the house sitter, am supposed to live in stylish debauchery. It embodies the designated life-style I am slated to experience. It is a place I don't like. But my clothes are there.

Inside the door from the garage, a pile of unopened mail had tipped over and now fanned across the floor, along with a pile of jackets and miscellaneous shoes. From the main living room, a space-age, minimalist monstrosity in white and silver, I heard Javier and his brothers laughing beneath the throbbing beats of Rock Band. I glanced at them gaming as I passed, then went upstairs into my spartan office and turned on my computer.

I began to Google things like "untranslated language" and "unknown language."

Within one minute, I found pictures of something called the Voynich Manuscript (fifteenth century, rediscover-ed by the modern world in 1912 by Wilfrid M. Voynich). Studious scholars had plastered sample pictures of the still-undecipherable text all over the web, replete with its bizarre illustrations of nude women emerging from pipes, goats eating stars, and plant roots entwined with eyeballs. Satisfied that this would fulfill the screw's requirement for a "lang-uage unknown," and encouraged by the easy success, I prin-ted several pages of it.

Then I Googled "rare language."

Mistake.

Never mind the details. Never mind the tedious tweaking of Boolean search terms, broken links, dead ends, poor-quality JPEGs, problems installing the latest version of Acrobat, email addresses that bounce and phone numbers that no longer work, or warnings from Wikipedia that this page does not cite sources. Instead, consider the cruelly double-pronged crux of the problem: (a) rare languages, by their nature, are elusive and undocumented; and (b) how rare must this thing be, anyway?

Frustrated moments strung themselves together into an entire wasted hour. I took a break to go downstairs and eat something, one hand on my pocketed phone in case Hanna called with news about the rare animal, which she didn't. In the living room, Javier and his friends played and banged around, then began a heated, multilingual discussion of Angelina Jolie. I heard beer bottles clink and topple musically, and someone curse. *"Chinga, tengo que mantener limpio este sitio—por las dudas que vuelva, ¿no sabes?"*

I went back upstairs, into my bedroom this time. Time to try something drastic. I opened the drawer in my nightstand, and from beneath my photograph of my mother I pulled a small box, wrapped in white paper and tied with a deceptively simple string. When I was first hired, Perihana'ii had given me the box at HQ as part of an orientation packet. "That," she had said, "is your Trail Crew 98 Emergency Kit, to be kept somewhere safe on the other side of your portal. Hopefully, you will never need to open it."

"Why?" I had asked.

"The packet contains some artifacts imbued with very powerful taps and screws, so the seal-break causes long-term damage to local reality."

"How much damage, exactly?" I'd asked, but Perihana'ii had just twisted her tail in dismissal.

Well. Let's just hope the neighbors don't get transmogrified.

I went outside, down the steps of my redwood deck and to the center of my backyard, stopping beneath a lone silver maple. The branches were alive with piping chickadees, as if they knew. I looked at the package in my hands, shrugged, and pulled apart the knot.

The seal broke. My backyard shuddered, the way a Plexiglas door shudders if struck too hard, and the chickadees took wing in alarm. Everything was normal within my next breath, but I could feel that the coalesced curtain here had just been stressed. The cycles were trying to separate into their essential, chaotic parts.

I didn't know if they'd succeed, so I figured I'd better hurry.

I opened the box. Great, roiling clouds of invisible zap poured over my fingers and rolled away over the grass. Inside the steaming box, a Stone awaited me, next to a Blade and a String. Good God. What had Perihana'ii been thinking? With one incorrectly tied knot in that String, I could send away the entire sentient population of the Western hemisphere.

Better just use the Stone. Worst that one could do was cause global madness.

Gingerly, I picked up the Stone with my free hand. I could feel it breathing. I daren't put down the box, in case I knocked it over and caused the Blade to touch something living, so with my hands full, I sat down beneath the silver maple and crossed my legs.

I closed my right hand over the Stone, then did something that I am forbidden to talk about.

Soon, a different sort of Internet lay before me.

My breath came quick. This thing was ugly. A lurching, throbbing mass of color and neuroses, needs and fears and perverted hungers. Memories branded with vulnerability and shame. Faces. Places. The landscapes of recurring dreams. Riddles, jokes, melodies; flavors, dirty fantasies; facts and factoids, urban legends and lies.

Boolean search terms don't work here.

Instead, I thought about the concept behind the pronoun "I," divorced from language, and skipped this concept over the muck like a rock across the surface of a pond. Words bubbled up with each point of contact, and I searched for any I did not recognize. *Je, ÿ, watashi, mim, ik, magamat, io, jeg, mimi, jag, minä.* Each time I found an unfamiliar word, I held it and thought of the concept of language, to dredge up any linked English words for the mystery tongue. *French, Russian, Japanese, Portuguese, Dutch, Hungarian, Italian, Norwegian, Swahili, Swedish, Finnish.* But I needed a language rare. I couldn't be sure, but I didn't think these were rare enough.

Ergo: lather, rinse, repeat. More times than I care to count.

The sunlight in the backyard shifted further and grew long. They say that the Earth has somewhere around 6,000 languages.

I believe it.

My right hand was beginning to grow uncomfortable when I came across the word *"nika."* Language: Chinook Wawa.

Oh?

The word was fuzzy and irregular, like the concept of *I* was sloppy. I tried another: *Pick up. "Mamook saghalie"* floated up, but the boundaries here were also blurred and watery. Something was wrong. Languages are sharper than this.

But I was running out of time. So Chinook Wawa it was.

I (or was it Me, He, She, Mine, Him, Hers?): *"Nika."* Pick up (or was it Raise Above, Uplift, Make High?): *"Mamook saghalie."* I went through all the words I'd need to

say for my screw: "I pick up the corner of the net... I pick up
the corner of the net... I pick up the corner of the net... I
pick up the corner of the net, and bind the strings." Then I
tried to think of them together, all at once, to see what a
grammatically correct translation would be, but I couldn't
get anything to focus. Was this correct? Was this guy a
novice speaker?

The translation flickered in and out. I memorized it
anyway, the cheap and dangerous way, copying the little
entanglements in this anonymous donor's head into my
own. Associations rode over on the words: the warmth of
family, a burst of excitement, a flavor I had never tasted.
Dust inside a corral somewhere. Sunlight.

I felt the terrified donor shouting and holding his
head, as he stood on a sidewalk outside a convenience store:
"Get out, get out, get out!"

Done.

When I opened my eyes, I saw that the Stone had left a
sunburned patch within my palm, and the silver maple's
leaves had turned snow white.

★★★

I wandered back into the house, clutching my
restocked white box. My own thoughts felt tidy and small. I
don't like telepathy. It reminds me of my loneliness and
limited understanding.

I went back into my office. I Googled Chinook Wawa,
as a check, and uncovered the worrisome source of the
"blurring" problem.

It wasn't that the donor had been a poor speaker. It
was that Chinook Wawa was an old pidgin language used by
Northwest Native tribes and Europeans, for the purposes of
diplomacy and trade with each other. By its very nature, the
tongue was inexact and makeshift.

How effing splendid.

I looked at the clock on my monitor. 7:54. I checked

my cell phone, but Hanna still hadn't called with news. Why hadn't I asked her for her new number?

I dialed her old one out of futile anger. To my shock, a phone rang. Her voicemail kicked in. "Hey kiddies, it's Hanna. Leave me a message, 'kay?"

"You didn't change your number again?" I sputtered. "This whole time, I've been waiting for you to call me with any news, and you've still got your old—"

My phone beeped. I switched to the other line. "Ramshead."

"Rammy Pa-jammy!"

"Hanna!" I sat up straight. "You're there!"

"Where else would I be?"

"Forget it. Have you—did you—"

"That thing you wanted? Yeah, it's fine. You haven't gotten it yet?"

I sagged with relief. "It's fine?"

"I just said."

"But you didn't call me."

"Call you? Oh—I forgot that part. Hey, I got you a snail—is that okay?"

"A snail's perfect. Hanna—thank you."

I heard her say, "Actually, do you have it in white?" and then to me, "Oh, it was no problem. I mean, it was, but that's okay, because I'm really curious about what's going on. Is the guy really not there yet? He should be. Like, any minute."

"What guy?"

"I'm having a guy come to the house and drop it off, to make sure you get it."

I sat up straight again. "Hanna."

"Yeah?"

"What house?"

Pause.

"*Which house*, Hanna?"

"Rammy, what's the big deal? Dad's house. Cuz that's where you usually are when you're around, right?"

I was already running down to the garage.

***

Sunset now. I drove fast, but each passing minute still shrank my world into a ball of idiocy and ugly consequences. Of course Hanna had sent it there—why wouldn't she?

I reached the gate and got buzzed in. I drove up to the house like I meant to ram into it, but instead I parked, badly, at the foot of the main steps.

No other cars were there. I got out and leaned against the hood of the Jag, staring at that priceless coat of Coronado paint in the gathering darkness. The Daytona on my wrist read 8:13. Had Hanna given me a time? Had she given me his name?

I mounted the stone steps of the house and went inside, dialing Hanna's number.

"Who are you calling, Ramshead?"

My body stiffened. In my ear, Hanna's voicemail message said, "Hey kiddies, it's Hanna. Leave me a message, 'kay?"

I closed my phone and slid it into a pocket. Then I looked up at him, leisurely, as though everything were normal. "I'm waiting for someone. He's late. What are you doing by the door?"

In a doorway across the entrance hall, my father smiled. It was more like a grimace. "This friend of yours. Is he an older gentleman? Bearded?"

I didn't say anything.

"Ramshead. How about you come upstairs with me to my office?"

It was not a question.

He turned and stalked down the hall, and I followed him. I don't know why. I could've just turned and run away.

No I couldn't.

He led me into his private office on the second floor, the one directly off of his bedroom, full of rare treasures and strange gifts from around the world. My father seated himself at his desk (English, mid-seventeeth century, carved by Grinling Gibbons himself), crossed his legs at the knee, and swiveled to look at me.

I did not sit.

"Ramshead," my father said pleasantly. "What in the name of Christ do you want with a snail?"

Stay calm. "I beg your pardon?"

"Your colorful hippie friend," he said, still pleasantly. "The bearded gentleman. Before you decided to grace me with your presence this evening, he arrived with a snail for a Mister Jones. It's not Alan's. It's sure as shit not mine. Well?"

"Where is it?"

My father paused, as if he hadn't heard me and something else had just occurred to him. He glanced at his desk, at his framed photograph of my mother, then raised his eyes to one of the mysteries on the wall—a framed silver bird feather from a species I could never identify, something fantastic that looked more like it belonged in the other life I lived. "Ramshead," he said, "I am trying my absolute hardest not to lose my temper. Do you know how difficult that is for me?"

I did not reply.

"Now then. Please answer my question."

"It's none of your business."

"It's my house."

"It's my purchase."

"It's my property."

"Where is it?"

My father rubbed the bridge of his nose. It was a theatrical gesture only. He never got headaches. "This moment we're having right here? This is precisely indicative of the ongoing problem that I am having with you. What did I tell you this afternoon, Ramshead?"

I didn't respond. I felt a flush creep up my skin, some ugly synthesis of self-consciousness and fear.

"I said, 'I suggest that you grow up.' Didn't I?"

He was waiting for me to nod. I did not.

"Aren't you going to answer me?"

I didn't want to, but silence was the losing move. They were all losing moves. "Yes."

"That's right. Now, have you taken my suggestion yet?"

I closed my eyes. I felt sick. "Where is my snail?"

"No?" My father made a *tsk-tsk* noise behind his teeth. "Someday, I'm hoping, you'll finally realize what's good for you. In the meantime, why don't you let the grownups make the big decisions, hmm?"

I opened my mouth, but where could I even start?

My father abruptly turned to his desk and shuffled through a few papers. His tone dropped to one of boredom. "The Morro Shoulderband Snail. Indigenous to California and endangered, and found only in Montana de Oro State Park, under coastal scrub and chaparral, as well as some places in nearby Los Osos. Recognizable by the thick brown stripe running around the outside of its lighter, tawny shell, which is globular in shape, and marked by deep grooves. Or so your bearded friend told me. That's cute, Ramshead. Very cute. 'Accidentally' finding an endangered snail under the bushes out back would mean that I couldn't do a damn thing to the land until they assessed it, wouldn't it?

"Too bad for you, but Los Osos is a long way from L.A. It may seem close if you're desperate, but honestly, nobody would buy that sad sack of crap. So forget the snail. It wouldn't've worked anyway."

I said nothing.

"Ramshead, look—this is my house. I own it. I do

what I like to it. You have your own house, which I bought you several years ago, to which *you* can do whatever *you* like. You're that attached to the hedge maze? Fine. Build one of your own. Jesus, build a Neverland Ranch over there for all I care. But here? Don't even try to fuck with me. This house is not a democracy.

"I don't know what your problem is, Ramshead, but though I've tried, it's clearly nothing I can address. So get out of here. I've better things to do than talk to someone who never listens."

I whispered, "My snail?"

He scribbled on some papers. "I sent it away, back to wherever it came from. Good night, Ramshead."

I stared at his hands. He would not look up and acknowledge me, even though I stood there in the crucifying silence.

I left his office. I went into a drawing room somewhere on the first floor and collapsed onto the couch. Around me, the house settled further into nighttime, as unseen staff opened windows to let in the cool air.

When I felt able to speak with a steady voice, I called Hanna.

"Hey kiddies, it's Hanna. Leave me a message, 'kay?"

"Hanna. Hi. The guy you sent over? Is he—do you have his number? Can you get him to come to my house instead? Hanna, please, pick up..."

I trailed off into silence. I hung up and dialed again.

"Hanna. Okay, goddamn it, the snail *is* for a spell. The most important one I've ever done. Hanna. Please. Send him to my house. Please, pick up!"

I hung up. I twitched for ten more minutes, then called again.

"Hanna, I'm begging you. I'll tell you everything if you'll call me back. I don't want to, not like this, not over a fucking cell phone, but Hanna, please, you don't know all the things at stake here. I'm sorry—that sounded patronizing and stupid. Just—call me back..."

I hung up and waited, and dialed again.

And again.

I finally pulled my feet up onto the couch and hugged my knees to my chest, as if I were a child curling up in the shadow of the rose garden, expecting that someone would care enough to comb the monstrous yard to find me. And now?

And now—what?

Now I kick myself without moving. Now I ask myself why I ever thought that I had anyone here I could rely upon. I had kept The Maze a secret for nine lonely years, after my first accidental entrance one drunken night at age sixteen, and I should've just kept going.

Why had I thought that exposing my secret would change things? My family would continue to weave their shifting nets around me and themselves, and not even my greatest need was sharp enough to cut through the old hurtful patterns. May as well just go out and hide under the bushes in the rose garden again, looking for answers there.

Wait.

The bushes.

Answers under the bushes.

I closed my eyes. "Montana de Oro State Park," my father had said, speaking of the endangered snail's habitat. And there was a GPS in my car.

Time to be a Space Cowboy Hero.

★★★

Night. Route 101, winding north against the edge of the sea, the wind in my ears and salt in my nose. Hours rolled by beneath my tires, and by 11:29, I hit Los Osos. From there I entered Montana de Oro State Park, a place of soft darkness and hungry silence. The road dead-ended in a parking lot. I swung into a space too hard, my tires rolling over the pavement and into the scrubby dust beyond, but I was already climbing out.

I felt under the seat for the flashlight, and once I had it, I walked across the lot to a random trail. My light lanced feebly into the chirping, clicking darkness, and I followed.

The night swallowed me with ease.

I walked slowly. Snails of any kind are tiny, and the park was huge. To better my odds, I worked out a system: take a step or two. Bend over. Shine light under some likely-looking vegetation. Take another step or two. Bend over. Shine light.

Step. Bend. Light.

I inched my way into trail-scored wilderness. I got discouraged fast. Weren't they more likely to be hiding under places away from the trails? Dare I step from the path to search and maybe, accidentally, step on one?

It was cold here. I slid my free hand into a pocket and felt the hard edges of a small box. My Trail Crew 98 Emergency Kit. A fat lot of good something that powerful could do me here.

Step. Bend. Light.

Behind me, some small animal rustled in the brush. Something broke a twig, and something else took flight. The little lives in this place made it breathe and shift, barely, and I felt a rush of homesickness for The Maze. Why is it that I find the maintenance of chaos so attractive?

Step. Bend. Light.

Again. Again. Ad infinitum. All the way to the coast, and along it some, in the breathing darkness. And all the way back to the Jag.

And, six hours later, while sitting on the sandy earth near the driver's side door, with the rest of my life scheduled to be spent in an artificial world with no escape, waiting for me, under the front tire, hidden from someone who would not think to look so close to home—

—a snail.

***

The Morro Shoulderband Snail oozed along for a leisurely inch. I was too numb to react with emotion. I just reached over and picked it up. It felt how you'd expect a snail to feel: cold, slimy, light.

Fragile.

I ripped up a chunk of grass with my free hand. With my other, I gently placed the snail onto the roots, where it was cool and moist. Then we stood and climbed into my car. I started the engine and put the top up.

Four thirty-six A.M.

I drove back to L.A. with the muddy clump of grass placed on the dashboard. The snail oozed and appeared to sleep. I watched it and barely dared to breathe.

By the time we drove through Santa Ynez, the sun was rising.

We got snared in Santa Barbara traffic, broke free, and drove down the edge of the world. We turned inland at Ventura, moved on to Oxnard, Thousand Oaks, Calabasas, and the home stretch. I passed the big park nestled between Route 101 and I-405, and then remembered that I couldn't just roar up the street, saber rattling, to his backyard. I needed the rest of my blocks for the portal-moving screw to work.

I made a detour to my place and parked the car. With one hand, I scooped up the life rare (and the grass it rode in on) and unlocked the door with the other. We banged into the house.

On the couch, a strange man without a shirt awoke with a start and sat up. *"¡Puta que lo parió!"*

I ignored him and ran upstairs, snail habitat cupped against my chest, spraying dirt and roots on the floor with each footfall. I burst into my office and scooped up the printed pages of the Voynich Manuscript. And the language rare was in my head, and the life unknown—oh.

Right. I needed some homunculi.

I cursed, set down the snail's life raft on my desk, wiped my palms on my pants, shut the door, and unzipped my fly.

As I worked, I heard footfalls. Doors opened and closed. *"¿Alguien subió aqui, fué el tipo?"*

"¿Tipo blanco?"

"Sí."

"¿Donde fué?"

"Al cuarto, alli."

Footsteps approached my office door. A tentative knock sounded, along with a faintly accented voice. "Mr. Jones?"

I shut him out and focused, savagely, and pulled the pages of the Voynich Manuscript closer, like readied sheets of tissue. Combine the language unknown with the life unknown, the screw instructions had said.

As I finished, the handle turned.

"DON'T COME IN!"

The handle froze. "Mr. Jones? You want me to clean up all this dirt?"

I distributed my homunculi across the pages and fought to keep my voice even. "Yes, fine, whatever!"

"And Mr. Jones? Diego says he's very sorry for falling asleep on your couch."

"I don't care."

"Mr. Jones, I'm very sorry. I did tell him he could stay a little, since you said visitors are okay, but I didn't say he could sleep on your couch with his shirt off."

"I still don't care." I composed myself and gathered my blocks.

"Mr. Jones—"

I opened the door. Javier stood in front of me, wide-eyed and conciliatory. "And listen, about the mail?"

I pushed past him. "It's fine."

"But—"

I fled from the house. "It's fine!"

When I climbed back into my Jag, my hands were shaking. My snail was still safe on his weedy clump. My pages were primed and ready. I put the pages on the passenger seat and the snail on the dash, and looked back and forth between them, unable to believe that I was succeeding.

My Daytona read 8:16 when we roared out into the street.

***

Rush hour descended, full and hard. My ballooning panic got trapped in gridlock and the wails of horns. Eight twenty-seven. Contractors always started early, before nine o'clock, while the morning was cool.

We broke free of traffic and I kicked the gas pedal, and the Jag's supercharged V8 roared awake. My blocks and I flew down the asphalt, nearly bottoming out. Home stretch now, for real. The long upward slope of the hill, the houses growing more sprawling and ostentatious, with the summit holding the grandest one of all.

We made the final turn. I took the service road that loops down the hill's other side. The gate had been left open, and an ominous caterpillar tread was imprinted in the grass.

We drove all the way down. I slid my Jag behind a parked bulldozer, before they could see me, but not before I saw them: rough men toting chainsaws, circling the hedge maze's bushes and settling into position. Someone started a chainsaw, and the calls of two more answered.

I grabbed the pages and the tuft of grass, and ran from my car without even shutting the door. Sprinting to the first thing that looked like a corner, I crumpled up a ball of manuscript and ripped up a piece of lawn and half-shoved the paper under the turf to make sure it would stay. Then I plucked the snail from its haven and thrust the startled animal against the page, and formed the alien but somehow intimately charged words that could cage the zap and funnel it down, into that curling shell:

"Nika mamook saghalie kushis yahka tenas sitkum."

I felt a jolt. I drew a breath. My magnetism was rising, fast, so close to the wall of leaves. The zap was spinning close and hot around me. A man without a chainsaw noticed me crouching there, and he frowned and started to shout me away. But I was already up and bolting along the southern wall of the hedge maze, fanning zap in my wake, moving east to the next corner.

I shoved a page halfway beneath a rock and tapped it with the snail. *"Nika mamook saghalie kushis yahka tenas sitkum!"*

A second jolt, stronger, with an almost audible hum. Someone else saw me. "Hey! Hey you!"

North. I moved low and hard, like an offensive tackle, knocking someone's hips with a shoulder and sending him spinning into the grass. Someone else popped a dirty transceiver from his belt and shouted into it. I sprinted to the third corner, zap fanning out like flames, within view of the cherry orchard and three other men. They glanced at each other and then trotted toward me. I tossed down a page and ground it into the earth with my heel, then dropped onto my knees and rubbed it with the snail and shouted, *"Nika mamook saghalie kushis yahka tenas sitkum!"*

"Who the hell is that? Hey, bozo!"

One more. I ran west with all the terror of my soul, final page clenched in a fist, snail in my half-closed palm, $1,000 Christian Dior shoes ripped, beaten, and filthy, Yves Saint Laurent jeans muddy and torn, the zap hot enough to ignite air, and not giving a fuck about anything, anything, *anything*, except making that final corner before *he* ordered all those chainsaws forward.

Ten feet from the corner, I had to pass him.

"RAMSHEAD!"

I dove into the earth, zap hitting me like a sonic boom. I mushed a page into the grass and bumped it with the snail, gasping, "*Nika mamook saghalie kushis yahka tenas sitkum —pee kow klapite!*"

One last jolt.

Next to me, the coalesced curtain shook. Some meta-pattern *slid sideways*, into me, into us. Into the startled little ball in my palm. Suddenly, the hedge maze before me was just a bunch of tidily groomed bushes.

The spinning zap had vanished.

I looked down into my palm, at my snail's curling shell, but now, when I tried to follow that inwardly curving spiral, my eyes got lost in The Maze's beckoning edge. And my snail felt warm. It wiggled its little eyestalks at me. In bewilderment?

My portal was bound.

I lay in the grass, too relieved to stand. I held my hand curled near my chest, keeping my life rare hidden and safe, while around me, he shouted at them in annoyance. "Did I tell you to stop? Get your crew back to the south side! Get out of the way! Yes, I still want it done! And this time, don't you move forward a goddamn inch until I say go."

My father squatted in the grass in front of me. "Do I have to call the police?"

I closed my eyes. "No," I murmured. "I'm done here."

"That's for goddamn sure." He gripped my arm, cruelly. "Do you have any idea what I had to miss this morning, just so I could stand out here and make sure you didn't try anything stupid at the last minute? What is it with you? Really, Ramshead?"

"Nothing." I pushed myself up into sitting with my free hand. "I'm fine now. I'll go."

"And what have you got there?"

Slowly, I raised my head. I pulled my hand closer to

my chest.

"I asked you a question!" He grabbed my elbow and yanked. "Jesus Christ. You aren't still trying to pull that endangered-snail bullshit, are you?"

"No." I jerked back.

"You *are!*"

I roared. I rolled over and curled into a ball, holding my snail close to my chest. He roared back and threw himself on top of me. "You stubborn son of a bitch!"

He grabbed my wrist and, like an animal, bit into it.

I yelled. My hand jerked. His fingers slid into mine like a knife blade, and he pried apart my grip and plucked my snail from my grasp. "No, Dad!"

He scrambled back from me and stood. With a sneer of disgust, he threw the snail onto the grass, then ground its secret shell into oblivion with the heel of his John Lobb Oxford.

Finis.

The bound strings ripped. The portal began to disperse, but so close to its former home, it just snapped back into place and restabilized. And the ambient zap once again charged the air.

And beneath it, the chainsaws waited, all over again.

"Okay," said my father coldly, wiping his heel on the grass. "*Now* you're done here."

Inside me, something much more terrible than magnetism began to rise.

"Well?" he demanded. "Get up. And for Christ's sake, go take a shower before anyone sees you. What have you been doing all night? Wallowing in a pigpen? You look like shit."

Higher.

"And on second thought, I think I *will* call the police. If I ever see you on my property again, I swear to God I'm going to have you arrested. I have had it with your selfish, manipulative crap. Enough is enough."

Higher.

"Do you think I'm kidding? Look at me. Do you think I'm kidding? Do I look like a man making a joke?"

I stood.

"Well?"

I said, "Duck."

"And what the fuck is that supposed to mean?"

I punched him in the face.

His head snapped back. His eyes widened and a hand flew to his nose. The other flailed uselessly for balance before he tumbled backward onto the grass.

Then I jumped on top of him and went for his eyes.

I fought with zap. I spun it into the first, the second, the third degree of visible, arching and sizzling, inflicting damage on what should have been his soul. I went for his confidence and faith, mangling them. That is, I meant to.

But when he fought back, he used zap, too.

We tried to maul each other. Ripping, tearing, shredding, destroying, breaking and pounding and bleeding. Hair. Teeth. Skin. But when we reached each other, fingers slid uselessly over flesh and clothing, rarely landing a real blow. The protective properties of zap. How did he know? How did he know?

We rolled into the opening of the hedge maze.

I was half-blinded in one eye. I tasted blood. Something in my foot hurt. I didn't know where I was, couldn't even pay attention to where I was, because I was too busy— no, not even trying to shield myself anymore, but trying to murder him.

Above us, the single sun smeared into an uncertain polynomial of light.

He spat blood. He favored his left fist. His jacket was shreds of useless fabric. I went for his eyes again, he went for mine, and I snapped at deadly fingers and clawed his face, my assaults deflected with zap's oily smoothness.

We rolled over something that purred.

He tried to smother me with his body, to lock me up in his limbs and rip off the flesh from my face and neck with his teeth, but I was too strong. I wriggled away, over mud, then over something hollow that rang out like a xylophone.

I was getting weaker. So was he. My gouges got clumsy; his punches, weak. He tried to pull my hair, and it slipped through his fumbling fingers. The zap around us thinned and cooled.

Somewhere, I heard children singing.

I took a swing at his face. He was too exhausted to block, and I was too exhausted to hit. My loose fist bounced uselessly off a shoulder.

We collapsed onto a bed of moss.

I breathed, my body throbbing and on fire. Above our heads, The Maze breathed too, sculpting a roiling canopy of branches, vines, flowers, fruits, and birds, melting into each other as fast as they separated into anything distinct. A frantic kaleidoscope of light and shadow played over our bed of moss as the canopy danced. At our sides, the jungle behaved the same, as the trunks of the trees mingled with the sudden hides of elephants.

The moss beneath us did not shift. One of us had screwed it in place, and it wasn't me.

"You son of a bitch," he rasped.

I realized that we were entangled, like shoelaces tied by a frustrated child.

"You son of a bitch," he rasped again. "How long have you been hiding this?"

"Hiding what?"

He made a sound of pain. "This." He tried to gesture around himself. "Why didn't you tell me you knew?"

"I—*what?*"

"Why do you *never* answer any of my goddamn

questions!"

"You knew about this place?" I panted. "You *knew?*"

"I knew." He tried to move and moaned. "Get off of me."

I rolled away, onto my back, wincing. He pulled himself up into sitting, his back against a large and unshifting rock. His expression creased in pain. "I knew."

"Jesus."

"Of course I knew."

"How could you?"

"I'm sorry."

"How *could* you?"

"I didn't know you'd been here."

"How does that change anything?"

My father looked down at me. Somehow, he seemed more human, exhausted and beaten like this. He raised a trembling hand to his mouth and wiped away some blood with the cuff of his shirt. "I've never been in here. Do you know that?"

I stared back at him.

"I never actually went inside," he said. "She just taught me some things when we stood close—how to defend myself, mostly, in case anything unwelcome came out. The closest I ever came was standing in the entrance, when she —"

"Who?"

His head dropped forward. Exhaustion or defeat? He didn't answer me.

"Dad. Who?"

He shook his head.

I closed my eyes. We let the silence stretch. As The Maze resettled itself, its sounds overlapped and mingled too: birdsong, wind in leaves, children singing, water chuckling over stones; lions roaring, monkeys chattering.

"Listen," he said. His voice was thin. "I didn't know.

What do you do in here?"

"What?"

"Damn you, Ramshead—"

"I work."

"You work?"

"I'm on a Trail Crew. I help maintain things. I make everything behave how it's supposed to... it's complicated."

"Have you seen her?"

"Who?"

Silence again.

He asked, "What is this place?"

"You don't know?"

"No."

I spat out some blood. "It's the place between worlds."

He closed his eyes. "So she could be anywhere."

I didn't bother asking again. He said nothing else. I made my painful, laborious way to the big rock, pulling myself along, and then up into sitting beside him.

He coughed. "What else do you know about this place? What can you tell me?"

"Why do you want to know?"

He rolled his head over the surface of the rock to look at me. "Because I'm finally ready to know."

"But—what do *you* know?"

"Let's start with you, okay?"

"Let's not. 'Finally ready to know'? What are you hiding?"

"Ramshead." His eyes closed, in pain. Physical or emotional? "This is hard enough as it is. Okay?"

"This is my place. You understand me?" I raised a hand, weakly, to gesture at the swallowed path we'd used to come here. "That place back there? That world? Where you already have everything? That's yours. You can choke on it. You can live in it and die in it. I stopped caring about it a long time ago.

"This place is *mine*. In a sense you can never understand. And if you try to destroy my one way into it—and everyone else's way into Earth—I *will* kill you."

The pain on his face sharpened. "I can see that," he said. "But even though it's yours now, it was your mother's, first."

The second of my shock stretched into ten. "Wait."

"Your mother's," he repeated.

"No. Oh no. You—"

"Shut up." He tried to resettle himself and winced again. "You never listen to me. You know that? What have I been saying all this time, about letting go and moving on? What exactly do you think I'm trying to do here, for myself, by doing this? Do you think I'd plow a link to a place like this under if I really knew exactly what it was? What do you take me for?

"No, don't answer that. I know exactly what you take me for.

"You know what the sum total of my knowledge is about this place? Only one thing: this is where your mother came from. And she didn't even tell me that until later. At first, I just thought she was a tourist, lost in my backyard somehow.

"You know the rest. I could never tie her down. She told me she liked California, but she still came and went, and was never around much. And the last time she went, she just never came back.

"And I'm ready to give up hoping she ever will."

I didn't know what to say.

"Do you think this is easy? Do you think it's easy knowing that something from beyond this Earth, and probably better than this Earth, once thought you and the children you shared were worthy of attention, and then changed her mind?"

Okay—now I really didn't know what to say.

"I know you hate me. Okay? I know all of you hate me. And believe it or not, I don't blame you. I'm trying my damndest to give each of you the world and a strong role in it, but for her, a place in this world wasn't enough either. Okay?

"Okay?"

I didn't know how he expected me to digest all of this so fast. But maybe it wasn't about digestion—just acknow-ledgment—so I said, "Okay."

He nodded.

We listened to The Maze a while longer: chirps and song, rumbles and laughter. Twigs breaking. Distantly, the beat of drums. Above our heads, the branches entwined, melted, and separated again, in a reiterative, never-ending net, needing each other to exist.

"Okay," I finally said. "I'll tell you everything I know."

***

We stepped out of The Maze almost three hours later, limping and holding onto each other. Most of the workers were still there, waiting, looking bored and pissed off in turns, their chainsaws silent in the grass. My father had a short talk with the foreman, and twenty minutes later, the bulldozers and trucks were rumbling away up the service road.

"Should we go to a hospital?" I asked him.

"Probably. If you looked like shit earlier, you look like reheated shit now."

***

In the aftermath of this, as one might expect, things changed. In a way, it was more terrifying than before. Then, I knew what to expect, but now the pattern had been broken and there were no maps.

I suppose it began in The Maze, with my father's unusually quiet attention, but became truly noticeable in the hospital. Instead of phoning Juan from his room, my father read a number of newspapers and took no calls. And over the next few weeks I got a trickle of further reports from Alan. Our father was quieter at the office, too. His violent temper had not changed, but now he'd only stare at the offender and say, "I have no time for you," before turning away.

Alan broke his own pattern. Instead of determinedly living as my father's desperate, bitter echo, he began to drift from his designated life. Perhaps because he saw something different in our father's silence than I did—something forgiving, or at least tolerant. I saw Alan at the house more often on weekends. A couple of times, I saw him head out with a shy smile on a Saturday night, to try moving in the exotic world he'd always been so jealous of me for being told to inhabit.

Hanna's pattern was something I had never fully understood, so perhaps it changed and perhaps it didn't. However, I did see her at the house again, often grinning and whispering things in the male staff's ears.

A few times, I saw Alan and Hanna actually talking.

A few other times, I saw Hanna and my father actually talking. "For God's sake, cover yourself—you're supposed to be elegant," he'd said, but at least they were speaking again.

And me?

I broke my own silence. Once home, I recounted my three-hour-long talk in The Maze to Hanna, which spawned more talks in turn. I talked with Alan, too, although these conversations were far more painful. I suspected that his childhood, year-long nightmare of the hedge maze eating everyone was a distorted memory of our mother's final exit, and easing that pain would take more than just words.

I tried to talk about The Maze again with my father, but it was not successful. I still wanted to feel some kind of cathartic honesty. I still couldn't bring myself there. All the final things I had to say could only be said within an entirely new pattern, one which neither of us yet knew how to move in.

We did agree, however, that for the sake of convenience and his peace of mind, the portal ought to be moved.

So, I hired a landscaping company to build a hedge maze in my own backyard. I drew up no blueprints, and told the foreman to design it himself. When it was ready, I had Hanna's source bring me one Morro Shoulderband Snail, and I bound the old portal. In my backyard, by the new hedge maze's entrance—the place beneath the white-leaved silver maple—I released the corners of the net, and unbound the strings.

***

A week after I transplanted the portal, Hanna came over.

"Ready, Rammykins?" she asked.

We stood in my backyard. Around us, the day was sunny and warm. I heard Javier and his friends in the side yard, playing Frisbee, though from where we were, I couldn't see them. Above Hanna and me, the boughs of the silver maple drank in the sun, the snowy leaves somehow photosynthesizing anyway with the aid of the ambient zap.

Before us, the opening to my hedge maze receded into shifting infinity.

Hanna cleared her throat. "Do they have cigarettes there?"

"Sort of."

She peered into the portal. "What are they like?"

"You'll be fine."

"Daddy's right—you really don't like to answer questions, do you?"

I shook my head in dismissal. Hanna pulled out her wallet and flipped it open to our mother's picture, as if she hadn't memorized her face by now. "Well, we'll find some cigarettes somewhere. It'll be a heck of a lot easier than finding her, anyway."

"It was your idea."

"I'm not saying it's a dumb idea. It'll just be hard."

"No doubt. She probably won't even be in her human form."

Hanna's expression turned uncomfortable. She put away her wallet. "And on that creepy note..."

I smiled. "I'm ready. We better go before I attract too much zap anyway."

"Wait!"

We turned. Alan, wearing beat-up Levi's, work boots, and a man's work shirt—more or less the same outfit Hanna and I wore—came huffing over the wide lawn, his backpack flopping up and down with his clumsy strides.

"Wait." He stumbled to a stop near us, then leaned over and placed his palms on his knees as he gasped, "Wait. A second. Okay?"

Hanna smiled at him, almost shyly. "Al'ligator. I thought you didn't want to come."

"Changed. My mind."

Her smile widened. "Rammy says it's kinda rough in there. You sure you don't want to just join a gym instead?"

He freed a hand to give her the finger.

I pretended I hadn't seen this, and resettled my familiar slouch hat (Yuri: "It's a cowboy hat, right? And you're a hero in space, right?") on my head. "Al, don't listen to her. She's going to spend the whole time asking if there are any cigarettes."

"Will not."

Alan straightened, still breathing hard. "Forget it. Let's just go."

I nodded.

"What do we do?" he asked.

I glanced between them, then turned to face the way

home. I extended my hands. "Each of you, take a hand. Close your eyes and run with me. I'll pull you through this first time."

I felt them glance at each other behind my back, but they took their positions, Alan on my right, Hanna on my left. I took their hands: broad and sweaty, slender and fine.

We closed our eyes. I led them forward, and together we turned side.

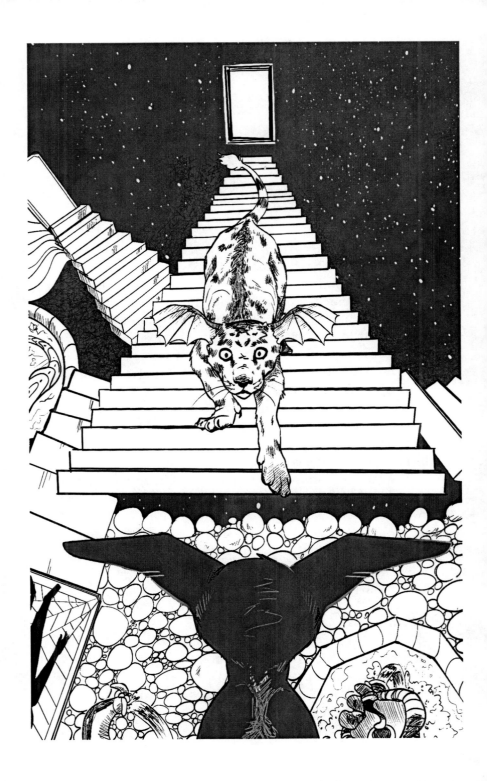

NIGHT AND DAY

Night.

It's Lokifur's turn. And it's always the same awakening. Whether he dreams of being alone in a Marriott hotel room, with a woman in his Back Bay apartment, or camping in the Adirondacks with his nephews, Lokifur awakens riding a floating block of granite through warm and perfect clouds. The stone sinks, the clouds clear, and his vessel docks at the top of a granite staircase.

Lokifur alights. Lokifur descends. Around him are a hundred other staircases with a hundred other floating blocks, each gently docking and departing, like monolithic bees. Each block holds someone else. But Lokifur is the only person who walks down a staircase, because Lokifur is the only person who is awake.

At the bottom, which is never more than four stories away—the staircases are not tall, and the island is not large —is a rambling series of courtyards, with benches and statues and fountains. The statues are all animals. Lokifur himself is an animal, a sort of large, white, black-spotted, cat-like thing. He has batwings for ears. His tail has a tuft on it. In the dream, this is normal.

"Hello," says Lokifur, to the other animal at the bottom of the staircase.

"Hello," says the other animal. In color, she is his opposite: white where he is black, black where he is white. Her own ears are the wings of doves.

She walks up the stairs then, and the floating stone takes her away, up into the clouds.

***

Day.

Jonathan William Pembroke goes to work. He works at One Financial Center, that tall, tall building in Dewey Square, right by South Station.

A few years back, Occupy Boston set up their tent city in the park across the street. This was an unpleasant time for Jon. Because he wears a suit (Brooks Brothers) and because he makes a lot of money (securities law), Occupy did not like him. Every time Jon left the building, the unwashed mob of cardboard-waving hippies would bellow YOU GOT SOLD OUT, BANKS GOT BAILED OUT, or maybe RESIST, RESIST, RAISE YOUR FUCKING FIST. To which Jon always thought: *I'll raise my fist, all right. Right into your mouth. Christ, why can't you just take a shower and get a job?*

"It's gotta be hard on you, man," one of the hippies said to Jon one day. They were standing in line for the Momogoose food truck. "You're a Republican, right?"

"We are not having this conversation."

"No, no," said the hippie, scratching his armpit. "I'm not trying to pick a fight, or anything. I'm just saying. Boston's practically the bluest town there is, and if I lived somewhere where nobody ever agreed with me... well, I bet you feel sorta lonely, sometimes."

Jon laughed. "I do."

The hippie picked a grasshopper out of his beard. "So are you, like, more of a fiscal conservative or a neoconservative?"

***

Night.

Lokifur alights. Lokifur descends. It isn't always the same staircase—today, he's docked at the shortest one, by the western point of the island. Above, the sky is purple-black, horizons limned in pink. Clouds roll below brilliant stars. Lokifur has never seen the sun here, but every night comes the moon.

"Hello," Lokifur says.

"Hello," says the other animal.

"This is driving me crazy," says Lokifur. "Since the beginning of time, this has been our job. I wake up every night on a flying rock, I dock and come down to the island, I watch the sky go black and the moon come up, and the moon go down and the sky get light, and you show up and we switch. Every single fucking night. Aren't you ever curious? Don't you ever wonder where all these other people come from, or where they go? Or why we're the only ones who ever wake up?"

The other animal stares at him. In confusion? It's tough to read the facial expressions of a cat.

"Don't you have the dreams?" asks Lokifur. "I have the craziest dreams. And they're all consistent and tied together, like one long story."

"I have... fewer dreams now," she says.

Lokifur goes quiet.

"I used to dream like that," she says. "Now I can hardly remember my dreams. They're all so mundane. It's like... I'm in a hospital bed, and I'm always tired. Sometimes it's sunny, and sometimes there are people smiling and holding my hand." A white wing on her head twitches in dismissal. "That's all."

"Do you believe in that old urban legend?" Lokifur asks. "That if you die in your dreams, you die in real life?"

She laughs.

Ascends. Boards.

★★★

Day.

"Oh," the woman laughs. "You're one of *those* people."

Her name is Bulbuli. She's an Indian postdoc at Northeastern, studying chemical engineering, though right now she's studying the curlicues of hair on Jon's chest, lightly swirling her nails over his skin. "I never understood that. How can some people literally never remember their dreams?"

Jon runs a hand up and down her bare back. "I don't know. I used to be able to, when I was a kid. But then sometime during high school or college I just... stopped dreaming."

"Mmm," says Bulbuli. She kisses his nose. "You never dream of me?"

Jon smiles and cups her hips in his hands. "When I'm awake, I do."

***

Night.

There is no animal waiting at the bottom of the staircase.

Lokifur is gripped with a profound, instinctual terror. He sprints through the courtyards. He wants to call her name, but he has never learned it, and all he can shout is, "Hello! Hello!"

There are no buildings on the island—only stairways, arches, benches—and therefore no walls. No places she could hide. There are no plants or living things, no trees she could climb, no patches of earth in which to dig. Just stone, and all around that, the infinite lake, eight inches deep and smooth as a mirror.

Lokifur cannot find her.

He curls up at the base of the stairs and cries and cries.

***

Day.

Jon calls in sick. His manager is surprised. "Jesus. You got the norovirus that's going around, didn't you? Well look —you better not come in on Monday either."

Jon calls his mother, his father, his sister, his favorite cousin, his best friend from college, his other best friend from college, and his first-love-from-high-school-and-now-they're-very-close-but-it's-complicated. "Are you okay?" he asks each of them. "I have this funny feeling that something's wrong."

"Are you sure you don't have that ESP?" Jon's mother asks, again. "Because your gram-gram had it, you know."

"I know, Mom."

"She'd call us up and say, 'I was just thinking about you...' and we'd say, 'Okay, Ma, what's gonna happen? What should we watch out for?'"

"Kathy got it," says Jon. "Not me. You know that."

"Well, if you're sure," says his mother.

★★★

Night.

Lokifur wakes on his floating stone, sweating, heart pounding. He can't bear another night on the island alone.

Of course, essentially, they're all nights alone. Book-ended between each, "Hello... hello," there are hours and hours of unchanging time, where the only movement is the water in the fountains, the stones and clouds in the sky, and the passage of the impossibly bright moon. There is no wind to ruffle the surface of the infinite lake. Even the stars stay fixed. It is the loneliest place on earth.

If it's on earth. If it's even a place.

In the beginning—was there a beginning?—Lokifur tried to find ways to entertain himself. He could splash in the fountains and splash in the infinite lake, but he never found pebbles or coins or shells. He discovered that, if he opened his batwing ears and held them a certain way, he could levitate and move like the rocks, but after a certain height, he became swallowed in cloud, and could see nothing on the horizon in any direction. Lokifur even frisked the sleepers on their slabs of granite, and while he did find interesting things in their pockets, he couldn't help but feel that the passengers carried these talismans for a reason, the way ancient Egyptians equipped their beloved dead. Who knew what purpose was served by this old woman's rubber-band ball, that old man's pocketknife, this child's action figure? And anyway, Lokifur wasn't a thief. He merely picked pockets, examined the contents with a longing sigh, and replaced them.

In the end, Lokifur was left with his thoughts, eyes up on cloud and rock. Sometimes the weather changed, and the clouds fell low and covered the island in mist, and sometimes the floating stones changed too, growing large and holding pairs or even whole families of sleepers. Sometimes stones floated past the island entirely, never stopping at all. A few times, Lokifur had even seen stones come and go from the infinite lake, extruded and absorbed as easily as bubbles of soap.

Sometimes, Lokifur took naps.

Sometimes he sang and talked to himself.

Never had he imagined that one night, he might descend a staircase, find a different, other animal waiting at the bottom, and want to change everything.

★★★

Day.

Jonathan William Pembroke runs errands, because he is the kind of man who Has His Life Together. His apartment is tidy, his eating is regimented, his gym habits are regular, his clothing clean and freshly pressed, and his person well-groomed. All of these things are terribly important, because they are what make a functional, independent adult.

Here are some things that functional adults do *not* do:

—wear skinny jeans

—watch cartoons

—text in a movie theater

—read any book that has dragons or vampires in it

Better alternatives would be:

—wear polo shirts

—watch crime dramas

—watch the Pats game instead

—read biographies of historical and scientific figures

There are some gray areas, of course. Like having a picnic in the park. That's a little silly, but if the weather is nice and your family wants to, why not? And it's only human to eat a big pile of barbeque once in a while, cholesterol be damned.

Then there's that ESP. Or rather, belief therein. Family joke or family truth? The July that Kathy turned 10, she called home from summer camp, crying about a nightmare in which the house had burned down. Her father said *Don't be ridiculous;* her mother said *We'll change the batteries in the smoke alarms.* At 2 a.m., the carbon monoxide detector went off, the family exited the house, and the fire department was called. *She didn't actually get the facts right,* Dad grumbled afterwards, but still. Everybody saw the look on his face.

"Well!" says Kathy. "Calls from my brother two days in a row? What special cold front must be moving through Hell?"

"Come on."

"What's up?"

"Have you Felt anything about me? Lately?"

Jon can picture her shrug in the silence. "Not really. I dunno. I don't think so. You know it doesn't work like that."

"I know. I just thought I'd ask."

***

Night.

This animal is different. She's cat-like and spotted, yes, but her fur is brown, and the spots and tail-tuft and funny tabby markings shine like gold. Her ears are pterodactyl wings.

She smiles. "Hello. I'm Solifur. What is this place?"

Lokifur opens his mouth.

He could pounce upon her, knock her on her back, press his face into her throat and sob YOU'RE HERE, YOU CARE, THANK GOD, THANK GOD.

Lokifur can't shut up.

"I'm Lokifur. I live here when I'm awake, I mean I wake up and come in on a stone and then go away on a stone and fall asleep in the clouds, and I have these crazy dreams. I dream I'm one of the sleeping people. Is this too much? I'm sorry. I've only ever seen one other animal here. Maybe she had your name too but I think... I'm sorry. I think she's... sorry."

Solifur raises a shining eyebrow.

Lokifur laughs. He knows he sounds crazy, but he feels crazier. "I watch this island at night. It doesn't have a name, but one time I found some charcoal in someone's pocket and borrowed it to make that graffiti on that archway there. 'The Sleep Palace of the Mind.'"

"Why?" says Solifur. "Because we're all just dreaming ourselves?"

Lokifur almost says, 'I love you.' Instead he says, "Listen—do you really have to go right away?"

***

Day.

"Listen," says Henry. "You call in sick, you come in late, and you're dropping balls. But I know you. You're not some idiot intern and you're not a slacker, and you've done a lot for this firm and you've been with us a long time. And that's why I'm getting worried instead of pissed off.

"Also, and there's no way to put this delicately, but you don't look great. I mean you actually look sick. I'd never be such a dick that I'd tell you to hit the road if you tell me you got cancer—you know that, don't you?—so you have *got* to tell me what's going on.

"So tell me."

Jon can't meet his manager's gaze. What's going on is:

he can't stop sleeping. 9, 10, 15 hours a night sometimes, and when he finally wakes, he feels confused and exhausted. Doctors have been consulted. It's not anemia, narcolepsy, mono, hypothyroidism, sleep apnea, diabetes, celiac disease, dehydration, fibromyalgia, head trauma, or fifty other things.

Jon says so.

"Oh, fuck me," says Henry, leaning back. "You've got depression."

"I'm not depressed," says Jon, too quickly. "What've I got to be depressed about?"

"That isn't how it works," says Henry. "You get depressed, you just stop functioning for no reason." He shakes his head. "That's some serious shit, Pembroke. That shit ruins people. You've got to get that taken care of."

"I'm not depressed," says Jon again, but he's afraid Henry is right.

***

Night.

He has shown her how to fly. Bat and pterodactyl wings extended, they float up among the stones, trying to race, trying to play tag. They smack cartoonishly into rocks, laughing and unhurt.

They chase each other in the infinite lake. The water is not quite warm, but it is not quite unpleasant to shake off on dry land, shiver a little, and smile at how fun and stupid it all is.

They pick pockets and make up stories about the discovered contents. "This paperclip," Solifur proclaims, "once clipped together the pages of the Magna Carta." Lokifur says that the Magna Carta is one page long and was made before the invention of paper clips, and everybody knows that. "Maybe it's that way in *your* dream world," says Solifur. "But not in mine."

They borrow charcoal, chalk, pens, paint, pencils, pastels, and pocketknives. They write, paint, draw, and scratch jokes and poetry and quotes over all the granite surfaces of the island. One bench becomes covered with all the vulgar synonyms for genitalia that they can think of. Another contains prayers. Another, nursery rhymes. "We'll do an experiment!" says Solifur. "We'll mark the stones in some way and keep track of when they come and go. Let's see if we can learn something!"

This time, Lokifur does say, "I love you."

Solifur laughs.

Time stops when they're together. The stones and clouds keep rolling, but the sky is always purple, limned in pink, empty of sun or moon. They get tired and they don't care. "We should just stay here," says Solifur. "What if we just stayed here?"

"I don't think we're supposed to," says Lokifur.

They are by the northern shore, curled together in the basin of a fountain that has always been dry. "You don't know that," says Solifur. "Nobody's ever given you a rule book, or anything."

"No," says Lokifur. "But I just know. You go when I come, and I go when you come. That's how it *is.*"

"I know that too," says Solifur. "But just because you know something doesn't mean that listening to what you know is always the best idea."

★★★

Day.

They try Celexa, Zoloft, and Paxil.

Jon still wants to sleep.

"Can we have a serious conversation?" Bulbuli finally asks, and Jon says yes, with a resigned disappointment. Here is the part where Bulbuli will make dramatic statements about how Jon has been conducting his life lately, set forth ultimatums and unreasonable personal requirements Jon cannot meet, and thereby initiate the beginning of the end of their relationship.

Damnit, Bulbuli, Jon thinks. He is more upset than he expected to be. *I really liked you.*

***

Night.

Sometimes, a sleeper rolls over, and some talisman falls from a pocket and into the island. If it's discovered, it's added to a small pile of things kept in a dry bird bath by the southern shore. 'The Toy Box,' Lokifur calls it.

One night they find a pair of condoms, joined at the line of sealed foil. That's good for a laugh. "Do you think we should use one?" Solifur asks, and the question is so natural and direct, Lokifur wonders, *Why is it always so difficult in my dreams?*

"I don't think I love you like that," he says. "Do you?"

"I don't think I do either," says Solifur. "But maybe we should try, in case we're wrong."

They don't succeed. But that's okay. That's good for a laugh too.

***

Day.

"I think you should take some time," says Henry. "Call us when you're ready, okay? Door's always open."

***

Night.

The Stone Project, as Solifur has dubbed it, is yielding intriguing results. They are developing a taxonomy of stones, a hierarchy of staircases, a map of the rockwinds of the Sleep Palace of the Mind. Lokifur is no thief, but Solifur is, and she has no compunctions about stealing paper from the pockets of the dreamers to take her notes and outline her theories.

They place objects on the stones, to see if they come back. (They do.) They place foreign objects in pockets, to see if those come back as well. (They don't.) "Are you sure that's ethical?" Lokifur asks. "Giving a person someone else's talisman?"

"They aren't talismans," says Solifur. "Talisman implies that they serve some function, but even when people drop theirs, they still float away after a while, right? And we don't find their bodies in the lake or on the stones when they come back, right?"

"I'm tired of screwing around here," says Lokifur. "I want to pilot a stone and see where it goes already."

Solifur smiles. "You know we can't steer them. But maybe we could see what happens if we both leave on a stone together."

Lokifur shakes his head. "You know we can't leave this place unguarded."

"There's no rule book..." Solifur begins.

"We *can't.*"

"It was unguarded for a while when the other Solifur died," she points out.

"We don't know that she died. We don't know *what* happened." Lokifur lashes his tail. "For all we know, she vanished while doing some dangerous experiment, too."

Solifur lashes her own tail. "For all we know, we could do something here to change the world, or... or the fundamental nature of reality, or something. You say you've always been dying to learn about the nature of this place—well?"

"And I *am* learning about it," says Lokifur. "I'm just saying that certain avenues of inquiry aren't a good idea."

Solifur pulls back her pterodactyl wings. "In my dream world," she says, "I'm unmarried with two kids, and I have to work twelve hours a day as a maid. I clean houses for a living."

"So?"

"So my subconscious is obsessed enough already with yearning after things and spaces I have to take care of but can never have, and I'm gonna be damned if I can't have that satisfaction in my waking life."

Lokifur looks up a staircase, uneasily, where a large stone docks and eclipses a piece of sky. "So, what," Lokifur says. "You're just going to... walk me to my stone one day, and then jump on when I least expect it?"

Solifur smiles.

★★★

Day.

The phone on the house line rings.

Jon doesn't answer. He floats through his apartment. *I should do something,* he thinks. The place doesn't look at all like a functional adult lives here, but there is no telling what is more important—the dishes in the sink, the laundry by the door, the desolate state of the fridge, the gym bag gathering dust. His ungodly reflection.

I am sick, he thinks at last, looking at the ghost in the mirror of the medicine cabinet. *And I don't know how.*

The phone rings again. Jon answers this time.

"Jon," says Kathy. "Listen to me. Don't get on the boat. Whatever you do, don't you dare get on that fucking boat."

"I don't have a boat," says Jon.

"I had a dream. DO NOT GET ON THE BOAT."

"I had a dream too," says Jon. "I was—" But like always, it slips away.

"Okay, well, there's gonna be a boat," says Kathy. "And you better not get on it." She makes a noise that's almost a sob.

"Okay," says Jon, confused and concerned.

"Promise me you won't." She's crying now. "I've never had a dream like this in my entire life."

"I'm sorry. Uh, I won't get on any boats... I don't know what else to say."

Kathy cries harder. "When I woke up, there was a

piece of paper in my pocket. There's writing... don't even leave the house. Don't you even leave the fucking house."

The hairs on Jon's forearms stand on end. He doesn't know why, but he says, "Solifur."

Her cries smother. In a bare whisper: "What did you just say?"

"I don't know. What *did* I say?"

"The paper..." Kathy's whisper is painful. "Don't get on the boat."

"Kathy?"

Dial tone.

★★★

Night.

The stone descends to the island, taking its place among gentle twilight traffic and granite staircases. Lokifur is comforted by the familiarity. *Sometimes,* he thinks, *you're given a task in life, and there's just no way around it.*

He thinks of Solifur's theories. He thinks of his dream world. He feels, surprisingly, sorry for agreeing to The Stone Project, and wonders if asking what it's all *for* is in fact not the proper question.

His dreams are getting bad. Unhappy and monotonous.

He alights.

"My name is Lokifur. I have been assigned to guard this place at night, whatever this place is, whatever guarding it might mean."

He descends.

"I dream that I am human and my name is Jonathan Pembroke. My dreams used to be much better than my real life, but now it's all backwards. I suspect I'm fucking up. I think my reward for doing my job well here—which, if I do it correctly, is a boring job that nobody wants—is great dreams over there."

She is waiting at the base of the steps. "Thinking

aloud?"

"What are we?" Lokifur asks. "What are we, *really?*"

Solifur twitches a pterodactyline ear.

"You say you think we're gods in training, or something else, or that we're dead and we're remembering our lives piece by piece before we can move on, or I only exist in your imagination, or..."

Solifur straightens and curls her tufted tail about her paws. She looks cloudward. "My current best guess?" She sounds sad. "We're people who can't dream. We're walking around backstage, where we aren't supposed to be."

"But why are there only two of us?"

"I'm sure there aren't." She nods at the traffic. "Considering how few staircases there are and how slow those stones move? This is barely a drop in the bucket, as far as humanity's numbers are concerned. We're probably spread out across hundreds of islands. Or thousands. Maybe the other islands don't even look like islands, or maybe other people who can't dream get to go to different places."

Lokifur looks away. He doesn't know how to argue because he doesn't know how right Solifur might be. *Whether Jon dreams Lokifur or Lokifur dreams Jon,* he thinks, *when I'm here, I'm here to guard something. Or prevent something. I'm sure of it.*

"Look, it doesn't matter," Solifur says. "We're the only people who'll ever notice or care what happens here. And I'm tired, so I'm going to sleep." She nods at the stone, waiting two flights up. "Are you coming with me?"

Lokifur looks back over the island. He feels sorry for the coming moon, so bright and beautiful, unseen by all except him. And whatever Lokifurs came before.

"I'm sorry," he says. "I had a dream. I'm not supposed to get on any boats."

Solifur shakes her head.

Ascends. Boards.

Lokifur watches her stone disappear, then runs to the Toy Box for pen and paper. The entire time that lovely, secret moon crosses the unchanging sky, he writes and writes and writes.

When he is done, he opens the foil packet containing that second condom. He turns the condom inside-out, wads up the papers as neatly and as tightly as he can, stuffs them inside, and ties up the condom's end.

He hides it under his tongue.

***

Day.

Jonathan William Pembroke awakens with his mouth full of Christ knows what. He spits and coughs, and the Christ knows what plops onto his pillow like a dead fish.

He swears. The handwriting inside of it is his.

It is, hands down, the most terrifying morning of his life.

***

Day.

"I believe you, actually," says his first-love-from-high-school-and-now-they're-very-close-but-it's-complicated. "Remember when I said you started talking in your sleep, senior year? It was all stuff about flying rocks and mirrors and stairs."

***

Day.

"That paper you found in your pocket," says Jon, "when you woke up from that dream. Do you still have it?"

She does.

"What does it say?"

Kathy tells him.

***

Night.

When Solifur asks Lokifur to go with her again, Lokifur has a vision: accepting her offer, stepping onto the stone with her, and then saying, "It's you... I'm protecting this place from people like you" before pushing her over the edge.

But that would be far too violent.

Instead, Lokifur asks for one last turn, and that she leave with him.

Solifur is excited. She accepts.

As they lie on that final, ascending stone together, Lokifur feels ashamed. Of course he does: he loves her. She has brought thirst and excitement into this quiet, lifeless place, but it is that same thirst and excitement that will tear off the protective mysteries, one by dangerous one, until the stones fall, the stairs crumble, the lake dries, and everyone awakens.

He doesn't think he'll ever fall asleep, but the clouds come down and the stars go out, before he can even say he's sorry.

★★★

Day.

Jon awakens alone.

Of course he does. In this universe, you can't paper clip the Magna Carta. Certain things have never existed.

★★★

Night.

There is no other animal waiting at the bottom of the stairs.

Of course there isn't. But Lokifur curls up there and cries and cries anyway.

★★★

Day.

Jonathan William Pembroke gets a haircut.

These things are terribly important.

★★★

Night.

The clouds are high tonight, and Lokifur drops below

them to see a spectacular view of the island. Stones float in pink, majestic silence, their sleepers curled alone and in pairs, as families and with tribes. The hunks of granite dock and wait anywhere from seconds to many long minutes, and then float away, satisfied with the exchange of whatever arcane energies The Stone Project had been unable to measure.

Tonight, Lokifur's stone docks at the smallest and westernmost staircase. He alights. He descends. At the bottom, he finds a new animal waiting. Her coat is the deepening purple of twilight, and her markings are the pink of a sunset. Her ears are diaphanous, the wings of giant dragonflies.

"Hello," says the animal. Her eyes are wide and baffled.

"Hello," says Lokifur.

She looks about to speak, then perhaps thinks better of it, and hesitantly creeps up the stairs. *Give her some time,* Lokifur thinks. *She doesn't know how she knows these things. She has to settle into it.*

When her stone is gone and the sky has resumed its plunge to black, Lokifur wanders the island and studies the graffiti by starlight—the couplets, the vows, the bits of lyrics, the sketches and jokes, in colors that fade to the same lonely gray with the silvering appearance of the moon. He comes upon the arch where hangs the beginning, 'the Sleep Palace of the Mind.'

With a rag from the Toy Box, it is the first thing he erases.

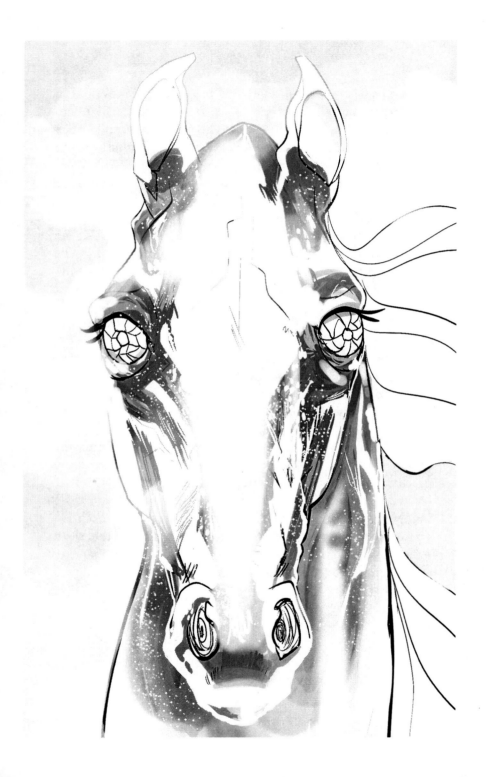

THE FLIGHT STONE

"Never forget, ladies, how lucky you are," says Miss Reeper all the time. "You could have died in an alley from plague or starvation, or grown up to become disgusting harlots. But The Harkish Crown, in its wisdom and mercy, has lifted you out of the gutters and has given you a great destiny instead. The least you can do is repay its kindness. So *pay attention.*"

Miss Reeper is the Headmistress. Her school, outside of Hark's city walls, is where you go to become an Air Knight.

You can only be an Air Knight if you're a street orphan first. A landhorse can carry a big man and all his gear, but an airhorse can only take off with a really light load.

I heard they tried regular kids at first, but they always grew too big and got too heavy.

They have to use starving ones.

★★★

Sairee is my friend. She is shorter than me, even though she's much older. Her upper arms are skinnier than her forearms, and her thighs don't touch together. She'll be an Air Knight forever.

"I heard they're going to start using *dwarves*," she whispers to me one day, over breakfast. "Isn't that *stupid?*"

We always eat outside, in the assembly yard, so Miss Reeper can make sure we don't cheat. We have to eat exactly what they give us: no more, no less. "Light and strong, light and strong," Miss Reeper says, "like little butterflies."

"Why would they use dwarves?"

Sairee wrinkles her nose. "They think we can't decide for ourselves. Like we're too *young*."

Kaiya leans forward. "But they let us decide about whether to go back. They took Linn back to Hark last fall when she said she wanted to leave, remember?"

"Exactly," says Sairee.

"Remember, ladies," Miss Reeper says, pointing to the Flight Stone in the center of the yard. "Little butterflies. Not big, clumsy rocks."

★★★

Sairee will graduate and be a full Air Knight when the next Accounting comes. We all know she's ready—she's old enough and she's stopped getting taller. But I haven't. I worry about it all the time. I'm not like Linn. I don't want to go back to Hark and sleep in a doorway under crawling rats.

I want to keep riding airhorses.

The airhorses are the most beautiful things there are. You can see through their skin, like glass. They have narrow heads, like hunting dogs, and their eyes change color every time they blink.

When they open their wings, it's silent and cold, like mist going over the moon.

I want to be an Air Knight forever, too. But I only will if I stop growing in time. Airhorses can't take off with anything heavier than the Flight Stone, and if the pan you stand on come Accounting Day goes down to the grass and the Flight Stone's pan goes up, you go back to Hark, whether you want to or not.

I learn from Kaiya how to cheat.

I don't like making sick, but I like it when I take off on all that beautiful flying glass, and all I can hear is wind.

★★★

"Calife," says Miss Reeper, during lunch one day.

"Come with me."

She leads me away from the yard and into the Doctor's building.

"I've been watching you at morning drills," says Miss Reeper, as Dr. Hatch looks hard at me and pokes my skin all over. "You seem to be tiring out easily. Why is that?"

"I'm not tired," I lie. Dr. Hatch examines my fingers and touches my hair.

"Mmm-hmm," says Miss Reeper. "Maybe you have a cold. Starve a fever but feed a cold, they say."

"I'm not sick."

"I daresay you are."

I don't answer her. I look away, at Dr. Hatch's tools. She has a lot of them—big scary scalpels and big scary bone saws.

"The Harkish Crown is not in the business of abusing children," says Miss Reeper. "We select you girls for your naturally smaller size, innocently begotten from your early, harsh life on the streets. Do you understand? We do *not* want girls to behave contrary to Nature, if Nature can remedy what your earlier misfortune has brought."

Oh, yeah, Linn used to say sarcastically. *They take real great care of us now. I had more to eat back when I stole bones from the butcher.*

"I understand," I say.

"From now on, at the end of meal times, you will come straight to Dr. Hatch. She will watch you and make sure you behave yourself, until you have proven to me that you can be trusted to keep down everything you've been given. Is that clear?"

"Yes, Headmistress."

Dr. Hatch talks. "It's not bad," she says. "She hasn't been doing it for long."

"Good," says Miss Reeper. "You must always nip these things in the bud."

***

Sitting in Dr. Hatch's office, sometimes I think about nipping buds. I feel like a branch with most of its buds already nipped off, but even like this, I'm still too big and clumsy to fit into my vase.

And I think about how my legs are kind of like branches, coming out from my knees, and my feet are like big clumsy buds. And how loud and cold it is inside the wind when you fly, and how warm the glass airhorse is underneath you, and how airhorse harnesses are different from landhorse saddles. You don't need anything below your knees to ride an airhorse.

Dr. Hatch gets up from her desk and says, "I'm going to the latrine."

I watch her leave.

There's a rumor going around that Miss Reeper goes into the assembly yard every night with a chisel and takes an itty-bitty piece out of the Flight Stone, like a kind of secret game.

Either way, I'm not going to lose.

I go to Dr. Hatch's tool case and take out the bone saw.

STEADY ON HER FEET

The day before her sister Molly's birthday, Holliday noticed the new shop in Watchmaker Alley.

Its display windows held no watches—nor tiny ballerinas that danced at the twist of a key, nor birds that sang when you pumped their tails, nor instruments that played themselves. Indeed, the windows were bare entirely, save for two large placards that read as follows:

Fond of Drink? Weak for Sweets? Lusty for Ladies?

OR PERHAPS you are
Slothful? Gullible? Deceitful? Mewling? Dull?

WOULD YOU LIKE TO BE
Energized! Committed! Upright! A Moral Champion!
In Full Possession of Your SELF and Your FACULTIES!

THEN
RECEIVE DR. SVARTLEBARRT'S SURGICAL
AUGMENTATION
OF THE CHARACTER

Dr. Svartlebarrt, a Most Distinguished Gentleman from Lands Afar, has teamed with Dr. Mortleaus, a Brilliant Local Surgeon of Impeccable Family History, to provide Character Prostheses for Those In Need. Much as a Man who is missing a Leg can gain ambulatory Benefit from the application of a False Appendage, a Person who is missing

Key Components of His or Her Character can make up the Difference and radically Improve, even Overcome Entirely (!) a Host of Moral Deficiencies with SVARTLEBARRT'S SURGICAL AUGMENTATION.

—Only the Finest and Most Advanced Micro-Clockwork, DESIGNED and PERFECTED by Dr. Svartlebarrt himself, is used to create our Prostheses
—Our Happy Customers include Statesmen, Businessmen, Dignitaries, Tradesmen, &c.
—Come inside for a Consultation and ASK how YOU CAN BENEFIT
SVARTLEBARRT'S SURGICAL AUGMENTATION OF THE CHARACTER:
SUITABLE FOR EVERYONE!

Holliday struggled through the display's difficult words, her lips moving soundlessly. The public schoolhouses of the great city of Runsdown were free, but that didn't mean the marms took kindly to a girl like Holliday turning up. Many a time had she demanded a reading lesson at a schoolroom threshold, a salvaged and waterlogged book in her hands, while the sour-mouthed marm planted herself between Holliday's bare feet and the giggling froth of pink, beribboned school children beyond.

"Well?"

Holliday started. A boy, perhaps 10 years old, had opened the door from within and stuck his head outside. "Well, what?"

"Aren't you coming in?"

Holliday tightened her grip on a small clock she held in her hands—not because she thought the boy would take it, even though it was prime salvage, but to remind herself that she hadn't time to waste gaping at marvels today. The Arto Road Market was only two blocks down. "I'm sorry. I haven't any money."

"Today's consultations are free," said the boy.

Holliday hesitated. According to the grown-ups in her family, there was an awful lot wrong with Holliday's character. And being examined by a doctor was supposed to be good for you. "Well... all right. If it won't take long."

The boy led her inside. The interior was as barren as the display windows. Plain wooden chairs and a plain wooden bench sat arranged around a low, plain wooden table with a pan of sawdust beneath. The floor had no carpets. There was a glass vase upon the table, but instead of flowers, it held cat's eye marbles.

"What lovely marbles," said Holliday, trying to be polite.

The boy grinned. "Those aren't marbles."

Holliday saw more of them in identical vases in the cubbies across the back wall of the shop, up behind a wooden counter. "Then what are they?"

A linen curtain behind the counter flapped aside. A handsome man, his face made cold by the severe cut of his clothing, strode into the room. "What is that *thing* doing in my shop, Nevinn?"

Holliday clutched the clock to her chest and braced herself for a fight.

"I—sir?" said the boy. "She's here for a free consultation...?"

"She's tracking in the filth of the Marmouth River, is what she's doing," said the fellow. His hair and eyes were dark, and when he peered at Holliday, he reminded her of a hawk. "Don't you have eyes? We don't serve the likes of *her.*"

Holliday squeezed her salvage, the casing of the clock digging into her palms. "With your pardon," she said carefully, "not all of us mudlarkers are like you think."

His eyebrows leapt in disbelief. "So you have proper

society in your sewer pipes, then? Or perhaps you have schemes to live in real houses someday, and eat your river rats with little pewter forks and little pewter knives?"

Holliday's face grew hot. "I go to the schoolhouse, same as anyone here in the up-there, and the marms give us history lessons. I know all about revolutions and what like. And guess what? We all *will* live in real houses someday. One of Runsdown's mudlarkers will get too angry, and they'll start everything, and you and everyone else in the up-there will be sorry."

The man laughed. "A river-dog who attends lessons! Well, I never. Fancy yourself the great philosopher of this someday-revolution, do you? Hasn't anyone ever told you that a bit of knowledge is a dangerous thing?"

"What's all this, Mortleaus?" The linen curtain pulled aside again and a second gentleman waddled into the room. He was old, and very fat, with an untamed beard the color of the Marmouth's ice in winter. His right eye rolled in milky blindness.

"A mudlarker," said the handsome fellow, who must've been Dr. Mortleaus, "supposedly here for a consultation."

"Mmm," said the other, who must've been Dr. Svartlebarrt. He squinted at Holliday through his good eye. "Well, it gives us something to do, then, doesn't it?"

Dr. Mortleaus grumbled.

The boy, Nevinn, darted into the back. Dr. Mortleaus pushed the vase of not-marbles to the edge of the table and smacked the surface. "Have a seat, then, Miss Revolutionary," he said to Holliday. "What've you got there?"

"A clock," said Holliday, pulling it to her chest again. "It's river salvage. I was on my way to Arto Road to trade it. My sister Molly turns six tomorrow, and she should have some licorice as a present."

Their faces cracked in surprise. Holliday fell silent. Nobody, not even learned doctors, deserved to know more about poor Molly. She was a fragile, obedient little girl, and it broke Holliday's heart to never see her smile. Molly's favorite game was to draw pictures in the river mud with sticks—very good pictures, too, of strange monsters and funny people, and fish the size of boats. The pipes and tides of the Marmouth ate such gentle dreamers alive, and if this was the nature of Molly's soul, she would not survive long without kindness and a fierce protector. The rest of their family could provide neither. The duty fell to Holliday, and it was a solemn task she would not have parted for, not for all the world.

Nevinn returned with a doctor's bag that he handed to Dr. Svartlebarrt. The old man opened it and removed a case, which in turn contained twenty thimble-like things with fine, stiff wires attached to their bottoms. Dr. Svartlebarrt slid half of them onto his fingers while Dr. Mortleaus did the same with the rest. "Dr. Mortleaus and I are going to ask you a series of questions while we examine you." He wiggled his capped fingers. "Ready?"

The examination was not what Holliday expected. Instead of touching her, they floated their hands in space about her person, as a puss uses its whiskers to suss out shapes, and they asked the queerest questions. Could she please relate her happiest memory? Her saddest? What had she dreamed about last night? What was her favorite food? Had she ever kissed a boy? How did she react to stray dogs? What was she most afraid of?

"Hum," Dr. Mortleaus finally said. He frowned, lowered his hands, and removed his devices. "Well."

"Indeed!" said Dr. Svartlebarrt.

"Am I sick?" Holliday asked.

Dr. Svartlebarrt removed his own objects. "No no, child. Dear me—young woman. How old are you?"

"Thirteen."

"Well." Dr. Svartlebarrt put away the case. "I am delighted—shocked, really—to report that your character is in thoroughly excellent condition. Of course, there is always room for improvement, but isn't that true of us all? In your case, had you the financial means, I would suggest a minor prosthesis for your temper. You have a great deal of anger, and your character is not *quite* strong enough to harness it completely. But other than that—"

"I'm sorry," cut in Dr. Mortleaus, "but these results don't make any sense. She's too kind, conscientious, and intelligent. She can't possibly be a born mudlark."

"But I am," said Holliday. "My uncles were all there when Mamma had me. They can say so."

"Is your mamma a born mudlark, too?" asked Dr. Mortleaus. "Did she belong to a good family before running off to the sewers?"

"I don't know."

"What about your papa?"

"Mudlarks don't have those. We just have uncles."

Dr. Mortleaus gave her a funny look.

"Now is not the time to fuss about her pedigree or degenerate family life," said Dr. Svartlebarrt. "We barely know her, don't we?" He turned to her. "Listen, my dear... what did you say your name was?"

"I didn't. It's Holliday."

"Well, Holliday," said Dr. Svartlebarrt. "How would you like to help out in our shop?"

Dr. Mortleaus' eyes bulged. "Bart—"

"You may come in whenever you have a little time, so that you may take care of whatever small tasks are on hand," said Dr. Svartlebarrt. "Changing the sawdust after surgery, sweeping the floor, things like that. This will free up Nevinn to better focus on his apprenticeship."

"You mean..." Holliday could barely speak. "You mean, do I want... a job? That pays money?"

"No," said Dr. Mortleaus. "Absolutely not."

"Yes," said Dr. Svartlebarrt. "That is exactly what I mean."

"But Bart, look at her, for Smoke's sake! She stinks, she's wearing rags, her hair is a pigeon's nest, her feet are black—"

"So what?" said Dr. Svartlebarrt. "We'll give her some nicer rags. And a membership to the bath house up the street, where she may bathe and keep her work clothes."

"This is ridiculous!"

Dr. Svartlebarrt's voice turned soft, but it was a dangerous softness—the softness of Marmouth mud, covering a sinkhole that goes down and down. "To what exactly are you objecting, Mortleaus?"

Dr. Mortleaus fell silent.

"We've examined her character. We have seen that it's excellent." Dr. Svartlebarrt's good eye glared. "Unusually, compellingly, *valuably* excellent."

Dr. Mortleaus' face changed in some subtle way.

"Should I go now...?" Holliday asked.

"Nevinn," said Dr. Mortleaus. "Take her to Arto Road. Let her attend to her clock business and buy her some better rags." To Holliday, he said, "Welcome to our staff."

★★★

Holliday had never had an occupation that paid wages. All she had known was mudlarking alongside the dangerous rhythms of the Marmouth—its fickle tides, so close to the estuary; its disease-carrying refuse; its few surprises half-buried in gravel sandbars. To have tasks to do that did not involve digging in mud or carrying a sack was quite glamorous, and for many days, Holliday was hard put to hide her excitement.

The rules were so different, working in a shop. Instead of clawing through filth, Holliday ran rags over the furniture and floor to keep the shop clear of it, and instead of keeping a sharp eye out for things in the muck that didn't belong, all

Holliday had to watch for was the marble-like things. If she found a stray one outside of a vase, she was to give it to Dr. Svartlebarrt personally—and never, ever, ever put it back into a vessel. If she did this, they would beat her and throw her out. Did she understand?

"Yes," Holliday said. "But what are they? The marbles?"

Dr. Svartlebarrt raised a bushy eyebrow. "Those are my micro-clockwork augmentations, suspended in air-resistant, haemo-reactive, aqueous solids. And I am the only one qualified to distinguish them from each other, and Dr. Mortleaus and I are the only ones who know which vessel contains what type. So I will thank you not to disturb them. Can you imagine what would happen were Dr. Mortleaus to accidentally augment a violent man not with self-control, but with an overabundance of courage?" Dr. Svartlebarrt shook his head with a stentorian wheeze. "Such unbalanced personalities are the forces that disrupt the world, child. And we are here to keep our beloved world steady on her feet."

The most exciting task was assisting with surgery. While Nevinn tied the patient to the table, Dr. Svartlebarrt prepared the ether, and Dr. Mortleaus inspected his instruments and said encouraging things to whatever nervous soul lay sweating on the wood, Holliday was tasked with fetching them anything they might need as they worked—a glass of water, a certain tool, a handkerchief. If they needed nothing, which was usually, she was permitted to stand and watch. All Runsdown mudlarkers, whether by birth or choice, have strong stomachs, and Holliday was not perturbed in the least by the calmness with which Dr. Mortleaus sliced and stitched flesh.

And what fascinating lessons he gave Nevinn as he worked. "The incision need not be deep—the augmentation, recognizing where it is most needed, will burrow home gradually over time, repairing the tissue in its wake. So to conquer timidity, you must merely place the augmentation below the skin but somewhere above the spleen, like so... to bolster energy, you must find a place with much phlegm, such as the sinus cavity... for strength, what you want is proximity to the stomach. The process begins upon contact with blood and body temperature, at which point the aqueous solid encasing the augment begins to dissolve, at a rate dependent upon the patient's age. The lump will disappear within one to three weeks, indicating that the aqueous solid has fully dissolved."

Willing but thick-headed Nevinn required much repetition. Holliday required but a glance at the back wall, to note which glass vase was missing from the cubbies when Dr. Mortleaus delivered each lecture during each procedure. For a mind accustomed to noting the placement of dozens of different piles of wreckage with each turn of the tide, creating a mental map of the vases was easy. And for a pair of eyes trained to scan millions of stones for bits of ship-wrecked gold, discerning the subtle differences between the augmentations was even easier.

But there was one group of augments whose purpose Holliday couldn't deduce: the group in the vase that was left on the table as decoration, outside of surgical hours. She daren't ask, for fear of revealing what she shouldn't know about the micro-clockwork already, and nobody offered. Nevinn caught her looking at it and began to make up silly stories. "Those aren't augmentations that get put in—those are things they've secretly taken *out*. They kidnap poor people, like you, and they cut out all the good parts, and they sell them to the very rich. Didn't you know?"

The thought frightened her—that someday, without warning, kind Dr. Svartlebarrt might tie her down and cut her open, and rip all her courage and compassion away, leaving Molly with no one to protect her.

So Holliday said, "I think they knocked you out one

night and used those burrowing machines to take out your brain, piece by piece, and that's why you say such stupid things."

That finally shut him up.

★★★

Holliday was careful with her secret employment. Mostly.

She kept her hours at the shop irregular, and she always changed back into her Marmouth clothes at the bath house, and she let her furious mamma and jeering uncles assume that she was sneaking away to frolic with boys. "If'n you're old enough now to let some pimpled sot shoot a baby into your belly, why not let one of us?" this or that uncle would joke, and Mamma would screech and hit them, and they'd laugh.

Holliday was even careful with the coin she earned. Some of it she stuffed into Fairy, Molly's ragdoll and favorite toy, through a burst seam in Fairy's bottom. A little, Holliday sprinkled throughout the family's sewer pipe—a slipcrown here, a halfmark there; enough to be the plausible result of a trip to the market that someone had forgotten about, but not so much as to raise suspicion.

But in the end, it was Molly that undid her. The rest of Holliday's coin went to her, secretly and in roundabout ways —in the form of apples, pork buns, peppermint candy, toffee, a less-worn dress, a sturdier sack for carrying salvage, a tiny hat for Fairy. Gentle Molly never questioned these gifts. She only stared at them with round, startled eyes, and then smiled—so sweetly and brightly, Holliday's throat ached ever harder each time.

Their drunken uncles didn't notice the gifts either, but sharp-eyed Mamma did.

"And what's this, then?" Mamma demanded one night.

The tide was high, and the Marmouth's oily waters lapped at the lip of their great pipe. A smoky fire sputtered

in the back, where a pot of stray dog stew bubbled un-
attended. Mid-way through the pipe, Holliday's uncles
passed a bottle and sang, in between declarations that Holliday should take a swig and invent a verse or two, because
she was old enough now. Holliday felt strangely proud, but
Mamma didn't like that at all. It made her angry. Then again,
Mamma was always angry when Holliday's uncles drank and
laughed, as if a good time were the one thing in this hard
world that Mamma couldn't abide.

"It's just a little sip n' song, Benevolence love," said
Uncle Tails.

"I wasn't talking to *you*," Mamma spat. She pointed at
Molly. "I was talking to *her*."

Holliday's good feeling vanished. She pushed away
from her uncles. Molly crouched at Mamma's feet, obviously
interrupted mid-game. One of her little hands held Fairy;
the other, a tiny wooden horse.

"She's going for a ride," said Molly.

"What is that?" Mamma demanded again. Her voice
cracked. "Where did you get it?"

The singing trailed off. "What she got up there, a dead
kitten?" asked Uncle Tails. "Just have 'er add it to the stew."

"That toy!" Mamma cried, her voice growing louder.
"That horse."

"I," said Molly. She looked around, bewildered. "Holliday gave it."

"My arse," Mamma shouted. She grabbed Molly's
wrist and wrenched. Molly cried out, dropping the horse to
the floor of the pipe. "It ain't broke and it's all clean. That's
no salvage, you poor little liar. It's *thieved*."

Every uncle fell silent now. Uncle Jagged sucked in a
stern breath.

"No, it weren't!" cried Molly. "Let me go! You're hur-
ting me, Mamma!"

"Mamma, stop," begged Holliday. Terrible heat flooded her heart. "I got it for her, and I did it honest. I did."

Mamma ignored her. "You're big enough by now to know better," she sobbed at Molly, "so you did it on purpose —don't tell me you didn't. Decided you're too good for what the Marmouth gives you freely, is that it? You poor little fool. Paying for thieves' wares is the same as thieving direct!"

Holliday grabbed her mother's other arm. "It weren't bought from no thief! It was got fair. I traded salvage and got coin, and I bought it for Molly new."

Mamma released Molly, whirled, and shoved Holliday. Holliday flew backward to the opposite wall, falling against her shoulder. Fireworks of pain arced over her back. *"New?"* Mamma screeched. "You didn't never. I didn't raise no powder-faced, fat-pursed princesses who chase whatever fancy, toity, dainty what-you-please they want, and think to have everything *new!"*

"It's not like that," Holliday gasped. Below the pain, a quaking, simmering anger rose. "I'm not a... I just had... she's only..."

"And this," cried Mamma, tearing the new hat off of Fairy's head. "And this." She ripped the hem of Molly's new dress. "Think I don't got eyes? Think I don't know you're turning into some criminal's yap-dog, going after the little thievings what get sold off?"

"You know what they do to them that keep stolen things, in the up-there," said Uncle Jagged darkly. "Same as what we honest people do down here, poppet. We cuts off their hands what they paid with."

Holliday forced herself up. She staggered to Molly, but Mamma shoved her down again with a bony hip. Tears pulled muddy streaks down Mamma's face, the Marmouth in twin miniature. "Find them bandages, Spade. And Crab-rock—give us your knife."

Uncle Crabrock pulled out his knife. Molly screamed.

Holliday launched herself at Mamma, catching her

legs and making her fall. Mamma cursed, and Holliday shoved away, grabbed Molly, and rolled around her, tight tight tight. "No!" Holliday ordered.

"You little banshee!" Mamma howled back, and her lean, hard hands fell upon her, prying and pinching, pulling at clothes and tearing already-frayed cloth. "Get off!"

Mamma's pinching hands found Fairy. Molly wailed and refused to let go. Like an infant torn apart by wild dogs, poor Fairy split into pieces.

From within the remains, a pile of glinting, ringing coins fell to the floor of the pipe.

Mamma froze in shock. The uncles froze in wonder and greed.

With Molly weeping in her arms, Holliday rolled off the edge of the pipe and splashed into the oily Marmouth.

"And don't you come back!" shouted Uncle Jagged, but Holliday and Molly were already paddling back around to the Marmouth's confining walls, where a rusting line of rungs embedded in the stone could lead them into the yawning world of the up-there.

There was only one place Holliday knew of to take her.

★★

She banged upon the door with both fists. "Doctor Svartlebarrt! Doctor Svartlebarrt!"

On the floor above the shop, light scratched between the slats of a shuttered window. Molly kept weeping. Holliday pounded harder. "Doctor Svartle—"

"Grave take you, you flea-wit," said Dr. Mortleaus as he shoved open the shutters and leaned out over the street. He squinted down, blinking sleep from his eyes, his night-dress trembling in the breeze. "Don't you know what hour it is?"

"You've got to let us in!"

"Quiet!" hissed Dr. Mortleaus. One building over, a

second light flared behind a pair of shutters as some other disturbed shopkeeper lost his patience and readied a harsh word. "Are you trying to wake the neighborhood?" He looked over one shoulder. "Ah, Nevinn, you're up. Good. Let her in before she brings the constabulary on our heads."

Nevinn opened the door and Molly pressed her sobbing face into Holliday's shoulder. Holliday set her jaw and pulled Molly inside. "Who's that?" asked Nevinn.

"Good Heavens," said Dr. Svartlebarrt, emerging from the back. He pulled a waist-coast over his shirt, one tail of which he'd failed to tuck in. Dr. Mortleaus, looking similar, was right on his heels. "Whatever is the matter?"

Holliday blurted out the events of the evening in a disjointed rush. Dr. Svartlebarrt ordered Nevinn to fetch the girls a glass of cordial, to calm their nerves, and Dr. Mortleaus didn't even grumble about the filth of the Marmouth when the sisters sat down upon the bench.

"There now," said Dr. Mortleaus gruffly, as Holliday passed the half-drunk glass of cordial to Molly. "That should help."

Molly sipped from the glass between hiccups. "Where are we? I want Fairy."

Holliday pulled her close. "We're in the up-there. We're with good people, my friends. I earn wages here. That's where I've been getting the coin for your presents. It's all fine, Moll. It's fine." Holliday looked up at the men, her eyes hardening. "Examine her. Give her a job."

Dr. Mortleaus raised an eyebrow.

"She's got no other way to take care of herself now. My wages alone here won't be enough."

"That is not our responsibility."

"Morty," said Dr. Svartlebarrt. "She's upset. You cannot expect politesse from the desperate." To Holliday, he said, "Please calm yourself. We can examine your sister, certainly—she's already here, so why not?—but we can't make any promises. Nevinn? My bag?"

Holliday coaxed Molly to sit on the table. While Molly sniffled and wiped her nose on her sleeve, the doctors plucked the air about her with their enhanced fingertips, murmuring questions and nodding at Molly's answers. Around them, Nevinn gathered and lit lamps until the room felt almost cheery.

At the conclusion of the examination, the doctors exchanged a long look. They removed their devices in silence. "Well?" asked Holliday, past a knot in her throat.

Dr. Svartlebarrt shook his head. "I'm sorry, Holliday."

"You sister is obedient, trustworthy, and creative," said Dr. Mortleaus, "but she is also too shy, fearful, and unconfident. Employment in a shop would not suit her."

Holliday's eyes prickled. She squeezed her sister's hand. "Dr. Svartlebarrt, you've *got* to give her a job. You've *got* to. Or—" Holliday looked around, blinking away tears. "If not—if not a job—maybe you could make her so she, so she'll be better—" Her eyes fell upon the cubbies of vases behind the counter.

Dr. Mortleaus followed her gaze. With surprising gentleness, he said, "No, child. Our wares are far too expensive. Dr. Svartlebarrt's operation cannot afford that kind of charity."

Molly began to cry again. "I want Fairy."

"Hush, Molly."

"I want Fairy. I want Mamma."

"Hush, Moll, I'm trying to think!"

"I want Mamma and I want to go home."

"We can't go back home, Moll. Not ever. They'll hurt you."

"Fairy," Molly cried, wringing her tiny hands. "Fairy."

"Smoke me alive, but I can't watch this," said Dr. Mortleaus. "Bart, can't we—"

Dr. Svartlebarrt held up a finger.

He turned to Holliday. "Young lady. There is... maybe... one thing we can do."

"*Hush*, Moll. What is it?"

As one, the doctors turned to the mysterious vase on the table and regarded it in silence.

A chill, icy as a river breeze, swept up Holliday's back.

Dr. Svartlebarrt pulled out a marble and rolled it between his meaty fingers. "This," he said.

Holliday pulled Molly close. "What is it?"

"It's for the best, actually, that you arrived in the middle of the night," said Dr. Svartlebarrt. "When it comes to application of this particular type of treatment, the importance of discretion cannot be overstated. And if we act before dawn, there's no chance of anyone interrupting."

"Act how? And interrupt what?"

Dr. Svartlebarrt replaced the marble. He didn't answer.

Molly wiped her nose. "I'm thirsty," she said. Nevinn disappeared into the back. He returned with a tray, upon which sat a glass of water.

And surgical tools.

"*No*," said Holliday. She pulled Molly off the table. "If you don't tell me what it does, I won't let you put it inside of her."

Dr. Mortleaus looked down at his shoes.

"Child," said Dr. Svartlebarrt, gently. "You have to trust us."

"Why won't you tell me?"

"It's complicated."

"Do you think I'm too stupid to understand it?"

"Hardly," said Dr. Svartlebarrt. "But it's a trade secret."

"What'll it do to her?"

"You wanted us to make her better, didn't you? Well, this will serve that purpose."

"How will it do that?"

Dr. Svartlebarrt's voice dropped into that dangerous, Marmouth-mud softness. "Young lady. Do you want our assistance—or not?"

Holliday squeezed Molly's hand. Molly, who was too shy and too fearful—who would get attacked by street dogs, assaulted by older children, spit upon by the wealthy, harassed by commoners, ignored by tradesman, and harmed by her own blood. As she was, no place on this earth was safe for her.

Holliday couldn't say no.

Dr. Svartlebarrt read her eyes. "Well then," he said. "Morty, let's go wash up for surgery. You too, Nevinn."

They left the sisters alone in the front of the shop.

Molly sniffed. "If we can't go home, where will we go?"

"I dunno." Holliday's eyes darted around the room. "I'll think of something." Maybe Dr. Svartlebarrt would at least let them sleep behind the counter at night, so they wouldn't have to fight for a doorway out in the street?

Molly sniffed again. She touched the vase on the table. "Can I play with the marbles?"

"Those aren't marbles," said Holliday. "They're—"

She stopped.

Listened.

She heard no footsteps. She had time. Holliday jumped up and scurried back behind the counter, to the wall of cubbies and vessels. What might Molly need? Bravery. Confidence. Aggression. Resilience. Heroism. Scheming intelligence. Maybe even anger. Holliday swept up vase after vase, taking an augment from each. She couldn't know what the vase on the table contained, but this way—this way—

Somewhere, a footstep creaked. Holliday darted back to the table. From that final vase, she removed and pocketed seven augments; into that final vase, she placed the seven augments she had just stolen, in an even layer over the top. Surely, Dr. Mortleaus would reach in and happen to select one of these useful seven. They'd wind up helping Molly in a way that Holliday trusted whether they had intended to or not.

The curtain to the back flapped aside. Nevinn and the pair of doctors entered, freshly scrubbed, shirts tucked in, sleeves rolled up to the elbows.

Their eyes gleamed like those of rats.

Holliday clung to Molly's hand, murmuring over and over *It's all right, it's all right, they're going to make you feel better* until she believed it herself. She relaxed a bare fraction when Nevinn pulled the cloth ties from a bag, but Dr. Mortleaus said, "No, we shan't need to tie her down."

Ever-obedient Molly lay back on the table when Holliday told her to. She inhaled ether from Dr. Svartlebarrt's little cup, and her tiny hand relaxed within Holliday's grip.

"It's all right," whispered Holliday one final time, as she stroked Molly's slender wrist with a thumb.

Then brutish hands fell upon her.

Holliday squealed. Dr. Svartlebarrt pinned her back against the table as Nevinn grabbed her legs. "What are you doing? Stop it! Let me go!" She kicked Nevinn away, but Dr. Svartlebarrt heaved her up beside her unconscious sister, and ah, it was no wonder they hadn't tied Molly down. They needed the strips of cloth to restrain *her.*

"What are you doing?" Holliday screamed.

Cloth jammed into her mouth. She roared and bit around the gag, but to no effect. The hoary face of Dr. Svartlebarrt, shadows digging deep into his wrinkles, loomed above her.

"Pity," he said. "You were such a help in the shop. Ah well. We shall simply hold a free consultation day to lure someone else."

Holliday's fury soared. She kicked within her bonds,

uselessly, while Molly lay beside her, as limp and as foolishly trusting as a kitten placed into a drowning sack. "It's such a rare opportunity for us to have the chance to experiment upon siblings, you see," said Dr. Svartlebarrt. "And when something good falls into your lap like this, you must take advantage of it."

Nevinn shoved his hand into the final vase and pulled out a whole handful of augments. His grin crackled with glee. "We're upping the dose this time, right?"

Holliday's most vengeful roar was but a murmur within linen.

One of Dr. Svartlebarrt's massive hands gripped her jaw, forcing her head to be still. Dr. Mortleaus stood over her, a scalpel cocked in his clever fingers, his handsome face near-melted with sadness.

The lamplight traced a fat, red scar along the underside of his bare wrist.

He nodded at the scar. "I'm sorry, child," he said softly. "But I am Dr. Svartlebarrt's right-hand man. And his previous surgeon, before his mysterious disappearance, inserted into me a double augment for obedience."

Dr. Svartlebarrt's other hand, the ether mask cupped within, came down upon Holliday's face, and all sank into hazy darkness.

***

Floating.
Floating.
Heat.

Floating. Something strange. A rush, in fact—a great infusion of fire and brightness, some titanic frisson of feeling that did not make sense. Bravery. Confidence. Aggression. Resilience. Heroism. Scheming intelligence.

Anger.
So much anger.

***

When Holliday opened her eyes—

Her shirt was torn. A bandage lay over her heart. Only bravery was supposed to be inserted there. Holliday did not know, but oh, pray tell, great Dr. Svartlebarrt, what happens when many different augments are inserted together into the wrong place? Who knows? Do *you*?

Nevinn had undone her bonds. "Hey," he said. "Holliday's awake. You said they wouldn't wake 'til—"

Holliday was a bird, a tide, a wind. She was off the table and moving, the final vase flying from her fingers, shattering over the floor and spilling augments, augments everywhere. People slid and crashed. Dr. Mortleaus lay on the hardwood, moaning and gripping one knee; Nevinn hid behind the counter like a coward, and Dr. Svartlebarrt—why, he lay under Holliday, wailing, as her suddenly clever hands bound him up.

"Mortleaus, you damnable buffoon! You've put the wrong—"

"But you *saw* me!" His words were sobs. "You *saw* me draw from the vase!"

"Then how do you explain—"

It was Dr. Svartlebarrt's turn to wear the gag, now. And Nevinn's turn to be dragged out from behind the counter, mewling. And his turn to be tied up, too.

Dr. Mortleaus, still crippled, pleaded where he lay. "I'm sorry. Oh child, forgive me. Forgive us all."

No.

On the table, Molly still lolled. "Take them out."

"I can't," cried Dr. Mortleaus. "She's too young. They've already begun to dissolve."

Below the bandage on Molly's chest, a ghostly blue light arose.

All the vases, now, came smashing down below Holliday's hands. The floor sparkled with lamplight, glass, rolling augments, drops of blood and crazed spittle—hers? Molly's?

mewling Nevinn's?—while Dr. Mortleaus screamed out some apology or doomed bargain.

On the table, Molly moaned, a split, overlapping sound no human throat should be capable of making. Her eyes opened into radiant slits.

Holliday picked up a scalpel, still wet with Molly's blood, and faced her captors. Simple incisions, simple stitches. Simple to tell all these scattered augments apart. Not so simple to tell whether there was much ether left in the canister, but you didn't need ether, not really. You just needed one person who was angry enough to start cutting. And cutting. And cutting.

Every revolution started that way.

THE SOUL IN THE BELL JAR

Ten lonely miles from the shores of the Gneiss Sea, where the low town of Hume rots beneath the mist, runs a half-wild road without a name. Flanked by brambles and the black, it turns through wolf-thick hollows, watched by yellow eyes that glitter with hunger and the moon. The wolves, of course, are nothing, and no cutthroat highwayman ever waited beneath the shadows of those oaks. There are far worse things that shamble in the dark. This is the road that skirts Long Hill.

So the coachman declared, and so Lindsome Glass already knew. She also knew whose fault the shambling things were, and where their nursery lay: in the great, moaning house at Long Hill's apex.

She knew anxiety and sorrow, for having to approach it.

"Can't imagine what business a nice young miss like you has with the Stitchman," said the coachman.

Lindsome knew he was fishing for gossip. She did not reply.

"A pretty young miss like you?" pressed the coachman. Their vehicle was a simple horse trap, and there was nowhere to sit that was away from his dirty trousers and wine-stained smile. "You can't be, what, more than eleven? Twelve? Only them scienticians go up there. Unless you's a new Help, is that it? The ol' Stitchman could use a new pair of hands, says me. That big ol' house, rottin' up in the weeds with hardly nobody to tend to it none." He laughed. "Course, it's no wonder. You couldn't get Help up there for all the gold in Yorken." He eyed her sideways. "So what's he have on *you?*"

The road wound upward, the branches overhead thinned, and the stones beneath the wheels took on the dreary glow of an overcast sky. November in Tattenlane meant sunshine, but Lindsome was not in Tattenlane anymore.

"Eh?" the coachman pressed.

Lindsome turned her pale face away. She fought against the quiver in her jaw. "Mama and Papa have gone on a trip around the world. They didn't say for how long, but I'm to stay here until they return. The Stitchman is my great-uncle."

Startled into silence, the coachman looked away.

The nameless road flattened, and the mad, untamed lawn of Apsis House sprawled into view. It clawed to the horizons, large as night, lonely as the world.

***

When Lindsome alighted with her single hat box and carpetbag, there was only one sour-mouthed, middle-aged man to meet her. He was tall and stooped, with shoulders too square and a neck too short, giving him an altogether looming air of menace. "Took your time, didn't you?"

Behind Lindsome, the coachman was already retreating down Long Hill. "I—I'm sorry. The roads were—"

"Where are your manners?" the sour-mouthed man demanded. "Introduce yourself."

Lindsome bit her lip. The quiver in her jaw threatened to return. *I must not cry,* she told herself. *I am a young lady.* Lindsome gripped the hem of her white dress and dropped into a graceful curtsey. "I... beg your pardon, sir. My name is Lindsome Glass. How do you do? Our meeting is well."

"s'well," the man replied shortly. "That's better. Now take your things and come inside. Ghost knows where that lack-about Thomlin is. Doctor Dandridge is on the cusp of a singular work, one of the greatest in his career, and he and I have far more valuable things to do with our time than coddle you in welcome."

Lindsome nearly had to run to keep up with the man's long, loping strides. "The house has three main floors, one attic, and two basements," he said, leading her past a half-collapsed carriage house. "Attic is dangerous and off-limits. Third floor is Help's quarters and off-limits. Basements are the laboratories, so they are *definitely* off-limits, especially to careless little children."

The man pushed through a back door that cried on rust-thick hinges. Lindsome followed. The interior had a damp, close smell of things forgotten in the rain, and the air was clammy and chill. A small, useless fire guttered in a distant grate. Pots and pans, dingy with age and wear, hung from beams like gutted animals. Lindsome set down her hat box and touched a bunch of drying sage. It crumbled like a desiccated spiderweb.

The man grabbed her wrist. "And don't. Touch. Anything."

Lindsome fearfully withdrew her hand. "Yes, sir."

A middle-aged woman, generous in girth but mousy in the face, hobbled out from a pantry, wiping her hands on her flour-smeared apron. "Good afternoon, Mister Chaswick, sir." She turned to Lindsome. Her smile was kind. "Is this the young miss? Oh, so pale, with such lovely dark hair. You'll be a heartbreaker someday, won't you? What's your name?"

"This is Lindsome Glass," said Chaswick. "Mind you watch her."

"Yes, Mister Chaswick."

"Don't trouble to see her up. I'll do it."

"Thank you, Mister Chaswick."

"Don't thank me. With your knees it takes you a century to get up the bloody staircase."

Chaswick led Lindsome deeper into the house, under moldering lintels, through crooked doorways, past water-damaged wainscoting and rooms hung with peeling wallpaper. The carcasses of upturned insects lay in corners, legs folded neatly in rictus. Paintings lined the soot-blackened walls, and Lindsome thought that perhaps they had portrayed beautiful scenes, once, but now most were so caked with filth that it was hard to divine their subjects. Here, a lake? There, a table of hunting bounty? Many were portraits with tarnished nameplates. Any names still legible meant nothing. Who was Marilda Dandridge, anyway?

"Are you paying attention?" Chaswick demanded. "Breakfast's at seven, supper's at noon, and dinner's at seven. We don't have tea or any of that Tattenlane nonsense here. Bath day is Sunday, wash day is Monday, and if you'd like to occupy yourself, I suggest the library on the second floor, as it contains a number of volumes that will ensure the moral betterment of a young person such as yourself."

"Do you have any picture books?" Lindsome asked.

Chaswick frowned. "I suppose you could borrow one of your great-uncle's illustrated medical atlases. Perhaps Porphyry's *Intestinal Arrangements of the Dispeptic* or Gharison's *Common Melancholia in the Spleen of the Breeding Female.*"

Lindsome looked down at her shoes. "Never mind."

"You may also explore the grounds," Chaswick continued. "But don't cross paths with the gardener. Understand? If you ever hear the gardener working, turn around and go back at once.

"And mind the vivifieds. Doctor Dandridge is a brilliant, highly prolific man, and you'll see a great many examples of his work roaming throughout the area, many of which do not have souls consanguineous to their bodies. However, none of the vivifieds that Doctor Dandridge and I have created for practical purposes are chimeric, so you may safely pat the house cats and the horses in the stables. If you'd like to go for a ride..."

Something colorful moved at the edge of Lindsome's vision. Surprised at something so bright in so dreary a place, she stopped and backtracked. She peered around a corner, down a short hall sandwiched between a pair of much grander rooms.

The door at the end of the hall stood ajar. A hands-breadth of room beckoned, sunny-yellow and smelling of lavender. A bookcase stood partially in view, crammed with spinning tops, painted wooden blocks, tin soldiers, stuffed animals, rattles, little blankets, papers cleverly folded into birds...

Lindsome stepped forward.

A woman exited the room. Her movements were quick, though she was old and excessively thin, with dark circles about her despairing eyes. She grasped the doorknob with bloodless talons, pulling it shut and locking it with a tiny iron key.

She turned and saw Lindsome.

Her transformation into rage was instantaneous. "What are you doing?" the woman bellowed, baring her long, gray teeth. "Get out of this hall! Get away from here!"

Lindsome fled to Chaswick.

"What's this?" said Chaswick, turning. "What! Have you not been following me?"

"There was a woman!" Lindsome said, dropping her things. "A thin woman!"

Chaswick grabbed Lindsome's wrist again. He bent over and pulled her close—lifted her, even, until she was nearly on her tiptoes and squirming with discomfort and alarm.

"That's Emlee, the housekeeper. Mind her too." Chaswick narrowed his eyes. "And that little hallway between the study and the card room? Definitely, *absolutely* off-limits."

***

Chaswick deposited Lindsome in front of a room on the second floor. As soon as he had withdrawn down the grand staircase, Lindsome set her things inside and made a survey of the rest of the level. The aforementioned library was spacious and well stocked but poorly kept, with uneven layers of dust and book bindings faded by sun. Many volumes had been reshelved unevenly, incorrectly, or even upside-down, if at all.

Most of the other rooms were unused, their furniture wholly absent or in deep slumber beneath moth-eaten sheets. Two of the rooms were locked, or perhaps even rusted shut, including one next to what she assumed were her great-uncle's personal quarters, since they were the largest and, she could only surmise, at one time, the grandest. Now, like all else in Apsis House, their colors and details had darkened with soot and neglect, and Lindsome wondered how, if Dr. Dandridge were so brilliant, he could fail to control such misery and decay.

While exploring the first floor more thoroughly, she came across a squat, surly man in overalls who was pasting paper over a broken window in the Piano Room. He introduced himself as Thomlin, the Housemaster. Lindsome politely asked how did he do. Thomlin said he did fine, as long as he took his medicine, and as an illustration produced a silver flask, from which he took a hearty pull.

"May I ask you something, Mister Thomlin? What's at the end of the little hallway? In the yellow room?"

The house'm scowled as he lifted his paste brush from the bucket and slapped it desultorily over the glass. "Nothin'," he said. "Nothin' that a good girl should stick 'er nose in. How a man wants to grieve, that's his business. No, no, I've said too much already." Juggling flask and brush, he took another medicinal dose. "I know everything that happens and ever did happen in these walls, you understand, inside and out. Wish I didn't, but I do. Housemaster, that's me. All these poor bastards—oops, pardon my language, young miss—I mean all these poor folks walk around in a fog a' their own problems, but a Housemaster sees everything as The Ghost sees it: absolute and clear as finest crystal, as not a soul else can ever understand. But good men tell no tales anyway. An' a gooder man you won't find either side of this whole blasphemous Long Hill heap. Why don't you go play outside? But don't never interrupt the gardener. Hear?"

Lindsome did not want to explore the grounds, but she told herself, *I must be brave, because I am a young lady,* and went outside with her head held high. Nonetheless, she did not get far. The weeds and brambles of the neglected lawn had long since matured into an impenetrable thicket, and Lindsome could barely see the rooftops of the nearby outbuildings above the wild creepers, dying leaves, needle-thin thorns, and drab, stenchful flowers. The late autumnal blossoms stank of carrion and sulfur, mingled with the ghastly sickly-sweetness of mothballs. Lindsome pulled one sleeve over her hand and held it to her wrinkled nose as she picked her way along a downward-sloping animal trail that ran near the main house, the closest navigational relief in this unrelenting jungle, but she could get no corresponding relief from the smell.

She rounded a barberry bush. A little scream squeezed from behind her hand.

The stench wasn't the flowers. It was vivifieds.

In her path, blocking it completely, stood a white billy goat. He did not breathe or move. His peculiar, tipped-over eyes were motionless, his sideways pupils like twin cracks to the Abyss.

His belly had burst, and flies looped around his gaping bowels in humming droves.

Heart pounding, Lindsome backed away. The goat did

nothing. Its gaze remained fixed at some point beyond her shoulder. As she watched, bits of its flesh grew misty, then resolidified. *It's all right,* Lindsome told herself. *It's just an old vivified, rotten enough for the soul to start coming loose. It's so old it doesn't know what it is or how to act. See? It's staying right there.*

Push past it. It will never notice.

Lindsome shuddered. But she was a young lady, and young ladies were always calm and regal and never afraid.

So Lindsome lifted the hem of her dress, as if preparing to step through a mud puddle, and inched her way toward and around the burst-open creature.

Its foul-smelling fur, tacky with ichor, brushed the whiteness of her garment. Lindsome closed her eyes and bit her lip, enough to bring pain, and a fly buzzed greedily in her ear. *I am not afraid. I am not afraid.*

She passed the goat.

At the first possible moment, she dropped her hem and sprinted down the path. The thicket thinned out into a place where the trail wasn't as clear, but she kept going, crashing through brittle twigs and dead undergrowth, prompting vivified birds to take wing. The corpses were poor fliers, dropping as swiftly as they'd risen. One splatted onto a boulder at the edge of the path, hard enough for the stitched-on soul to be shaken loose entirely in a shimmer of mist; the physical shell, without anything to vivify it, shrank in volume like a dried-up fruit.

The faint trail turned abruptly into a long, empty clearing that stretched back toward the house. The vista had been created with brisk violence: every stubborn plant, whether still verdant or dormant for the season, had been uprooted and laid in careless, half-dried piles, revealing tough, rocky soil. A second path connecting to this space had been widened and its vegetation thoroughly trampled. Lindsome silently blessed the unseen gardener's vigorous but futile work ethic and, slowing to a breathless, nervous walk, crossed the clearing. Despite the portending stink, there were no vivifieds in sight.

But as the path resumed, the stench grew stronger yet. Rot and cloying sweetness clogged Lindsome's nose so badly that her eyes watered and she breathed through her mouth. Young ladies remained calm and regal, Lindsome supposed, but they were also not stupid. Perhaps it was time to turn back.

The path ended at a set of heavy double doors.

To be truthful, a number of paths ended at these doors, with at least four distinct trails converging at the edges of the small, filth-caked patio. Lindsome imagined that her great-uncle, along with the unpleasant Chaswick, exited from these doors when making expeditions into the haunted thicket for the few live specimens that must remain. *Do they only catch the old and injured*, she wondered, *or do they murder creatures in their prime, only to sew their souls right back on again?*

Lindsome tried the doors. They opened with ease.

The revealed space was not some dingy mudroom or rear hall, as Lindsome had expected, but a room so wide, it could have served as a stable were it not for its low ceiling and unfinished back. Instead of meeting a rear wall, the flagstone floor disintegrated into irregular fragments and piled up onto a slope of earth.

Three long tables ran down the center of the room to Lindsome's right, the final one disappearing into the total blackness of the room's far end. The tables were stone, their surfaces carved with deep grooves that terminated at the edges, above stained and waiting buckets.

Melted candles spattered the tables' surfaces. There were no windows.

The stench of the place flowed outward like an icy draft. Lindsome left a door open behind her, held her nose, and took a step inside. Even when breathing through her mouth, the vivified odor was a soup of putrification that clotted at the back of her throat, thick enough to drip into her belly. The sensation was unendurable. Surely that was a stone staircase leading up over the unfinished back wall, into less offensive parts of the house?

Three steps toward the staircase, Lindsome made the mistake of glancing behind her.

The entire front wall, lined floor to ceiling with cages and bars, bore an unliving library of vivifieds, every creature too large for its pen. Stoats stood shoulder-to-shoulder with badgers and owls, and serpents had no room to uncurl in their tiny cubes. Rabbit fur comingled with hawk feathers. Paws tapped and noses twitched, and bodies lurched gently from side to side, but that great wall of shifting corpses, scales and hide and stripes, made no sound. Each rotting throat was silent.

Three hundred pairs of eyes watched Lindsome, flashing yellow and green, white and red. She fell into a table, hitting her shoulder against the stone.

Get up. Run away. She daren't breathe. *You silly fool. The ground was sloping outside. Remember? This is a basement.*

You cannot be here.

A door squealed open. A trickle of light dribbled down the steps.

Lindsome dove away from the table and behind the staircase's concealing bulk.

The door at the top opened fully. Candlelight flowed down the steps now, making hundreds of vivified eyes sparkle. "The sea lion, I think," said a voice. It was papery and thin, like a flake of ash that would crumble at the barest touch. "At the far end."

"Really, Albion," said Chaswick, stepping down onto the flagstones. He held high a five-branched candelabrum, his shadow stretching behind him. "We're overpreparing, don't you think?"

"Oh no, not hardly." An old, old man shuffled in Chaswick's wake. His head, wreathed in a wispy halo of white and framed by sizeable ears, seemed bowed under the weight of constant thought across many decades. His knobby fingers would not stop undulating, like twin spiders in a restless sleep. "One last test, before Thursday. I'm certain that a Kell Stitch at the brain stem, instead of a Raymund, will surprise us."

Chaswick's back heaved in a sigh. "I maintain that the original protocol would have sufficed. The first time around —"

"I was lucky," interrupted the man. "Very, very lucky. That ghastly knot was nothing but shaking hands and fortunate bungling. And besides—" He sighed, too, but instead of deflating, the exhalation appeared to lift him up. "Think of the advances, Chaswick. The discoveries I've made since then. How all these newer elements might work in concert —well. We cannot be too careful. I don't have to tell you what's at stake."

The two men moved into the blackness of the room's far end. The candelabrum revealed that the distant third of the wall was hidden behind a heavy black curtain.

"Of course, Doctor Dandridge," said Chaswick.

"The sea lion," Dr. Dandridge repeated.

Chaswick passed the candelabrum to his superior. When he turned to grip the curtain, Lindsome noticed what he was wearing.

Waders?

The curtain hissed partway aside upon its track. The candlelight fell upon tanks, tanks and tanks and tanks, each filled with an evil, yellowing liquid. Each held a shrunken animal corpse, embalmed and barely recognizable. The lowest third of the wall was but a single tank, stretching back behind the half-closed curtain.

A great, bloated shadow rolled within.

Lindsome shivered. She had never seen the dread creature's like. It must have been a specimen from the continent to the east, but whatever it was, it was not what they wanted, because Chaswick knelt by a tank on the second shelf, obscuring the monstrosity. He fitted a length of rubber hose to a stopcock at the bottom of his chosen tank, then ran the hose along the floor and out the open door. "Door's blown loose again. That useless Thomlin—I've asked him to fix the latch thrice this week. I swear to Ghost, I'd stick him in one of the tanks myself if he weren't a man and would leave behind anything more useful than ghost-grease."

Chaswick returned and opened the stopcock. The end of the hose, limp over the edge of the patio, dribbled its foul load into the weeds. The large corpse within the tank settled to the bottom as it drained, a limp, matted mess. Chaswick did something to the glass to make it open outward, like the door to an oven.

He gathered the dead thing to his chest and stood. Ichor ran in rivulets down his waders. "I don't mean to rush you, but—"

"Of course." Candelabrum in tow, Dr. Dandridge shuffled back to the stairs. "I'll do my best to hurry."

They ascended the steps, pulling the light with them and the squealing door shut.

Lindsome fled outside. After that chamber of horrors, the sticking burdock, Raven's Kiss, and cruel thorns of the sunlit world were the hallmarks of Paradise.

★★★

At seven o'clock, some unseen, stentorian timepiece tolled the hour. Lindsome, who had elected to spend the rest of the afternoon in the library in a fort constructed from the oldest, fattest, dullest (and surely therefore safest) books she could find, reluctantly emerged to search for the dining room.

The murmur of voices and clink of silverware guided her steps into a room on the first floor nearly large enough to be a proper banquet hall.

Only the far end of the long table, near the wall abutting the kitchen, was occupied. A fire on the wall's hearth cast the head of the table in shadow while illuminating Chaswick's disdain.

"You are late," Chaswick said. "Don't you know what they say about first impressions?"

Lindsome slunk across the floor. "I'm sorry, Mister Chaswick."

From the shadows of a wingback chair, the master of the house leaned forward. "No matter," said Dr. Dandridge. "Good evening. I am Professor Albion Edgarton Dandridge. Our meeting is well. Please pardon me for not arising; I'm an old man, and my bones grow reluctant, even at the welcome sight of a face so fresh and kind as yours."

Lindsome had not expected this. "I... thank you, sir."

"Uncle Albion will do. Come, sit, sit."

Opposite Chaswick, Lindsome pulled out her own massive chair with some difficulty, working it over the threadbare carpet in small scoots. "Thank you, sir. Our meeting is well."

Chaswick snorted. "Mind her, Doctor. She's got a streak in her."

"Oh, I don't doubt it. Comes from my side." The old man smiled at her. His teeth were surprisingly intact. "Are you making yourself at home, my dear?"

Lindsome served herself a ladle-full of shapeless brown stew. "Yes, sir."

"Don't mumble," said Chaswick, picking debris from his teeth with his fingernails. "It's uncouth."

"I am delighted that you're staying with us," continued Dr. Dandridge. Outside of the nightmarish basement, he looked ordinary and gentle. His halo of hair, Lindsome now saw, wandered off his head into a pair of bedraggled dundrearies, and the fine wrinkles around his eyes made him look kind. His clothes were dusty and ill-fitting, tailored for a more robust man at least thirty years his junior. She could not imagine a less threatening person.

"Thank you, sir."

"Uncle. I am dear old Uncle—" Dr. Dandridge coughed, a dry, wheezing sound, and put an embroidered handkerchief to his mouth. Chaswick nudged the old man's water glass closer. "Albion," he managed, taking a sip from the glass. "Thank you, Chaswick."

"Yes, Uncle."

"And how is your papa?"

Lindsome did not want to think of him, arm in arm with Mama, strolling up the pier to the great boat and laughing, his long legs wavering under a film of tears. "He is very well, thank you."

"Excellent, excellent. And your mama?"

"Also well."

"Good, good." The doctor nibbled at his stew, apparently unfazed by its utter lack of flavor. "I trust that the staff have been kind, and have answered all of your questions."

"Well...," Lindsome started, but Chaswick shot her a dangerous look. Lindsome fell silent.

"Yes?" asked Dr. Dandridge, focused on teasing apart a gravy-smothered nodule.

"I was wondering..." dared Lindsome, but Chaswick's face sharpened into a scowl. "...about your work."

"Oh!" said Dr. Dandridge. His efforts on the nodule of stew redoubled. "My work. My great work! You are right to ask, young lady. It is always pleasing to hear that the youth of today have an interest in science. Young people are our future, you know."

"I—"

"The work, of course, builds on the fundamentals of Wittard and Blacke from the '30s, going beyond the Skin Stitch and into the essential vital nodes. But unlike Havarttgartt and his school (and here's the key, now), we don't hold that the heart, brain, and genitals, a.k.a. the Life Triad, are the necessary fulcrums. We hold—that is, I hold—that is, Chaswick agrees, and he's a very smart lad—we hold that a diversified architecture of fulcrums is key to extending the ambulatory period of a vivified, and we have extensive data to back this hypothesis, to the extent where we've produced a curve—a Dandridge curve, I call it, if I may be so modest, ha-ha—that illustrates the correlation between the number of fulcrums and hours of ambulatory function, and clearly demonstrates that while *quality* of fulcrums does indeed play a role, it is not nearly so prominent as the role of *quantity*. Or, in layman's terms, if you stitch a soul silly to a corpse at every major mechanical joint—ankles, knees, hips, shoulders, elbows, wrists—you'll still get a far better outcome than you would had you used a Butterfly Stitch to the heart itself! Can you imagine?"

Lost, Lindsome stared at her plate. She could feel Chaswick's smug gaze upon her, the awful look that grownups use when they want to say, *Not so smart now, are you?*

"And furthermore," Dr. Dandridge went on gaily, setting down his fork and withdrawing a different utensil from his pocket with which to attack his clump of stew, "we have discovered a hitherto unknown role of the Life Triad in host plasticity, which also beautifully solves the mystery of how a very small soul, like that of a mouse, can successfully be stitched to a very large flesh mass, like that of a cow, and vice-versa. Did Chaswick explain to you about our chimeras? The dogs with souls of finches, and the blackbirds with the souls of chipmunks, and in one exceptional case, the little red fox with the soul of a prize-winning hog? Goodness, was I proud of that one!" The old man laughed.

Lindsome smiled weakly.

"It is upon the brain, you see, not the heart," Dr. Dandrige went on, "that the configuration, amount, and type of stitches are key, because—and this is already well known in the higher animals—a great deal of soul is enfleshed in the brain. You may think of the brain as a tiny little seed that floats in the center of every skull, but not so! When an animal is alive, the brain takes up the *entire* skull cavity. Can you imagine? Of course, the higher the animal, the more the overall corpse shrinks at the moment of death, a.k.a. soul separation, due to the soul composing a greater percentage of the creature. This is why Humankind (with its large and complex souls) leaves no deathhusk, or corpse, at all— nothing but a film of ghostgrease. Which, incidentally, popular doggerel will tell you is absent from the deathbeds of holy people, being that they are so *very* above their animal natures and are one hundred percent ethereal, but goodness, don't get me started about all *that* ugsome rot."

Dr. Dandridge stopped. He frowned at his plate. "Good grief. What am I doing?"

"A Clatham Stitch, looks like," said Chaswick gently. "On your beef stew."

"Heavens!" Dr. Dandridge put down his utensil, which Lindsome could now see was an aetherhook. He removed what looked like a monocle made of cobalt glass from a breast pocket, then peered through it at his plate. "There weren't any souls passing by just now, were there? The ley-currents are strong here in the early winter, dear Lindsome, and sometimes the departed souls of lesser creatures will blow into the house if we have the windows open. And when *that* happens—"

The lump of beef quivered. Lindsome dropped her fork and clapped a hand to her mouth.

From beneath the stew crawled a beetle, looking very put out.

Dr. Dandridge and Chaswick burst into guffaws. "A beetle!" cried the old man. "A beetle in the stew! Oh, that is precious, too precious for words! Oh, how funny!"

Chaswick, laughing, looked to Lindsome, her eyes saucer-wide. "Oh, come now," he said. "Surely you see the humor."

Dr. Dandridge wiped his eyes. The beetle, tracking tiny spots of stew, crawled off across the tablecloth at speed. "A beetle! Oh, mercy. Mercy me. Excuse us—that's not a joke for a young lady at all. Forgive me, child—we've grown uncivilized out here, isolated as we are. A Clatham Stitch upon my stew, as if to vivify it! And then came a beetle—"

Lindsome couldn't take it anymore. She stood. "May I be excused?"

"Already?" said Chaswick, still chuckling. "No more questions for your great-uncle, demonstrating your *very* thorough interest in and understanding of his work?"

Lindsome colored beneath the increasing heat of her discomfort. This remark, on top of all else, was too much. "Oh, I understand a great deal. I understand that you can stitch a soul to an embalmed deathhusk instead of an unpreserved one—"

Chaswick stopped laughing immediately.

"—even though *everybody knows* that's impossible," said Lindsome.

Chaswick's eyes tightened in suspicion. Dr. Dandridge, unaware of the ferocity between their interlocked stares, sat as erect as his ancient bones would permit. "Why, that's right! That's absolutely right! You must have understood the implications of Bainbridge's supplemental index in her report last spring!"

"Yes," said Chaswick coldly. "She must have."

Lindsome colored further and looked away. She

focused on her great-uncle, who, in his excitement, had picked up the aetherhook once again and was attempting to cut a bit of potato with it. "Your mama was right to send you here. I never imagined—a blossoming, fine young scientific mind in the family! Why, the conversations we can have, you and I! Great Apocrypha, I'm doing it again, aren't I?" The old man put the aetherhook, with no further comment or explanation, tip-down in his water glass. "We shall have a chat in my study after dinner. Truth be told, you arrived at the perfect time. Chaswick and I are at the cusp of an astounding attempt, a true milestone in—"

Chaswick arose sharply from his chair. "A moment, Doctor! I need a word with your niece first." He rounded the table and grabbed Lindsome's arm before anyone could protest. "She'll await you in your study. Excuse us."

Chaswick dragged her toward the small, forbidden hallway, but rather than entering the door at the end into the mysterious yellow room, he dragged Lindsome into one of the rooms that flanked the corridor. Lindsome did not have an opportunity to observe the interior, for Chaswick slammed the door behind them.

"What have you seen?"

A match flared to life with a pop and Lindsome shielded her eyes. Chaswick lit a single candle, tossed the match aside, and lifted the candle to chest-level. Its flicker turned his expression eerie and demonic. "I said, what have you seen?"

"Nothing!" Lindsome kept her hand over her eyes, pretending the shock of the light hurt worse than it did, so that Chaswick could not see the lie upon her face.

"Listen to me, you little brat," Chaswick hissed. "You might think you can breeze in here and destroy everything I've built with a bit of flattery and deception, but I have news for you. You and the rest of your shallow, showy, flighty, backstabbing kindred? You abandoned this brilliant man long ago, thinking his work would come to nothing, and that these beautiful grounds and marvels of creation weren't worth the rocks the building crew dug from the soil, but with The Ghost as my witness, I swear that I am not allowing your pampered, money-grubbing hands to trick me out of my inheritance. Do you understand me? I love this man. I love his work. I love what he stands for. Apsis House will remain willed to *me*. And if I so much as see you bat your wicked little eyes in the doctor's direction, I will *ensure* that you are not in my way.

"Do I make myself clear?"

Lindsome lowered her hand. It was trembling. Every part of her was. "You think I'm—are you saying—?"

The vise of Chaswick's hand, honed over long hours of tension around a Stitchman's instruments, crushed her wrist in its grip. "Do I make myself clear?"

Lindsome squirmed, now in genuine pain. "Let me go! I don't even want your ruined old house!"

"What did you see?"

"Stop it!"

"Tell me what you've seen!"

"Yes," announced Dr. Dandridge, and in half a second, Chaswick had released Lindsome and stepped back, and the old man entered the room, a blazing candelabrum in hand. "Yes, stitching a soul to an embalmed, or even mummified, deathhusk would be a tremendous feat. Just imagine how long something like that could last. Ages, maybe. And ages more..." His expression turned distant and calculating. "Just imagine. A soul you never wanted to lose? Why, you could keep it here forever..."

Chaswick straightened. He smiled at Lindsome, a poisonous thing that Dr. Dandridge, lost in daydreams, did not see. "Good night, Doctor. And good night, Lindsome. Mind whose house you're in."

★★★

Surviving the fervid conversation of her great-uncle was one thing, but after just five days, Lindsome wasn't sure how long she could survive the mysteries of his house. Chimeric with secrets, every joint and blackened picture was near bursting with the souls of untold stories. Lindsome was amazed that the whole great edifice did not lurch into motion, pulling up its deep roots and walls to run somewhere that wasn't bathed in madness and the footsteps of the dead. She searched the place over for answers, but the chambers yielded no clues, and any living thing who might supply them remained stitched to secrets of their own.

The only person she hadn't spoken with yet was the gardener.

Lindsome finally set off one evening to find him, under a gash of orange-red that hung over the bare trees to the west. She left the loop trail around the house. Bowers of bramble, vines of Heart-Be-Still, and immature Honey-locusts rife with spines surrounded her. A chorus of splintering twigs whispered beyond as unseen vivifieds moved on ill-fitted instinct.

"Hello? Mister Gardener?"

Only the twigs, whispering.

Lindsome slipped her right hand into her pocket, grasping what lay within. A grade-2 aetherblade, capped tight. She'd found it on the desk in Uncle Albion's study one afternoon. Lindsome couldn't say why she'd taken it. An aetherblade was only useful, after all, if one wanted to cut spirit-stitches and knew where those stitches lay, and Lindsome had neither expertise nor aetherglass to make solid the invisible threads. It would have done her just as much good to pocket one of Cook's paring knives, which is to say, not much good at all.

"Hello?"

Beneath the constant stink of corpses came something sweet. At first, Lindsome thought it was a freshly vivified, exuding the cloyingly sweet fragrance of the finishing chemicals. But it was too gentle and mild.

A dark thing, soft as a moth, fluttered onto her cheek. A rose petal.

"Mister Gardener? Are you growing—"

A savagely cleared vista opened before her, twisting back toward the house, now a looming shadow against the dimming sky. The murdered plants waited in neat piles, rootballs wet and dark. Lindsome squeezed her stolen aetherblade tighter in relief. The things were newly pulled. He'd be resting at the end of this trail, close to the house, preparing to come in for the evening.

But he wasn't.

At the end of the vista, Lindsome halted in surprise. It was as if the gardener had known that Lindsome would come this way, and had wanted to present her with a beautiful view, for in front of her lay another clearing, but this one was old and well maintained. Its floor held a fine carpet of grass, dormant and littered with leaves. The grass stretched up to the house itself and terminated at the edge of a patio. The double doors leading out were twin mosaics of diamond-shaped panes. Through them, Lindsome could see sheer curtains drawn back on the other side. Within the room, a gaslamp burned.

Its light flickered over yellow walls.

Lindsome's breath stuck in her throat like a lump of ice. She could see the shelves now, the stacks of toys, the painted blocks and tops and bright pictures of animals hung above the chair-rail molding. A tiny, overlooked chair at the patio's edge. An overlooked iron crib within.

Nobody had said the room was forbidden to approach from the outside.

Lindsome drifted across the grass. As she drew closer, she noticed something new. In the center of the room, between her and the iron crib, stood a three-legged table. Upon the table sat a bell jar. Perfectly clean, its translucence had rendered it invisible, until Lindsome saw the gaslight glance from its surface at the proper angle.

Within the bell jar, something moved.

Lindsome drew even closer. The bell jar was large, the size of a birdcage, but not so large as to dwarf the blur within. The blur's presence, too, had been obscured from behind by the stark pattern of the crib's bars, but it was not so translucent as the bell jar itself. The thing inside the glass was wispy. Shimmering.

Lindsome stepped onto the patio. The icy lump in her throat froze it shut.

Within the bell jar, a tiny, tiny fist solidified and pressed its ghostly knuckles against the glass.

Lindsome's scream woke Long Hill's last surviving raven, which took wing into the night, cawing.

★★★

Thorns tore Lindsome's dress to tatters as she ran. "Chaswick!"

She fled toward the squares of gaslight, jumping over a fallen tree and flying up the main steps into the house. She called again, running from room to empty room, scattering dust and mice, the lamplight painting black ghosts behind crooked settees and broken chairs. "Someone help! Chaswick!"

Lindsome reached the kitchen. Cook was kneeling by the hearth, roasting a pan of cabbage-wrapped beef rolls atop the glowing coals. "Cook! Help! The yellow room! There's a baby!"

Cook maintained her watchful crouch, not even turning. "Sst!" She put a plump finger to her lips. "Hush, child!"

"The yellow room," cried Lindsome, gripping Cook's elbow. "I saw it. I was outside and followed a path the gardener made. There's a bell jar inside. It's got a soul in it.

A captured human soul. He's keeping a—"

Cook planted her sooty hand over Lindsome's mouth. She leaned toward her, beady eyes pinching. "I said hush, child," Cook whispered. "Hush. That was nothing you saw. That fancy gaslight the doctor likes, it plays tricks on your eyes."

Lindsome shook her head, but Cook pressed harder. "It plays tricks." Her expression pleaded. "Be a good girl, now. Stop telling tales. Lock your door at night. And don't you bring the gardener into this—don't you dare. That's a good girl?" Her eyes pinched further. "Yes?"

Lindsome wrenched herself away and ran.

"Chaswick!" She ran to the second floor, so upset that she grew disoriented. Had she already searched this corridor? This cloister of rooms? She could smell it. Fresh vivified. No—something milder. Right behind this locked door...

A hand touched Lindsome's shoulder. She squealed.

"Saint Ransome's Blood, child!" Chaswick said, spinning her about. A pair of spectacles perched on his nose, gleaming in the hall's gaslight. His other, dangling hand held a half-open book, as though it were a carcass to be trussed. "What's all this howling?"

Lindsome threw her arms about him. "Chaswick!"

He stiffened. "Goodness. Control yourself. Come now, stop that. Did you see a mouse?"

"No," said Lindsome, pressing her face into Chaswick's chest. "It was—"

"How many times must I tell you not to mumble?" Chaswick asked. "Now listen. I was in the midst of a very important—"

"A BABY!" Lindsome shouted.

Chaswick grew very still.

"It was—"

Chaswick drew back, gripped Lindsome's shoulder,

and without another word marched her down the hall and through a door that had always been locked.

Lindsome glanced about. The place appeared to be Chaswick's quarters. The room was in surprisingly good repair, clean and recently painted, but all carpets, tapestries, cushions, and wallpaper had been removed. The only furniture was a desk, chair, and narrow bed, the only thing of any comfort a mean, straw mattress. The fire in the grate helped soften the room's hard lines, and Lindsome's fear of this stern and jealous man melted further under her larger one. "I'm sorry, Mister Chaswick, but I was walking outside, and there was a path that took me past the yellow room, and inside I saw a bell jar. And in it was an infant's soul. It solidified a fist and put it against the glass. I swear I'm not fibbing, Mister Chaswick. I swear by Mama's virtue, I'm not."

Chaswick sighed. He placed his book upon his desk. "I know you're not."

"You *know*?"

Chaswick shook his head, the flames highlighting the firm lines around his mouth. "I have said. The doctor is a brilliant man."

"But he—but you *can't* just—" Lindsome sputtered. "You can't stop a soul from going to Heaven! It's wrong! You'll—The Ghost will—you'll freeze in the Abyss! Forever and ever! The Second Ghostscroll says—"

"Don't quote scripture at me, girl, it's tiresome." Chaswick withdrew a small leather case from a pocket in his trousers, removed his spectacles, and slid them inside. "The Ghost is nothing but a fairy tale for adults who never grow up. Humankind is alone in the universe, and there are no rules save for those which we agree upon ourselves. If Doctor Dandridge has the knowledge, the means, the willingness, and the bravery to experiment upon a human soul—well, then, what of it?"

Lindsome shrank back. "He's going to—what?"

Chaswick set his mouth, the firelight carving his sternness deeper. "It's not my place to stop him."

Lindsome took a full step backward, barely able to speak. "You can't mean that. He can't. He wouldn't."

"In fact, I rather encourage it," said Chaswick. "Fortune favors the bold."

"But it's illegal," Lindsome stammered. "It's sick! They'd think he's gone mad! They'd put him away, and then they'd—"

She stopped. She stared at Chaswick.

They'd take away all of Uncle's property.

And they'd look in Uncle's will and give it to...

"You," Lindsome whispered. "It's you. You put this idea into his head."

Chaswick sneered. "His wife Marilda died in childbirth, and the doctor chose his unorthodox method of grieving, well before I ever set foot on Long Hill. Not that you'd know, considering how very little your ilk cared to associate with him, after the tragedy. Ask your precious mama. She doesn't approve of the yellow room, either." Chaswick's laugh was nasty. "Not that she thinks it's anything more than an empty shrine."

Lindsome backed toward the door. Chaswick advanced, matching her step for step. *You monster. You brute. What has my poor uncle done? What awful things has he already done?*

And what else is he going to do?

The door was nearly at her back. Chaswick loomed above her. "Go to bed, little girl," he warned. "Nobody is going to listen to your foolish histrionics. Not in this house."

Lindsome turned and fled.

She ran down the hall and into her own bedroom, where the bed sagged, the mold billowed across the ceiling like thunderheads, and the vivified mice ran back and forth, back and forth against the baseboards, without thinking, all night long.

Lindsome locked the door. *Cook would be proud.*

Then she lay on her bed and wept.

★★★

The night stretched like a cat, smothering future and past alike with its inky paws. Lindsome tossed in broken sleep. She dreamed of light glinting off of curved glass and something lancing through her heart. Chaswick above her, flames of gaslight for eyes, probing her beating flesh with an aetherhook. "What's all this howling?"

Under everything, roses.

★★★

An hour before dawn, Lindsome dressed and left the house. The sky was too dark and the clouds too swollen, but she couldn't stand this wretched place another moment. Even the stables, which held nothing but vivifieds, would be an improvement. The matted fur of dead horses is just as well for sponging away tears.

In the stables, Lindsome buried her face against the cold nose of a gelding. Did he have the same soul he'd had in life, she wondered, or did some other horse now command this body? What did it feel like, to be stitched imperfectly to a body that was not yours? She remembered the grade-2 aetherblade in the pocket of her coat. She recalled the few comprehensible bits of her great-uncle's post-dinner lectures. Lindsome drew away from the horse, wiped her face on her sleeve, and produced the aetherblade.

The horse watched her, exhibiting no sign of feeling.

Lindsome plunged the tool behind the horse's knee, between the physical stitches of a deep, telltale cut that could never heal. She circled the creature, straining to see in the poor light, plunging the aetherblade into every such cut she could find.

The horse's legs buckled. It collapsed to the floor.

Its neck still functioned. The horse looked up at her,

expressionless. Lindsome searched through its mane, shuddering, trying to find the final knot of stitching that would—

Set it free.

Lindsome stopped.

The horse did not react.

"Wait for me," Lindsome said, setting down the aetherblade on the floor. "There's something I have to do. I'll be right back."

The horse, unable to do anything else, waited.

But she didn't come back.

★★★

Something was wrong with the sky, Lindsome thought, as she trotted toward the house. It was too gray and too warm, after last night's chill. There shouldn't be thunderheads gathering now. Not so late in autumn.

And something was wrong with the vivifieds. Instead of rustling in the depths of the thicket, they lurched up and down the irregular paths in a sluggish remembrance of flight. A snake with a crushed spine lolled in a hollow. A pack of coyotes, moving in rolling prowls like house cats, moved single file in a line from the stables to the well, not even swiveling an ear as Lindsome squeezed past.

Near the main steps of the house, the burst-open billy goat had gotten ensnared in a tangle of creepers, its blackened entrails commingling with blackened vines.

Lindsome resolutely ran past it.

A dead sparrow fell from the sky and pelted her shoulder, and a frog corpse crunched beneath her foot. A hundred awful things could smear her with their putrescence—but oh, let them, because she was a lady. And ladies always did what needed doing.

There.

The gardener's careful path to the yellow room.

She was at the final vista, now. Then the private patio.

The sheer curtains were closed, but one of the patio doors was open, swinging to and fro on the fretful breeze.

In the center of the room, the three-legged table waited, but the bell jar was gone.

Lindsome slumped in gratitude. Uncle Albion had finally come to his senses. Or Chaswick had felt guilty about their talk last night, or careless Thomlin had knocked it over and broken it, even.

But then Lindsome remembered.

Today is Thursday.

Her throat made an awful squeak. She turned back and ran, up the vista and through wilderness to the ring path.

To the basement. Where ranks of monsters rotted as they stood, and the flesh of nightmares yet to be born floated in tanks, dreaming inscrutable dreams.

One of the doors to the basement stood open, too, swinging in the mounting wind. Lindsome ran inside. By now, she was panting, her back moist with sweat, her heart fighting to escape the hot prison of her chest. The foul air choked her. She bent double and gagged, falling to her knees on the icy stones.

Scores of waiting eyes watched her.

The wall of bodies began to moan, hundreds of bastard vocalizations from bastardized throats that had long ago forgotten how to speak. Pulpy flesh surged forward against bars and railings, jaws unhinging, the sound rising like the discordant sirens of an army from the Abyss.

Beneath them, Lindsome began a keening of her own, tiny and devoid of reason.

She did not know how she stepped to that far corner, where the future nightmares waited, but step she did, into a forest of burning candles. Some had toppled over onto the floor, frozen in sprays of wax. Some had melted into puddles, now aflame. The plentiful light showed all the tanks and that long, black curtain pulled fully back.

The giant tank on the bottom, as long as two men laid end to end, was drained, empty, and open.

The moaning grew. Lindsome's keening grew into a wail, though she could not hear it, only watch as her feet pointed her around and sent her across the basement and up the stone steps.

The door at the top was already open.

Lindsome's wail squeezed down into words, screamed loud enough to tear her throat as thorns will tear a dress. "Uncle Albion!"

Someone emitted a distant, ringing scream.

Lindsome couldn't breathe. She stumbled through the first floor, gasping, her uncle's name a mere whisper on her wide-open lips.

She found a door that Chaswick had forbidden, the door to the other basement-cum-laboratory. Or rather, she found the space where the door should have been. Both door and molding had been torn away.

As if the unseen gardener had entered the house, signature violence in tow.

"Uncle," Lindsome gasped. Outside, lightning flickered, and Lindsome saw four steps down. Dark smears daubed the floorboards. Further within, the glitter of metal and broken glass.

A bloody handprint on the wall.

The scream came again, an animalistic screech of distilled and mortal terror. Lindsome backed away from the stairs. Her legs quaked too much to run now.

She walked to the grand staircase. A painful flash of lightning illuminated the entire house—the puddles of ichor through which Lindsome trod, the monstrous gouges in the wood and wallpaper on either side of her, the gaslamps torn from their mounts.

The mental image of a tiny fist, its knuckles bumping

the inside of a tank as long as two men laid end to end.

Lindsome found Chaswick on the staircase. He had ended up like the billy goat outside, his stomach torn open, his entrails tangled in the shattered spindles of the banister.

"Linds..." One of his hands, slimy and bright, pawed at the banister.

She stared at him.

"Up...," Chaswick whispered. "Up..." His head twitched in the direction of the second floor. "If you... love... then up..."

Lindsome's head nodded. "Yes, Mister Chaswick," her mouth said.

His gaze clouded. The room flickered, as if under a second touch of lightning, and the pools of blood below him flashed into a sizzle.

Lindsome blinked, and Chaswick was gone. In his place, a pile of clothing lay tossed against the spindles, commingled with heavy black ghostgrease.

Somehow, Lindsome was running.

Sprinting, even. Up the stairs. "Uncle Albion!" she cried, and realized that she could speak again, too. Yet again, Lindsome heard that scream, that inhuman terror.

"Albion!" someone else called. Emlee, the gaunt old housekeeper. Third floor. The devastation continued up the staircase. "Get out!" Go!"

"No—not when she's—" A crash.

"Run, damn your miserable old hide! If ever you loved me as I loved you, Albion, then *run!*"

And that scream. That Ghost-forsaken scream.

Lindsome ran, up and up and out, tripping over shredded carpet, torn-down paintings, shattered vases and urns. From around a corner came a ghastly crunch, then booms and bangs, the sound of something mighty hurtling down a staircase.

"No, Marilda! Stop!"

Lindsome rounded the corner. The servants' staircase lay before her, walls half-ripped asunder, ichor on the steps.

Lindsome took them one flight down. At the bottom lay the housekeeper's clothes, black with ghostgrease.

"Uncle!" Lindsome wailed. "Uncle, where are you? We have to hide!"

His bedroom. Outside in the hall. Uncle Albion's door was open.

So was the door next to his, the one that had looked rusted shut.

The stench inside was unspeakable. Lindsome fell to the carpet and vomited, despite her empty stomach, hard enough for bile to dribble over her lips. Vivified. An ark of freshly vivified. They had to be stacked to the ceiling, packed like earth in a grave.

But when she looked up, all she saw were briars.

Roses. Thousands upon thousands of roses. Fresh, dried, rotting, trampled, entire bushes of them, as though a giant had uprooted them and brought them in here.

They were woven into a gigantic nest.

In the center sat Thomlin. His eyes were rolled up, showing nothing but white. He grasped his knees to his chest and rocked, like all those windblown, yawning doors, moaning like that wall of rotting flesh. A frothy river of drool dribbled down his chin.

Lindsome did not speak to him. It was clear that Thomlin would never speak again.

The siren song of that inhuman scream rang out, and Lindsome ran out into the hall. She called her uncle's name, shouted it, even, but received no answer.

She ran into his room, searching. The knobs of a rope ladder lay bolted into his windowsill.

"Uncle!" Lindsome peered over the sill. The ladder still wobbled from a recent descent, trailing down into a tight copse of saplings. Lindsome scrambled down. "Uncle Albion! Wait!"

Lightning cut her shadow from the air. The boom that answered split the sky, a rolling bang that made Lindsome squeal and cover her ears. In seconds, its echoes vanished under static, the sound of a million gallons pouring down. Lindsome was immediately soaked. The tatters of her dress slapped at her legs as she ran, and so heavy was the downpour, Lindsome couldn't see.

The path became slick. Lindsome slipped and went sprawling, face-first, and a fallen branch tore a gash in her arm. Lindsome screamed and rolled aside, curling around her wound, blinded by rain and tears.

Get up.

The thing will get you. Get up!

Weeping, squeezing her arm, Lindsome struggled to her feet. She stumbled along a trough of mud. She ripped off a strip of her soaked dress and tried to tie it around her wound to protect it.

A vivified hunting dog lumbered past, Cook's sodden apron hanging from its jaws.

The sky lit up again, illuminating a great gash in the thicket. Uprooted plants, unearthed rocks, and crushed branches paved the way. How dare anyone keep working in the shadow of such horrors? Lindsome yelled for her uncle, for the gardener, for someone and anyone as she stumbled down that fresh avenue, arm throbbing and poorly tied scrap of dress soaking through with red.

No creature hindered her. The fleeing vivifieds had disappeared.

Instead came roses. Thicker and thicker still, the tangled walls burst with roses, like puddles of gore on a battlefield. She moved in a forest of them, boughs bending to enclose the path overhead, their stink so strong not even the downpour could erase it. It was black beneath the boughs, black and dripping. Torn-off petals dribbled down between the branches, sticking to her hair, her hands, her face.

The tunnel turned and opened.

Not even the looming branches of this deadly forest could cover a space so large. The clearing was a pit of trampled thorns and bowed-in walls, canes of briars thrashing in the gusts, petals smeared everywhere like a violent snowfall. It stank of roses and death, water and undeath, and though naked sky arced above this grove of wreckage, the light was not strong enough for Lindsome to understand the pair of shapes that waited at the far end.

But then the lightning came.

Its brilliance bore down, and Lindsome understood even less, though what she saw burned itself into her vision with the force of a dying sun. One was large, impossibly large. An alien mountain of fur and rot, waiting on trunk-thick limbs, bearing eyes that knew—even if the throat could not speak, even if those ghastly hands could not move with the mastery and grace that memory still begged for.

And one was small. A baby of that species. The size of two men, laid end to end.

Lindsome did not know that she kept screaming. There was only feeling, a single feeling of eclipsing terror so hot she felt her own soul struggling to tear free. The pain in her arm disappeared. She felt neither cold nor wet. Only this searing moment, as the small one rolled in its nest of thorns and flailed, as though its soul had never learned to walk.

The mountain of rot took a step forward, until it towered protectively over the wriggling thing below.

It reached out a hand toward Lindsome.

The eclipse reached totality. Lindsome went down, her heartbeat a ringing roar.

★★★

"Miss?"

Something struck the front of her thighs with brisk

force. Lindsome grunted.

"Miss?"

"Leave her. She's a woodcutter's child, innit? Girl a' the woods?"

"In woods like these? Not on yer hat. An' look at her bleedin' arm, ye piece-wit. That's no small hurt. Miss?"

Lindsome opened her eyes. She was lying on her side in the sodden leaves, at the edge of a nameless road. The earth smelled good, of dirt and wind and water, and the branches of the bare trees overhead swayed and knocked in the bleak sunshine.

Two men stood over her, one holding the reins of a pair of horses. The other held a staff, with which he rapped Lindsome's thighs again.

Lindsome's eyes went to the horses. They were the horses of poor men, witless, subpar animals bought for cheap with zero cost of upkeep: vivifieds.

Lindsome began to cry.

One of the men mounted, and the other placed Lindsome at his comrade's back. She clung to his coat and sobbed as they rode out of the deserted wood.

They asked her questions, but Lindsome did not answer. They rode to the low town of Hume and deposited her on the steps of the orphanage, where kinder, cleaner, better-dressed men and women asked her the same things, but Lindsome only wept. She did not protest when they steered her inside, bathed her, tended her arm, dressed her in worn but clean things, and gave her a bowl of oatmeal and honey. She hardly ate half before falling dead asleep at the table, and barely noticed when a pair of strong, gentle arms lifted her up and placed her upon a cot.

The streets of Hume were buried in the snow of the new year before Lindsome spoke a single word.

★★★

She had to tell them something. So Lindsome, in the

course of explaining who she was and that she did in fact have living parents who might someday appear to fetch her, decided to say that the household of her Great-Uncle Albion had succumbed to a foolish but gruesome accident. He had planned to perform a stitching experiment on a pack of wolves that were not yet dead, Lindsome claimed, and the rest of the household, making heated bets on whether this holy grail of vivology was in fact possible to obtain, had gathered in the laboratory to watch. Lindsome had been spared from the ensuing tragedy because she did not care about the bet and had been playing outside, alone. The constable's men, who went to Apsis House to investigate as soon as the spring thaw came, found evidence to corroborate her story. The interior of Apsis House was torn apart, as if indeed by a pack of infuriated wolves, and not a trace of anyone living—including the great Professor Albion Edgarton Dandridge himself—could be found.

The spring after that, Lindsome's parents returned, refreshed from travel but baffled and scornful of the personal and legal complications that had evolved in their absence. At the conclusion of the affair, the judge gave them the property deed to Apsis House. They wanted to know what on Earth they were supposed to do with such a terribly located, wolf-infested wreck, and told Lindsome that she would have it, when she came of age.

The day she did, Lindsome attempted to sell it, but nobody could be persuaded to buy. She couldn't even give it away. The deed finally sat unused in a drawer in her dressing table, in a far-away city in her far-away grown-up life, next to the tin of cosmetic power she used to cover up a long, ugly scar upon her arm. Her husband, to whom she never told the entire truth, agreed that the property was probably worthless, and never suggested that they visit Long Hill or take any action regarding Apsis House's restoration. Nor did their three daughters, once they were grown enough to be told the family legends about mad Uncle Albion, and old enough to understand that some things are best left where they fall.

And besides—now that Lindsome knew what it was to have and love a child, she couldn't bear to interrupt what might still move up there, within that blooming forest of thorns. If they were both intact, still, the least Lindsome could do was give them their peace; and if they were not, Lindsome could not bear the thought of finding one of them alone, endlessly screaming that desperate, lonely scream, until however long it took for Albion's sturdy handiwork to unravel.

As Chaswick had said, Uncle Albion was a brilliant man.

It could take a very long time.

HEAVENTIDE

Daybreak-under-Clouds stood and faced her grandmother. Heads in the assembled crowd turned. Were they staring at her boldness? Or—still—the fact that Daybreak wore a dress?

Daybreak didn't like it either. One short year ago, she had been certain that she'd grow up to be a man instead. So had everyone else, for that matter, until Daybreak began to dawdle outside the Traveler House and eye the bodies of Traveling men with obvious desire. *Daybreak's no boy,* the whispered rumors went. *She's a girl, ready to become a woman.* What else could explain Daybreak's obsession? Men didn't lie with men, after all; everyone knew that.

Daybreak forced her chin to stay up. Though her palms were damp and her heart banged like a galloping rockhorse, she said, "I, Daybreak-under-Clouds, approach the Council."

From beneath the low, heavy bows of the boneoak, five pairs of ancient eyes regarded her. "Approach," said Thunder-within-Sky.

Daybreak stepped to the shadow's edge. The morning was sticky with heat. She longed to remove her much-hated dress and bare her flat, muscled chest to what little breeze there was, but the unmarried women and girls in Lionfjord did not have that privilege. "I wish to talk to the Council again about my Traveling."

Ashes-in-the-Garden, all the way on the left, spoke as though Daybreak were an imbecile. "Only young men Travel. Women and girls stay in the village."

"But my papa—er—before Spring-from-the-White-Rocks died, we talked about his Traveling, and he *swore* that someday I'd go, and surely you wouldn't dare break the promise of a father to his—"

Grandma Thunder-within-Sky raised her hand. Her expression was stone. "Daybreak-under-Clouds. One year ago, you consorted with a Traveler in the Traveler House, did you not?"

"I did, Councilor, but—"

"And you do know, do you not, that such an act is a confirmation of femininity? Namely, womanhood?"

"I do, Councilor, but—"

"And you have since continued to consort with the Travelers that pass through Lionfjord, have you not?"

"I have, Councilor, but—"

"Then there is no discussion to be had. The far-away lands that run south, north, and east are the destiny and domain of men. You have consorted with men, and are therefore a woman. And women do not have a Traveling." Grandma clapped her hands twice. "It is settled. Who is next?"

"It is *not* settled," said Daybreak, her hard tenor carrying through the startled silence. "You know that all my life I've dreamed of my Traveling, of seeing the Lands of Salt and the Mile-High Tower, and going where the houses —"

"Enough," ordered Grandma, rising to her feet. "You will shut your ungrateful mouth, you willful child, and go back to the Maiden House. You need to spend your time there far more than you need to waste it here."

Daybreak's powerful hands tightened into fists. Her vision clouded not with a woman's tears, but a man's rage.

"It is settled," said Grandma firmly. "Now who is next?"

Daybreak turned on her slippered heel and stomped

south, through Council Field and past the boneyard to the Maiden House in the village proper. The worst of it was that Grandma was right. Daybreak had only been a woman for a year, and while her body continually ached for consort with men—their big hands, their broad shoulders, their full desire hot alongside hers—in every other womanly art, she was an embarrassing failure.

***

After nightfall, Daybreak took the trail on the north bank of the Twine River and followed it west to the sea. It was too late for fishermen, so she saw no one. But that was fine. That was what she wanted.

She stopped at the mouth of the fjord. South and north, the fjord's steep arms, Howltongue and Roartongue, stretched into the ocean, ignoring the volatile froth that churned between them. Gibbous Heaven was just climbing down from the sky, sinking toward the silvery blocks of light that awaited it upon the maddened water. Heaven's own luminous, blue oceans were no doubt churning, too. Daybreak gazed with sickened longing at its distant continents, its arcs of snowy clouds. Earth looked the same from Heaven, old Priest Shell-in-the-Sand taught. If so, it did no good to gaze up at it, for it was nothing but another mocking reminder of what Daybreak could not have.

Here on Earth, the outgoing tide was picking up speed, following the eternal call of Heaven. Each wave pulled back farther and farther, revealing great strides of the fjord's bottom with each wash. But as Daybreak eyed the steady revelation of the slick, shimmering rocks, she received the strangest impression.

Heaven was showing her a way.

South, north, and east—that was the destiny and domain of men.

But the old rule said nothing about going west.

Daybreak approached the high-tide zone, where she

stared with a predator's hunger at the rapidly receding sea. Only suicides and imbeciles chased after it past Warning Rock, so certain was the death that awaited when the returning tide came to pounce upon the exhausted. Even the fishermen only dared to go out far enough to set their traps.

But suicides, imbeciles, and fishermen had all given up on Traveling.

★★★

"Perhaps I should try riding there," Daybreak mused to Boneoak-within-Forest. "If I rode a rockhorse along the riverbed into the fjord—Brambles-by-the-Twine has a gelding that's very sure-footed..."

Boneoak cocked his head. He was a Traveler, aged twenty-six years. His hair was a lighter brown than hers, and his eyes starmoss green. He smiled at everyone, but it was an odd smile of caution, or thought, or serious secrets. When Daybreak had boldly told him that she was going to Travel across the ocean-bed someday, he hadn't laughed. Only asked how it might be done.

"Why not a boat?" he asked.

"What's a boat?"

Boneoak's eyebrows went up. "Other Travelers haven't told you? Or the settled men in your village?"

"No."

"Your mama? Your papa?"

"No. I can't ask them, either. They've crossed to Heaven. And I'm... not good... at talking with farparents."

Boneoak rolled onto his side in the bed they shared. He propped his head up with one hand, gray-green gaze tracing the hard lines of Daybreak's naked skin. From beyond the greenreed mats that hung around Boneoak's pile of furs, gentle conversations and cries of pleasure floated as other unmarried women of Lionfjord tried to entice their chosen Travelers to stay and wed. "Surely your papa must've told you of his own Traveling before he crossed?"

Daybreak sat up. "Oh yes. And he promised me that someday I'd—I mean—yes—the cave with no bottom, and the Lands of Salt, and a place where the grass is so high, it grows past the head of a rockhorse. And he said there's a region to the south where the tops of the mountains spit fire, and—"

"He never told you about Giant's Lake? Or the Infinite River?" Boneoak's cautious smile emerged. "There are places where the rivers are so large, they're wider than ponds, and ponds so big, it's hard to see the opposite shore. To cross these, a bridge isn't enough. So, you use a boat. Think of a leaf floating on the surface of a puddle, with whirl seeds fallen on top of it. But picture it made large, so the seeds are the size of people. The leaf would be your boat."

Daybreak leaned forward. "How do you make one?"

"Out of wood."

Daybreak gripped Boneoak's arm, the muscles of her forearm jumping. "Show me tomorrow."

★★★

The simplest kind of boat to make, Boneoak explained (as he drew diagrams in a soft clay shore of the Twine with a stick), was called a trunk boat. "All you need is the trunk of a fallen boneoak tree," he said. "You cut a section, strip off the bark, and burn out the center. Then you pare it down further into the right shape."

Daybreak shook her head. "How will we ever move a boneoak trunk to the water's edge?"

"Oh, we won't work alone. There are plenty of other Travelers who can spare an hour or so from their work for Lionfjord. And anyway, other people's work is always so much more interesting than one's own."

From the path behind them, Daybreak heard giggles and whispers. Sunlight-off-of-Water had sent some of the other girls from the Maiden House to spy on Daybreak, no doubt, to see what crucial task she could possibly be doing that was more important than practicing her sorely under-developed womanly skills. A flush crept though Daybreak's ears, but she staunchly ignored the giggles. Travel, as long as it was west, was completely womanly.

"I saw what could be a good trunk around here a few days ago," said Boneoak.

"East of here on the opposite bank?"

"Ah, you know the one." Boneoak stood and discarded his stick. "Wait here. I want a closer look at it, but I'd hate to make you stomp through the briars in that pretty dress for nothing, in case it isn't suitable." Before Daybreak could even smile, Boneoak sprang lightly across the Twine's exposed rocks and vanished into the undergrowth on the opposite shore.

"Pity the dress is the only thing that's pretty."

Daybreak's teeth clenched within her neutral mouth. She turned. Most of the other girls were up the path some ways, clearly ready to go home with the intelligence they'd already gathered. But one girl was picking her careful, fastidious way down the long slope toward the water's edge, smoothing the route before her with a self-satisfied smile. "I'm only saying what's true."

"Leave me alone, Skill."

Skill-with-Laughter stopped near Boneoak's diagrams. She frowned at the dark clay. "You know he's only humoring you."

"I don't care."

"He feels sorry for you." Skill raised her head and tilted it prettily. "Once he's satisfied with his charity, it'll be me he comes after."

Shame and longing churned in Daybreak's guts. Skill was slender and willowy, with a higher tenor and a graceful, rolling walk. She could tend a garden, quiet a crying child, roll the bones and speak with the farparents, train a rock-horse, weave a greenreed mat, and tame a waveraptor.

Bones, she could probably build an entire Small House on her own. But Skill had known since she was four that she'd grow up to be a woman. It wasn't fair.

Skill leaned in. The plumpseed oil on her lips made them glisten. Even her makeup was perfect. "You know he's the sort of man who only likes front-tailed women. And you know you don't stand a chance against me." Her smile turned indulgent. "*If* I decided I wanted him back. Which I'm still not sure about yet. What's he worth to you, Daybreak?"

Daybreak's eyes tightened into slits. "What exactly are you saying?"

"It'll do!" Boneoak emerged from the jungle on the far bank and jumped back over the rocks. "Come see, Daybreak. You'll have to risk your dress after all. Who was that?"

Skill was already floating up the slope, back to the path and her tittering escort. Daybreak's lip curled. "Nobody."

Boneoak watched Skill climb. Of course he did—no man could resist watching her do anything. "You sound upset. Did she say something to you?"

"No." Daybreak dropped her eyes to the mud. "Boneoak—am I pretty? Do you... do you really want me?"

Boneoak closed the air between them. His strong hands slithered around the small of Daybreak's broad back. "I want you all day," he breathed into her ear, "but seeing as how I'm Traveling, I'll have to be satisfied with having you only at night." He took her earlobe between his teeth, gently, in claim. "Hmm?"

"I'm not..." Daybreak felt her desire rise beneath her dress. Boneoak ground into her, once, teasing. "I'm not a very good woman."

Boneoak pulled back. He offered her his closed, mysterious smile. "You're a fine woman, Daybreak. Now come —we've a boat to build."

★★★

The boat came faster than Daybreak would've thought, but the constant stream of assistants helped. So did their stories. Boneoak and the other men were more than happy to tell and retell their tales of lands wide and deep. Daybreak listened with an insatiable hunger (more than once at the expense of the direction of her chisel), asking questions that had no end. Did the wolves in the Red Forest really have saber teeth? Did the snow on Skytouch Peak really never melt? Was there really a lake of floating mountains? How could a mountain spit fire? Was it true that the birds in Jewel Fen could speak like people? The men's answers were as colorful as their tales, ranging from blunt and cryptic to elaborately poetic, and listening to them only made Daybreak's yearning burn hotter. She didn't just want them, she wanted to *be* them—to be surrounded by them, to wander in spontaneously formed tribes from village to village, chiseling out her essential self with the long blows of the road. Every morning, when whatever Travelers felt the urge waved good-bye and mounted the trail up Boarder Hill, Daybreak's heart cried out after them, sick with envy and imagination and loss, for the conclusions of their stories that she'd never get to hear. Blown like windweeds, they came, thrived, grew a little bit larger, and rushed on, across who knows how many wild and lonely lands before their roots finally came down, in some unknown, exotic soil.

Never had the towering arms of Lion Fjord felt so oppressive.

"You're spending a lot of time with that Traveler Boneoak," said Daybreak's grandmother one morning. "And he's spent a long time in Lionfjord. Are you going to propose?"

Daybreak looked up from the rows of crisp-roots she was weeding. She and Grandma Thunder-within-Sky were crouching in the dirt of the Maiden House's garden. They had been out since sunrise, the Councilor stubbornly rebuking her granddaughter for every vegetable seedling she accidentally pulled up. "I... I don't know."

"You should. That's a crisp-root, child, another crisp-root."

"I'm sorry." Daybreak scrutinized the tiny root for some telltale crisp-root-like quality. Her eyes wandered to the ridge of callouses below her fingers, thickened from her hours of holding a chisel. If only Boneoak hadn't agreed to help muck out the rockhorse stalls this morning, they could be working together on the boat right now.

"Well, are you going to put it back into the ground?"

"I'm sorry." Daybreak sought the crisp-root's native hole.

"Honestly, Daybreak, you aren't even trying." Grandma's voice softened. "You should ask him, you know. He likes you."

Daybreak suppressed a shiver. "I can't get married now, Grandma."

"What? Why in The Mother's name not?"

The west. Aloud, Daybreak said, "Well," and gestured to the battle-scarred crisp-root patch.

"Oh, Daybreak." Grandma raised her creaking bones with a sigh, stepped across the row, and resettled beside her. "You're just a late-bloomer. Keep trying. You'll get it right." Her tone took on a wandering, dreamy quality. "You won't go Traveling, like your older brothers. You'll stay here and get married, and take in a babe of your own. And I'll have great-grandchildren." She held Daybreak's strong, calloused hand. "When I heard you'd consorted with that first Traveler, I was so happy. When Clouds-beyond-Thunder crossed to Heaven, I thought she'd taken with her my only chance to have a granddaughter." Grandma squeezed her hand. "But then The Mother gave me you—who you really are. Don't give up, child. You'll be happy someday."

Daybreak dared to look Grandma in the eye, but

Grandma's far-away gaze did not hold love. Rather, it held a calm satisfaction, as if this arrangement pleasing her was all that mattered.

Despite the sun's merciless heat, the pit of Daybreak's stomach grew cold.

"Everything will work out," said Grandma, releasing Daybreak's hand. "Now try weeding the shortpeppers."

★★★

Four days later, the boat was complete. The current crowd of Travelers, laughing and singing, helped drag the thing to the Twine, rolling it over small logs and sliding it across makeshift roads of fanleaves. Daybreak watched, giddy with triumph. *I'm really going to do it. I'm going to become like you.*

The boat, which Boneoak dubbed *Runner-after-Heaven*—for all boats had names like people, the men explained—sat high and confident in the Twine, even when Boneoak helped Daybreak climb inside and then climbed in himself. The men on the south bank whistled congratulations as Boneoak fit the oars into the oarlocks, maneuvered *Runner*'s nose downstream, and pulled.

"We'll moor him high on the delta, just before the beach at the mouth of the fjord," said Boneoak, "so nothing but a Heaventide can reach him. And then—!"

"Then?" asked Daybreak, leaning forward.

"Then—well, you tell me." Boneoak's eyes twinkled like Heavenlight on the sea. "This is your Traveling, isn't it? You decide when and where and how to go."

Power surged through Daybreak's veins. She inhaled and sat up straight, and for a moment believed that her will was mighty enough to propel her anywhere. "I—well, I—"

"Think about it carefully first," Boneoak laughed, steering them around a rock. "The ocean is no play-yard. There's a reason nobody's ever gone where you're about to."

★★★

Instead of fumbling with the Maiden House's loom or getting scratched by irate hatchlings in the waveraptor mew, Daybreak spent her early evenings on Stony Beach, one hand on *Runner*, watching the fishermen beneath the lowering sun. When the thunderous tide turned tail, they'd trot out to the seabed and snatch up their traps. The more daring went farther with buckets and dug through the exposed muck for shellfleshes and mudmeats. And the foolhardy Travelers distinguished themselves from the settled men of Lionfjord by racing out even farther, prying rockmeats from the slick boulders with whoops of triumph. Once Daybreak hiked out to the top of Roartongue Ridge and watched. At that vantage point, she could see fields and fields of dark-green stones, covered in clumps of rockmeat like lumps of moss. Any fisherman—or Traveler—who could bring back such bounty would be much respected indeed.

"I've decided," said Daybreak to Boneoak that night. "I'm going out to the center of the fjord, past Warning Rock." They were in Boneoak's bed, facing each other, both of them drowsy but unwilling to sleep.

"Hmm?" Boneoak roused himself. "And how are you going to do that?"

"Easily," said Daybreak. "I'll ride the ebbing tide out past the shellflesh diggers, drop anchor, and climb out and take all those rockmeats. And when the tide turns, I'll just ride *Runner* back in."

"That's quite a plan."

"I don't care if you think it won't work."

It was too dark to see, but Daybreak was certain that Boneoak was grinning his secret grin. "I know."

***

The next day was Heaven-Half-Empty, the time when the Dark tides cycled too far into the evening and fishermen switched back to the Bright tides that would cycle through the day during the next quartermonth. Daybreak would've rather made her move on a Dark tide, unseen, but trying to gather rockmeats at night in unfamiliar territory would be foolish.

So, early the next morning, Daybreak went down to Stony Beach with the Lionfjord fishermen and any Travelers scheduled to help. While the others carried the usual buckets and nets, she carried a sack of provisions and the determination to ignore their inquisitive glances. The Father bind them. She was going.

While the fishermen milled around on the shaded beach, chatting and eyeing the slack tide for signs of turning, Daybreak readied *Runner-after-Heaven*. When the waves looked to be starting their retreat, Daybreak pushed against *Runner*'s stern with everything she had, until he ground down the bank of the delta and into the shallow mouth of the Twine.

Waveraptor-in-the-Air turned around at the noise. "Daybreak? What are you doing?"

Daybreak ignored him. She pushed *Runner* farther, down to where the Twine spilled over the beach and melted into the waves. The icy water bit into her slippered feet, then calves, then knees. The ocean surged and sucked, and it was hard to keep her footing. She lifted the sodden hem of her dress and clambered into the boat, to the sound of muffled exclamations and giggles at her peculiar actions, but one determined glare from her and their amusement turned into confusion.

Daybreak lifted the oars, like Boneoak had showed her, and dipped their blades into the frothing salt. "Fine day for a Travel, isn't it?"

Because she had to sit backward to row, Daybreak had the gleeful pleasure of watching their confusion turn to shock, just moments before the ascending sun blinded her.

"What is she—she's—roll the bones! Daybreak! Daybreak, don't!"

Daybreak laughed. Heaven loomed behind her, pulling, half of its mysteries shrouded in dark. The turning sea began to gather speed and strength, and it was all she could do to row to keep from being grounded. In moments, the frantic shouts of the fishermen were muted beneath the whoosh and hiss of the waves. A handful of Travelers sprinted into the water, but going more than thigh-deep in such accelerating forces meant death. Once the tide receded past Warning Rock, they cupped their hands and wailed, but dared not follow farther.

The sun slipped behind a fleecy cloud. Daybreak's vision cleared. The bountiful ocean-bed opened up before her, revealing more treasure than she ever could have guessed at from her perch atop Roartongue Ridge. Rockmeats as big as juicemelons, writhing longfish trapped in tide pools, slimy fjordapples carpeting the ground. Occasionally, a muckdiver swooped down and snatched one away in its shovel-shaped beak. And when an especially violent wave nearly grounded Daybreak, she saw a creature no one in Lionfjord had ever seen alive—a sea hedgehog— uncurl itself from within a now-exposed rocky crevice and go on the prowl, hemmed in by canyons painted with wilting seaweeds of fantastic colors. At its approach, strange insects popped up from the mud, leaping like bushhoppers before burrowing into the drooping weeds.

It was magnificent.

At Drowning Rock, Daybreak dropped the anchor. The waves of the still-receding ocean pulled hard but the anchor held, and in twenty waves, *Runner* was resting on the revealed alien jungle.

Leaping from the boat, flatknife ready, Daybreak dared to sing a fishermen's song.

The rockmeats fell like hay beneath a scythe. Daybreak heaved them into the boat with glee. A single round of work out here and she could gather enough to feed the entire village. Yes—when she returned, they'd have a feast, and everyone would be so impressed that the next time the Council met, surely Grandma would acquiesce to letting Daybreak Travel like a man, and—

Something stung her.

She flinched and looked down. A sea hedgehog stood by her ankle, barbed tail waving. Daybreak snorted. "It'll take more than your little beesting to stop me now."

Something stung her other ankle. A second sea hedgehog waved its tail at her, spikes bristling.

"Oh, stop it," said Daybreak. "What are you out hunting? Minnows trapped in tide pools? Well, don't worry. I'm not here for something so small."

The rocks around her came alive. Dark cracks cleared as tens and twenties of sea hedgehogs, tails raised and ready, scuttled toward her.

Daybreak yelped and dropped her flatknife. She scrambled toward the boat, but rocks sharp with bladeflesh slowed her down, and patches of stinking mud sucked off her slippers. The sea hedgehogs rushed her bare feet. They stung her insteps and the sensitive places between her toes. Her yelps turned to yells. Her skin was turning red. By the time Daybreak reached the boat, her feet and ankles were swelling.

She climbed in. The sea hedgehogs swarmed around her, scrabbling at *Runner's* sides, searching for flaws in the polished, oiled wood that their hooked feet could catch. Daybreak picked up a rockmeat and began the fight in earnest, trying to mash it down upon them as they scaled the outer hull, but they were tough as sunlobsters, and as stupid. Daybreak couldn't discourage them, only lunge around the boat and knock them off—over and over and over.

Her lower legs tingled. It became hard to breathe. Though the tide was still receding, the roar of the ocean somehow got louder and the sky became strangely dim. Time for an eclipse already? The sea hedgehogs multiplied and splintered into shadows, and Daybreak lunged at them with her rockmeat but struck nothing. The tingling in her legs grew to prickles, then biting fire. Darkness and light popped before her eyes. Each breath was like drowning.

The rockmeat slipped from Daybreak's hand. Both it and she fell to *Runner's* bottom.

★★★

Jumbled dreams rolled beneath her—scorching sun, the earth rocking, the stench of death and salt. She'd gotten too close to the firepit and the hem of her dress had caught. Stinging shadows crawled over her body, and Boneoak asked her, "Where do you want to go?"

West.

Daybreak opened her eyes. It was twilight, the sunset dark blood in the west. Her head throbbed. The earth rose and fell beneath her, gently, like the chest of a slumbering giant. Her lower legs pulsed with agony, and when she wiggled her ankles, the pain was enough to make her scream.

Her throat constricted around the sound. So dry.

Daybreak pulled herself up into sitting. Around her was glimmering dimness delineated by liquid splinters of light. Dark shapes bracketed it to the south and north. Above, half-full Heaven had vanished, leaving an empty nest of a million stars.

The Dark tide had come in. She was still in the boat.

Daybreak pulled her waterskin from her sack of provisions and sipped. Once her throat was wet enough, she started laughing.

★★★

When Daybreak rowed into the mouth of the Twine at dawn, pushed by the waves of the rising Bright tide, the fishermen did not cheer.

Instead, they gasped and shouted. Some stared in open-mouthed silence. Daybreak rowed *Runner* onto a gravelly bank, then hefted the biggest rockmeat she'd gotten, masking the agony in her legs with a fierce grin. "Who wants rockmeat stew?" she asked, but nobody laughed or whistled.

Wind-beyond-Boughs took one look at Daybreak's feet and ran back to Lionfjord to get the Priest. A handful of fishermen turned their backs, mouths sour and nets wrapped around clenched fists. The rest stared at her. A sick feeling began to build in Daybreak's gut, but she kept her head high and moved to the edge of the boat to climb out and stand, even though she didn't think she'd be able.

The crowd of fishermen looked at each other uncertainly. Only one face, in the back, was smiling.

Boneoak.

Daybreak didn't have to climb out and stand after all. Boneoak carried her all the way back to Lionfjord, whistling.

***

Hearing the talk outside the Priest House was enough to close up Daybreak's throat again.

"Is she well enough for me to see her?" demanded Grandma, on the other side of the oilbark walls.

"Give her some more moments," said Priest Shell-in-the-Sand, in her measured, quiet way. "Let her rest with her lover."

"She doesn't need a few moments! She needs guidance!"

"Of course she does," Shell said, "but the poultice I've put on her feet is uncomfortable enough, and it'll take some time before—"

"I want her while she's hurt," said Grandma sharply, "so she can't deny to herself the idiocy of what she's done."

A voice Daybreak didn't know interrupted. "Did Waveraptor tell you what she brought home? Rockmeats as big as your head!"

"You will be quiet, Traveler. This is a Lionfjord affair."
To Priest Shell-in-the-Sand: "Will her feet heal?"

"To be honest, I'm afraid I'm not sure. We don't know
what a sea hedgehog sting can do. But the flesh, though
firm, is red, not purple or black, so I'm optimistic."

"That's almost a shame. Losing her feet would prevent
her from trying this again."

Daybreak's heart squeezed within her chest, even as
Boneoak, kneeling by her bedside, squeezed her hand.

"Do you hear me in there, Daybreak-under-Clouds?"
Grandma Thunder-within-Sky shouted. "I forbid you to go
out in that boat!"

★★★

It took days for both Daybreak's feet and courage to
recover. But while her body needed many of Shell's uncomfortable concoctions, in the end, her courage needed but one
furtive conversation.

"You should just go out when the high tide's at night,"
Boneoak said to her, beneath his breath.

It was the deep night of the Near-Heaventide Summer
Eve Festival. Heaven's slender crescent had just risen into a
sky patchy with clouds and now hung behind them in the
east like a silver flame behind a screen. All of Lionfjord had
been waiting for it at Council Field since sunset, feasting and
swapping tales of the next world in between poems to honor
those who had crossed over during the previous year. With
Heaven's appearance, the late-running Festival was finally
winding down, and old Councilor Springtime-chases-
Summertime was indulging in his annual retelling of the
final story. In years past, Daybreak had been enraptured by
the tale of Fox-dancing-with-Snow, wondering at the brave
spirit who dared cross to Earth without a Heaventide before
his next body was ready to receive him. But Daybreak's
mood was too low to be distracted by tales, and her mind

wandered. She'd barely heard Boneoak's interruption. "Hmm?"

"At night," repeated Boneoak. He spoke without looking at her, scooping up bites of shellflesh stew in his bowl with his stonebread. "Go out in the boat when the tide's up at night. You've walked on the fjord bottom once before, so you know what's there now. And the fishermen won't be working. Who would stop you?"

Daybreak looked sideways at him. Boneoak was still focused on the remains of his meal, but the edges of his mouth curled upward, cupping his proposed secret.

"But anyone would stop me," said Daybreak. "The whole village is terrified of Grandma, and everyone knows what I've done. If anyone saw me, they'd raise the alarm and I would never make it."

"*If* anyone saw you. A lookout would prevent that."

Daybreak glanced sideways at him again. The curve of Boneoak's smile bent deeper, like the far-away bottom of the fjord.

"...Boneoak?" Daybreak asked.

"Yes." It wasn't a question.

★★★

They snuck away together from Lionfjord the next night, witnessed only by the unblinking eyes of the stars. Priest Shell-in-the-Sand was out in the boneyard with Lionfjord's pregnant women, readying their wombs for the wave of souls that would ride the next Heaventide back to Earth. But the boneyard was at the northern end of the village, and they were nothing but gravid shapes swaying against distant firelight. Daybreak and Boneoak padded to the beach unseen.

Once there, Boneoak helped her load the boat. Daybreak was better prepared this time, with double the provisions, an extra knife, a hatchet, a spear, a net, a bucket, and most importantly—and unexpectedly—a pair of knee-

high Traveling boots made of tough Ahatchipan leather.
They were Boneoak's. He handed them to her once
everything else was settled, and Daybreak sat on a rock to
put them on, her heart aching. Overhead, a few wisps of
cloud drifted between the constellations. The starlight
hugged Boneoak's broad shoulders and handsome face, and
watching him carefully oil the oarlocks with a handful of
rockhorse fat, Daybreak's heartache became unbearable.
"Boneoak."

"Yes?"

"Why are you doing all this?"

Boneoak looked up, quizzically. "Because I love you."

The spent waves hissed their jealousy atop the beach's
gravel. "Do you? Is this what love looks like?"

"Well, what would you call it?"

Daybreak stood. "Come with me."

"What?"

She wrapped her arms around his waist, pressing her
face down into the nape of his neck and inhaling the smell
of him, starmoss and old leather. "Come with me. I want—I
want—"

Dreams of the road clouded her vision, she and
Boneoak side by side, marching out together into the wide
and deep. Together they'd scale the Diamond Mountains and
descend into the Open Abyss, and build more boats and row
the entire length of the Infinite. They'd cross rivers of ice
and forests of lightning. They'd run with beasts. They'd
wrap up the world in a history of footsteps, laying them
down in tandem, paving the miles with their cyclic breaths.
And at night, their paths would dovetail and become one.
Again and again, in a rainfall of days, a thunderstorm of
days, until they found a far-away that was meant to become
home.

"You want?" Boneoak asked. His hands had gone still.

"I want you to be with me, Boneoak."

For a moment, his breath stopped. "Daybreak. Are you asking me if I'll—will I marry you?"

Daybreak's heart clenched like a fist. *No. Yes. Not like that.*

"Daybreak?"

"I don't..." Her voice sounded small and defeated. "I don't know."

Boneoak squeezed her fingers with a fat-greased hand, then swiveled in her grasp and embraced her, his breath quick and hot against her neck. "I'll be here when you get back. But look—the tide is beginning to turn. I'll help you launch *Runner*. Come."

They parted, Daybreak avoiding his eyes. For ten precious steps, their hands on *Runner*'s stern, they moved side by side in tandem, but then Boneoak said, "I'll help you in," and Daybreak sat in the boat, alone.

She watched his face as the tide pulled her away.

Movement flashed at the trailhead to Lionfjord. A second shape strolled partway down the beach, beneath the shadows of the trees. Emerging into the cold starlight, Skill-with-Laughter, with her graceful, seductive walk, approached Boneoak. She put a hand on his arm. Boneoak turned.

Daybreak stood. "Boneoak!" she shouted, but his name was eaten by the ocean's roar.

★★★

Daybreak returned on the next high tide, in late morning, her heart as heavy with worry as *Runner* was with catch. Boneoak was nowhere to be seen, not even farther up the Twine, when Daybreak rowed *Runner* up and grounded and anchored him at his usual place. In fact, the beach and river mouth were empty.

Daybreak covered her prizes with netting, as much to discourage the wheeling muckdivers as to busy her nervous hands. As she worked, the boughs at the trailhead nodded. Councilor Springtime-chases-Summertime emerged, followed by Councilor Muckdiver-on-the-Cliff.

"Councilors?" Daybreak asked. She stepped from the boat. "Where are the fishermen?"

More Councilors came—Ashes-in-the-Garden, and Longrass-near-Burrows—and only then, the fishermen. But the fishermen had no buckets or nets, and more people kept coming after them. Hunters, Travelers, mothers, children, stone- and wood-carvers, rockhorse handlers, waveraptor tamers. Almost all of Lionfjord.

Last to emerge was Grandma Thunder-within-Sky, Skill-with-Laughter at her elbow.

Daybreak's worry turned to anger. "What is this?"

"Daybreak-under-Clouds," said Grandma, "you are charged with disobeying your sirepeople. Not two hands ago, I expressly forbade you to go out in this—this *boat*—"

"I'm fine!" Daybreak looked wildly from assembled face to face, but all were closed and serious. "It doesn't matter—I took Boneoak's boots and I'm fine! I didn't get hurt at all!"

"—and you flagrantly disobeyed me. Skill-with-Laughter witnessed everything."

"Well, Skill-with-Laughter is a greedy, conniving pig," Daybreak shouted, "who could have any man she wants, but that's still not enough for her!"

"Young lady," said Muckdiver-on-the-Cliff, "you *will* be silent. Or must we also charge you with disobeying your Council?"

"We find you guilty," said Grandma. "And for punishment, you will burn that evil boat on Heaventide Night before the entire village."

"Wait!"

Heads turned. Boneoak shoved his way down to the beach, panting, the Priest's two apprentices in hot pursuit. "Wait! If I may approach the Council!"

"You may not," said Grandma. "Why is the prisoner

not being restrained? You have already been convicted of assisting in a crime, Traveler, and you have no right—"

"She is my betrothed!"

Gasps were swiftly muffled.

Skill's smug demeanor blanked to shock. But Daybreak could take no pleasure in it, for it was nothing but, at best, a terrible misunderstanding, and at worst, an ugly lie. "Boneoak—"

"Silence." Thunder-within-Sky turned to Boneoak, eyes narrowed. The panting apprentices finally caught up with him and grabbed his arms, but he ignored their presence and mirrored the elder's stoicism. "Wait, apprentices. Traveler, you may approach."

"She is my betrothed," said Boneoak, "and Lionfjord will be my far-away. Please—let me help make up for what I've done to all of you. I'll burn the boat myself. It was I who taught her how to make it anyway."

Quick as Daybreak's anger had flooded in, it ebbed away, leaving her ragged and painfully empty. *How could you?* she tried to say, but even her breath had disappeared.

Grandma's whitened eyebrows rose. She spoke slowly. "You're going to marry my granddaughter? And raise my great-grandchildren?"

"With all my love and will."

"Hmm," Grandma said.

"I think his proposal is reasonable," said Springtime-chases-Summertime.

"And a sincere apology is always a good foundation for a new beginning," said Longrass-near-Burrows.

"Very well," said Thunder-within-Sky. "Boneoak-within-Forest, you shan't be required to leave Lionfjord tonight after all. Instead, in five days' time, you'll burn the boat. And Daybreak-under-Clouds—you will watch him do it."

Daybreak's breath wouldn't come back. She collapsed

to the beach on her knees, the sharp stones biting hard.

Grandma clapped her hands twice. "It is settled. Apprentices, let my grandson-in-law go. And get rid of whatever my fool granddaughter's brought back with her again. It's ill-gotten, and likely to be cursed."

★★★

While Daybreak sat nearby in misery in her place of honor upon a longgrass mat beneath a fanleaf umbrella, the married women of Lionfjord laughed and worked on the latest Small House to join their number. Many took breaks to chat with Daybreak and congratulate her. They all agreed that she was very lucky. Boneoak, while undeniably mischievous and hard to read, was hard-working, generous, and handsome, and a latecomer to womanhood like Daybreak would never do better.

Her nights were still spent with Boneoak in the Traveler House, but now her desire filled her with shame. It was this lust that had doomed her to stay chained within Lionfjord's limits. They would make love in silence, her face pressed to his neck, taking sick comfort in the very thing that poisoned her.

"Don't you love me?" Boneoak whispered.

Tomorrow, the sun and blackened Heaven would rise together. They'd climb the sky, Heaven overlapping and fusing with the sun into The Mother's womb, until, imbued with the heat of Life, soul-gravid Heaven pulled aside and spilled all those quickened souls straight down. Heaventide. The earth might quake, and the ocean would surge with the incoming vitality, all the way up Stony Beach and into the freshwater reeds of the Twine.

"I said, don't you love me?" Boneoak whispered.

Runner-after-Heaven was waiting there, high on the bank, awaiting the bonfire that Boneoak would build around his flanks.

Daybreak didn't answer.

"Daybreak?"

She rolled away. "The Mother help me. I do."

"Then please—what's wrong?"

"What's *wrong?* You're going to destroy *Runner!*"

"Hush." Boneoak sat up. "Listen to me. Do you think I want to do this?"

"Then why are you doing it?"

"Because I can't stand to watch you annihilate what you've always dreamed of."

Daybreak fell silent.

"Burning that boat would be like cutting off your own hand," said Boneoak. "It would kill you."

"I'm dead already." Daybreak got to her feet and dressed. "I'm getting married. I'll be trapped in Lionfjord valley for the rest of my life, and the most Traveling I'll ever do will be to cross to Heaven when I die. I *wish* I would die. Then I'd finally get to go someplace new, where nobody would care if I used to be a man or woman or what."

Boneoak looked as though she'd struck him. "Is a life with me so terrible?"

"No," said Daybreak, in almost a shout. "Don't you get it? I want to Travel, Boneoak, and I want to Travel with *you.*"

Daybreak ran outside.

Her feet led her down to the beach. The sky was rain-pregnant and thickly overcast, without any starlight to guide her, but she'd know the way with her eyes closed. She climbed into waiting *Runner* and doubled over on a bench, not knowing whether to cry or scream. She wanted to punch Skill in the face. She wanted to burn her half-finished Small House to the ground. She wanted to—

"Daybreak!"

"Go away."

His steps clattered across the stones. "Please. I'm sorry. Listen—"

"I said, go away."

"I have an idea."

"You and your ideas," shouted Daybreak. "Making me think I can actually get what I want! I'm a woman, Boneoak, and women stay home!"

"I'll go out with you."

Daybreak rubbed a wrist across her eyes. "What?"

Boneoak stepped to *Runner's* side. He laid a broad, calloused hand upon the wood, rippled with the countless chisel strokes of his and Daybreak's, overlapping and dovetailing into an indistinguishable whole. "At Heaventide," said Boneoak quietly, "when everyone's praying in the boneyard tomorrow, you'll have time to take *Runner* out one last time. And... I'll go with you."

Daybreak shook her head. "But—"

"I know," said Boneoak. "When they find that we've gone missing, they'll be furious. And I can't say what they'll sentence us to when we come back. And it isn't much, I know, especially when it's sure to come at such a terrible cost. But... it's what we can have.

"So..." Boneoak paused. "Daybreak-under-Clouds— will you Travel with me, for a while?"

Those distant foothills, unknown rivers, black woods and waterfalls, deserts of red sand that piled up in the wind like mountains, frozen wastes and lush deltas full of exotic serpents and monsters—this was what Traveling with Boneoak should've been.

Not a halfcycle of the tides, in a trunk boat.

But they'd walk in places no one else had ever walked in, and marvel at the things they found there, and go wherever the wind would pull them.

The history of their footsteps would be so short.

Daybreak blinked back tears. "I will."

***

Heaventide dawned thick and cloudy, the air nearly

tense enough to crackle. Rain was coming, everyone agreed, but breakfast came and went, and no drops fell.

Skittish winds arose, darkening the clouds to purple-black. Praying out in the boneyard under this sky was asking for ill luck, the Priest and the Council agreed. The Priest would say the prayers on behalf of everyone, but the rest of Lionfjord was to remain indoors.

"We're still going," said Daybreak to Boneoak, outside the door of the Traveler House. "Aren't we?"

Boneoak eyed the blackening sky in silence, the wind roughing his hair. "Are we?"

"We have to. It's our last chance."

Boneoak nodded. "It is, isn't it?"

They went inside to wait. Boneoak lay in bed on his back. Daybreak lay atop him, and with his arms around her hips, they softly told each other stories. What Boneoak's parents had prayed he'd become ("quiet but wise—they didn't get either wish, I think"). What Daybreak had been like as a child, when she was so sure she'd grow up to be a man, and all the manly arts she'd excelled at—trapping, skinning, haggling and bargaining, singing and poetry. What Boneoak's childhood village was like. What bodies they'd had in former lives, according to the Priests who'd seen their births, and what body they might expect next. They talked as though they'd never talk again. Perhaps they wouldn't, Daybreak thought, at least not like this, because once they Traveled together, a sediment of good memories would drift down onto Boneoak's ever-thickening past, but Daybreak would have nothing new to reminisce over—only this single, stormy Heaventide, rushing further and further away.

When Daybreak guessed the time was right, they dressed, snuck out the side door, and took their pre-gathered supplies to the beach.

In its cage of the Lion Fjord, the ocean was roaring. Brave *Runner-after-Heaven* stubbornly stood his ground upon the Twine's grassy bank. The Heaventide was at its apex, the frothing ocean raised to overflowing, and Daybreak tried not to stare at it as she readied the boat.

Instead, she eyed Boneoak's slipper-clad feet. "Are you sure I can wear your Ahatchipan boots again?"

"Yes. Whoa!" A wave rushed up the swollen Twine, fanning outward and licking *Runner*'s belly. "Quickly, Daybreak! Get in!"

They climbed aboard. The next wave was enough to float *Runner* where he sat, and Boneoak pulled up the anchor. He had to yell to be heard above the wind. "Let me row him!"

Daybreak moved to the seat in the bow. Boneoak took the oars, maneuvering *Runner* to stay in the center of the river. "The tide will take us when it turns," he shouted. "Are you ready?"

Before Daybreak could answer, the ocean changed its mind. *Runner* shot forward as though hurled from a waterfall. Daybreak nearly fell backward, and Boneoak almost lost an oar. *Watch out!* his mouth said as the ocean thundered.

The sky answered.

Daybreak looked up. A pair of fat raindrops hit her cheek. The ocean began to chop and wrestle, and *Runner* pitched and rolled in alarm.

To the west, lightning flickered.

Boneoak's face was gray. He should've had to row hard to keep pace with the retreating tide, but he had found a strange current that was sucking them away at an effortless, alarming speed. Howltongue and Roartongue rushed past in dark blurs. Crazed waves banged into *Runner*, exploding upward against the wood and drenching Daybreak within seconds.

"Start bailing!" shouted Boneoak. "The bucket—scoop the water—"

Thunder boomed and ate his words, and an entire

second ocean dropped from the sky to join the first. The
world vanished beneath a dark gray veil. The frenzied ocean
heaved, and *Runner* crested a mountain of water only to
plunge down the other side, into a waiting abyss.

Hold on, Boneoak's mouth might've shouted, behind
the rain and chaos, but Daybreak couldn't see. She locked
one arm around the seat, the other around the bucket, and
bailed. The water struck like an avalanche, ripping away
nets, knives, knapsacks of food. Something banged into her
knuckles. *Runner* crested another soaring mountain. The
arms of Lion Fjord were nowhere to be seen. As the boat
dove into the far abyss, an oar tore free and vanished into the
frothing maw.

The next mountain erupted with such force, it tossed
Runner into the air. The uniform noise fused into a
weightless silence. They floated in nothing. Daybreak stared
ahead, down the barrel of gray eternity.

She locked eyes with Boneoak—one hand on the
remaining oar, the other gripping a net he'd wrapped
around the rear seat, his face white, jaw set, and mouth dead
serious.

His eyes blazed with love.

Runner banged down. Daybreak's head struck the
seat, the bucket flew from her arm, and the storm around
her plunged to full black.

★★★

Pain throbbed at her temple.

Daybreak moaned, then sputtered. Her mouth was
full of sand.

She opened her eyes. Her right hand, knuckles scraped
and bloody, rested in front of her face. Beneath her was a
beach, but it was all wrong. The pebbles were tiny, like river-
bottom sand, and the sand was gold-brown, not gray.

Daybreak struggled to her knees, breathing shallowly.
She was aching and in pain in a hundred different places.

Daylight blazed above her. Her clothes were stiff and half-sodden, and chafed badly against her skin.

The movement was too much. Daybreak retched, and the agony in her head flared. Seawater dribbled from her mouth. She retched again.

Empty, she risked raising her head again. The coastline was all wrong, too. Smooth gold stretched south and north, bordered by a shallow swath of land and low brown cliffs.

The arms of Lion Fjord were nowhere in sight.

"Boneoak?" Daybreak called, and winced at the painful dryness in her throat.

She moved to kneeling again. Ten strides away, one of the waterskins lay in the alien sand, half-buried. She crawled to it and took cautious, feeble sips. Other things were half-buried in the sand, too: a net, the bucket, pieces of wood. "Boneoak?"

She hurt everywhere. These awful, chafing clothes. She took everything off, wincing. Salt and sand had gotten trapped beneath the fabric and in many places she was nearly rubbed raw.

She needed to wash with fresh water. She needed to find the food. She needed to find Boneoak. Unsteadily, Daybreak stood and limped up and down the beach, from one end of the wreckage to the other.

She didn't even find his footprints.

At the broken oar, Daybreak collapsed. The distant low tide hissed like a mild breeze through grass, revealing a near-infinite field of featureless, rippling sand. The empty land stretched in all directions, like the sky.

"Hey," called an unfamiliar voice.

Daybreak turned. A man emerged from the savanna at the edge of the beach, a hunting bow in his hand and surprise on his face. As he came closer, Daybreak saw the cluster of bright feathers in his hair and realized how young he was. She also noticed his boots. Ahatchipan hide. Like

Boneoak's.

"Hey," he said. He stared at her nudity, at her scrapes and thunderhead bruises, and scanned the wreckage on the beach. "What happened here? Are you all right?"

Daybreak was too overwhelmed to speak.

"Father's Bones," said the man. "And I thought my Traveling was starting out rough. Here—I'll help you salvage your things. Did you go too far down the Snakeback River? Everybody says that estuary is tricky, and you wouldn't be the first to get swept out on a turning tide. You'd be the first to come back, though, that I've ever heard of. It's a miracle you're even alive."

"I'm... what?"

The man set down his pack and withdrew a piece of stonebread. He offered it to her. "Here," he said. "It's stale, but it's what I've got. Looks like you could use it. You're a Traveler, right?"

Daybreak stared at him. He was addressing her casually, like a man, the way the Travelers of Lionfjord used to speak to her, when she would beg them for exotic treasures and stories, and they'd laugh and say, "You just can't wait to grow up and see for yourself, can you?"

Up the beach, Boneoak's empty boots waited, ready to entwine their steps with Daybreak's.

"Yes," said Daybreak slowly, accepting the stonebread. "I am a Traveler."

WE DON'T TALK ABOUT DEATH

Allie goes to the door without even saying goodnight.

My toes clench inside my shoes. The medical assistant isn't finished typing up her assessment of me, so I have to sit there on the exam table and pretend like Allie leaving doesn't bother me at all.

The door slides open. Allie stops there, and because of the lights in the outer corridor, this nimbus glows around her springy red hair. She looks at me for a second. Any time now, she's going to invite me to come with her after one of our post-run medical clearances to get some food or coffee or whatever, and I'm going to have to say no.

I mean, I could say yes. But then I'd have to talk about myself, and Allie would finally learn the truth.

Which is this: I am boring. Boring as dirt. According to my mom, the only thing I've ever been good at is sitting around like an idiot, and she's 100% right. Pilots—people like Allie O'Donovan—are the interesting ones, with their calibrated synesthetic schizophrenia, and their ability to perceive Ureality the same way every time and use those percep-tions to navigate it. Whereas Passengers—people like me—are the ones whose brains are so lethargic, we can't experience Ureality at all.

"Laurel?" Allie says.

My toes clench harder. I don't want to fuck up Allie's idea of me as someone who's likable, but Mom has a saying about this, too: *Nothing good lasts forever.* "Yeah?"

Allie looks down at her hiking boots. You don't need to wear anything special to fly an Overship, and I always just show up for runs in my boring old regular clothes, but Allie likes to dress up like she's tromping through a wilderness. To her, I guess she is. "Good job today."

Was it? "Thanks."

She hesitates.

"Listen..." I say. But I have no idea what, exactly, Allie should listen to. What is my mouth even doing?

Thankfully, Allie doesn't hear me. She turns and walks out.

"Okay," says the medical assistant. She pounds in a couple of hard returns. "Any tingling-numbness-pain in the extremities?"

* * *

I've been a certified Passenger with Close Companions for twelve years. Before joining the agency I majored in General Studies in college, in between lying there like a broken robot while boys crawled over me and I hoped to feel something. (Spoiler alert: I never did.) I still keep in touch with some people from my college days and I know some people through work and around various orbital stations. But I wouldn't say I have friends, exactly. Friends share their deepest darkest secrets, and I'm not interesting enough to have any.

I mean, there is all the stuff about my mom. But that's her stuff. Not mine.

* * *

At 4 a.m., my Phalm rings. For a second I don't know where I am—my mom's house in Cincinnati?—but then I remember that I'm on Friedman Station, a good 6,000 light years away from her.

And if it's 4 a.m., it must be the hospital calling.

My guts clench. I fumble for my Phalm. Despite all this call data squeezing through the wormhole network from Earth and back again, this near-instantaneous signal transfer still feels far, far too late. "Hello. This is Laurel.

Coco's daughter."

"Embers," says a voice that's definitely not a hospital person. "Get down to the launch bay and bring an overnight bag."

I blink. It's Karen Jadhav, Allie's boss (and by extension, mine) for as long as Allie and I are in port here. My heart's still pounding. "Geez, Karen, what the hell? I thought you were—I thought this was an emergency."

"It is," snaps Karen. "Bag. Launch bay. Meeting room. Come."

The call ends. I'm wide awake now. For three weeks now, ever since Allie's agency subcontracted mine and I got paired up with her, we've been doing a series of runs between all the stations in the Marchante-Friedman corridor, carrying sedated riders in mega-comapods. (It's an easy job, if creepy.) And if you're poor enough to be willing to buy an FTL ride in a shared comapod, jammed shoulder-to-shoulder with twelve other people, you're not important enough to merit an emergency ride at 4 a.m.

Well, whatever. I just work here. I root around in my trunk for some clean underpants.

***

Allie's face is pale, even paler than usual. "You want us to... what?"

Karen Jadhav faces us from across the meeting room's table. She looks like hell. I look like hell, too—half my hair is a ball of static, and even though I found my good bra it's underneath yesterday's dirty shirt—but then again, this is basically how I look every day. (Am I rock-solid confident or just slovenly? You be the judge.)

Karen's jaw tightens. She's a skinny little woman, and right now, she reminds me of a determined terrier. "You don't have to accept, of course," she says. "You are private citizens, not military. And besides that, a run from here to Barahna Station 6 would be entirely outside the scope of your current contracts."

I pick at the dirt beneath my fingernails and look out the window into the corridor. A lot of unhappy-looking people in Commonwealth Fleet uniforms mill around outside.

"Is there really nobody else?" asks Allie.

"Considering that Kagan Base Station is still literally on fire, full of dead and dying people, and being evacuated as we speak, I would say no. No, there is nobody else."

Allie makes a hissing noise between her teeth. Outside in the corridor, a trim gray-haired guy who has a lot of shiny bits on his uniform says something to the others. They look even more unhappy.

"If we don't get that ship full of seeds to Barahna Station 6 today, terrorist attack or no terrorist attack," Karen continues, "we will be in serious breach of our trade pact. And right now, with tensions with the Barahna being what they are, the Barahna are looking for any excuse to..."

She shakes her head.

"Look. The Barahna are demanding the seeds. All the Fleet's Pilots that were on Kagan are now too injured or dead to fly. Friedman Station is mixed-use, not military, but it's the closest source of backup Pilots, and you are the *only* registered Pilot here who has both the training and clearance to fly Darter-class military Overships.

"I'm sorry, Allie. Admiral Bettencourt wouldn't have asked us, and I wouldn't be asking you, if we had a better option."

It's 4:30 a.m. now. Allie has had no more sleep than the rest of us, but she still looks fantastic, dressed as usual for a wilderness adventure. She's got a vest on, for Christ's sake, the kind with all the bulky pockets. And a necklace of some kind of animal teeth. "But Barahna Station 6 is across a war zone..."

"It isn't a war zone yet," Karen says.

"And how 'not a war zone yet' right now is Kagan Base Station?"

Even at the best of times, interstellar politics make my head swim. And this is not the best of times. "Look, does all this really matter?" I interrupt. "You need a crew to fly a thing to a place, right? I can do that. Sure."

They turn to stare. "You would go?" asks Karen. She says it like I'm crazy.

"Yeah."

Allie keeps staring. It's the stare of a child looking with awe upon a grown-up hero.

"What?" I say, my face getting hot. "It's no big deal. They won't hurt us or anything—we're just two civilians, and we're flying a ship full of stuff they want."

Karen leans over and, to my further embarrassment, clasps my hand. "Embers," she says, her voice full of emotion. "Thank you. But you know we can't go ahead without your Pilot."

"It's fine," mumbles Allie. "I'll go." Before Karen can effuse in her direction, too, Allie gets up and leaves the room.

Karen frowns at me. "Be careful out there, Embers. You know the perceptions of Pilots can become more... intense... when they're under stress."

Do I.

***

Allie and I fly a Hopper-class Overship to Kagan Base Station, which looks not like a giant futuristic hubcap (which it should) but like a disintegrating donut (which it really, really shouldn't). Unmoored ships float around it like dazed bees.

Only one ship is still docked: a Darter-class Overship.

We fly there, to the part of Kagan that's still intact, and dock next to it. Inside, this part of the base is nearly deserted. There are a few terrified-looking people in Fleet uniforms who order us around, but other than that, it's a lot like business as usual.

Except that Allie's a wreck. Her face goes pale and red by turns, and a couple times I think she might cry. And Allie is not a Pilot who cries. She's built like a sled dog, short and thick but full of muscles, and she stomps and bellows and declares.

I don't like to see her like this.

"It's, uh…" I say.

We wait in a Kagan Base Station airlock. When the light turns green, we'll open the hatch at the bottom, climb down the tunnel, and enter the airlock on *The Luunpa*, the Darter-class ship that holds the Barahna's seeds, and (by extension) the Commonwealth's Get-Out-Of-War Free card.

"It's what?" says Allie.

I think about taking her hand. But the idea is so childish and stupid. I almost blush as I say, "It's gonna be okay."

Allie looks away. Her necklace of teeth is like a frozen smile.

Green light.

★★★

We strap in. We launch.

The Luunpa makes the usual noises. Outside, as we enter Ureality and tesseract across space-time, the usual stars wink out. I'm left sitting like an idiot next to Allie, who does all the work: sensor-rich Flygloves cover her hands, and her fingers pluck at the air in front of her in some baffling way that translates into commands that make the ship go. Or pull Ureality around it. Whatever.

She sucks in a deep breath. Her head drops forward, as if she's falling asleep. Her hands never stop moving.

She mumbles something.

"What's that?" I ask.

"The barn," Allie says.

"We're sitting on the Overship *Luunpa*," I say. "Do you see a barn?"

Allie doesn't answer. Her head lolls.

Outside, of course, it's dead black. But not to Allie. Like all Pilots, she experiences a whole synesthetic wonderland out there. And it's my job to keep her focused on how to make decisions in the face of it. "Do we need to go closer to the barn?" I ask.

Allie's fingers twitch. "Ohh," she says, in an almost-moan. "Oh no. No no no no."

"Should we go a different way?"

"This is the barn," says Allie. "She's over there."

I sit up in my harness. There's no gravity in Ureality, so the motion is functionally useless, but ol' biological habits die hard. "Wait... you're perceiving a *person?*"

"She's over by the barn," says Allie, "in the shadow of the wood, where the paint on the siding flakes to gray in the sun. Her hand is on the wood, her nails are on the wood, and she's drumming her fingers.

"Look at them. Her nails are polished, and so, so pink. I want those nails. I want them."

This is mega wrong. "There are no people outside, Allie. We're in the Overship *Luunpa*, flying to Barahna Station 6. Remember?"

Allie's chin drops to her chest. Her hands keep plucking.

"Do you know where you are?" I ask.

"Yes."

"What's my name?"

"Laurel."

"And do you know there are no people outside?" I glance out the windows, spooked. "And that no Pilots perceive people in Ureality? Just stuff like, I dunno, colors and soundscapes? The dreamscape thing you do is already really rare. But perceiving other *people*... nobody does that. It's not possible."

"It's not possible," Allie echoes.

"Right. So just... go back to flying us through swamps or libraries and all that stuff you normally imagine."

"But her nails," says Allie, "are perfect and pink, and she's hiding. She's run through the wheat. You can't see her behind the barn. The sun's going down behind the chestnut trees and they'll never, ever find her."

"O'Donovan!"

Her voice gets thick. "This is a bad place. I don't like it here."

"Keep moving your fingers!"

Allie starts. Her fingers pluck faster. No kidding do Pilots' perceptions get unhinged under stress. Allie must be convinced that we're flying straight to our deaths, to perceive all this wild shit. "O'Donovan, listen to me. It's your ol' buddy Laurel. I'm telling you that we are flying to Barahna Station 6, and although the Barahna might look like the lovechildren of an armadillo and a nightmare, we have something they want and it's going to be *fine*. Trust me. But for us to even get there, you've got. To stay. Focused. There's no woman outside. No people. Only your usual... your usual whatever. And if you forget that, you're going to freak out and get lost, and then you really are going to fly us to our inevitable deaths. So stay with me. Okay?"

Allie shudders.

"Okay?"

Allie says, "Okay."

We fly for about ten awful seconds in silence.

Then Allie says, "There's a stream."

I relax by tiny increments. Allie talks about streams, a forest, a dirt road, and a hardware store. She does not talk again about people. So we don't talk about death.

We don't talk about a lot of things.

★★★

I know the Barahna are happy to see us, but they put up a good warlike front—yelling, opening their frills, feinting at us with their shockprods, and so on.

I don't speak whatever language they're using, but I've learned you can get by pretty good with screaming, brandishing weapons, and pointing. So we scream and point our way to an understanding, and soon, Allie and I enter some type of living quarters while a big group of angry armed Barahna wait outside, presumably while the rest of them do their thing to *The Luunpa* and its cargo of seeds.

Allie sits on an ottoman and quakes.

I stoop over—Barahna are short compared to humans, and if I stand on my tip-toes, my head bumps the ceiling— and look around the room. There's a low table, a pair of sleeping nests, some visual art on the walls (at chest height), and something that looks like a glass bouquet of lilies. "It's fine," I say, poking one of the 'lilies'. "Look, they gave us a chemical lick." I gesture to a screen and its slideshow of nebulae. "And some type of computer access. Not that I know how to work that thing. But the point is, they're treating us more like guests and less like prisoners."

Allie says nothing. She squeezes her hands between her knees and looks at the floor.

Distance yawns between us. Like a moron who thinks she can throw a rock across a canyon, I ask, "Uh... you okay?"

Allie looks up at me, then, her face anguished. The expression stabs at me. It's the way my mom looks at me, sometimes; a look that says: *you betray me with the fact that you exist.*

"No," she says. That's not how you're supposed to answer that question. I don't know what to say.

She gets up and goes to the bathroom. "I'm taking a shower. Then a nap. Wake me up if they bring us some food."

I listen to her bang around. I'm so unsettled, I don't even think, *We're going to share a room—it's like a sleep-over* until a full minute has passed.

★★★

I shower after Allie and burrow into the other nest. It's bad enough trying to sleep when you're attempting it under a literal pile of rags instead of a blanket, but it's even worse when your brain won't shut up.

I look over at Allie, a lump under a crack of light from the nearly-closed bathroom door. I wonder if she can't sleep, either. I feel too stupid to ask her.

Outside in the corridor, someone honks, and a few other Barahna join in. Are they laughing? Arguing? Gearing up to run in here and zap us until our hearts stop? I wonder if when we get back, Admiral Bettencourt will try to debrief us. He's gonna be real disappointed when all I can tell him is, "The shower in our room had great water pressure."

I wonder what my mom will think.

Or if she'll even know. Will some news organization cover this, the heroic journey of two civilian volunteers who averted a diplomatic melt-down between the Common-wealth and the Barahna? If there is news about it, and Mom does hear it, will she even care? I can see it now. The next time I call, I'll tell her that I literally helped stop a war, and she'll go, "Oh, that's nice. Have you talked to Tiana lately?" And then she'll gush about the latest accomplishments of my sister, who is younger, thinner, prettier, smiley-er, and more perfect than I am in every possible way, and who doesn't need to involve herself with the tedious work of saving the galaxy.

Ha ha. Moms.

I wonder what's happening. I wonder if the hospital finally called—I'm too far away from the closest wormhole for my Phalm to tell. What if they did try to call? What if I've missed it? I dig my fingers into the ultra-soft rags around me. I don't know which is worse: the thought of talking to my mom again, or the thought of never talking to my mom again.

It's funny, what impending finality does to a crappy relationship. Which is: nothing. Absolutely nothing. You think there'll be some honest conversations, or these little sparkling moments of Truth and Meaning, but there's not. All the awful things remain the same, except all the old bullshit now gets coated in rising panic, thicker and thicker, like layers of candy on a jawbreaker that's become too big to fit into your mouth.

Allie rolls over in her nest. My chest hurts to look at her. I want to go over and slide in next to her and talk, the way I did with my little sister when we were both too young to understand just how crazy Mom was, and Tiana wasn't yet old enough to be crowned Better Than Laurel For Always, Amen. I want to ask Allie if she has a sister. I want to ask her if she'll be my friend.

The door to the hall slides open. A Barahna, its frill open in alarm, slides a tray of food inside. It snatches its arm back and shuts the door.

Groggy, Allie sits up. I kick off my rags and fetch the tray, heart pounding from more than my sudden leap from bed.

I kneel beside her and remove the cover on a dish with a flourish. "Madam. Your bug paste has arrived."

***

After we eat our insect paste, Allie figures out how to work the computer. The Barahna have graciously given us access to some entertainment. The videos don't have Human Xenospeak as a subtitle language option, so we settle on subtitles in Mmur, which is an Aainen language that Allie speaks kind of and I speak almost not at all, except for like ten words.

We binge-watch some kind of incomprehensible

series, barely speaking.

We receive more insect paste. We sleep.

The next morning, just when I'm starting to wonder if we are in fact prisoners, several Barahna come in to our quarters. They've still got weapons, but their frills ripple in a subdued sort of way. They point to us, then out the door.

We pack up our things. I grin with relief, but Allie looks miserable.

I don't know what her deal is.

"Come on," I say, as we wait in the Barahna airlock for the light to turn green. The hatch to *The Luunpa* waits under our feet. "They're letting us go. We did it."

Allie shakes her head.

"If they wanted us dead—"

"It isn't that."

I raise my eyebrows.

Allie's hand tightens around the strap of her overnight bag. "I have to go back. Through that." She gestures out the porthole.

I remember our run here, and how Allie was so stressed out, she thought she was perceiving people. "It'll be fine," I say. "You're less worried this time, so your Ureality perceptions should be normal. Right?"

Allie locks eyes with me. She's got a Mom look again, but a different one, the one that says: *I have a lot of opinions and you can't handle them.*

Green light.

***

This time, Allie doesn't talk.

She moans.

I look over at her, uneasy. "Allie. What's up?"

"No," says Allie.

"What do you see?" I ask.

"I want to go inside. I want to go back inside."

"You are inside. You're in the Overship *Luunpa*, with

me, and we're flying back to Friedman Station."

Allie's head rolls. Her fingers keep fluttering.

"Do you believe me?"

"Yeah."

"Do you remember *The Luunpa*?"

"Yeah. But I have to see." Allie's voice turns shrill. "I have to see! Don't you see her? She's waiting. By the barn."

Oh, hell. Not this again. What is she so worked up about? "Allie, there is no woman."

"I want to go there."

"Take us to Friedman Station, Allie."

Allie kicks at the hull with her booted feet. "No!" she shouts. "You can't make me! I won't let him!"

I have no clue what this means, but it can't be good. Afraid of bumping her still-working hands, I grab Allie's thigh. "We're going to Friedman Station." I swallow. "You need to take us to—"

Allie lunges out and slaps her hands at me.

"Allie!" I shriek. "What are you *doing*!?"

With no hands to control *The Luunpa*'s position in Ureality, we drop down and the stars pop into existence. But they're horrifyingly wrong, swirling like the fake snow in a snow globe. Allie shouts something. She slumps in her harness.

"Allie." My heart crawls into my mouth. I tear off my own harness and swim to her, crookedly, the spinning *Luunpa* throwing me off like I'm drunk. I squeeze her shoulders. "Allie. Wake up!"

Her eyelids flutter. Then she jolts awake, notices the spinning stars, and flaps her fingers like the world's most desperate shadow puppeteer.

The stars slow. Go still.

"Holy Christ, Allie, are you okay?"

Allie gapes at me. A few of her springy curls lay plastered to her forehead, and her many-pocketed vest heaves with her breath. "You... you're out of your seat."

"*Are you okay?*"

"You can't..." She stares at my hands, now grasping her harness so I float in place. I can tell she wants to pry them off, but thank God her own hands stay up and ready, a finger twitching now and then. She's in control, and physically pushing me away would mean losing it again. "Get back into your seat, Embers."

I don't. "Where are we?"

"Don't know."

"Well run up and check, goddamnit!"

Allie looks at me like: *What insane thing are you even talking about?*

I swear again and push off to the console in front of my chair. I can't fly a Darter-class ship like Allie, but certain Fleet systems are pretty universal, and I can at least figure out how to access the map. "We're almost 3,000 LY off course!"

Allie's lips press together. She stares straight ahead. "Find us another way."

"Me? I'm the goddamn Passenger!"

Allie shakes her head.

"This is some absolute horseshit." I brace myself against my chair with a leg and slap the console. "What kind of mental episode are you even having? We have to go back! The Fleet is gonna think the Barahna electrocuted us after all!"

Allie lunges forward like a dog on a short leash. "I have to go through that!" she shouts. "You think that's easy? You think I *want* to?"

"I'd think you'd want to go home, but evidently not!"

"Fuck you," says Allie bitterly. "You don't know anything."

I seethe into silence. She's right—I don't know anything, both now and not in general—but she most definitely didn't have to point it out.

"Look," Allie snaps. "I don't know you. And you don't know me. And I'd rather it stay that way."

"Well..." I sputter. "Well... that's what I think, too."

Allie turns her head completely away from me. "Hooray for you."

What are we even fighting about? Not knowing just makes me madder. I pull myself back into my seat, strap in, and stab my console like what I'm doing makes a difference. She wants me to find another way back? Fine. I'll plot the course through regular space. And we'll get home in about 16,000 years.

Allie deflates a little. She still won't look at me. Well, that's fine, because I'm not talking to her.

Her shoulders twitch in a silent sneeze.

Then again.

She sniffs. It's a wet sniff, the kind you make when you're crying. But I'm *not* talking to her so I don't ask.

Allie finally closes her hands into two fists—one of the few Pilot gestures I know; "engage smart status maintenance"—and digs into one of her vest's many pockets for a tissue. She blows her nose a few times, and I sit there and hate myself.

"Laurel."

I'm not talking to her. But I say, flatly, "What."

Allie pockets her tissue and takes out another one. "Do you... are you seeing anyone?"

I look at her like: *Have you lost your mind?*

"I'm not asking you like *that*," says Allie. She sniffs. "I just wanted to know... I just... when I was young, maybe eleven or twelve, I had a crush on an older girl. Violet Rascone. I followed her around and... you know how it is."

I don't. "I'm ace."

"Oh. I'm sorry."

I roll my eyes. "It's not a *disease*."

"I didn't mean it like that! I meant I'm sorry I *assumed.*" Allie clenches her tissue into a wad. "Look, what I'm *saying* is that I... there was this girl, okay? And I liked her, and I was naïve enough to believe that she liked me, but she was just using me to get to my older brother. She came over one afternoon, and I thought... why am I even—you know what, just forget it." She turns away again. "Forget I even said anything."

I stare at the back of her head. Allie tried to stuff her hair into a braid this morning, but all these wild corkscrews have come loose, and it's like solar flares around her, illuminating places you expect to stay dark. "It's memory."

Allie's shoulders stiffen.

"It's not a dreamscape for you at all. It's memory." I can hardly believe it. "When you're in Ureality, you perceive it as... as a memory map."

She looks down.

I suck in a breath. "That's..."

Her shoulders twitch again. She sniffs a bitter laugh. "Horrible?"

Consider that. Having your memories, your entire life, broken up into little fragments and exploded all over the cosmos. And you being unable to control, or choose, which fragments you get to relive—and when.

And being forced to have strangers go with you, every time it happens.

"Because it is," says Allie. She turns back to me, a little. "Abso-fucking-lutely horrible."

I nod.

"Shitty runs always make me think of shitty memories," she says, "and then, because that's just the way it works, they're stuck in that part of space forever. So now, every time I fly between Friedman Station and Barahna Station 6? It'll be Violet Rascone, waiting behind the barn, and me watching while the inevitable happens, powerless to change anything or make even the act of remembering stop. Isn't that *great?*

"Incidentally, I'm not seeing anyone. Because I have zero clue how to form intimate relationships with people while I'm forced to be intimate with strangers every single run of my professional life. What do I even have left for the people I'd care about?" She sniffs a laugh again. "You're lucky. You don't have to tell *anyone* who you are, if you don't want to."

Now I laugh. "Lucky? Are you kidding? It'd be great if I could tell someone who I am. It'd be even better if I was interesting, but I'm not. I'm the most boring person in the universe."

Allie shakes her head. She blows her nose one more time, but it's a hiss of dry air, so she crumples up the tissue and blots her eyes. "You're not boring, Laurel. You're funny. And you're brave."

My ears get hot. "I'm just a chump with no imagination. A weirdo. You're the one who's cool."

Allie makes a noise with her lips. But she smiles. "I'm cool?"

"Sure. You've got a necklace of alligator teeth. What kind of person wears a tooth necklace to work?"

Allie says, "Well," and fidgets with the flaps of her vest pockets.

By this point, I don't know which of us is more embarrassed. Which is great and all, but we're still 16,000 years from home. "Listen, uh," I say. "About getting back to Friedman Station?"

Allie's smile fades.

"Do you, uh, want to go ahead and do that? And prevent the Fleet from starting a war over our actually-not-murdered bodies?"

"Technically, no. I don't want to."

"What I *meant* was—"

"I know."

I nod at the stars outside. "I'm sorry, Allie. But there's only one real way back, and you're it."

Allie fidgets with her pocket flaps again. "I know. It's fine. I'll just need a Passenger who's..." She clears her throat. "Really engaged."

I scratch the back of my neck.

"It's okay if I don't remember later on what we talk about," says Allie quietly. "I know most Pilots have a hard time recalling anything that happens in Ureality that isn't Ureality itself. But just... talk to me this time. Like you're willing to be there with me. Please?"

It seems unlikely that my existence could matter to someone so much, but I say, "Okay."

Allie nods. She raises her fists and flashes them open, closed, then open again, her fingers ready.

★★★

Violet Rascone waits behind the barn. Allie O'Donovan can't tell if she wants her, or wants to *be* her, or what's even happening inside her eleven-year-old brain.

It's early August. The sun is setting. Allie O'Donovan hides behind a bunch of wild rhubarb, gathering her courage, when suddenly, Jon O'Donovan, two years older, comes around the barn from the other side.

Violet Rascone and Jon see each other and smile. Violet kisses Jon.

They kiss a lot.

Allie O'Donovan watches until it gets dark. Her legs fall asleep, and fireflies come out. Finally, her grandma comes out onto the porch, and she calls into the night for Allie and Jon to come inside.

Violet and Jon hush each other and giggle, but Allie jumps up and runs.

Twenty-five years later, grown-up Allie O'Donovan tells this sad little story in a really confusing and disjointed way to Laurel Embers, a Passenger who isn't exactly up for that kind of unhappy personal journey, but Laurel feels bad for Allie, so she, you know... tries. And I guess she does good enough with the questions she asks, because Allie doesn't freak out. She just cries a little.

And they make it home, and nobody starts a war.

So, happy ending.

★★★

We stand in the airlock of the Hopper-class Overship, watching the lights on the hatch above us. Allie's eye-fucking the ladder up out of here, and I don't blame her. She looks damp and worn out, and to be honest I feel the same way.

"Thanks," she says.

What she means is: *Thanks for watching me relive a crappy evening from my childhood.* It's a weird thing to thank a person for, but then again, I'm a weird person to thank. I smile. "No problem. Everyone's, you know... got their stuff."

Allie nods.

"If I were the Pilot and you were the Passenger," I say, "I'd bore you to death for fifteen hours straight with stories about my mom and my sister. So really. Don't worry about it."

Allie presses her palms to her forehead and smears them back, pushing loose, sweaty curls away from her face. "I wouldn't be bored."

I laugh. "You wanna bet?"

"Yeah. I do." Allie glances at me quickly, almost furtively, like she's doing something risky. "Let's talk about it over a drink."

Ah.

There it is.

Allie coughs. "If you want, I mean."

"I do," I blurt. "If you really... if that's okay."

"Sure." Allie wipes her palms on her pants. "It'll be

fine."

It'll certainly be something, for me to be the one to steer a conversation for once. I feel like I'm about to do something important, like I really am a Pilot. "Okay. Yeah."

Green light.

ALL SOULS PROCEED

The unfamiliar townscape rolls past, a glare of light and bleached-bone stone under weedy mesquite. I don't know where I am. The whole town is low-slung and the same, framed by raw mountains on every side, and the sun is always hard.

I roll down a big road. At the side of the road stands a bike.

It's nestled in bright silk flowers. Every inch of it, pure white.

What are those bikes, I say, to a local friend who knows better. I keep seeing these abandoned bikes that've been spray-painted.

Ah, says my friend. Those are the ghost bikes.

For people on bikes who get killed by cars? I ask.

She smiles. She says, Sometimes.

***

In early November, my friend carefully paints my face in black greasepaint and bone-bright makeup. It's the All Souls Procession, she tells me. You'll love it. Everyone paints their faces like skulls, and we all dress up, and at sunset, we march through town and think about all the people who have died over the past year.

I wear black. I think about the dead, as instructed. My friend wears her wedding dress and a sky-blue wig, rhinestones in the black-painted sockets of her eyes, like stars. She is well-versed in the ways loss can be beautiful.

On the edges of our silent procession, I glimpse the bikes. They wobble slowly. I can't see who rides them

because night has fallen, and the solemn-faced crowd is thick
with skulls and bones and ghosts.

The ghost bikes used to be full-sized, says my friend,
but people would steal them to ride. So now, all you see are
the bikes of children.

A bike rolls past. The training wheels rattle like teeth. I
see an empty seat, and I assume that the bike is pushed by a
hand I cannot see.

***

Near my new house, there is an accident. A boy has
snuck into the back of a FedEx delivery truck, and when the
truck backs up, he falls out. The rear tire crushes his skull.
His death is instantaneous.

For weeks, his family conducts a fruitless vigil at the
roadside. Neighbors bring out threadbare recliners and
folding chairs. The desert at their feet collects empty bags of
Taquis and glass bottles of tamarind soda. The police leave
them alone. It's nice of the cops to let them mourn at their
own pace, I say, and my friend says, This is the south side.
You think the police even come here?

By February, the furniture is gone. The empty bottles
have crumbled into a million stars, and in the place of the
family stands a bike.

***

On a cold night with a lean, bright moon, I see a ghost
bike rolling. Just rolling along the never-used sidewalk, like
me, out for a head-clearing stroll.

Hello, I say to the bike, but of course, bikes don't talk.
It rolls on past me, stiffly, in non-acknowledgment.

I see it again when I pass the old shrine for the dead
boy. The bike is poised on its bed of glass stars. Is this what
you do? I ask it. You just go out at night and…?

When I ask my friend, she only says, Shhh.

***

Next year, I do my own make-up. I tell my friend that

I'll meet her there, but we both know there are too many people and we'll never find each other.

The All Souls Procession begins. I'm near a group of people holding signs for victims of school shootings when I see a flash, the slow-rolling tires glimmering with fragments of star. I push through the mourners, but the bike keeps dancing away, so I ease off, and we walk side by side across a great, human, breathing distance, content to let things go.

★★★

The next morning, I start to tell this story to my friend. She asks for the name of the boy whose skull got crushed, those many months back, but to my embarrassment, I can't remember.

It was—I say. It was—it was—

★★★

The next time I walk past the old shrine, the bike is gone.

There's nothing there at all, now. Nothing but stars.

YOU CAN TAKE IT WITH YOU

1. Perfectia

When I lurch into awareness, I expect my heart to pound with fear. But when I put a hand on my chest—which is too cold and too hard—I feel nothing.

Then I remember: I don't have a heart anymore.

I sit up. My Afterlife has begun in a gigantic bedroom. Everything is a chilling, pure white, like some hack programmer's idea of Heaven, which I guess is what this is. Somewhere in this simulated wasteland is Michael Fain, and wherever *he* is, it's probably a colorful Paradise, but I'm not Michael Fain. And unlike him, I don't have to be made comfortable, because I haven't paid obscene sums of money to play on this Afterlife server for all of eternity.

I'm only here so Michael Fain's private Afterlife can meet a legal requirement.

And I've only got ninety days before I'm deleted.

***

I leave the bedroom. Walking feels weird, like I've just stepped off a moving walkway at an airport. Moving, period, feels weird. All my pain is gone, but my body is alarmingly insubstantial, like if I bent the wrong way I could uncover a glitch in the programming and reach inside my own bones.

I find a bathroom (what a joke—who poops in Heaven?) and I look into the mirror there. I don't recognize myself—my nose is too small and my skin's too light, like they didn't have the right template for my ancestry, and they made me younger than I wanted. I asked to be forty. I was happiest at forty. Do middle-aged people offend Michael Fain's aesthetic?

And then there's the music. It permeates everything, and even though the violins and chimes aren't particularly offensive, the volume is the same no matter how I stand or whether I cover my simulated ears.

I've got to get out of here.

But I get lost trying. The house—my house, now—is gigantic. There are bedrooms, bathrooms, game rooms, sun rooms, ballrooms, living rooms, side rooms, day rooms, dining rooms, sitting rooms, drawing rooms, receiving rooms, guest rooms, card rooms, TV rooms, and rumpus rooms. The house has five stories. And everything is white. Even the window panes are white: they emit diffuse, uniform light, like lightboxes, and they don't show any outside views.

Finally, I find what I think is my front door. Afraid, I stop there. I want to cry. But I'm sure Michael Fain's Afterlife won't simulate tears.

Just fifteen minutes ago, while they made a digital backup of my consciousness—all that I am now—Daniel held my hand, and we tried to be brave.

I sit on the tile and cry anyway.

***

In the good Afterlives, they let you send chats to the real world, so you can talk to the living.

In the good Afterlives, they tweak the physics engines so you can finally fly, like in your dreams.

In the good Afterlives, you're allowed to stay there as long as you can pay for your server space. It's far from perfect—don't get me started on the ethics of the commodification of consciousness—but at least some people get more time than they'd have had if they'd died with their bodies. And besides, you can always ask for donations to help keep your digital self around. Heck, you can even work, if there's still demand back in the real world for what you do.

But I'm not in a good Afterlife. I'm in Michael Fain's. And if the current set of regulatory laws tells Michael Fain that he must have a minimum of twenty-five people in his private Afterlife because socialization is a basic human right, then by god, is Michael Fain going to cut corners on the experience of every placeholder soul he's got in here, until he can eventually fill up his paradise with his special, chosen, eternal few.

***

When I finally get up the courage to leave my house, I find a giant, rambling lawn, with flowers and fruit trees and benches and fountains. The grass is freshly cut, and the sun is warm. But the air doesn't smell like anything, and I don't see any birds. And the music has only changed, not left.

My throat should be dry. It's not. I feel like I'm choking, like Daniel's absence has taken away all my air. His name is a scream, repeated, in my head.

He's gone. He's gone.

I'll never speak to him again.

"Where are you?" I say, and hearing the plaintiveness in my own voice is almost enough to make me cry again.

"I'm right here!" chirps a feminine voice.

I turn around. A naked white woman, blond-haired and blue-eyed, stands behind me. She's slender and tall, with a long neck. I guess straight people would think she's pretty. "Hi there, Lehann!" she says. "I'm Angela, your personal AI assistant."

She's not the one I need. Not at all.

"What can I help you with?"

I grip the trunk of a nearby tree. It's ugly and not real. The leaves are all different, impossible shapes, like stars and fish and cupcakes, and the trunk is crayon-brown. "You can tell me why I ever wanted this."

"I'm sorry, but I don't understand your request."

As I lay dying in the cardiac ward, I had told Daniel, "It'll be fine. I'll only be there for three months, and then he'll cycle some other retired former employee in as a place-holder. How bad can it be?"

"If it weren't bad," Daniel had said, "They wouldn't be bribing people to go there."

"Don't think of it as a bribe. Think of it as a stipend."

Daniel had looked away.

"We need that money," I had said quietly. "This room alone costs—"

"Stop it. Listen to yourself. You're... you're like this, and you're worried about money?"

"I'm worried about you. All of my problems are about to end."

"I said stop it. Don't..."

I can't handle the memory. I squeeze my eyes shut. In Michael Fain's Afterlife, squeezing your eyes shut doesn't make sparkles in your vision.

"Could you please rephrase that?" Angela asks.

"Never mind." I knew what my heart failure treat-ments had cost—in all senses of the word. "I've remem-bered."

★★★

My mind won't stop screaming his name. The urge to go to him consumes me. He's not here, I tell myself, and you can't go to him anymore, but my heart cannot accept this.

I can't stay in this place.

Angela watches me as I look through my mammoth house's closets, cabinets, cubbies, storage nooks, and drawers. "Can I help you with something?" she asks.

I find white sneakers, white underpants, white regular pants, white socks, and white tee-shirts. White button-downs, white sweaters, white hoodies, white shorts, white fedoras, white vests... white fur coats and white tuxedos, for god's sake. "I need a backpack."

"I'm sorry, but that's a prohibited item. Can I help you with something else?"

"How the hell is a backpack a prohibited item?" I kick shut a closet door. "How about a duffel bag?"

"I'm sorry, but that's a prohibited item."

"A suitcase?"

"I'm sorry, but that's—"

"Luggage." I sit on this guest room's bed. The white comforter makes no sound as I move, not even a rustle. "You're telling me that we can't have luggage."

"That's correct!"

"I have to get out of here." Panic rises inside of me, but my body feels as light and as breezy as ever, like I'm on some drug that blocks me from physically feeling everything I want to feel. "I need—" But his name would mean nothing to her. "I need... I can't be alone right now. And I know there are other people here. It's a law."

"That's correct, too!"

I stand and strip the bed. "If Michael Fain wanted us to stay isolated inside these houses," I say, as I knot the bed's top sheet into a bindle, "he should've made them less shitty."

★★★

"Where are you going, Lehann?"

I'm walking. To my right is my gigantic lawn, stuffed with whole football fields' worth of unconvincing decadences, like tennis courts and sculpture gardens and swimming pools (but would the water even feel wet?). Over one shoulder is my makeshift bindle, full of clothes and bottles of water and other stupid shit I probably don't need.

"Lehann? Where are you going?"

But then again, I might need the clothes after all. Would I get grimy in Michael Fain's Afterlife? Would I get thirsty? What about food? I found four massive kitchens back in my massive house, but none had anything edible in the fridges or cupboards. Just gadgets and stacks of china.

"I'm looking for a path," I say.

To my left is the forest.

I saw it when I climbed up the exterior of my house half an hour ago to get the lay of the land. The forest slopes up to every horizon, like my mansion is in the center of a little bowl-shaped valley, which I suppose it is.

"There are laws," I say. "Nobody's default location—nobody's 'home'—can be more than an hour's travel time, at most, from somebody else's."

"That's true! But—"

"And that path of travel has to be marked somehow." I wish for a rock to kick aside in irritation, but my lawn is too perfect. "And I don't see any roads or vehicles on my property—do you? So it's got to be on foot, through the forest. Somewhere *here* is a path that leads somewhere *there.*"

"To where?"

Nowhere, I think, imagining Daniel's face. I can see all the details of it with such painful clarity.

"To where, Lehann?"

"To everyone else."

Angela cocks her head, like a child who cannot understand. "Why do you want to find other people?"

How long ago has it been, now, since I've held Daniel's hand? Two hours? Three? They didn't program a watch onto my wrist or a phone into my pocket. And while the sun has moved in the sky—I think—and the length of any Afterlife day has to be twenty-four hours, there are no rules that state how the sun has to behave when it's up. For all I know, five hours could've gone by.

I picture him. Is he still in the hospital? Are they making him fill out paperwork? Does he sit and stare out a window, his pale hands tucked under his knees, the way he does when he's at a loss?

Is his own mind screaming my name, in answer?

All the places inside of me pull toward my center, as if I have heartstrings everywhere, and they're all getting sucked into a black hole in my belly. "If you have to ask, you'll never know."

***

"What do you think of Afterlives?"

It was May, 2135. I was twenty-seven, and we were on our fifth or sixth date. The first Afterlife, the Elysium server, had only been open for five years, and the Mythic server was set to open that fall.

Daniel bent over and scraped together a few pebbles at the foot of the bench we sat upon. "They're a cool idea. But I doubt I'll ever have one."

"Yeah?"

He sat up and tossed a pebble into the nearby duck pond. He didn't mind the dirt on his fingers or the sun in his eyes, but I wanted to stand over him and let my shadow fall on his face, so he could open his eyes fully, and look up at me, and smile. "First of all, I'm never going to be that rich. You don't get rich teaching pre-kindergarteners how to glue feathers onto toilet paper rolls. And second, I dunno if I'd want to live in a place where you can't get hurt. What's the thrill in that?"

I laugh.

"I'm being serious."

I take his other hand. I don't mind the dirt on his fingers, either. "I know."

***

I almost miss the path. It looks like an animal trail, barely a parting of the weeds, and it's marked by a tiny sign the size of a playing card, on a wooden stake six inches high. The sign has nothing on it but a green arrow pointing into the woods.

"The law says the paths have to be obvious," I say.

Angela beams. "No other walkways in all of Perfectia are marked with this signage."

Perfectia? Is that Michael Fain's name for this awful place?

I step into the woods. The forest is thick and dark, and it does not smell like forest. Instead, it smells like garbage, or sewage. I put a hand to my nose. "Jesus."

"Why do you want to find other people?" Angela asks again. "Perfectia has been designed to ensure maximum privacy for all of its citizens, and by exiting your encouraged personal zone, you may be violating the wishes of other community members."

I don't answer. I keep walking.

The ever-present music in my skull turns more ominous. "This forest is an unpleasant place," says Angela. "Would you like to go back?"

I ignore her.

The outlines of the tree trunks waver. Then shimmer.

"Are you sure?" asks Angela.

Insects—thousands and millions of insects—rush to the fore from behind every branch and trunk. Each tree stands coated in a shivering carpet of shells and clicking mouthparts.

I stop at the sight. My knees should wobble, but of course, they don't. "This isn't real."

A beetle falls upon my shoulder.

"This isn't—"

All those insects pour down around me like hailstones. I panic and bolt. Insects crunch and splatter under my soles, leaving patches of slime and spasming pieces of chitin.

A hornet flies into my mouth.

I scream and spit, but it won't come out. More hornets land on my face and the back of my neck, and they crawl up my sleeves and pant legs, stinging all the way. But there are laws. Unless the future resident signs a waiver, you can't have more than a certain amount of pain per minute programmed into your Afterlife.

And I hadn't signed one.

Don't get me wrong: the hornets are terrifying. But when I force myself to be still and pay attention, I realize that their assault barely hurts, like brushing up against a blackberry cane.

"This is very alarming!" shouts Angela, to be heard above the shrieking soundtrack and the clacking of the insects. "You should run back home!"

I stand my ground, quaking while hornets crawl over my hair. "You can go back if you want," I say, "but I won't."

★★★

Before the Elysium server, I remember, things were very different. Back then, Afterlives were small-time charities, usually for kids with terminal cancer. Children were getting robbed of time on earth, the reasoning went, so we should give them something in compensation.

But things didn't stay that way. As soon as the regulations got loosened, the dying of all ages—and even the not-quite-dying—signed up. Sure, it means that nobody inherits anything anymore, what with Mom n' Dad liquefying all of their assets to stay in digital bliss, but human nature being what it is, I can't say I'm surprised.

Who doesn't feel—no matter their wealth, their advantages, or their accomplishments—that their time is too short?

★★★

The forest finally releases us.

We stand at the edge of another ostentatious lawn. It's identical to mine. We cross it, and I see that the sprawling house in the center is identical to mine, too. The only difference is a note taped to the front door:

TOOK PATH MARKED WITH PAIR OF DIS-

CARDED PANTS

I frown. I picture the owner of this house waking up as I did—alone, frightened, their mind screaming someone else's name. Or maybe many names. Did they have kids? Grandkids? How many loved ones have they been cut off from? How much pain did they, too, carry with themselves when they fled their abyss of an empty house?

I strike the doorframe. "Michael Fain is a cesspit of horseshit."

"I disagree!" says Angela.

I clamp down on my outburst. For all I know, Angela will send him reports on what I say about him. "I should've left a note, myself," I mutter. "I don't guess you could go back to my house and tape a note to my door for me?"

Angela cocks her head. "I'm sorry, but that's not an action I'm authorized to perform."

I stalk back to the edge of the forest. I circle this lawn, too, but with more patience than I circled my own. I ignore the first trailhead sign I see, waiting for the tiny sign with a pair of white pants knotted below it, like a fat albino python.

***

I go down path after path, trying house after house, even doubling back to my own sometimes. They're all empty, or at least, all locked. Some doors have notes, with questions, maps, or directions, e.g., "I came from the western path. Will try next path clockwise." Angela says that I cannot enter houses that the host has deliberately locked, so I fetch a paper notebook and a couple of pencils and tape from my own house, to decorate strangers' doors with notes of my own.

I learn that I don't need sleep in Michael Fain's Afterlife. The sun sets, but I don't get tired. Instead, deep into the night, I find it harder to move, like I'm trying to walk through neck-deep water. It's spooky, especially on the treacherous forest paths. I have a flashlight in my bindle, but it's not a good one.

I also learn that I don't need showers, food, or water. My skin feels clean and I have no hunger or thirst. Experimentally, I sip one of my waters anyway. The action feels pleasant, but has no apparent lasting effects.

By dawn, I'm no longer sure how many houses I've been to however many times. Too late, I make a map of my own. I'm sure it's wrong. It gets easier to move again, but I'm not as fast as I was yesterday, as if walking all night has depleted my batteries. It takes longer to go down the paths, and I get frustrated. I yell a few things at Angela that I don't mean, but fortunately, she seems incapable of feeling offense.

Around mid-morning, my mind finally stops screaming Daniel's name. Instead, it cries it in a painful keening. Through it all, I wonder if the programming required to duplicate a mature human consciousness in an Afterlife is so very complex already, why they don't bother to program the grief out of you.

Maybe they do, in the good Afterlives.

***

Around late morning, I get a breakthrough: a pair of people sitting on a blanket on a lawn, chatting, the remains of a picnic between them.

I spot them from the forest path I've just exited. "Hey!"

They see me. One of them, a woman in a white dress, jumps up.

"Hey!" I sprint onto the lawn. Or try to. My movement is still frustratingly sluggish. "Hey! Are you people?"

The other person jumps up. She wears a dress that's blue—not white. My sense of urgency sharpens. "Wait! Don't—"

They run away from me.

"My name is Lehann Margrove," I shout, but they run

into the house and slam the door.

I finally make it there, too. I strike the door with my fist, which in Perfectia, doesn't hurt at all. "Listen to me! Please! I've been looking all over for you!" I grab the door-knob. To my shock, it turns. Because there are people inside? "Please—"

They shove themselves against the door to stop my entrance. Their eyes glitter like the backs of beetles.

"Please," I say, forcing myself to speak calmly. "I'm sorry. I just want to talk."

"Go away," says the woman in the white dress.

The woman in the blue dress frowns. She's clearly older than the other one, in her late forties or early fifties, and has a few streaks of silver in her dark brown hair. A couple of lines cup her mouth. How did she get away with being old in Michael Fain's Afterlife?

"I just want to talk," I repeat, as I let go of the knob.

Gently, the woman in the blue dress shuts the door.

I press my cheek against the doorjamb and speak into it. "I'm sorry. Let me start over. My name is Lehann. I'm seventy-nine—well, I was seventy-nine—and I'm from Buffalo. I have a husband and two cats, and a brother and three nieces and two grand-nephews. And all of our friends.

"Look. We can't chat or text anyone. We're stuck here. I'm just trying to..." His face swims into my vision. Nothing on earth—or anywhere else—will replace him, or make the obsessive thoughts stop. "We don't have anybody anymore. Not in here.

"We've got ninety days until we're gone for good, and unless we talk to each other, we've got to... to wait until that happens alone. I didn't sign up for that. Ninety days in purgatory, fine, but not that.

"So please. Talk to me. Have you met anyone else?"

Silence.

"Did you two come here together?"

Again, but muffled: "Go away."

I open my hand and place my palm on the door. The not-exactly-wood feels warm with the sun, but too smooth, like I'm touching glass. "I've got nowhere to go *to*. Everything I care about is..." I see Daniel's crooked front tooth. For fifty years, that tooth gave his smile that goofy charm.

I can't talk anymore.

Mumbling conversation hums within. Finally, the door cracks open. I straighten up, but the young, pretty woman says, "I'm sorry. I really just want to be left alone."

The door shuts again, and a deadbolt clicks.

So much for breakthroughs.

★★★

"You should take some time to enjoy your new home," Angela says. "Your own private Perfectia Mansion consists of over 40,000 square feet of pure, modern luxury, with features such as a private movie theater, a private bowling alley, and a 200-foot-long infinity pool."

I ignore her. The sun is setting, and unless the map I've constructed is completely off, we're approaching the front door of one of the last houses.

"Your new home also includes private tennis courts and a private climbing wall," Angela says.

I ring the doorbell and refuse to look at her. "What's even the point of tennis courts if there isn't anyone to play against?"

The door opens.

A white guy who looks like an action movie star—rugged, short hair, strong jawline, big shoulders—looks down at me and sighs. "Oh. You're new."

My hope struggles awake. I stick out my hand. "I am. My name's Lehann, and I just got here a couple of days ago."

"Lehann, huh?" He leans against the doorframe, and it rumples the shoulder of the white bathrobe he wears. "Well listen, buddy, I don't want to be rude or anything, but I'm pretty busy here. I got a good thing going and I'm focused on that, and I'm not interested in hanging out with anyone else."

I withdraw my hand. "I'm sorry?"

He waves. "Don't worry about it. You're new, so how could you know?" He backs up and starts to close the door.

"Wait!" I shove into the crack. "Please. What's your name? Where are all the others?"

"Buddy." He looks over a shoulder. Feminine laughter floats behind him. "Come on."

"Is someone else in there with you?"

Within the mansion, a woman—no, two women— stroll into the foyer, naked and holding hands. One is Korean, and the other is Filipina, maybe. They glance at me, then giggle conspiratorially.

Another naked woman, this one pale-skinned and red-haired, walks out from an archway to meet them. She smiles and holds up a silver tray. The first two women select a pair of shot glasses from among the cocktail offerings.

The man pushes himself in front of me, blocking my view and forcing me out. "Buddy," he says firmly, "your own AI can give you as many girls as you want. I'm not into sharing."

"That wasn't what I—"

"I got one week left, and I'm gonna make it count. Okay? You take care now." He shuts the door.

Angela touches my arm. Her fingers, like my own body, are too hard and too cold, nothing like the touch of a living human. "Shall we go home, Lehann?" she asks. "It's true that I can provide you with many partners for your personal enjoyment, each to your own specifications."

We have blinds in our bedroom. And when Daniel rolls over in bed, in the mornings, bright stripes of sun slide over his naked back.

I jerk my arm away and run back to the forest.

***

By nightfall, I have been to approximately twenty different houses, including my own, over multiple trips.

I think Michael Fain's Afterlife looks like this:

I shuffle east, now, toward the question mark. I'm moving more slowly than ever, so I have a lot of time to think about how stupid I am.

Why *had* I let them talk me into this awful place? I'd had everything I wanted. I'd had Daniel. But I let him go—I let fifty years of meaning and connection go—just to pay a goddamn hospital bill.

And now I've become a lurching zombie, my skin thirsting for his and my mind latched onto his name. And I'll remain such until my contract is over, and I can be deleted.

I should have just fucking died the first time.

My shuffling takes me to the end of the path. It opens onto yet another sprawling lawn, ghostly blue under moonlight too bright from a moon too large. But I don't care about the moon. I care about the mansion.

This one is lit up from within.

I shuffle to the door like my shoes are on fire.

When I ring the doorbell, a short young woman answers, and the sounds of a house full of people—talk, laughter, a TV on somewhere—float out into the artificial night.

"Oh!" she says. "Hello there! You've found us. Please, come in."

Do I ever.

2. The Last House

The woman sweeps her long hair away from her face, the better to see me. Her eyes are striking: gray and sharp. "I'm Kathrin. Welcome to my home." She ushers me inside. "Have you come a long way?"

"Yes," I say, but I'm too stunned by her house to elaborate. Kathrin's mansion is different from the others. It holds pops of color—a tangerine lamp, a teal accent wall, an Oriental carpet with an un-Oriental color palette. Kathrin herself wears blue jeans and a Pittsburgh Steelers sweatshirt. "How did you get colors?"

She makes a "follow me" motion with her upturned hand. "Your timing is perfect. We all just sat down to dinner, so everyone can help answer your questions."

Dinner? "How did you get food?"

Kathrin coaxes me past a TV room, where the screen plays a football game for no-one, and into one of her mansion's dining rooms. At the table, whose red placemats blaze like poppies in snow, sit about a dozen people. They serve themselves from white platters and bowls. I'm unsure what the fare is. Some of the foodstuff looks like rolls, or maybe potatoes. The meat might be sausages or hotdogs? Is the green stuff supposed to be broccoli?

"Everyone!" says Kathrin.

Heads look up. Nobody's over thirty, everyone has great skin, and everyone fits neatly into five different body types: average, slender, toned, fit, or muscular. For a moment I feel like I don't belong here, until I remind myself that, in Michael Fain's Afterlife, physical appearances mean nothing. They probably looked into their own mirrors after they arrived and felt as disappointed as I did.

Kathrin rests a hand on my shoulder, in a motherly sort of way, though I'm half a foot taller. "What's your name?" she asks.

I stare at her. Then at all those curious, friendly faces. "I'm Lehann. And I'm... I've been looking for you."

People grin. Several hold up champagne glasses. "Welcome to The Last House," someone says.

Kathrin pushes a full champagne flute into my hand. To be polite, I take a drink.

I'm shocked. It's the most delicious champagne I've ever tasted.

"Nice, isn't it?" says Kathrin, smiling. "We've happened upon a few surprises. The champagne is one. Mia, could you please move over...?"

They make a place for me. I sit and sample the food, which smells odd and tastes odder, and I listen to the soundtrack's string quartet. Nothing about this makes sense. I'm so rattled, I drop my roll-or-maybe-it's-a-potato before I can taste it. It disappears before it can hit the white carpet, which rattles me more.

The man seated to my right turns to me. He looks eerily like Captain America. "Now before you even ask a thing," he says, "let's take care of the FAQs. Mmkay?"

"Can I have another—" I start to ask, but everyone around the table pipes up.

"You don't need to eat or drink, but it feels good."

"You get food to appear in your kitchen by ordering groceries online. Well, it's not really online, but it's like, you know. A simulation of the internet."

"You can change the colors of things, but only things in your house that you own. You just have to ask your AI."

"And you can change how your body feels when you touch it, so you feel more like a mortal and less like a vampire."

"Javi, you have no idea how vampires feel."

"Sure I do," says a smiling man, who I assume is Javi. "They feel like the default flesh settings you have when you get here. Haven't you ever played '3D Vampire Battlefield

Five: The Reaping'?"

Kathrin clears her throat. "Let's not get sidetracked, Javi."

"Okay, okay."

"Anyone else?"

"You can talk to the programmers." This remark comes from a slender guy with a thick beard at the far end of the table. He hunches over and pokes his maybe-potato, and I get the impression that he was always the weird kid in school who sat in the back corner and drew disturbing pictures during class.

Captain America shakes his head. "That's not actually true," he says to me.

"Yes, it is," Weird Kid says sullenly. "If it isn't, then where do the notes go?"

"Never mind about that," says Kathrin firmly. She's seated herself opposite me. She pours herself a glass of champagne, and when she sets the bottle down, it remains full. "We're still running tests to settle that particular issue. Let's stick to what we know for certain."

The woman seated at Kathrin's right squints. With her light skin and thick eyebrows, she looks like my half-sister did when she was younger, except for the shaved head and intimidating muscles. She points over my shoulder. "Is that your AI?"

I turn. Angela still stands behind me, as naked and as blue-eyed as ever. I feel embarrassed, like a mom whose clueless toddler has pulled off its clothes at a grown-up dinner party. "I... uh..."

"You can make it go away. And when you want to call it up, you can change its default appearance," says Not My Half-Sister. She plucks, from thin air, a white rat, and she sets it on the table. "See? Mine's a rat."

The woman on her other side holds up a hand to block the rat from view. "Jesus, Marisa."

"What?"

"Marisa," warns Kathrin.

Marisa sighs and waves her hand over the rat. It disappears.

Captain America touches my elbow. "And you can change your clothes," he says. He himself wears a white tuxedo dinner jacket with black dress pants and a black bowtie. "Honestly, you just have to ask. Try it."

Everyone looks at me. Is my white tee-shirt really so bad? "Angela, can you make my shirt... uh... red?"

Angela cocks her head. "Why do you want that?"

"These Michael Pain-in-the-ass AIs can go fuck themselves," says Marisa, and I decide that I like her.

"Just tell it anything." Captain America slices a sausage into dainty bites. "They aren't very smart."

I look at Angela and clear my throat. "Because I said so."

Weird Kid rolls his eyes, but Angela smiles. "Okay!" she says, and the surface of my shirt ripples, flushing as red as the placemats.

For the first time, I can almost see an Afterlife's appeal.

"I suppose it's a start," says Captain America.

★★★

Much later, I sit outside on a deck lit with strings of party lights. A few of the others join me—Kathrin, Marisa, a man (from Brazil, I think?) whose name I don't know, and a shrimpy-looking white guy who doesn't say much. It's the equivalent of 2 a.m., and the grounds beyond the deck are rich with moonshadow. I wish it smelled like flowers and the night breeze out here, but of course, it doesn't smell like anything.

The Brazilian man produces a cigar, deftly slices one end with a cigar cutter, and somehow lights it with his index finger. Marisa catches me staring. "You can only burn certain items here," she says, "but you don't need any special tools to do it."

Kathrin sips more champagne. She's brought out the never-ending bottle and a tray of glasses that clean and dry themselves whenever they're empty. "Is there anything else you want to know, Lehann? If not, you can always ask us questions later. It's not like we're going anywhere."

My head swims with all the advice they've given me already. "Is this all written down somewhere? Like on a wiki on your simulated internet?"

The Brazilian man sucks on his cigar, coaxing the other end to glow, and pushes out a mouthful of smoke. The smoke is scentless, too. "Nope." He sits back in his Adirondack chair. "No wikis, no word processors, and no apps that'll save blocks of text. Pen and paper works, but Jeff's got a theory about that."

"Jeff?"

"Beardy guy," says the Brazilian. "Mumbles a lot. Looks like he was That Moody Kid in school, if you know what I mean." He blows a smoke ring. "Jeff believes that when you die—ha, sorry, when you *move on*—all your 'possessions' in Perfectia are erased too. So if you wrote down everything you learned in a notebook that you found in your house, in the hopes that future residents could read it, it wouldn't matter, because the notebook would disappear once you do. And the contents of whatever house you 'lived' in would be reset to the defaults for the next owner."

"Why does Jeff believe that?" I glance among them. "I thought you all said that nobody here has been in Perfectia for longer than six weeks, because Michael Fain is still doing the initial fill-up."

"We did," said Kathrin. "Because it's true."

I think, *That's an odd way to put that,* but I continue. "So if nobody here has... moved on yet, how do we know for sure that any documentation we make will disappear with its owner?"

"We don't know for sure," admits the Brazilian. "Jeff

says that's how some of the more cut-rate Afterlives in the Middle East operate, and considering how cut-rate this place is, that will probably apply here too. But that's another thing we're testing." He looks up at the too-large moon. "Lei has been here the longest. When she moves on, Jeff says, we'll have more data."

"Okay."

Kathrin sets down her glass. "Are you all right, Lehann? I know all this information is a little overwhelming."

I look at the moon, too, and then, the stars. The night sky is a senseless scatterplot of light, with no constellations I recognize. They said it changes every night. According to Michael Fain, the heavens should be the product of a randomization algorithm and nothing more. "I'm okay," I say, although I'm not. "You said... you said there were only thirteen of us in this house. Including me."

"Correct."

"And that Perfectia is still filling up."

"Correct."

"What about the others?"

Marisa and the shrimpy guy share a glance.

"Others?" asks Kathrin, leaning forward.

"I saw three other people, in other houses. Two women somewhere. And a man, in the house before this one, over there." I point west.

"Oh, him," says Kathrin disdainfully.

"He said he had a week left. So technically, he's been here the longest."

"Maybe he has." The Brazilian blows another smoke ring. It's too symmetrical and fades too uniformly at the edges. "He's probably a holdout. There are a few of them, out there."

"Holdouts?"

The Brazilian shrugs. "I think it's better to live together in one big house, and obviously so does everyone else here, but not everybody sees it that way. And hey, you can do whatever you want in an Afterlife. That's the whole point."

I cross my legs. I haven't been flexible enough to do this in decades, but here, the gesture is effortless. "So Perfectia might have all of its twenty-five residents by now, and we just don't know it."

The Brazilian shrugs again. "That's a possibility. But that map you showed us only has twenty houses."

"I'm sure parts of it are wrong. Besides, didn't you say that a whole bunch of you came to Kathrin's house from the east?"

The Brazilian taps his cigar to knock the ash loose, but only out of habit. Cigars don't ash in Perfectia. "We did. But I'm sure that many of the empty houses on those side paths on your map are decoys. Think about it logically: if you owned an entire Afterlife and were trying to keep two dozen people apart within the confines of the 'one hour of travel at most' law, what would the best physical arrangement of those people be?" He doesn't wait for me to answer. "A ring. With each node being one hour of travel from the next. This way, when someone is erased and their 'node' is unoccupied, the houses on either side still connect to at least one other house, and the proximity law isn't—"

Kathrin shoots him a warning look. I don't have the mental resilience for this analysis right now, either. And it doesn't matter how the houses here are arranged, because the end result is the same: isolated, terrified people struggling to find each other.

Kathrin stands. "It's getting late," she says to me. "We don't need sleep, of course, but we've found that if you lie quietly on a bed in the dark for about two hours every night, you don't suffer the movement-speed penalty for the next twenty-two hours. So it's close to sleep, functionally speaking." She yawns, though this seems a pointless affectation. "I like to rise early, so I'm done for tonight, I'm afraid." Kathrin sets her empty champagne flute on the tray, and it turns to pristine crystal before my eyes. "It was wonderful to meet you, Lehann. I look forward to having you stay here. If that's what you want, of course."

Where else was there? My mausoleum of an empty house, without any other voices but the weeping one inside my head? "Of course."

Kathrin heads toward the house. One last question pops into my mind. "Kathrin?"

"Yes?"

"Earlier in the evening, someone called this place The Last House. How come?"

Marisa and the shrimpy guy look at each other again.

Kathrin smiles. Under the eerie mix of moonlight and party lights, the expression seems forced. "Because it's the last house we'll ever live in, of course."

The Brazilian laughs, sadly. I get the feeling that even though Perfectia is new, it's an old, old joke.

***

At The Last House, I, along with everyone else, do things that are supposed to be luxurious and fulfilling.

We lay by the pools in the sun. We jump from the rooftops and float gently to the ground. We eat as much as we want. But my inaccurate body does not sweat or tan, and the experience of being in water is wrong, like floating in air. Most food tastes waxy, and I don't get hungry and I don't get full.

While I try hard to feel something good, the Brazilian man, whose name (I finally learn) is João, sits under the cartoon-perfect palm trees with charcoal and a sketch pad. The landscapes he draws are Hephaestian, full of thick, fiery lines, too raw for this bright and toothless world.

"I thought that anything we make here will disappear," I say.

João just shrugs. He keeps on drawing.

At night, I pretend to "sleep" for my allotted two
hours, but I don't want to be alone with Daniel's name in
the dark. To better hear the anchoring sounds of humanity
in the night—the whispers, the muffled sobs, the quick gasps
of pleasure—I keep my door open a crack. I listen closely for
some sign of feeling in this soulless place, while the
immortal soundtrack plays its version of soothing white
noise, and I wonder if the others have crept to each other's
beds, like children bunking together to brave a storm.

★★★

"I want to tell you something."

Marisa, myself, and the shrimpy-looking quiet guy,
whose name is Fields, sit on the edge of a stone fountain.
The trees around the fountain blaze with fall color, because
Marisa discovered that leaf color was a setting we could
change, even though this isn't her house.

I trail my hand in the fountain's basin. The water feels
the same as the water in the swimming pools: insubstantial,
like mist. "Sure. What is it?"

She hesitates. I look up. She sits with her rat AI in her
lap, stroking its head, as if she's in need of comfort. Maybe
she is. "Do you remember how you got here? To Kathrin's
house, I mean."

I make a gesture with my hand, which I've told my
own AI means, 'please appear'. My Angela, which I've recast
as a morpho butterfly, begins its randomly-generated flight
around us. I still don't like talking to the thing, but watching
it can be nice. "Yeah. I took the path to the west."

Marisa glances at Fields, who says nothing. "There's
another way."

"The path to the east? Doesn't that one go to more
houses, too?"

"I'm not talking about that path."

I raise my eyebrows.

Marisa scoots closer to me. Her muscular thigh

touches mine, and I note, with visceral pleasure, that she's changed the settings on her body. Her flesh feels human and warm. "There's another way out," she says quietly. "Well, not out, exactly. There is no way out of Perfectia. But it does lead to... something different."

I lean toward her.

"To him," she whispers.

Thoughts of Daniel seize me. But that isn't what she means—how could it be? Besides, there's one other 'him' here whose name we don't need to say.

"You can't see his path," she continues, in a near-whisper. "It's invisible. There's a sign on the eastern end of the lawn for it, but the sign points straight up. And it isn't really a path. It's a glass slide with no walls. You have to ask your AI to make your hands and feet sticky, so you can climb it." She presses her lips together. "They have all these shitty tricks to discourage us from taking it."

It sounds like a story a child would make up. But her shoulders are tight, her head is down, and she isn't kidding. "How do you know all this?"

"We've taken that path anyway."

Fields speaks. "Other people, too."

My eyebrows go higher.

"Me and Fifi—" Fields' face betrays no reaction at Marisa's nickname for him— "and João and Mia. We went up and we took it to the end, but we didn't step off. We just saw."

I think my eyebrows are under my hair. "You saw...?"

Marisa picks up her AI and cradles it to her chest. "It's a train station."

I don't need to ask where it leads.

Marisa rubs her cheek against the rat's snowy fur. "Kathrin isn't telling any of the newer people, and... I just thought you should know."

***

On and off, I think about what Marisa said. I don't know what to do with the information. I'm still trying, desperately, to feel something good, and thinking about that sign with the straight-up arrow makes me feel anything but.

We drink wine. Play board games. Watch movies. With each passing night, the mansion's bedroom doors crack wider. When I go to my chosen room to rest, now, everyone's doors hang partway open, like morning glories that anticipate the sun.

One night, good-looking Captain America, whose real name is Charlie, comes to my room. He stands in the half-open doorway and taps the doorframe, and I'm so surprised, I bid him to come in.

He closes the door and sits on my bed with his legs folded. "Did you have someone?" he asks.

Daniel's softness echoes painfully on my arms. "Yes."

Charlie nods. He looks away. "Mine was named Bryce."

I feel bad for him. So we talk about Bryce.

Then, because my own mind can't take crying in the dark anymore, we talk about Daniel.

It's not good. I talk and talk and can't shut up. I feel like a wound, raw and open to the unkind air. And I feel lonely and I hate myself, because fussy Charlie isn't the sort of person I'd ordinarily befriend. But in this moment, he's all I've got.

I can't keep going on like this. So the next night, I go to Marisa's room. "Come in," she says when I knock. "Oh, hi, Lehann."

Marisa wears a set of pajamas with snowflakes on them. Next to her lies Fields, wearing his regular clothes, minus shoes. I suddenly feel like an idiot. How can I talk about a lost love to a pair of people obviously falling in love themselves? "Never mind. I don't want to interrupt."

"No no, it's fine," says Marisa. "Come in." She and

Fields scoot over on the giant bed.

Feeling weird, I lie down next to Marisa. This isn't right. I listen to the soundtrack's white-noise rainfall, unable to speak.

Ashamed, I try other people. I visit Haylie, a sweet woman whose powerful instinct for mothering makes me feel both special and embarrassed—too embarrassed to really talk. Twice I stay with Javi, whose room is right next to Marisa's. He's a good-natured man whose colorful stories make me smile, but what I need is to talk myself, not just listen, and Javi's charm is a distraction. I consider going to Marlena or Jagdesh, who arrived at The Last House after I did, but their bewilderment at this place is too fresh. And I want to go to João, but he seems too cool for me. Isn't that funny? I'm dead, and I literally have nothing left to lose, but the thought of him indifferently shrugging in my direction makes me shy.

So I go back to Marisa and Fields. She doesn't mind, and he doesn't judge. After an hour without speaking, I gather my bravery and tell them about Daniel, at last.

They're both good listeners.

***

"I'm only thirty-four, actually," says Marisa, the next night. "Michael Drain has fucked me over even more than the rest of you. One of his shitty trams at the San Jose campus derailed, and I happened to be walking by at the time."

It's an ugly way to die. "Jesus."

Marisa sighs at her moonlit ceiling. "At least, I assume that's what happened, because one second I'm walking to work, and the next second, I'm waking up here. I'd bet you a million dollars that the Billionaire Bastard's lawyers took one look at my mangled, brain-dead body lying in a hospital somewhere and sold Mom on the Perfectia deal to smooth everything over. Not that I'd call spending the last ninety days of my existence in this reheated excuse for a Disneyland resort a 'smoothening over'.

"But whatever. Mom's never given a shit about what I wanted anyway. I bet if I *had* wanted an Afterlife, she would've refused to upload me into it, just to spite me."

Fields speaks. "What about Shuruq Alshshams?"

I ask, "What's Shuruq Alshshams?"

Marisa ignores me. "Shuruq Alshshams doesn't count," she tells Fields. "And anyway, it doesn't matter. I'm dead."

I let it go. So does Fields. "What about you, Fields?" I ask. "What's your story?"

Fields says, "Cowboy."

I lift up my head. "You were a cowboy?"

"Yup."

"I, uh... didn't think Fain Enterprises employed cowboys."

Fields does not explain.

I look out the window. Kathrin has altered the windows in her house to permit actual views outside. The forever-full moon hangs within sight, nestled among the unpredictable stars.

"This is nice," says Marisa. "Just talking."

"Yeah."

We watch the night together. The soundtrack plays the rustles of an invisible rainfall.

"It's too bad other people are so fucking hard to find here," Marisa says. "Do you know how long I wandered in the woods before finding Kathrin's house? It was almost a week. I got stung by those hornets, and, I dunno, I just lost it and sprinted off into the trees. And I couldn't find any of the paths. And if my AI hadn't turned me around, I'd still be out there, probably getting crazier and crazier."

Fields touches her on the shoulder.

Marisa rolls over and shoves her face into his collarbone.

Bitter feelings churn within me. What's even the point of this place? How can Michael Fain honestly believe that a 40,000-square foot mansion is an acceptable replacement for human connection?

I slide out of bed. Somebody has to answer for this. There are laws, and they are technically being obeyed, but the presence of laws is not the same thing as the presence of justice. And there is no justice in a world into which everyone comes confused, isolated, and frightened—and which tries to keep everyone that way.

Field looks at me questioningly. I shake my head. "I'll see you in the morning."

"Where are you going?" Marisa mumbles into Fields' chest, but I've already left them.

I go to the fifth floor.

There is only one occupied bedroom on this floor. I know where it is, though I have never been there. It's well known that the occupant likes her privacy.

I knock.

"Come in."

Kathrin's room is small, with two dormer windows and a slanted ceiling. Spots of white glow on the walls, like sophisticated glow-in-the-dark star stickers. I get the eerie impression that I'm looking at a copy of her childhood bedroom. How hard we search for comfort in this place. "Oh. Hello, Lehann. Do you need something?"

Kathrin's small space has a small bed. I dread being invited to lie so close to her, so I preemptively seat myself at the desk. It's cramped, sized for a child. "I want to talk to you."

"Sure. What's going on?"

Where is the monster who is responsible for all this?

"I... wanted to ask you something." I struggle to keep it light. "There's a sign on the eastern edge of your lawn, the kind that indicates a pathway between houses. But the sign points straight up...?"

Kathrin pauses. She rolls over in bed to face me. "And?"

"And I'd like to take it."

Kathrin is quiet again, for longer. The dim shape of her hand moves to rest near her face, and her fingers drum atop the mattress. "Would you."

"Yes."

"Do you know where it goes?"

"I have my suspicions."

"And?"

"And I'd like to hear yours."

"Why?"

"It's your yard, isn't it?"

"What does that have to do with it?"

"Seems you're the one who's most likely to know the truth."

"Have you heard what you assume are lies?"

"Why won't you answer my question?" I stand up. "What's on the other end of that path, Kathrin?"

Her fingers still. She tucks her chin. "Please sit down."

I don't. I wait.

Kathrin says, "I was the second person here. Did you know that? The second person to ever arrive in Perfectia. There was only one other house, and the owner was too terrified to open the door."

"Lei?" I ask. Kathrin had said, on the first night I'd arrived at The Last House, that Lei had been here the longest.

"Hush," says Kathrin. "Don't worry about all of that. Just listen.

"The next person to arrive in Perfectia wouldn't come to his door at all when I knocked. In fact, two entire days passed before anyone spoke to me face-to-face. It was a horrible time."

"I can imagine."

"Can you?" Kathrin sits up. "When Eliza found me, I could have cried. We must've talked for the entire afternoon. I left behind three children and three grandchildren. And my sisters. And my nieces." She chokes up. "I had a family. And then I had nothing. Of course, you've left people behind, too, but a whole new family was waiting for you once you came this far."

The comment feels like a jab. I like Marisa and Fields a lot, but it's a stretch to call them family.

"More people came," Kathrin says. "And everyone was just as frightened as I had been. He's placed us so very far apart from one another, and he's placed so many obstacles in our way to finding each other, it's inhumane. I don't care if it's technically legal. It's ethically unacceptable.

"And some of us decided that we couldn't let things go on like this. The only way he'll know that we don't accept this arrangement is if we tell him. So we decided to do just that."

These are my feelings exactly, and this is exactly what I want to do, myself. But Kathrin stops her story. I fold my arms. "And?"

Kathrin looks down. Then up again. "And we tried."

"And?"

She crosses her legs and leans back against the wall. "Lei and João stayed behind. The rest of us started on that path you're asking about. We got a bit turned around up there, and somehow came back down to the house that's northeast of mine, but we tried again and got to the end of the path eventually. And the purpose of the train station was obvious, but instead of boarding the train, Tiernan insisted that we go through the gate and into the meadow."

"Who's Tiernan?"

Kathrin ignores me. "He led us through that meadow and into the mountains. We trusted him too much, and it was days before I confronted him about not taking the train.

I should have done so back at the station, because it wasn't until we reached the mountains that he came out with the truth: he didn't want to go talk to Michael Fain at all. He wanted us all to start over." Kathrin forces out a laugh. "Can you believe that? Tiernan actually thought we could out-smart Michael Fain.

"He said there must be a place in the wilderness where the programmers had... I don't know... some kind of secret Shangri-La waiting for us. Of course Afterlife programmers are the same as any others, always hiding puzzles and secrets into their code for their own amusement, but believing in something that miraculous is just downright desperation.

"And moreover? It was wrong. After another week, the footpath we were on disappeared. Tiernan insisted that he knew where he was going, and Olivia insisted that we would find an Extra Time Well any day now, and we shouldn't worry about how long we'd been traveling. But Tiernan had no clue where he was going. And we didn't find a Well.

"A few days after that, I'd had enough. I turned around by myself and aimed for home, and even though I lost a few extra days more, I made it. But I must've been the only one, because nobody else has ever come back.

"And if they aren't back a week from now, some of them never will be. Eliza only has nine days left."

Kathrin stops again. The wounded silence is aggressive, daring me to ask. But I've come this far. We've all come this far. "You said your friend Eliza came two days after you did."

Kathrin nods.

"So if Eliza—wherever she is—has nine days left, it means you must only have a week."

Kathrin doesn't reply.

Anger rises inside of me. "You lied. You and Lei don't have six weeks on the rest of us. You have months."

Her mouth tightens. I'm being cruel. Who cares if

frightened Kathrin needs to lie to herself about the looming truth of her erasure? Except— "What happens to your house, then? What happens to everyone who's staying here, inside of it? Do they know about this?"

"Jeff thinks that the houses are re-set only when nobody else is within the property."

"I thought you didn't believe in what Jeff thinks."

Kathrin stands. Her words are careful, shivering with restrained anger. "If you think that I am failing in my stewardship of this community, Mr. Margrove, you are welcome to lead another band of lunatics into the mountains."

"I never said—"

Kathrin raises her voice. "You are right. I have seven days left. And I am not about to spend them alone, again, wandering this artificial universe without what little human connection I have cobbled together."

"But you don't have to," I say. "We could all try boarding the train this time."

Kathrin hisses. "We're staying here."

"And if the others don't want to?"

"Then they would have come to me with this nonsense far earlier than you have." Kathrin points to the door. "This is the time of night that I reserve for my two hours of quiet rest. Since you've come into my bedroom, my night has been neither quiet nor restful. It is time for you to leave."

Coincidentally, I agree.

I exit Kathrin's room. I, too, still need another hour's rest for the night, and I shouldn't skimp on it.

I have an invisible path to climb tomorrow.

3. Perfectia Station

Marisa is in. So is Fields.

I grab my old bedsheet bindle, still full of stupid shit I don't need (but might?), and we're off. It's another plastic-perfect day. The fake trees don't rustle in the steady breeze, and the nonexistent squirrels don't chatter. No dew sparkles on the grass. The soundtrack is bright, peppy woodwinds.

We reach the sign for the invisible path.

And we begin.

★★★

The worst part about the climb is the wind. It hits me in the face, so hard I can't breathe, then changes direction and blasts me from the side. Sometimes it knifes down under my collar and blows up my pant legs simultaneously. It's surprising how vicious mere air can be once you throw physics out the window.

The second worst part is the irregularity of the invisible path itself. The slope stays roughly the same, about 60°, but its direction is not linear. The path bends right or left at sharp, 90° angles, and for several handholds I have to scuttle to the side instead of climb. If I forget to check the air above me, or to the side, I might just grab at nothing.

And fall.

We move single-file through blasting wind and white-out fog, our feet bare, rolling our soles and palms just so on the path's glassy surface so they'll stick and let go, stick and let go. I feel strangely naked without my supplies—Fields offered to carry them—and wish I had my bindle on my back so it could block the wind, at least.

Marisa, who is ahead of me, shouts something, but the wind is too fierce for me to hear. She pulls herself up and disappears.

I freeze. Has she fallen? I look down, to see if I can spot her plummeting, but the fog is too thick. Instead, the mist parts in a strategic spot directly below me, and I can see all the way down—an impossibly great distance, thanks to what I'm sure is a deliberate space-time trick—to the rolling fields beneath the path. The fields are enticing, with warm sun, sweet flowers, and fluffy sheep. I know the sheep are fluffy because I've touched them. This is the fourth time I've tried to climb this path because Marisa and I keep getting blown off. At least we know by now that the walk from the fields and through the woods back to Kathrin's yard is short?

In any event, it looks like Marisa will have to climb the path a fifth time. It's early afternoon by now, probably. We agreed that we'd wait for each other at the end—

My reaching hand hits air. The path bends away from me. I climb for a few more feet, and it crests an invisible horizon and flattens.

I crawl forward like a lizard, not daring to stand up. Bare feet with red-polished toenails stand in my way. "Hey!" says Marisa. She crouches in front of me and smiles. "We finally made it."

"We made it?"

She straightens. "You can stand up now. There's no more wind to knock you off."

She's right. Carefully, I stand despite wobbling knees. White-out fog still surrounds us. I look down, and even though the path itself remains invisible, I see a flat plane of — "Is that... glitter?"

"Yup. Fields did it."

Fields, who made it up on the very first try, shrugs.

Marisa gestures for her Angela, then orders the rat to return her shoes and socks. "The glitter's so we can see where the rest of the path is. Otherwise, we might acciden-tally take one of those—" she gestures to a stray fan of sparkles, marking the junction of another invisible path with our own— "and be lost up here forever."

I call for my own shoes and socks. "Fields, where did

you get a vial of glitter?"

"Come on, Lehann." Marisa laces up her shoes. "His Angela gave it to him. Not everything is a prohibited item."

I put on my own shoes.

We follow the glitter.

Gradually, the fogs lifts. The road becomes solid dirt. Our way back remains masked in fog, but a pine forest looms at our sides. The air smells like a drugstore's idea of a pine-scented candle, and I find the cheapness oddly re-assuring.

Ahead of us soar mountains. And I mean soar. They're harsh things, rocky and dusted with snow, and they appear concave in their extreme height, like the inner side of a breaking wave. I cannot imagine anyone climbing them. If Perfectia has a border, they're it.

The pine trees fall away. Our path ends in a cul-de-sac by a folksy-looking building, painted white with brown beams crisscrossing the outside. A low, freestanding sign waits nestled in mulch and zinnias: PERFECTIA STATION.

"This is it," says Marisa. "This is where we stopped last time."

We hesitate. But no hornets fly out at us, and the sky stays clear, and the soundtrack remains neutral.

So we go inside.

The double doors open directly into a lobby, which has wooden benches and a ticket booth. A pricing sign above the ticket booth reads:

One-Way: $Are you sure?
Round-Trip: $Unlikely

A handsome analog clock, hung above the exit door on the opposite side of the lobby, shows the time: 2:14 p.m.

"What are you doing here?" a man demands.

I start. A mustachioed gentleman in an old-timey suit

with a bowler hat stands before us, looking outraged.

"Uh... I'm sorry?" says Marisa.

The ends of his mustache quiver. "I should very much hope you are."

His mustache is gray. He's too old to be a citizen. "I don't think he's real, Marisa."

A handful of other fake people in the lobby, all wearing old-timey clothes and frowning, stop whatever they're doing to scowl at us most disapprovingly. I think: *Michael Fain* would *make all of them white.*

"Right," says Marisa to the bowler-hatted man. She grabs my arm, and Fields', and tugs us toward the wall. "Excuse us. We need to go buy our tickets."

But the ticket booth is empty. A sign taped on the inside of the glass reads, "Back in five minutes."

I look around. The old-timey people frown at us above their old-timey print newspapers, and for the first time, I wonder what the hell the three of us are doing out here, with my knotted-up bedsheet luggage and bad ideas.

I really should have waited to do this. I should have taken the time to calm down, tell everyone at The Last House the truth, and recruit more people to follow us. But what if it were like Kathrin had said? What if everyone already knew the truth about both her age and the existence of the invisible path, but were too afraid to take action?

And anyway, maybe Jeff is right. Maybe once Kathrin is deleted, everyone in her house will be unaffected and remain perfectly fine. Maybe I seriously overreacted this morning and never should have climbed here, and maybe Kathrin is right, too, and the smartest use of my remaining time would be to cling hungrily to what few quasi-friends I've made.

Because honestly, what's the likelihood of finding deeper fulfillment from the choice I made this morning? Probably none. My fantasy is that Michael Fain will receive us unto his bosom, listen with thoughtfully tented fingers, and finally announce, 'I'm so sorry you're too far away from each other and it's made you sad, so sure, I'll change everything.' But come on. Perfectia is his show. And in Michael Fain's universe, Michael Fain will do as he goddamn well pleases.

And we'll be more alone than ever.

I fidget and look to the exit. The time on the analog clock remains the same, but I'm sure at least ten minutes have passed. "I think the sign on the ticket booth and the clock are more tricks," I say.

"I think you're right," Marisa says.

We all go out the exit.

The door opens onto a platform. Alongside the platform waits a gleaming, gorgeous train, its many colors candy-bright, its locomotive hissing steam. The engineer in the locomotive wears a blue striped hat. She sees us standing on the platform and, like the dowdy people in the lobby, frowns.

A conductor rushes up to us. He looks like a boy of sixteen, except, because this is Michael Fain's Afterlife, he's completely free of pimples. "I'm sorry, sir," he says to Fields. "Only passengers are allowed on the platform."

"We are passengers," says Marisa.

The engineer sticks her head out of the window. "What's all this then?"

"I'll need to see your tickets, ma'am and sirs," says the boy-conductor.

"Nobody's at the ticket window," says Marisa. "Can't we just get tickets from you?" She gestures for her AI, and it appears in her hand. "Angela. How do we buy tickets for the train?"

Marisa, her AI, and the conductor get into a weird, circular argument. Fields stands there in his usual lump-like way, but I look around the platform and think. There are laws. There is a way around this trick, whether we know how to get our AIs to admit the solution or not.

That's when I notice the gate.

On the other side of the platform, a metal handrail descends to the unseen ground, accompanying unseen stairs. They lead into an alpine meadow, where an enticingly serpentine path winds up to a wooden fence with a wooden gate.

The gate hangs open.

Something about it pulls me. I walk to the top of the stairs and look. The path continues beyond the gate, veering off into the trees, toward the mountains.

Kathrin wasn't lying about this part.

I put my hand on the handrail. I forget why I wanted to ride the train. Kathrin's team must have been onto something when they went through that gate, because I get the spooky feeling that—

"Lehann!"

I turn. Marisa waves me over. "What is it? What's wrong?"

A handsome chestnut horse stands on the platform. Fields pats its nose and makes a gesture, and the horse disappears. "Fields got his AI to tell him the cost of the tickets," says Marisa. She and Fields exchange a glance. "It's ten days."

"Ten days?"

Marisa hesitates. "Of time."

I pull my head back. "Oh."

Marisa jams her hands into her pockets. "I've only got thirty-five left as it is."

Fields gestures at Marisa and holds up two fingers. Thirty-seven days left for him.

"Maybe we could get there by walking along the tracks," says Marisa, but she doesn't sound convinced.

I close my eyes. For myself, in current terms—with

sixty-seven days left—ten days is 15% of my remaining eternity.

On the other hand, in a place where the days are like this, what real loss is ten of them?

"Fuck it," says Marisa. "Michael Faint thinks he can intimidate me?" She waves at the conductor, like calling over a waiter. "Hi. Excuse me. I'll take a ticket, please."

Fields hold up two fingers.

I say, "Make it three."

★★★

The locomotive, for all its toy-like appearance, is bullet-train fast. Within a minute of us boarding, the trees outside blur into a smear of green, then black.

We've plunged into a tunnel. We're going under the mountains.

"We fucked up," says Marisa.

I don't know why I'm looking out the window. There's nothing but black—not even the simulation of my own inaccurate reflection. "Hmm?"

The seats are arranged in pairs that face each other, and Marisa and Fields sit opposite me. "We should've left a note," says Marisa. "Before we left Kathrin's house. She wouldn't've wanted anyone to find it, maybe, but we could've slid it under Javi's door. Or Fiyohna's. Maybe they would've come after us, or at least told other people where we'd gone."

I let my head fall against the window. "We should've done a lot of things differently."

"It's okay," Marisa says. "We'll figure it out."

"I guess we'll have to." I sigh. "I never was any good at quest games. That was Daniel's department." And god-damnit—now I had to go and say his name, and think of his face, and how I don't have him anymore.

Marisa sighs too. "Maybe Javi will wonder where we went and come looking anyway."

"Somehow, I wouldn't bet on it." I stand. "I'm gonna go look around."

The train only has two passenger cars. We're in the last one. I exit the car from the front and cross the jouncing space between, even though I don't know what it is I'm looking for.

The other car is empty, but otherwise exactly like our own. I walk to the front and take a seat, pondering the blackness outside and how poorly equipped I am for this endeavor, bindle of crap and new-found friends notwithstanding.

The bit of solitude is welcome. And, now that I think of it, Marisa and Fields probably appreciate the privacy. Despite Marisa swearing that my frequent presence is fine, I can't fully believe that, because I never see a physical side to their relationship—there's no kissing, no hand-holding, hardly any touching. Whatever touch they do exchange is chaste, or weirdly tender. They must be shy in front of others.

I think of Daniel. Him slipping a hand into the back pocket of my jeans at the supermarket, laughing, saying, "What's the fun in being an old man if you can't be a dirty old man?"

Daniel.

His shoulders in my arms.

I stand. I'd better not sit in solitude after all.

I turn and walk up the aisle. But I must've been in deep thought when I came through here the first time, because now I notice another passenger.

A woman in her forties or fifties sits by a window, reading a paper book. Her silver-streaked brown hair is pulled back into a thick braid that rests over one shoulder. She nudges a pair of glasses up onto her nose. To my even greater surprise, I recognize her—this is the same woman that I saw at that house with the picnic on the lawn, the older woman who was with the younger one in the white dress.

She doesn't react to me. I can't tell if this older woman is real or not. If she is, what is she doing here? "Hello."

She looks up with a start. "You can see me." She sounds horrified.

"Er... yes. Am I not supposed to?"

She claps her book shut, stands, and pushes her way to the aisle. "Clumsy," she mutters. "Excuse me."

"Wait. I'm sorry. I didn't mean to interrupt your reading. I'll just go back to my car...?"

She stops and turns to face me. "You shouldn't be here," she says. "Can't you people notice anything? Everything you want is right there, right in your faces, but no. You just have to board the train. You just have to make everything as difficult as possible for yourselves."

She's real. "I'm sorry, but who are you?"

She throws up her hands. Her book has disappeared. "Go back to your car. Press the call button. When the conductor comes, tell him you changed your mind, and as long as you stay on the train when it stops, he'll refund your ticket when you return to the station."

"That's a good tip," I say, with no intention whatsoever of following it. "Thank you."

"You're welcome." She turns again and exits the car from the front. But she shouldn't be able to use that door. That's where the coal bin behind the locomotive should be.

I go after her. When I open the door and step outside, I, too, do not stand in front of the coal bin. Instead, I'm in front of another passenger car—a programming glitch?—whose door is locked.

I stand between the cars for a moment. I don't know whether to be frustrated or intrigued. But the uneven jouncing between them isn't helping me make up my mind, so I go back inside, back to Marisa and Fields.

"Does the other car have a different soundtrack?" Marisa asks. "Please say yes."

I wish she hadn't said anything. I realize that we're listening to a muzak version of "Chattanooga Choo Choo."

***

We emerge from the tunnel's blackness to a slap of sun. Blurs of landscape begin to resolve as the train undergoes its long, slow braking.

An unseen announcer says, "You are now entering The Wilderness."

The train stops. We hesitate, uncertain. It doesn't look particularly wild outside. Behind us stands a smudge of purple-blue—either the soaring mountains are programmed to look much different on the other side, or we've come a long, long way. In front of us waits another train platform and a train station, twins of the ones we disembarked from, and around us rooftops of other buildings poke above the trees.

The trunks of the trees are not crayon-brown, but gray: natural gray.

"Look!" I say, but Marisa and Fields, with my bedsheet in tow, are already walking back to the exit.

Marisa disembarks. When her feet hit the platform, she yelps and pulls her arms to her chest. Fields leaps after her, but as soon as his own feet hit the platform, he jumps, as if stung.

I linger at the top of the stairs, alert.

Marisa sucks in deep breaths. Something about her face looks different. And not expression-wise: in the bone structure itself. "Angela, what is this?"

Her rat AI appears on her shoulder. "You've made the trip to The Wilderness!" it says. "Reality behaves differently here, so watch out!"

"No shit," Marisa gasps. "This isn't right. Jesus, Fifi, this isn't right."

I descend the steps and half-crouch on the bottom one, so I can touch my white-sneakered toe to the platform. Nothing happens. I shrug and step off all the way.

Then I wake up.

I'm not in an Afterlife anymore. I'm flesh and blood again, gasping, my pulse throbbing in my palms, the fresh wind pushing against my face, traces of water and earth and pollen creeping up into the tunnels of my sinuses. I can feel the cracks between my teeth with my tongue, the solidity of my limbs.

I crouch and touch the platform. It's concrete. Real, rough concrete, warm against my fingers.

"Jesus Christ," I say, and my words fall upon a thundering kind of silence. Except for my pulse, the inside of my skull is still.

The soundtrack is gone.

The train behind us is still shiny-new and candy-bright. "Where are we?" Marisa demands again.

The boy-conductor pokes his head out of the car, having materialized from nowhere, and tips his hat at us. "You folks have a good day. I hope to see you again real soon."

The engineer toots a jolly whistle, the smokestack puffs, and the train choo-choos on, down the track and around a forested bend.

"You're in The Wilderness!" Marisa's AI repeats. "Can I help you find something?"

"Yes," I say. I want answers, in addition to what we're seeking, but asking questions about this place would only be a distraction from why we're really here. "Tell us where to find Michael Fain's house."

***

There are laws. Michael Fain's house has to be close.

And it is—a short walk across the platform, through the train station, down the dirt road to the right, and just along the edge of a sudden, fantastic lake. The lake is heart-breakingly beautiful, with a sandy shore that the wavelets have molded into ripples. Now and then, a fish jumps; sometimes, a raptor on the hunt swoops down to meet one. Bejeweled dragonflies dart closer to home, pausing to hover in front of my eyes, then slip away from my outstretched fingers.

I have ragged cuticles.

"This can't be real," says Marisa. "I mean it feels real, but it can't be. Our AIs are still here."

"Of course this isn't real," I say. "What did you think that tunnel was, a portal back to earth?" My own words sting. On a childish level, that's what I'd hoped it was, too.

We stop walking in front of Michael Fain's house. In actuality, it isn't one house, but a whole compound of buildings ringing the lake: boat houses and guest houses and gazebos, and private canals and foot bridges, and all the other luxuriana back at our own mansions, only on a lakeshore. And two orders of magnitude larger.

"This isn't right," says Marisa.

Michael Fain's front doors are a pair of towering bronze monstrosities at the top of a flight of marble steps. "Looks about right to me," I say.

"No, no. I mean that it's taken us way more than an hour to get here. Doesn't it have to take no longer than an hour?"

"Probably would," says Fields, "if you knew all the tricks to start with."

I'm sure he's right. If we'd known the exact shape of the invisible path through the sky, if we'd found some way to disable the wind and climb it in one go at a sprint, if we had run through the train station without any resistance, hopped on the train, and dashed straight to Michael Fain's double doors—probably, like power gamers running through a memorized course, it would take us fifty-nine minutes and fifty-five seconds. There are laws, after all.

And I can only imagine what kind of lawyers are on Michael Fain's payroll.

Marisa squints at the doors. "I guess we just knock."

"I guess," I say, and I go up to the doors and knock.

Nothing.

I find what I think is the doorbell, an ivory-looking rosette couched in an elaborate platinum setting. It's gaudy as hell. I always felt like the Michael Fain aesthetic was over-blown art deco meets baroque bullshit, like what you'd get if a Versace home décor catalog threw up inside of King's College Chapel.

I ring the bell. No change. "I can't believe that nobody is home," says Marisa. "He's got two of his people here already, right? It's him and one of his ex-wives, or something, and there's that advisor guy?"

"Pretty big compound," points out Fields.

"It is," I agree. "And anyway, even if they can hear the doorbell, there's no law that says they have to answer." I test a handle, not expecting much.

The door swings right open.

4. The Wilderness

We creep through great and terrible hallways as the day wanes. The opulence on display is stunning, all the more so because this part of Perfectia is so real. Every one of the throw pillows I touch feels like real silk; every candle in every candelabrum feels like genuine wax. Marisa lights one with a finger, the way João lights cigars, and the wax melts at the base of the wick in exactly the right way.

Billiards rooms, steam rooms, music rooms, rooms whose purpose I can't fathom. Art galleries with twenty-foot portraits of Michael Fain in dark suits and red ties. Rooms with bucolic murals featuring Michael Fain, humble shepherd, herding his sheep, and rooms with carved wooden wall panels, showing scenes of patriotic Michael Fain crossing the Delaware, god-like Michael Fain bearing the earth upon his shoulders, and holy St. Michael Fain defeating the Dragon. One of the bathrooms has toilet paper upon whose repeating squares lay faint images of one of Michael Fain's ex-wives. Is that the face of the one who's here?

The sun sets. Lamps in each room illuminate as we enter and extinguish themselves as we leave. There are still many, many buildings we've left unexplored.

"Angela," I ask, as we stand in the center of an enormous ballroom, "where is everyone?"

"I'm sorry," my butterfly-shaped AI says, "but I don't have that kind of information."

Marisa touches my arm. "I bet he knew we were coming, and I bet he's hiding somewhere. We're not allowed to know where anyone else is in Perfectia, but *he* can know whatever he wants."

I look up, as if the gigantic, beaming face of Michael Fain edged in gold leaf on the ceiling is a god actively listening to my thoughts. Then again, in this place, Michael Fain just might be. *Is that what you want?* I think at the beatific face. *To have us piss around here for our ninety days, running out our clocks so you don't have to deal with us?*

"Hmph," says Marisa. "Hey. Now that we're in the 'realistic' part of this digital hell-hole, you wanna see if we can set more things on fire?"

It's not a constructive suggestion. But the thought makes me smile. We couldn't be punished for it—Michael Fain has to give us the full ninety days specified in our contracts—and the programmers could easily replace whatever we destroy.

"Wait a minute," I say.

"Hmm?"

"The programmers."

"What about them?"

"Jeff," I say. "The night I first came to Kathrin's, Jeff said there was a way to talk to the programmers." I look around, as if I can find a programmer's receptive face in gold-leaf, too. "Let's try it. Maybe one of Perfectia's programmers can tell us how to find Michael Fain."

Marisa's lips purse. "I dunno. Why would any of them help us?"

"I don't know either," I say, "but do you have any better ideas?"

Nobody does.

★★★

We crouch in the darkness of the ballroom as Marisa pulls out the paper notebook and one of the pencils from my bedsheet luggage. It's creepy in here. The moon in this part of Perfectia appears to have phases, because the moonlight that comes through the high windows is too thin. I keep standing up, to try to trip whatever motion sensor turned on the lights when we first came in, but nothing works. Maybe the lights don't work the same way, after a certain hour.

"Will you sit back down?" says Marisa. She tears a sheet of paper from the notebook. "This is dumb enough as it is."

I sit. Fields points my crappy flashlight at the paper as Marisa writes a note. The whole thing looks very ordinary. "How do you know that the programmers see whatever we write?" I ask.

"They don't," says Marisa. "Or at least, Jeff thinks they don't. To make them see it, you have to do this." At the top of the note, before the first line, she writes, "<!--". At the bottom, after the last line, she writes, "-->".

Fields chuckles. I don't get the joke.

Marisa opens my bedsheet and carefully tucks the paper inside, so it stands more or less vertically within the rest of my stuff. Then she folds the sheet over it, so it's out of our sight. "Jeff says they can't read the tags unless the text is oriented perpendicularly to the force of gravity," says Marisa.

Fields chuckles again.

"What's funny?" I ask.

He shakes his head. "Old-school, is all. Clever."

Explaining himself would probably take more words than Fields is capable of producing at one time, so I let it go. "How long do we have to wait?"

Marisa peeks into my bag. "We don't. They got it already—it's gone."

I'm surprised. But not more surprised than I am by anything else in Perfectia, I guess. "And how do they talk back to us?"

"Well." Marisa rubs her neck. She and Fields exchange a glance. "Technically, they, uh... that's why we're still testing it."

I exhale and sit back. "I see."

"Jeff thinks we haven't said anything interesting enough for them to respond to yet. Whereas some of us think they just don't want to answer Jeff specifically, because he's a tool."

A voice speaks from a dark corner of the ballroom. "Both ideas have merit."

We all jump. Someone approaches us, and for a second I think it's Michael Fain's poor ex-wife.

But no. A few lights finally turn on at her approach, and in their friendly glow, I see that it's the older woman from the train. The one who said I shouldn't have seen her.

"Jesus Christ," I say. "You're a programmer."

She sets her mouth. "And you're all idiots."

I notice her clothes now: a sky-blue blouse and jeans, both in a style that wasn't even popular twenty years ago. Her shoes are wispy ballet flats. I remember the blue dress that she wore when I first saw her—wasn't it sort of shapeless, sort of dowdy?—and I wonder why engineer-type people have such a hard time dressing themselves. "Come again?" I ask.

The programmer shakes her head. Her body does not neatly fall into one of the average, slender, toned, fit, or muscular body type categories, and I feel both annoyance and envy. "You are all idiots," she repeats, more slowly. "Because you each spent sixteen days on round-trip train tickets."

"We didn't buy round-trip tickets," says Marisa.

The programmer grips the hair at the sides of her head, like a comedian's pastiche of extreme frustration. "Argh! You bought them one-way? That's twenty days for two one-way tickets!"

"Yeah, well, we didn't know if we'd be going back," says Marisa. "Listen, uh—"

"Of course you'll be going *back*," says the programmer. "Why on earth would you want to stay?" She immediately winces. "Wait. Let me guess—it's the quality of the reality, isn't it?"

Marisa, Fields, and I exchange glances. I don't know about them, but this was not how I envisioned this conversation going. "Listen," says Marisa again. "Thanks for coming. Or making yourself visible? Anyway—thanks for answering our note."

The programmer fishes it out of a pocket and flaps it accusingly at us. "You said you wanted to see Michael Fain. Why?"

Marisa blinks. I too feel stumped. We didn't talk about what to say, precisely, if a programmer actually appeared.

"Because Michael Fain is not interested in any complaints, entitled attitudes, or sob stories," says the programmer. "The only people Michael Fain wants to spend time with in Perfectia are his friends and greatest fans."

"I mean—" begins Marisa.

The programmer's eyes are daggers. "Friends and fans only. Do you understand?"

Suddenly, I do.

I step forward. "Of course!" I smile big, like the gold-leaf face that peers down on us from overhead. "And we are. We adore Mr. Fain. Don't we, guys?"

Fields' face is a stoic blank. Marisa's eyes are saucers.

"We're huge Fain fans," I continue. "He let us into his Afterlife, didn't he? Ordinary people like us, who could never hope to afford any kind of Afterlife otherwise. It was such a kind gesture. Especially being among the first to be here, which is a real honor, let me tell you."

The programmer frowns at me. She cranes her neck forward and squints, in cartoonish, overblown suspicion.

"And the stipend," I add. "I mean: wow. I knew that Michael Fain was a generous man, but the stipend on top of the offer is what really blew my mind." I elbow Marisa. "Me and my new friends here, we just wanted to thank him personally. I know ten days, or twenty days, to ride the train is a lot, but the way I see it is, we're on borrowed time already.

We're only in Perfectia at all because of Mr. Fain. So I think twenty days is a small sacrifice for us to pay in service of a sincere 'thank you'."

The programmer squints further. "I see. And all of you feel this way?"

Fields blinks. His jaw works in thought. "Sure."

"Fifi!"

Fields taps Marisa's arm. "Don't be shy."

Marisa's mouth flaps. She looks between us, helpless, like a dying fish. "Come on," I say to her through my smile. "Don't you want to get the chance to *really talk* with Michael Fain?"

She finally gets it: the charade is probably our only way in. She cobbles a smile together. "I... ha ha. Of course I do. I just, uh... I'm so stunned, that we..." She forces her smile up a few watts. "That we might finally have a chance to tell him how we feel."

The programmer straightens up. "Hmph."

"We have a lot of feelings," adds Marisa, as Fields subtly steps on her foot.

"I can see that." The programmer nudges her glasses up. "Well. Mr. Fain is at one of his secondary residences right now, but he is always happy to meet devoted fans, so, all right. I'll take you to him."

My smile turns real. "Thank you. Truly. We're very—"

She stalks back to the shadowy corner she came from. "Meet me outside at sunrise tomorrow at the end of Dock #3. You can't miss it—it's the one with the diamond-studded yacht."

***

Come sunrise, we're in position. A jewel-studded craft bobs at our right, its trashy, sparkling prow nodding to the morning. The sunrise across the lake to our left takes up half the sky, pinks and oranges painting the underbellies of golden clouds.

The programmer is absent.

"Figures," says Marisa. She sits on the edge of the dock, swinging her heels through empty air. The lake below her feet is cobalt glass. "She's probably fled Perfectia for some other server."

I think, *We don't know that Michael Fain gave his programmers that particular job perk.* But then again, offering between-server travel is industry standard, and I don't see how Michael Fain could have ever enticed anyone to literally die for him and work here if between-server travel wasn't one of the benefits.

"Either that or we're at the wrong dock." Marisa waves at the sparkling craft. "I bet this is his diamond-studded whaling vessel. His diamond-studded yacht is parked somewhere else."

Fields sits next to her. "Boats are moored. Not parked."

Marisa touches his arm with a fingertip. The gesture is ambiguous, neither caress nor jab. "You know what I mean."

I shade my eyes and pivot in a slow, 360° turn. I want to believe that the programmer is merely running late.

"This sucks," says Marisa.

I'm so surprised, I laugh.

Marisa stops swinging her legs. "It's not funny. Perfectia sucks. Michael Fail sucks. I could be in—"

"In?"

She looks at her lap.

Fields nudges her.

"It's just..." she says, still not looking at me. "I know I said at Kathrin's house that I never wanted an Afterlife. But that's not really true. I did want one. I wanted to go to Shuruq Alshshams."

The phrase is familiar. "That's a server?"

"Yeah. In Dubai." Marisa gestures for her AI. She scoops up the rat and rubs its head with her thumb. "They let you do anything there. It's pretty unregulated. It's like the Wild West, or something, and I always wanted to go somewhere where the rules weren't really... where you could... I dunno. Never mind. It's stupid."

I shake my head. "No it isn't." Modern American life—responsible, adult American life, anyway—comes with a lot of rules and expectations. Some people struggle to say sane under a system like that. Daniel certainly does.

My mind whimpers his name.

"Ahem!"

Startled, we turn. The programmer stands behind us. Three coils of rope lie pooled at her feet, from which their ends snake up and tie to the front of her belt. "This is a long trip, and we've no time to waste. Everyone grab a tow rope. And don't let go—if you do, I'm not coming back for you."

"Hi," says Marisa. "I'm sorry, but where have you been?"

Fields nudges her. When he does it, it's more like a jab. "I was just *asking,*" she says.

Fields shakes his head. In moments, he takes the ropes and loops them expertly around us, to create surprisingly comfortable body harnesses.

"I have a great many responsibilities around here," says the programmer, eyeing Fields as he works, "and all of them are more important than you. Remember that. Aren't you ready yet?"

Fields-the-former-cowboy steps back from his work. He's tied his own harness to include my bedsheeted pile of crap on his back. "Yup."

"And why do we need ropes to—" Marisa begins.

The programmer puts her palms together, inhales, and sinks into a squat. Then she leaps.

She flies straight up into the sky, like a super hero.

The coils unspool behind her like mad. I have time to say, "Oh, *shit.*"

Then I'm jerked, I'm flailing, and I'm airborne, too, soaring over the lake with the others, leaving Michael Fain's empty estate behind.

★★★

Suspended at varying heights above the ground, I come to understand what The Wilderness—what Perfectia's massive, deceptive, labyrinthine trap—really is.

The Wilderness is lakes. And rivers. And plains and mountains. Jungles thick and green, shivering with wind and alighting birds. Rumpled, empty sand dunes. Stony moors with craggy tors, sheep grazing on heather and grasses, and glaciers that glimmer in the sun. Volcanic cones, even, that steam and spit threads of lava, and cooling fields of rock, as desolate as the surface of the moon.

There are whole oceans. Limestone cliffs. Archipelagos with palm trees that flap hello in seaside breezes. White sand beaches and black sand beaches, yellow sand beaches and cobblestone beaches, narrow fjords and plunging sinkholes, rapids and vast, vast deltas, ten times the size of the African Okavango.

There are lions and elephants, bison and eagles.

There are dinosaurs.

There are dragons.

In swarming, howling carpets, beast and birds crawl over and through the brush, fighting and hunting and fucking. Bears bellow warnings at saber-toothed tigers. 100,000 carrier pigeons flee from a pack of charging Allosaurus, spiraling up past us and blocking the sun with a smokescreen of wings. Humps of whales and prehistoric monsters emerge from blue-dark ocean, spurting their exhalations, and I am dizzy with glimpses of pterodactyls, gryphons, and hummingbirds the size of wolverines, whose blurred wings echo like hurricanes.

My rope emerges from my harness between my shoulder blades and stretches to the programmer's belt, high above me, and I don't have anything reassuring to cling to.

Fields' knots are good, I tell myself. And if you fall, you'll just float to the ground, like you do everywhere else. And the creatures here can't kill you.

Or can they?

This new Perfectia is enormous. We fly, suspended from the programmer's belt, for the entire day. The sun goes down, and we keep flying over savage landscapes painted in silhouettes and shards of lingering sun. The forests, the mangrove swamps, the marshes and reaches and wind-blasted wastelands—they all go on and on.

The moon comes up. The stars come out.

The Wilderness is a cradle of blackness below, from which endless waterfalls roar.

***

As we decelerate, I see the lights. They look like the lights of normal, developed human civilization, clustered together in a steep-walled valley.

We go lower. A winding line of darkness—a river—cuts through the lights and empties into a lake to the south of the valley. There are lights there, too, though not as many.

Lower. The lights outline magnificent building facades, manicured lawns, fountains and towers and rambling pathways. Everything looks old and hand-carved, in a European sort of way, but too large in scale, in an American one. The parapets of the buildings are crenellated. And the roofs of all the buildings are connected, by walkways or winding stairs, so this path of faux battlements remains contiguous.

It's a hundred gaudy buildings crowned with a half-melted, crenelated turd.

A freshly mowed courtyard drifts up from below. When my toes touch the grass, and my weight settles on my feet again, I sigh with relief. I don't know how Michael Fain will treat us, but at least we won't fall and get eaten by a

Liopleurodon.

Fields undoes our rope harnesses. The programmer winds the ropes back into coils. "You didn't fall."

Fields shrugs.

The programmer points down a crushed gravel path, ghostly white in the outdoor floodlights. "That'll take you inside. Ring the bell for the butler."

I rub my face to get some feeling back into my too-wind-blasted cheeks. "Thank you."

The programmer sighs. She looks tired. "I wish you would've just taken the gate."

"The gate?" I ask, but the programmer has already stalked off into the night.

5. Courant de la Lac Diamant

We follow the gravel path. It leads under a portico and into a building, into a kind of sitting room.

Marisa finds a brass call bell on a side table. She taps it.

"Welcome to Courant de la Lac Diamant. You rang?"

A slender, bald white man of middle height stands by a sofa, his hands clasped in front of him. He wears a tuxedo and white gloves. His clean-shaven face is slightly droopy, and his eyes are half-closed, as though nothing can surprise him anymore.

"You're the butler?" asks Marisa.

"Indeed I am. And to whom do I have the pleasure of speaking?"

He doesn't look capable of pleasure, but I already like this AI miles better than Angela. "My name is Lehann Margrove. And this is Marisa Dawson and..." I realize that I don't know Fields' first name. "Uh... Mr. Fields. We're from Perfectia's other end." I force a smile. "And we're here to meet Mr. Fain. We're huge fans of his."

"Very good, sir," says the butler. "Right this way, sir."

He leads us through Courant de la Lac Diamant, which is the estate by the train station times a hundred. This is a 'secondary residence'? The walls explode with god-awful art and the floors gasp beneath all the knobby-legged, crushed-brocade-and-velvet-with-tassels furniture. And every chamber seems to be a sitting room or lobby. But this makes no sense. There is nobody waiting anywhere, and nothing to wait for.

Finally, the butler leads us into a sitting room that makes even Fields choke. Every table, sofa leg, mirror frame, and decorative urn gleams a rich, brassy yellow, and I understand instinctively that every hard object in this room is made of solid gold.

"Please have a seat," the butler says.

We don't. He bows anyway, then retreats and disappears.

"I don't like this," says Marisa.

I don't either. But I say, "Just let me talk. Everything will be fine."

"What if he's..." Marisa begins, but trails off. We don't know how closely he's watching us, here.

I look away. The wallpaper is embroidered with gold thread, and the wainscoting made of solid gold paneling. His beaming face is stamped into the panels. I feel a tightness in my chest and a dampness on my palms, and I can't help but wonder: does he want people in this part of Perfectia to feel bodily fear, so that they can tremble appropriately before him?

My throat goes dry. This is really happening: I'm going to meet Michael Fain. He's going to hear my name and say things at me, things he'll forget or later deny or even somehow hear the exact opposite of, but for a brief and terrifying interlude, our spheres will intersect.

I'm going to meet the man whose caprices keep me from my husband.

My sweaty fingers convulse into fists. How many days has it been, now, since I held Daniel's hand?

At the other end of the room, a solid gold door swings open. "—by tomorrow," his voice says. "Listen, it was great talking to you, truly great, but I've got some people here. Yeah. Ask Usha. Bye now. Butler! Why aren't they coming in?"

From the room: "I don't believe you explicitly invited them, sir."

"Well, get them in here."

I glance at Fields and Marisa. They look terrified. At least I'm not the only one.

I walk to the open door, the others in my wake. What's the correct etiquette here? I have no idea. I knock on the door frame.

"Come in, come in!"

He wasn't this tall when he was alive, and his hair wasn't this blond and thick, and his skin wasn't so evenly tanned, even when he was this young. The hand he gestures with seems too large. But his eyes are the same: small and squinting. In calculation? Contentment? Confusion?

Depends on who you ask.

"It's great to meet you," he says, and his thick hand grips mine. It's a businessman's handshake, swift and sharp, and over before I can squeeze back. "A real pleasure. Why don't we sit. No, here, you take the other sofa. Isn't that terrific? Don't you just melt right into it?" He laughs. If his hands are too large, his mouth is enormous, a toothy, luminous abyss. His teeth physically glow, like tombstones under a black light.

Liopleurodon ahoy.

"You like it?" he says, gesturing to his teeth. "That's the whitest smile you'll ever see, guaranteed. Sitara's work. She's swell, just absolutely incredible, even considering what programmers can do nowadays. But you know I've got the best people." He beams at me. "Listen, I want to tell the three of you, Ariadne called me last night and told me everything. And I'm flattered. I'm very flattered. You wanting to come all this way to thank me in person, that's very kind."

Act your part, Lehann, you fool! I remember my own smile. "Of course. It's the least we could do."

"Of course," he says. "You know, when I talked to Usha—she's on my legal team, a real sharp gal, and great legs, too—she told me that you people would be happier in your own part of Perfectia, and do you know what I said? I said no. I said, 'don't do it, Usha.'" He laughs again. God, that abyss of a mouth just goes back and back. "But you know, for the most part, she's right? Almost none of you have come this way. I mean, why would you? It's a pain to get here. And I've already given you everything you could ever want. It's nice, isn't it? Perfectia?"

My smile hurts. "It's magnificent," I lie.

Michael Fain talks about how much he agrees. Details of the room filter into my awareness: all the laptops on his sprawling desk, the monitors on the two inner walls that aren't floor-to-ceiling windows. Actual filing cabinets. We're in the office of a working man. Of course, Michael Fain would continue to work from beyond the grave. Why would he want to give up an inch of influence to anyone with the paltry advantage of a body?

"But of course, it's even better on this side of Perfectia," he says, "because that's where I live." He beams. "And I only accept the best. Butler!"

The butler appears. "Yes, sir."

"Where's Vlad?"

"You sent him out for coffee, sir."

"I did, and my coffee's not here. What the hell is he doing?"

"Vladimir has acquired the coffee, and he is currently staring into the mirror in the Wilcox Room," says the butler. Goosebumps prickle on my arms. Vladimir must be that one advisor from Michael Fain's inner circle who is here already, but apparently not even this status earns him his privacy.

"Well, go get him," says Michael Fain, and the butler nods and exits. "Where was I?"

Marisa smiles sweetly. "I don't know. It's so hard to take in everything you say."

Michael Fain's squint deepens. He learns forward, to the couch where the three of us sit, and pats Marisa's knee.

She stiffens.

"Don't worry, honey," he says. "You're not the first woman to say that to me."

A muscle in Field's jaw jumps. He does not smile.

"Hey," says Michael Fain to him. "I know you from

somewhere. Don't I know you?"

That jaw muscle jumps again. "Maybe."

Michael Fain closes one eye, makes his right hand into the shape of a gun, and fires an imaginary bullet at Fields. "A man of few words," he says. "I like that. You always know where you stand with that kind of man."

I have no idea what Michael Fain means by this. I'm sure Fields doesn't either, but he inclines his head.

"Listen," says Michael Fain, standing, "it's been great, but I've got a real busy evening lined up, a lot of calls to make. You wouldn't believe the things those idiots are doing in Washington. Well, even if I did explain it, you wouldn't understand. But don't worry about it. I'll get it taken care of."

Marisa jumps up, her smile doggedly hanging on. "Hey, um... about you taking care of things. We—"

I touch her arm. "Marisa. What we mean is—"

But Michael Fain has already gone back to his desk.

"Mr. Fain."

He waves a hand and seats himself. "We'll talk later, okay? Bye now."

"Mr. Fain." I soften my tone and sidle up to the desk, like this is normal, like negotiating basic human rights is a special favor best asked submissively. "You've got a lot more fans back where we come from."

"Oh yeah?" He sits and taps at a laptop, ignoring me.

"Oh yeah," I repeat. I amp up my smile. I place a hand on his desk, hoping my sweaty palm doesn't leave a print. "Everybody loves you in that corner of Perfectia."

"Of course they do." He taps at another laptop. "I know that."

"We'd like to talk with your other fans more easily," I say. "But our houses are so far apart..."

Michael Fain waves in dismissal again. "You've got landline phones in your houses, don't you? And the phone directory?"

Stunned into silence, I stare at his tapping fingers. Do we?

Michael Fain looks up, squinting harder. "You did know about the phone directory, didn't you? That your AI knows?"

"The..." I struggle to say something redeeming. "I didn't see a landline phone in my house."

"Well you have to know where it *is,*" says Michael Fain. "And your AI can tell you that. Didn't you ask her? If you had a phone of some kind?" He looks between the three of us. His mouth tightens into disappointment. "Unbelievable."

"But, see, that's exactly our point," says Marisa. "It's too hard to—"

"Butler!" he barks. "Show these people out. I said butler—oh, there you are."

The butler enters Michael Fain's office from the Gold Room, a reedy, sullen man in tow. The man has pale skin but dark eyes and dark hair. He carries, of all things, a cardboard drink holder, the kind you'd get at a Starbucks or a McDonald's, with a pair of to-go cups nested kitty-corner inside. The cups say, "COFFEE: PERFECT" and bear a line drawing of Michael Fain's beaming face.

"What the hell, Vlad," says Michael Fain.

Vladimir scuttles over. His sullenness blends seamlessly into fear. "I'm sorry, Mr. Fain. Here you are."

"You'll never work your way up if you don't bother to work."

"I know. I'm sorry, Mr. Fain. I'll do better."

Michael Fain sips his coffee. "At least Sitara makes sure the coffee here stays hot. What, did you get one for yourself? You didn't earn that. Go outside and throw it away."

"Yes, Mr. Fain."

"And you." He gestures at me, Marisa, and Fields.

"What are you still doing in my office? Butler, get them out of here."

***

The butler escorts us out, down a hall, down another hall, and through multiple empty lobbies. He finally opens a door— "Step inside, please—" and unthinking, we do.

He closes it behind us. A lock clicks.

Marisa whirls. She throws herself against the door, banging it and yanking on the knob, but that supernaturally hard wood doesn't budge a millimeter. "Son of a bitch!"

I don't know what to think. Everything in Michael Fain's office happened so fast. But he didn't kick us out of his estate—I guess that's something?

Fields frowns and tests the knob on another door. This one opens. Apparently we're just not allowed to make our way back to his office. "Marie."

Marisa slaps the locked door. Her face crumples. "You slimy little shit," she says. "Like we're nothing. You didn't even ask for our *names.*"

"Marie," says Fields.

She wipes her face with the back of her hand. She's been weeping real tears.

It's not Paradise for Michael Fain if he can't make you cry.

***

A door opens. The lights come on.

I blink, roused from my dismal thoughts. Marisa, Fields, and I lay on leather couches, in a sort of library, taking our nightly two-hour rest. The lights, which are art deco reading lamps, illuminate the room's bookcases and their contents. They're mostly knickknacks. There are only a few hundred books, and they are all hardback copies of *Steal the Deal, Make 'Em Gasp,* and *Greatness Is the Only Option: A Desperado Approach to Success,* all autobiographical business self-help books by Michael Fain.

I see someone by a bookcase. It's Vladimir, the sullen man with dark hair who brought Michael Fain coffee yesterday. He pulls out one copy of each of Michael Fain's books.

Fields sits up. "Morning," he says.

Vladimir jumps. His books tumble to the floor. "Jesus! Oh, it's you. What are you doing here?"

Marisa bounces to her feet. "Literally nothing. Your butler dumped us in a room last night and locked the way we came, so we found a place to lie down."

He bends and gathers the books, grumbling about creased pages and cracked spines. "Yeah, well, now that it's morning, you can go."

"Go?"

He stands and looks at us like we're nuts. "Home. Your mansions. You know?"

"How?"

"The same way you came here. —Wait. Don't tell me they sealed the pad already?"

"The what now?" asks Marisa.

"The teleporter pad." Vladimir shifts the books to his other arm. "That is how you came to Lac Diamant from the other end of Perfectia, isn't it? You found one of the hidden teleporter pads?"

We all look at each other.

Vladimir shakes his head. "I'm not talking about the *transporter* pads that programmers use to move themselves to other Afterlife servers. Obviously, those are illegal and unsafe for non-programmers to access. I'm talking about the local *teleporter* pads. The ones that link places within Perfectia."

"Oh," says Marisa, carefully.

Vladimir sighs. "It's okay. They're not a secret, or anything. Mr. Fain knows the programmers are still hunting them down and deleting them. They're holdovers from an earlier build, if you were wondering."

"We were," I lie. "That explains a lot. Thank you."

"They shouldn't've sealed up your teleporter pad before he told you to go home, though," Vladimir says. "No wonder you didn't know how to leave." He smirks. "Maybe Mr. Fain will do you a favor and fly you back on his private jet. Ha! That'll be the day."

Marisa affixes her fake smile to her face. "I don't recognize you from the news. You're one of Michael Fain's friends, right? I know he has two permanent citizens here already."

"Oh. I'm not anyone. I'm just..." Vladimir shifts the books back to his other arm, as if preparing to shake hands and reintroduce himself, but he loses momentum. Instead, he smiles sheepishly and gives an awkward wave. "Er. I'm Vladimir."

"It's nice to meet you, Vladimir," says Marisa. "I'm Marisa, and this is Fields and Lehann."

"Hi," says Vladimir. "Listen, I've got to get—"

"When do you think we can talk to Michael Fain again?" she asks.

"Well listen, I'm really very busy, and—"

"Doing what?" grunts Fields. "Seems the butler can do all that."

Vladimir stiffens. Fields just stares at him, unperturbed. Finally Vladimir looks away. "He can," Vladimir says, shortly. "I'm working my way up."

Fields keeps staring, and now Marisa and I do, too. This is one of Michael Fain's most trusted advisors?

"Look," Vladimir snaps. "I'm not Lester van Dijk. He's in some other residence, I don't know where—somewhere with Kirsten, maybe.

"I'm just a guy. And I got into Perfectia the same way you all did. I took the bribe and got a ninety-day citizen contract, and I woke up in one of those cookie-cutter mega-mansions."

I raise my eyebrows.

"But I know how these things work," Vladimir continues. "What you see is never all that you get. Programmers always make a game of hiding goodies in Afterlives, no matter what the 'official' terms in the contracts are. So I went out with some other temporary citizens to look for goodies, and—"

Understanding finally hits me. "You were in Kathrin's party. The one that went into the mountains by the train station."

Vladimir smirks. "I was."

"What about the others?"

"What about them?"

"Where are they?"

"How should I know? I got sick of their crap and struck out on my own. And I was alone when I finally found some goodies, and one of the things I found was a hidden teleporter pad. And it took me straight here."

I hold up a hand. "And how did you get from 'here' to 'fetching coffee for Michael Fain'?"

Surprisingly, Vladimir laughs. He rests the stack of books on a khaki-clad hip. "How do you think? I begged him for a job. And as long as I do whatever he wants, he'll never delete me."

Fields and I stare again. Marisa gapes outright. "Do you really believe that?" she asks.

"My ninety-day contract's been up since yesterday," says Vladimir. "And I'm still here, aren't I?"

I open my mouth. I manage, "That can't be true. Kathrin said that Lei is the oldest."

"'Kathrin said'." Vladimir laughs again. "Can't you tell by now that that woman is a habitual liar?"

We have nothing to say to that.

Vladimir snorts—"Maybe if you beg, he'll give you

jobs, too"—and walks out.

Marisa sinks onto a couch, as if the truth of Vladimir's story is too heavy to carry. "Jesus Christ. It's a deal with the Devil."

***

We go outside, out of Michael Fain's turd-crenelated estate, and into the woods, on the eastern slope of the valley.

I admit it: I don't know what to do. If the real purpose of our mission here is to convince Michael Fain to change the living conditions on Perfectia's other end, then we should all do what Vladimir has done. If Michael Fain sees us every day, from now until the end of time, we have infinitely more opportunities to talk to him and change his mind.

On the other hand, Marisa is 100% correct. That arrangement is a deal with the Devil. Sure, I worked for Fain Enterprises in life, but at least I always had the option of walking away and looking for employment elsewhere. Here, Michael Fain would be the force that decides whether I literally live or die.

"Okay," says Marisa. She stops and sets down my bedsheet luggage. "This is far enough."

The woods are deep around us. The tree cover is so thick, I can't see into the valley below. I want to tell her that her paranoia is absurd, in that Michael Fain is neither less likely nor less able to spy on us if we're in the forest around Lac Diamant than inside of it, but at this point I'd just be repeating myself.

Marisa writes a note in my notebook—'Did you actually hide more bonuses for us in Perfectia, like Vladimir thinks you did? And if so, where should we look?'—tears out the page, and tucks it in among all the crap in my bedsheet.

"The programmer's not going to answer a question like that, you know," I say. "If they did hide things for us to find, what would be the point of telling us about them?"

"I mean, she's not going to *tell* us," says Marisa. "But she'll probably give us a hint."

I shake my head. "We're wasting our time with this. We should've just stayed in the compound."

"And do what there? Spend another two hours looking for a call bell for the butler, who won't take us to see Michael Fain again anyways? How about another two hours looking for a landline phone so we can call up Kathrin's, which she won't pick up because as far as she knows, it doesn't fucking exist?

"Look. Everything will be great. The programmer will show up, she'll give us a hint, and we'll find some bonuses that give us more options. Maybe we'll find email tokens or calling cards to other servers—or the real world. They have those in Shuruq Alshshams, you know, and on the Blå server in Sweden."

"That doesn't mean—"

"And if Perfectia has those kinds of things, too," Marisa continues, "we won't need to keep arguing with Michael Shit-Stain over the set-up in our crappy corner of reality, because we'll be able to use the bonuses to contact our living friends and families.

"And boom, no more loneliness. Love conquers all."

My ache for Daniel follows her words. If there are such bonuses somewhere in Perfectia, and if I could use one to write to Daniel—

If I could vchat with him again—

My heart can't take the hope. Not after all this. "It won't be like that," I say, sharply.

Twigs snap.

We all look up. Someone pushes through the under-growth to where we crouch around my bedsheet of supplies, but it's not the programmer.

It's an Indian woman, very tall, wearing a pantsuit. The pantsuit is cream and pink. Her bearing suggests that she should be in a General's uniform instead, and the contrast is unsettling. "How did you get to this end of Perfectia?" she asks, with no preamble.

We look at each other, confused.

"Well?" she demands.

I stand and brush off my pants. "We were invited." I offer my hand. "I'm Lehann Margrove. And you are...?"

Marisa makes a hissing, defeated noise. She puts her head in her hands. "Lehann. She's a programmer."

Feeling like an ass, I lower my hand. Of course she's a programmer.

Just not the one we wanted.

"Invited or not, you shouldn't be in this location," she says. The programmer raises her hand and flicks her fingers at us in a complex pattern.

The world goes dark.

6. Service Cluster Building 00

"Marisa?" I whisper.

"Yeah?"

I reach toward her in the total darkness, but I bang my hand on something metal.

"Angela," says Fields. "Give us a little light, would you, honey?"

Fire flares. Fields' Angela, that beautiful, chestnut-brown horse, stands next to us with a lit wooden torch in her mouth. Fields takes it from her and kisses her nose.

"Here you go!" says the horse, in Angela's bubbly voice. "Is that enough?"

Fields holds up the torch. The firelight illuminates a room with a concrete floor and gray cinderblock walls. Metal bunkbeds, bereft of bedding, line the space. To my left, behind Fields, a metal door stands ajar.

"This looks like... a barracks room?"

Fields shrugs. He leads us out, his Angela clip-clopping at the rear.

The next room detects our presence, and lights turn on. We stand in a wide, open space, the size of a high school gymnasium, its floor covered in dingy gray carpet. Clusters of pathetic furniture dot the space: overturned milk crates, folding metal chairs, a table made from a door propped up on cinderblocks.

No art hangs on the walls. Only a couple of analog clocks.

"Okay, where the hell are we?" Marisa asks. "Are we in some kind of Michael Fain jail?"

"Nope," says the horse. "You're in the Service Cluster!"

"And what the hell is the Service Cluster?"

"The Service Cluster is a collection of buildings on the shore of Diamond Lake at the mouth of the Platinum

River," Angela says. "It's designed to hold all of the future employees of Michael Fain's Courant de la Lac Diamant estate."

We all trade stares. Ice prickles down my arms.

"As employees advance, they are given more and more benefits and rewards, including improved living spaces," the horse continues. She flicks her tail. "You are in Building 00. That's for new employees who are being evaluated!"

"Oh no," says Marisa. She backs away and nearly trips on a milk crate. "No no no. There's been a huge mistake. We did *not* agree to be employees. We don't even want—"

"Wait," I shout, holding up my hands. "Everyone. Just wait. We need to hear this."

"Like hell," says Marisa hotly, but Fields taps her on the arm.

"Once your evaluation period is successfully completed," Angela chirps, "you'll be moved to Building 01, which features rewards such as quadruple-occupancy rooms and colors."

I lower my twitching hands. The ice prickles across my shoulders and down my spine.

"Of course, you always have the option of withdrawing from employment at any time," says Angela, "but if your initial ninety-day contract has been completed when you do, you'll face immediate conclusion."

Marisa's face contorts. She kicks a milk crate across the room. My own thoughts are sand in breaking waves, swirling every which way and unable to settle.

I thought Vladimir working for him was an exception. An anomaly.

I didn't think Michael Fain was deliberately planning... that he was just sitting here, across The Wilderness, waiting for people to...

I don't understand. What does Michael Fain want? Does he want peaceful isolation with his twenty-four best chums and nobody else? Or an entire army of once-living slaves for him and his loved ones?

Does he himself even know?

We're ants. Ants getting torched with a goddamn magnifying glass for a fickle boy's amusement.

"Angela," says Fields. His face is a stone. "How many Service Cluster buildings are there?"

She tells him.

I turn and run.

I wrench every doorknob and kick open every door, all around the perimeter of that dismal space. It's all barracks rooms. How many suckers like us will come? How many other teleporter pads are there? How many tricks and secret methods await for crossing The Wilderness, and how many sullen, angry Vladimirs will bunk here, yearning for a day when they can finally have... what? A room of their own? A Service Cluster building that has windows?

And how much of Eternity will that take?

Sunlight kicks back. I've finally found the door that leads outside. I sprint out into a crushed gravel yard, but I go nowhere except around and around, because Building 00 is surrounded by high cinderblock walls topped with loops of barbed wire, and the only door through the outer wall is locked and stamped with EMPLOYEES ONLY.

I fall to my knees, forehead against the door.

I couldn't even get Michael Fain to listen to me during a direct conversation.

How impossible will it be, when this prison camp fills up with a dozen, a hundred, ten thousand people clamoring for his favor?

***

When I finally go back inside, I find Marisa and Fields in one of the barracks rooms. They crouch by a flipped-open footlocker, which rests at the foot of one bed that has been made up, with white, scratchy-looking sheets and a gray, scratchier-looking blanket.

"I don't think we should," Marisa is saying to Fields. "Because even if we can get over the wall, I'd bet you anything there are alarms. We'll just get picked up again by the pantsuit mafia and dumped right back inside."

"Don't see how else we'll get out," says Fields.

"Yeah, well, I'm working on that. Maybe there's a steam tunnel."

"Don't need no steam tunnels in an Afterlife."

"I said I'm working on it, okay?"

Fields shakes his head. He notices me in the doorway, then gestures for me to come in.

"Hi," says Marisa to me. "You feeling okay?"

"No."

"Well, here," she says. "This should cheer you up. Look what we found." From the pile of clothes in the footlocker, she plucks a rolled-up scroll of paper and offers it to me.

"Is that Vladimir's footlocker? Why are you going through his clothes?"

"Because I wanted to," says Marisa. "Also, everything here technically belongs to Michael Fain, so rooting through Vladimir's footlocker doesn't count as stealing." Marisa waggles the scroll. "Aren't you curious?"

I take the scroll and unroll it. It feels thick and soft, not like ordinary paper.

It bears a few hand-written words:

Let the wind blow you.
Let the water close over you.
Let the well refresh you.

I stare at the handwriting. It's pretty.

"Well?" says Marisa.

"What is this supposed to be? Poetry?"

"Come on," says Marisa. She takes it back and rolls it up. "You know that's not what this is. It's a map."

"A map."

"Don't you ever solve riddles?" Marisa grins. "It's a clue to an Extra Time Well."

"Inside Service Cluster Building 00."

Her grin fades. "Well, no. I mean obviously Vladimir didn't find the clue here. I think he found it in the mountains."

I rub my brow ridges. I am way too emotionally exhausted for this level of conspiracy theory.

"Listen," says Marisa. "Vladimir said that when he was in the mountains, after he left the others, he found some goodies. Plural. He found at least one other thing aside from the teleporter pad that brought him here, and I think this is what he found."

I lay down on Vladimir's bed. The blanket is as scratchy as it looks. "Fine. So he found a clue to an Extra Time Well that's somewhere in the mountains on the other side of The Wilderness. How does that help us, at all, where we are right now?"

Marisa's mouth cracks in disbelief, like the answer should be so obvious that my question is offensive. "Don't you want more time to *exist?*"

"Sure," I say, though to be honest, if Perfectia is the place I have to do it in, I'm not sure at all. "But it doesn't do us any good if we can't get to it."

"But maybe we *can* get to it. What if the clue was in the mountains, next to the first teleporter pad, but the Extra Time Well itself is by the second teleporter pad—near Lac Diamant, where Vladimir landed?"

"I don't know," I say flatly. "What if it is?"

"Well..." begins Marisa. She looks at the scroll, then at Fields, then at the scroll again. "Well... we'd better ask him."

***

Long after midnight, the door to Building 00 bangs open. We're sitting in the common area, so we notice Vladimir slink in right away.

He spots us just as quickly. His face sours into disappointment. "So you did beg for jobs. Well, I guess I'd better give you all the lowdown, then, huh?"

He drags us through a gloomy orientation. No wonder he's depressed; the window into his routine is depressing. From 5:30 a.m. to 5:35 a.m., every morning, the door in the yard marked EMPLOYEES ONLY becomes unlocked, and Vladimir goes through and rides the train on the other side to the Lac Diamant estate. He must report to Michael Fain by 6 a.m., and he must work until midnight. The train back to Building 00 comes at 12:30 a.m. From 2 a.m. to 2:05 a.m., a door inside Building 00 marked 'BUTLER ONLY' unlocks and opens, and Vladimir is allowed to talk to the butler and ask for clothes and certain supplies. But the clothes and supplies must come from a pre-approved list, and they must all fit within his footlocker. At 3 a.m., all lights in the building turn off.

All days thereafter are the same.

"Until I get promoted," Vladimir adds. "Whenever that is."

We sit on overturned milk crates close to the BUTLER ONLY door. Once 2 a.m. hits, we will have to ask for our own footlockers and clothes, Vladimir has explained.

"That sounds awful," says Marisa.

"It's okay so far," Vladimir says, without conviction. "You'd be surprised how fast you get used to things."

Marisa nods. "Hey, uh, Vladimir. I have to be honest with you. When we got dumped—er, when we arrived at the building, we didn't realize at first that the one footlocker was yours, and we, um... we kind of went through it."

Vladimir frowns at her.

"Marisa—" I begin.

"Anyway," she adds, with all the subtlety of a sledge-hammer striking a wall, "we found your Extra Time Well map."

Vladimir hunches into himself. He regards us with hooded eyes.

"Excuse me," I say. "I had nothing to do with looking through his things. I wasn't even in the room."

"You looked at the map when I offered it to you," says Marisa.

"That's not the same!"

Vladimir ignores us. He watches the BUTLER ONLY door.

"How did you get the map?" Marisa asks Vladimir.

Vladimir doesn't answer.

"Did you find it in the mountains?" she asks. "Before you found the teleporter pad and came here?"

Vladimir's nostrils flare.

"I'm very sorry," I say. "We should've closed the foot-locker as soon as we realized it wasn't meant for any of us. I mean... Marisa should have closed it."

"Fuck you," says Marisa, conversationally. "No, I shouldn't have. Otherwise we wouldn't know that Vladimir has the map."

"We don't know that it's a map!"

Vladimir stands. His tone is ice. "Excuse me."

Fields jumps to his feet. "I'll buy it from you."

Fields' words startle everyone. "What?" Vladimir says to him.

"I'll buy your map," repeats Fields.

"We don't know that it's a map," I grumble, but Vladimir laughs. He says, "With what?"

"Blank paper," says Fields. "And a pencil."

Vladimir laughs harder. "Why would I want that?"

"Michael Fain don't give you paper, does he?"

"No. So?"

"Or the butler?"

"What's your point?"

Fields fetches my bedsheet luggage from another cluster of nearby milk crates. He pulls out the notebook and one of the pencils and jots down a message. He tips the notebook to show us all what he has written—"Why won't Angela give us clothes here? Why do we got to ask the butler?"—then rips out the page and tucks it inside the bedsheet. "Watch."

A door to a barracks room opens.

Out strolls yet another woman in yet another pantsuit. But this woman is old, with a face like wrinkled tree bark, and her pantsuit, I realize, is actually a man's suit. And maybe she isn't a she. But to be honest, I'm not sure.

"My darlings, I am so terribly sorry," says the programmer. They sweep their layered, gray hair away from their face with an elaborate flourish. "The low-end AI is a bit simple, poor thing, isn't it? That would be my fault, I'm afraid—the first version of anything is always maggoty with UI issues. But how lucky for you, at least, that it was me who happened to check the general inbox just now."

Vladimir's eyes are goldfish-round.

The programmer strolls to Fields. Their bearing is regal, like that of a Siamese cat. "Now. To answer the question you asked us. Angela *should* be giving you clothing, no matter where you are in Perfectia, but we went a weentsy bit overboard on her Service Cluster restrictions. That should be remedied with the next build, but there's no telling when that will be released, so I'm afraid you'll just have to grin and bear the inconvenience for now.

"In the meantime—oh, where did I put it—" The programmer pats down their suit jacket. "Ah, here we are." They hand a business card to Fields. "If you should encounter any other AI issues, and goodness me, I expect you will, please write to my personal inbox directly. Not that my personal inbox is any more private than the general one that Comment-tagged remarks get redirected into—Mr. Fain believes very strongly in transparency, *if you understand my meaning*—but there's no sense in bothering everyone with an inquiry that should be answered by me or my team anyway."

Fields solemnly accepts their card. "Thanks."

"Oh, thank *you*. Your feedback helps us build a better product. Just remember—if you write a general, Comment-tagged remark, Heaven knows who'll answer you." The programmer glances at their wristwatch, which is the size and shape of a man's wristwatch, but ringed in rhinestones. "Oh dear. I've got to dash. You've got my card, now, but don't abuse the privilege." They trot back to the barracks room—"Ta!"—and shut the door.

Vladimir sprints to it. He throws it open, darts inside, and swears at the deserted darkness. He runs back out. "Where are they? Where did they go?"

Fields pockets the business card. He shrugs.

I can't stop smiling. "That was a Perfectia programmer. And we can show you how to contact them. But first... you need paper."

"And a pencil," says Marisa. "Which are restricted items that Michael Fain and the butler won't give you. Fifi, you're too amazing."

Vladimir nods fervently. "You've got a deal. Show me."

★★★

Vladimir, giddy with his paper and new knowledge, tells us about the scroll. He, too, thinks it's a clue to an Extra Time Well, and he did in fact find it in the mountains. But no pool of water was waiting near the receiving teleporter pad at Lac Diamant, and he can't decipher the riddle, so he never found the Well.

We can't decipher the riddle, either.

At 2:03 a.m., Vladimir's expectations compel us to get

footlockers, clothes, and bedding from the butler. We choose a barracks room two doors down from Vladimir and make our beds.

Lights out comes.

Marisa says, "Since Vladimir will take us right to him, are we gonna try to talk to Michael Fain again tomorrow? Or...?"

The idea makes my insides tighten. Conversations with Michael Fain are like carnival games: they're not things that ordinary people can win.

"Because I think we should," says Marisa. "Since we'll have the chance. But if we still can't get him to listen to us at all, we should say we 'quit'. Then we don't have to stay in this crappy building, and we can walk around the valley and look for that Extra Time Well. I don't know about you guys, but I can't—and won't—work for Michael Heinous for an eternity."

Fields agrees with her plan. I say I do, too.

Lying to Marisa does not feel good.

***

At 5 a.m., the lights come on. We arise and dress.

At 5:27 a.m., we walk outside and find Vladimir waiting at the EMPLOYEES ONLY door. "I just realized," he says with a smirk. "I'm not the new guy anymore. Maybe he'll put me in charge of you—ha!"

At 5:30 a.m., Vladimir opens the door. A train platform waits on the other side, and we board an otherwise-empty train, which takes us to an empty station.

Vladimir leads us out and through the questionable majesty of Courant de la Lac Diamant. By 5:58, we reach the Gold Room abutting Michael Fain's office.

"When we go in, stand behind me and don't say anything," says Vladimir. "Now watch and learn." He knocks.

"Come in."

We enter. Michael Fain sits at his desk, engrossed in his

laptops. He wears a different suit from yesterday, and a mug of coffee steams at his elbow. "I want a new tie for my call to Seoul, so pick me one that isn't ugly. Make the Stewart Study look more elegant. At lunchtime, someone will fly you to The Lazy H Ranch for lunch with Kirsten—she's been sad lately, so pretend to care about whatever she says. And you forgot my coffee, didn't you?"

Vladimir acts like the steaming mug isn't there. "I did. I'm sorry, Mr. Fain."

"What else do I want? Butler!" The butler appears. "What does Vlad need to do?"

"I'm afraid I wouldn't know, sir," says the butler.

"You're useless." Michael Fain finally looks up, and he notices me, Marisa, and Fields. "What the hell are you people doing here?"

I think: I can't do this.

But Fields and Marisa have their mouths open, and it's clear I'm the only one who has a ghost of a chance. So I force a smile, along with some oily words to grease it. "We're sorry to bother you again so soon, Mr. Fain, but we wanted to follow up on our conversation yesterday while we had the chance."

Vladimir interrupts. "You gave them jobs yesterday."

"Ha ha," says Marisa. "Technically—"

Fields elbows her for silence. Michael Fain snorts. "No I didn't."

"That is," I say, stepping in front of Vladimir, "after we spoke to you, we met a programmer, and she—"

"Why?" Michael Fain sits back and sips his coffee. "You want jobs?"

"Of course they do," says Vladimir. "And they're willing to work under me."

Michael Fain ignores Vladimir. He stares only at me with those tiny, narrowing eyes as he slurps, and although this conversation has already spun out of control, I plunge ahead while that Liopleurodon mouth is occupied. "That is, we ran into a programmer yesterday who picked us up and put us in Service Cluster Building 00. And we've learned that that's where your employees... live. So Vladimir's a little confused. We never formally asked for jobs.

"But I'm still glad to be here. Because if we could just touch base with you about—"

Michael Fain sets his coffee aside. "Who picked you up? What programmer?"

"Oh, that's all right," I say. "We don't mind the confusion—"

"Is everyone around me stupid today?" Michael Fain points to me. "You. Describe the programmer who put you in the Service Cluster."

"I... uh..."

Michael Fain hisses. "Butler!"

The butler reappears. "Yes, sir."

"Check the teleportation records into Service Cluster Building 00. Who went there yesterday?"

"Sitara, sir."

"Get her in here. Now."

My smile is beginning to hurt. "We honestly don't hold it against her. You don't have to—"

Another door in Michael Fain's office opens. The tall Indian woman from yesterday steps through. She wears the same style of pantsuit in a soft purple, and her makeup is brighter. "Yes?"

"Sitara, sweetheart, do you know anything about these people?" Michael Fain asks, pointing to us.

Sitara ignores the 'sweetheart.' "They're the ones I asked you about yesterday."

Michael Fain snorts again. "I didn't even see you yesterday. So how could you have mentioned them to me?"

Sitara sighs.

"Well, look, whatever," says Michael Fain, turning

back to us. "You're all here now with Vlad, and you're dressed nicely for work, so do you people want jobs or not?"

"Yes," I blurt.

Marisa jerks back. "No!"

Fields just coughs.

Michael Fain squeezes his mouth into a line.

I step forward so far, I'm against his desk. My smile feels like a clown's, ostentatious and painted on, and my heart's flapping like a pigeon in a cage. "Once again, I'm sorry for all this confusion, Mr. Fain. I'd love to work for you."

Marisa yanks on my arm. "What are you *doing?*"

What I'm doing is the only meaningful thing anyone in Perfectia *can* do, in the end: stay behind. Fight.

And hope to god that someday, for the people who come behind, things get better.

"Ha ha." I worm my arm away. "Don't mind my friend. She—"

"I want to go home," Marisa shouts.

Sitara fixes her cold eyes on Marisa. "You don't have a home anymore, my friend. You're dead."

Michael Fain's eyebrows go up. "Well, sure she is, Sitara. We all are."

I raise my voice. "Everyone. Please." Sweat prickles at my temples, and dampness slimes the insides of my fists. "What Marisa means is that she and Mr. Fields would like to go back to their mansions, but I'm perfectly... I can be the one to stay—I mean... I'll happily..."

"Fields?" Michael Fain sits straight up. Then he stands. *"Fields?"*

Fields just looks at him.

Michael Fain bangs his palm on the desk, several times, in a triumphant "gotcha" gesture. The sound rattles me into silence.

And I know I've lost.

"Fields!" he bellows. "Of course! That's who you are. I knew I recognized you the other day. Didn't I? Of course I did."

My feeble bravery crumbles to ash. I can't talk at all. All I can do is watch in mute, miserable submission as Michael Fain bustles around his desk and claps Fields on the back.

"It's great to have you here, just absolutely great. You know I'm glad I can reward former employees like you? That's what this Perfectia program is all about. Rewarding my people for their loyalty.

"Now listen to me, because I'm going to do something for you. I'm going to have Sitara fly you and your friends all the way back to your homes, absolutely free of charge. She's got a great glass helicopter sort of thing she does, really remarkable. You'll get to see the whole Wilderness that way. It's just astounding. And even better—she'll fly you over the mountains. No need to buy a return train ticket. Think about that! I just want you and your new friends to relax and enjoy yourselves. Okay?"

Fields stares at him.

"Okay," says Michael Fain. He claps Fields on the back one more time. "Sitara, take them home."

I should not want this. But I desperately want this. *We can't. Somebody has to stay behind. Somebody has to do the hard work of convincing him.* My hands clench and my lungs suck air, but I cannot make my cowardly self say "stop" or "wait."

"Wait," says Marisa, and my heart leaps.

Michael Fain turns to her, eyebrows up.

"What, uh... what did Mr. Fields do for you?"

Fields' eyes grow haunted. He shakes his head.

Michael Fain laughs. "Look at that. He's shy. Can you believe that, Sitara?"

Sitara's expression remains frigid. "I couldn't believe a

lot of things until after I started working here."

"That's right," says Michael Fain. "That's absolutely right. Perfectia is a land of miracles. Everyone, it was so great to see you again, but I've got some calls to make. Bye now."

I still can't speak. My heart cries and my mind howls, and Sitara marches us out of his office and teleports us into darkness. And I hate Marisa for ruining my focus, and I hate inexplicable Fields for setting off inexplicable Michael Fain, and I hate myself, for being unable to remain brave when it mattered the most.

The darkness lifts.

We're back in Service Cluster Building 00.

"I have far more important things to do than spend twelve hours flying you across the landscape," Sitara spits, "and so does the rest of my team. You'll just have to wait. One of us will take you on your Wilderness tour... eventually."

She leaves.

I sit on a metal folding chair, quaking.

"Fifi," says Marisa. "What did you do?"

"A man does what he has to, sometimes," says Fields.

"What does that even mean?"

Fields won't say.

7. The Rolling Fields

"You know you couldn't have stayed."

It takes me a second to realize that Marisa has spoken. "Hmm?"

Marisa, Fields, and I sit aboard a wholly translucent vehicle, in a passenger compartment at the bottom. The space glitters with rainbows, like a multifaceted crystal in the sun. The vehicle itself is like a mashup of a helicopter and a double-decker bus. But its glass blades whir as softly as a ceiling fan's.

Our pilot sits on the "floor" above us. Coincidentally—or maybe not—they're the old, elegant programmer who gave Fields their business card. They showed up at Building 00 only ten minutes after we did and swept us aboard the conveyance, saying something about the desire to offer impeccable customer service.

"I said," Marisa repeats, "you couldn't have stayed. Behind, with him."

I look outside. Below us, unicorns stampede through mossy ravines.

Marisa comes over and sits next to me. Even the seats are translucent, though they are well-padded and feel nothing like crystal. "Working for him would've killed you."

"Nothing can kill—"

"I mean that you would've quit. Long before you could've convinced him of anything."

I shake my head.

We watch The Wilderness in silence.

Fields sits back in his seat opposite us. My trusty bed-sheet bindle rests at his feet, and he holds the programmer's card in his hand. He tilts it at us. "I used to do this, you know."

I'm surprised. I don't think I've ever heard Fields start a conversation.

"Do what?" Marisa asks.

Fields holds out the card to us. I take it. Instead of a name, job title, or email address, the card bears a mess of gibberish, greater-than and less-than symbols, along with strange punctuation and non-words. "Html," says Fields. "Dead programming language. The early internet used to use it."

"You were a programmer?" I ask.

Fields nods.

"I thought you said you were a cowboy."

"That too," he says. "Before. Grew up on the ranch."

Marisa shrinks away from the card. She covers her mouth. "You didn't," she whispers.

I'm missing something. "Didn't what?"

Fields' expression hardens. He points.

I don't know what he's pointing at. There's nothing out there but ravines and moss. And the entire Wilderness.

"I did," he said.

I almost understand. "You—?"

"A man's got to feed himself," says Fields. "And I worked for Fain Enterprises at the time. It was 2131. We didn't know hardly nothin' then. How old were you in 2131, Margrove? You remember? We had the Elysium server and nothing else, and it was all anyone talked about.

"Well, old Edward Fain had just passed on, and he was cozying up inside Elysium, and everyone assumed that Michael Fain would end up there too. But then, in front of a whole room of people before a meeting starts, I say, 'If the Fain family is so rich, why don't Michael Fain plan to get his own server someday?'

"It was supposed to be a joke. But my boss Ms. Li, she looks at me and she says, 'You know? I think you're onto something.' And she told her boss, and her boss told his boss.

"And that's how it started."

I blink.

"That's all?" asks Marisa. "You just had the idea?"

"I ain't no liar."

"I'm not saying you're a liar. I'm saying that if all you did was contribute an idea, then you can't feel responsible for *that.*" Marisa flings her arm at everything. "It's not like you helped build it."

Tension grips the compartment.

"Fifi," says Marisa. "You didn't help build it... did you?"

Fields rubs his neck. He looks outside. "Maybe a little," he mumbles. "In the beginning."

I don't know what to say.

Marisa moves back to the other side of the vehicle and sits next to Fields. She puts a hand on his arm.

"It don't matter," says Fields. "He got mad at some suggestions I made and booted me onto another project, and now he don't even remember that he used to hate me. You saw how he was.

"Forty-five years I worked for that mud-gulping bastard. But I told myself it was okay, because I saved a whole pile of his dirty money, and I was going to Elysium myself, where I'd never see him again.

"But then my granddaughter got sick. And it weren't the kind of sick you come back from. So when her time got close, she and I talked it over, and I sent her to Elysium instead of me, because there ain't any justice in an old man getting fifteen more years when his twenty-five-year-old granddaughter can't get none. And then Marie's mother got sick, too. So with their permission, I sent my Rose, my only daughter, after her. I didn't want them to be apart.

"And now I got nothin'." Fields' face screws up. "Nothin' but twenty-five days left and... and a helicopter ride."

Marisa hugs him. Fields' eyes glimmer, but he does not cry. I sit rooted, my face hot, feeling like stepped-on shit.

Here I am, feeling sorry for my own cowardice, when Fields had to kill both his daughter and granddaughter and leave himself alone in both the mortal world and the next—the perfect, heinous capstone to a lifetime spent assisting a monster.

Then again, I was guilty of assisting the same monster. Everyone in Perfectia was. That's why we were contacted; that's why we were chosen.

Perhaps there is more justice in the world than Fields realizes.

★★★

Many hours after nightfall, the programmer touches us down on an illuminated length of concrete. I realize that we are back at the first train station on the far side of the mountains.

The platform is deserted. No simulated people move in the lobby, either. "Here you are, dears," says the programmer, opening the door for us. "You're less than an hour from home, now."

"Thanks." I step out of the hatch and my feet hit the platform. Immediately, my body feels wrong, like air, and when I touch myself, my flesh is hard rubber.

And I hear the music.

Marisa and Fields wince when their feet hit the platform, too. Their faces and clothes change, smoothing out in a way I can't explain. As Fields stoically shoulders my bedsheet luggage, I look away. It feels disrespectful somehow to watch the simplification of their selves.

The programmer exits their helicopter and withdraws a key fob from a pocket. One tap, and the helicopter disappears completely. "I hope you enjoyed your flight," they say. "Teleportation is the most pleasant way to travel, in my opinion, but of course all teleportations are logged. And Mr. Fain did want you to get a good view of the countryside.

"Now don't forget: you can ping me if you have an

urgent question. But remember your sense of discretion! We are all so terribly busy. Ta." They walk into the station's empty lobby and through a door marked STAFF ONLY.

We listen to the eerie soundtrack and simulated crickets.

The others look at me. As if I know what to do next. Then again, this whole ill-advised Michael Fain adventure was my show, wasn't it?

I wander to the edge of the platform. I see, and remember, the open gate. The one that leads to the deeper darkness of the alpine field.

It calls to me. The dirt path is a thin curl of smoke in the starlight. I want to go there. I want to go there so, so bad.

But only Kathrin made it back.

And by now, she only has two days before she's gone, too.

There are forces at play in Perfectia that I do not understand. I can't even tell if I am meant to. I think that last programmer is on our side, but are they? If they were, wouldn't they have dropped us off at the mansions directly, or next to one of Vladimir's dreamed-off "goodies"?

The drugstore-pine-scented-candle smell of the nearby forest makes my head spin.

"Lehann?" asks Marisa. "Are you okay?"

"I'm fine," I say, and at the same moment, my mind sobs his name. Daniel.

I no longer have a ludicrous quest to distract me from his loss.

Fields nods at the empty lobby.

"Good idea," says Marisa. "Lehann, let's go inside."

The gate calls to me. I want to rip my luggage from Fields' back and sprint into the darkness, into the maze of mountain paths that will either be my final resting place or my salvation. I can see it now: a secret cabal of programmers who decided to program us all with an urge to run through the gate, so we can ferret out the hidden bonuses that will make this purgatory bearable. But they can't say anything to us directly, or they'll be caught. They can't teleport us there, or they'll be caught. And when flighty Michael Fain demands to know why they've programmed a bunch of hiking paths next to the train station, they'll trot out a party line about wanting to program another harmless distraction for the rabble, to keep the unwashed masses away from his more-perfect end of Paradise.

I can't imagine a conspiracy theory more desperate and pathetic.

"What?" Marisa asks. "What's funny?"

I realize I'm laughing. I'd forgotten that we have Vladimir's map, one of the imaginary cabal's gifts. It's how I know my conspiracy theory is wrong: extra time in this nightmare dimension will not make it any more bearable.

But nonetheless, Marisa wants it. And by extension, so does Fields.

And, now that I'm not allowed to have Daniel anymore, they're all I've got.

"Vladimir's map," I say. "The first line is about letting the wind blow you, right? I know where to find the Well."

Marisa leans in. "Really? Where?"

"If you found this map in the mountains, and you read a line about blowing wind, what's the first place you'd think of?"

***

We walk through the lobby, onto the road, and into the mist.

We follow Fields' old carpet of glitter, then remove our shoes and begin the descent down Kathrin's invisible path. But we don't hold on. We peel off our soles and let go.

The shrieking wind yanks us away, then dies, leaving

us adrift.

Hands clasped, we float down through calm air. The mist parts. We see dots of sleeping sheep by hillocks and glimmering pools.

We drift to the grass like snow. I look up, and see not clouds, but a clear, starry sky.

As seen from this one field, Michael Fain's algorithmic heavens are gone. The moon here is small and gibbous. And the circumpolar constellations of the northern hemisphere hang, like old, familiar Christmas lights: Ursa Major, Cepheus, Cassiopeia.

Ah yes—that's right. There's no crying in this part of Perfectia.

★★★

When the simulated dawn comes and the simulated sheep stir and munch on the simulated grass, we arise from our rest and begin.

There are many possibilities to test.

We go pool by pool. We take turns jumping in and sinking to the bottom. As in the swimming pools of our mansions, the water does not feel wet, and we can breathe beneath it. We aren't entirely sure what to look for, at the bottoms of these pools—different servers indicate their bonuses in different ways—but we'll know it when we find it.

Whenever I emerge from a pond, I see Marisa holding Fields' arm. How foolish I was, to ever think that they were a romantic couple. I can see it plainly, now, the innocent way Marisa touches him, and how firmly he stands by her side. Hadn't he said his granddaughter, just nine years younger than Marisa, was named Marie?

We test the entire field.

The western clouds burst with flower-bright color when I finally say, "I guess I was wrong."

We stand at the eastern edge of the field, the surrounding woodlands at our backs, the impossibly gorgeous sunset in our eyes. The ponds are pools of fire in this light. "That's all of them," I say. "I'm sorry."

Fields shakes his head. He hooks his thumb behind us. There's one pond left, the only one that isn't in the fields proper. Gold limns the ferns around its edge.

"That one's technically in the woods," Marisa points out. "But sure. We might as well."

We push through fifteen feet of saplings. Marisa, fully clothed, jumps into the black water and sinks.

We wait so long for her return, the gold that limns the ferns turns to watery red.

Marisa surfaces with a gasp. "Come down!"

Fields drops the bedsheet luggage. I say, "This is it?"

"Get in the water, goddamnit!"

Fields and I jump in. She grabs our hands.

We drift down and down.

Finally, our feet touch bottom. A round light, embedded in the rock wall of the pond, waits at the level of my eyes. I realize that it's a window, set into a door in the rock face.

Marisa breaks free from us, turns the knob, and swims through the new darkness.

We follow. Somehow, the water changes into air and we are on land again, walking through a cool, dim corridor. It smells like a museum that's just been built. The lighting suggests that of a museum, too, with gallery lights forming bright spotlights on the bare walls, as if art were supposed to hang there.

The corridor turns. We stop in a room with a raised, circular platform on the floor, in the center of which is a big green circle. The circle glows, its light gently pulsing, as if it were a giant power button on a piece of fully-charged electronic equipment.

"There," whispers Marisa.

I exhale. It's strange to have actually found the Well. Part of me had believed that Vladimir's map was yet another piece of subterfuge, somehow. "Did you try it?"

"Not yet." Marisa moves cautiously toward the circle.

Fields makes a sound. He grabs Marisa's arm. "Ain't no Well," he chokes.

"But what else could it be?"

He points.

On the edge of the circular platform stands a podium. Its face is tilted toward the center of the circle, and I see that a screen rests within the plane of its surface. It's some type of control console, but I can't tell anything further. "Fields, what am I looking at?"

He pulls us onto the raised platform and toward the control console. "Transporter. For programmers." He taps the screen. It awakens and displays the following text:

WHICH AFTERLIFE SERVER WOULD YOU
LIKE TO GO TO? WARNING: TRANSPORT
FROM THIS LOCATION IS ONE-WAY ONLY.

I'm spooked. If that's what this is, then I don't know how we accessed this room. "Only programmers can go between Afterlives. We all know that."

Fields shakes his head. "Only programmers are *supposed* to go between Afterlives. Only programmers are *supposed* to get access to transporters."

I stare at that green, green circle, vertigo swirling through me with its every pulse. We shouldn't have been able to enter this place at all.

And yet, Marisa did. And then did it again, with us.

If the map that we followed was meant to take us here —

"This is really, really illegal," Marisa whispers, and I think: *There are laws.* New laws about why only programmers can understand and accept the risks of moving between servers, and old, old laws that regulate trespassing, travel, and border crossings.

And yet... how many people throughout human history have ignored the latter?

If we could sneak onto any Afterlife server we wanted... and if Michael Fain demanded transparency, but was too fickle to delve into the data transfer reports the programmers gave him... assuming he knew how to read them at all...

A hundred objections block my throat. Nobody has tested this yet. It could be a trap. It could be unsafe. Or the other programmers could notice our usage of it and immediately shut it down. And what about the other side? If —when—we were caught trespassing on some other server, we'd be deleted.

True... but after how long?

Fields types one word onto the screen: ELYSIUM. "I could be with Rose. And Marie." His fingers still.

Marisa puts her hand over his. "And I could go to Shuruq Alshshams."

They look at each other, over a long, knowing distance.

Bittersweet pain flares within me. I can't picture the two of them without each other. I don't know how they can picture themselves without the other, either, but I remind myself that, even for them, it's only been about fifty days.

It's been, literally, another universe.

Marisa closes her eyes. Fields leans in and kisses her cheeks, each one.

I look away, at the screen. What about me? What would I choose? I have a handful of older friends in After-lives, and an uncle and a step-dad, but nobody I'm close with. Daniel's the one my heart needs.

And Daniel's still alive, on earth. In the one universe I

can never go to.

"Come on," says Fields. He gently takes Marisa's hand and pulls it away from the screen. "We can't do it yet. We each gotta do it sneaky-like. Leave the day before our contracts are up. This way, if you don't look too closely, it seems like we've been deleted proper, and nobody'll ever wise up.

"And besides, we need to tell the others about this place first, too." Fields releases her hand and smiles. "We got a whole world to save."

And moreover?

We can.

We exit the transporter room, go down the dark corridor, and swim through the secret door. We kick upward, though the warm, not-wet water, but somehow it doesn't feel like a climb. I feel like a kite, propelled upward by a steady wind, all the way to the top of the clouds.

Because we do have a world to save. And Marisa and Fields and all the others each have journeys to take. And I suspect I still have that little journey of my own, through that so-enticing gate in the alpine meadow. Maybe I can find a real Extra Time Well. Or something I can use to contact Daniel.

Maybe he can rearrange what little money we have, and he can someday afford a tiny Afterlife—twenty-four simple hours—and then I can...

We can be...

But I have to find the right bonuses first. I don't know if they even exist, or whether I can find the right programmers to give me hints on how to find them. Ultimately, I don't know how much time I really have, or how many chances await me.

Then again, isn't that what it means to be alive?

ACKNOWLEDGMENTS

So many people have helped me throughout my career that it's impossible to thank everyone by name— including all of my readers, both old and new, who deserve the greatest thanks of all.

Still, there are some people who come to mind in relation to this specific project, so I'd like to thank the following:

Scott Andrews, Gordon Van Gelder, Jonathan Laden, Michele Barasso, and Suzanne Vincent, the editors who originally took chances on, and helped improve, much of the work within this volume, along with Ellen Datlow, for her additional improvements to "The Soul in the Bell Jar."

Michael Takeda and Bill Racicot, the approachable, helpful, hardworking people behind the press responsible for this book, who wear many hats both cheerfully and well.

Joshua Bilmes, for generous legal assistance.

Dante Saunders, for gorgeous cover art and interior illustrations.

Myke Cole, Fonda Lee, and Lisa Janice Cohen, for invaluable advice about promotion and marketing.

Erin Wilcox, Linda Addison, Ed Hoornaert, Mira Domsky, Natalie Wright, Monica Friedman, and the many other artists in my local writing crew, for writing sessions, craft discussions, knowledge sharing, and support.

Erin Wilcox and Monica Friedman get a second "thank-you," along with the class of Viable Paradise 18, for many Tuesday night writing parties and digital camaraderie.

Monica Friedman gets a third "thank-you" for her incredible friendship and insight.

And lastly, my husband, for his ability to be endlessly entertained by a computer. "I really will need a lot of time alone to write," I warned him at the beginning of our relationship, to which he said, "That's okay. I can play a *lot* of video games."

ABOUT THE AUTHOR

KJ Kabza began selling short fiction in 2002, while earning his B.A. in Creative Writing from Antioch College. Since then, he has sold over 70 stories to places such as *F&SF*, *Beneath Ceaseless Skies*, *Daily Science Fiction*, THE YEAR'S BEST DARK FANTASY AND HORROR 2014, THE BEST HORROR OF THE YEAR, VOLUME SIX, and more.

KJ lives in sunny Tucson, by way of many other American towns too numerous to name. He is not great at hiking, swimming, and roller skating, but he enjoys all of these activities and does them regularly anyway. He shares a home with one husband, zero cats, and a number of trees that he is determined to sustain.

He invites you to visit him at kjkabza.com or follow him on Twitter @KJKabza.